For my readers.

Remember, no matter how many years you've been on this planet, your goddess energy shines strong!

(And you are never too old to fantasise about a hot guy in a balaclava showing you a good time.)

A NOTE FROM ELODIE

My FMC, Aida, is American but has lived in the UK for many years.

She thinks and speaks and narrates in US English, but I've stuck with British English spelling throughout the book for consistency.

CONTENT ADVISORY

This book contains discussion of marital infidelity by the FMC's ex-husband. It's an adult book with sexual themes, scenes and dialogue suitable only for adults. These include exhibitionism, rough sex, role play involving the wearing of a balaclava by the MMC and various forms of bondage.

There is the vaguest suggestion in one role play at the FMC's home that the MMC is playing an armed robber who has broken in, but no actual on-the-page depiction of a break-in or anything other than enthusiastic consent.

This book has no OW/OM drama and has a big monogamous HEA.

1

CAL

What is it with my co-founders and age gaps?

We're all in our mid-to-late thirties, yet Rafe and Zach have both found love with beautiful women in their early twenties. Incidentally, these are women who fooled around with me but fell for my friends.

The less said about that, the better.

The fourth member of our Alchemy team, my gorgeous mate Gen, has fallen head over heels for the formidable Anton Wolff, a fifty-something billionaire whose dodgy-as-fuck exploits earned him the nickname The Big Bad Wolff. But Gen's tamed him. He's as needy as a spaniel these days.

None of this bothers me, though it bothers them, because when you're loved up, you want to inflict that status on everyone around you.

No, thank you.

I mean, for fuck's sake, the four of us co-founded London's most exclusive sex club, yet I'm the only one who's really dabbling now. The others come in with their paramours and promptly disappear off to the private rooms.

It's down to me to fly the Alchemy flag after dark, and fly it I certainly do.

(I have a very impressive flag pole.)

Don't get me wrong. I adore seeing my mates so happy. Rafe's smitten with, and ridiculously overprotective, of the beautiful Belle. Her best mate, Maddy, has turned Zach's life around following the death of his wife. And Anton, despite my initial misgivings, has thawed out our favourite ice queen. Gen is delirious these days.

I'm just not in any rush myself. I'm thirty-six, I'm loaded, and the business I run affords me spectacular, kinky-as-fuck sex on tap every night of the week.

I suppose I'd like a wife and babies at some point. Just not now.

Not when I'm living every guy's dream.

~

'I NEED TO TALK TO CAL,' Gen says as we wrap up our regular morning meeting.

There's a collective—and immature—*ooh* from the others.

'Sounds like you're in trouble, mate,' Zach observes. He stands and stretches, and I don't miss the adoration in Maddy's eyes as she looks up at him. That our nerdy, rock-fucking-solid CFO makes our sexy little social media manager as happy as she makes him is obvious to everyone with eyes.

'He's not in trouble,' Gen says, crossing her excellent legs on our fancy Italian sofa. 'In fact, I have a fascinating proposition for him.' She shoots me one of her warm smiles, and I grin back. I'm generally up for anything, and she knows it well.

'If it's a threesome with her and Anton, say no,' Rafe advises me. 'You'd never be able to keep up with him, from what I hear.'

'Fuck off,' I tell him as Gen rolls her eyes.

'No threesomes. Anton's quite enough for me, thank you very much.'

Maddy sighs happily. She's a romantic who rooted for Gen and Anton from day one, long before I warmed to the idea of that dodgy fucker going anywhere near my friend.

'Go on.' Gen shoos the others away with her hand. Because it's her, they obey. No one ever does anything I ask, but you don't mess around with Gen.

They trail out of the airy meeting space at the front of Alchemy's building and through the double doors to our office space. Once they've closed it behind them and we're alone, I twist my body on the sofa to face Gen.

'What's this fascinating proposition, then?' I ask. Gen doesn't exaggerate, so her choice of words has my curiosity piqued.

'Well,' she says slowly, 'a couple of months ago, I met with a woman who wanted to sign up to Unfurl.'

'Right.' Unfurl is one of our flagship programmes and greatest achievements. It's specifically designed for people, usually women, who are inexperienced and want to change that in a safe environment.

Belle, who was Rafe's neighbour, signed up for the programme. Not only was she a virgin, but she'd been fed religious doctrine and purity culture bullshit all her life. She wanted to discover her sexuality in style, and she certainly did. I was in a couple of her early sessions, which were hot as fuck, but Rafe fell hard, and that was that.

'She's not inexperienced,' Gen continues. 'She's just got divorced, and she wants to spread her wings.'

'Good for her,' I say. I love that. But it sounds like there's more to this story, so I wait.

Gen smiles like she has a delicious secret, and not for the first time, I observe that Wolff's a lucky guy. She's one of my best and oldest friends, but there's no denying she's a knockout. That platinum hair and those killer curves are every guy's fantasy.

'What makes it intriguing for us,' she adds, 'is that she wants to film the experience. She's pitched me a documentary that follows her journey to reclaim control of her sexuality. She's forty-six, and she wants to show women it's possible to redefine their approach to and enjoyment of sex after a long-term relationship.'

My mind is whirring. I love this idea—I completely agree that this woman's message is one that needs to be spread, and I adore the idea of Unfurl being used in this way.

But:

'When you say it'll be filmed,' I ask, 'what exactly do you mean?'

'It won't be a porno,' she shoots back quickly. 'No way. She's been pitching it to Channel 4 and the big streaming platforms. It would be an actual documentary, focused heavily on interviews with her, with us, and with various sexperts who are qualified to discuss female sexuality. But there's one more thing you should know.'

'What's that?' I ask, grinning. Gen's circumspect by nature, but her obvious excitement is infectious.

She licks her lips. 'The woman in question is Aida Russell,' she says. 'And I thought you'd be just the man to unfurl her.'

Holy fuck.

2

CAL

Aida Russell.

Aida Russell, who is hot as fuck and one of the smartest, most articulate broadcast journalists we have in this country.

Aida Russell, whose habit of running that pink tongue of hers along her bottom lip has made her the subject of a million sexy gifs.

Aida Russell, who's interviewed everyone from King Charles to Joe Biden with her signature aplomb.

Aida Russell, whose wanker of an ex cheated on her with women half her age.

Aida Russell wants to get unfurled?

And Gen wants *me* to lead the charge?

Where's the nearest pen? Sign me *the fuck* up.

No, actually.

Wait.

Gen's grinning at me in undisguised amusement. 'That got your attention.'

I nod slowly. 'Yeah. Certainly did.'

'What's your initial reaction?'

'Um.' Wow. 'Dunno. I need some time to process. Spell it out for me?' I wipe my palms over my wool-clad thighs.

'Aida wants to do a documentary with us. She feels strongly about changing the narrative around her divorce and the prospects for women of a certain age as sexual beings.'

'Amen to that,' I say.

'And she's going to need a... leading man. Someone who can hold her hand through the programme and mentor her and also advocate for her cause on the documentary.' She pauses. 'I thought you'd be perfect. You're indecently attractive, you're a great ambassador for the Alchemy brand, and something tells me you wouldn't be camera-shy.'

I smirk. 'Indecently attractive, you say?'

'Please fuck off.'

'And when you say *hold her hand*, you mean...'

She rolls her eyes. 'Obviously, I mean fuck her senseless and show her what she's been missing with her crusty old husband, but I assumed you weren't obtuse enough to need it spelt out for you.'

Jeeeesus.

I certainly didn't expect my day to kick off with an invitation from Gen to fuck Aida Russell's brains out and discuss it on camera.

When it comes to women, my standards are sky high but varied. They have to be stunning, but I don't have a particular type. Unless you consider the fact that the vast majority of them think the sun shines out of my arse.

Yeah.

I like my women adoring.

Not that I'd necessarily admit that out loud.

But Aida Russell—it seems impossible to think of her on first-name terms only—is a fucking institution. She's a proper grownup, a serious power player with equally serious clout.

What the hell would I talk about with a woman who pulls all-nighters to cover every US general election for the BBC with terrifyingly astute political commentary for hours on end without breaking a sweat?

She wouldn't want to hear my thoughts on how the Red Bull team is faring on *Drive to Survive*, that's for sure.

'Cal.' Gen's voice cuts through my reverie, crisp and melodic. 'Stop spiralling. I'm assuming you find her attractive?'

'Everyone with a pulse finds her attractive,' I mutter. I feel like a schoolboy with an impossible crush on my most impressive teacher.

'Exactly. I sat down with her a couple of months ago, and—'

'A couple of *months* ago?'

'It was right before Cannes, and I was in the middle of that fight with Anton. I haven't had a chance to talk to you till now.'

'Fair enough.' We launched our seasonal pop-up sex-club in Cannes at the beginning of the summer through a JV with Wolff Leisure, one of Anton's businesses. It was an unqualified success, thanks to Gen.

'Anyway, she's warm and gorgeous and hilarious. I think you two would have a lot of fun together.'

'She's scary.'

'She's an incredibly cerebral human being who also has a great personality. She's had a really shitty time of it, and I for one would love nothing more than to give her that boost she deserves while also helping her spread her message to other women who need to hear it. How about you?'

'Yeah.' I nod. I don't know why I've got cold feet. My

knee-jerk reaction when Gen said her name was one of utter carnality. I'd fuck that woman six ways to Sunday.

But this is a partnership that Gen's proposing.

And it would be on camera.

I'm the fun one. The one who's bloody good at the marketing and promos side of our business. I'm the good-time guy who knows how to use his dick, but I don't think anyone would accuse me of having gravitas.

And Aida Russell has a fuck-tonne of it.

'Cal.' She lays a hand on my arm. 'Hon. We all adore you. You're exactly what she needs. Just have fun with this, and make sure she does too. That's all I ask. The rest is details. What do you think?'

3

AIDA

"Awake, arise, or be forever fallen!"
—Milton, *Paradise Lost*

Sometimes they call me *brave.*

Or *plucky.*

What the actual fuck? Am I a Dickens heroine? Who even says that?

Last month, after I stood on the steps of the courthouse in head-to-toe Stella McCartney as my attorney announced what I would call a major fucking win in my divorce from John, they called me *triumphant.*

Damn right I was triumphant. I liked that headline.

More recently, though, they called me *gaunt* and *drawn.*

That's right.

Aida makes a gaunt, drawn appearance post court case win.

Once again, I ask you: What the actual fuck?

Are you telling me there's not a single person on the

editorial team of a national newspaper who studied English long enough at school to know tautology when they see it?

Also: I had just been for a five-mile jog. Damn right I was gaunt.

And drawn.

I hate it.

I hate when the tabloids pretend to champion you when, really, they're waiting for you to stumble. Waiting for you to show that chink in your armour. They're all the same, and it fucking sucks. Even if I'm used to it after seventeen years in this country.

I'm not usually fodder for these guys. They're too busy with *Love Island* alums and the royal family. But when they get the scoop that your husband, who's a member of the British aristocracy, has been fucking his secretary and his intern and God knows who else, you can bet your life they'll be all over you both.

They may paint him as the fuckboy and me as the wronged wife, but it's never that simple. Because he's one of them, and I'll always be an outsider, an American who doesn't really get how things work here. The left-wing papers have annihilated him, but the right-wing ones have been slower to condemn.

I hate that they're so toxic, and I hate even more that I care. But it hurts, because I was always John's young, hot, glamorous, successful wife as well as being a power player in the TV industry in my own right. And now I'm the spurned wife. You know, the one who's gaunt *and* drawn, right?

I'm forty-six. I refuse to be portrayed as some cast-off reject who's past her prime while my fifty-nine-year-old ex-husband fucks his way around the Houses of Parliament.

I refuse to accept that my fate is single-parenting two

boys while bemoaning the fact that guys my age all have their Tinder matches set to women of thirty-five and under. I'm a smart, attractive, successful woman in my sexual prime.

There's only one solution, and that's changing the narrative.

Unfortunately for John, that's where I'm a fucking pro.

I have a plan so audacious it'll make Tinder look like LinkedIn.

~

THE AUDACIOUS PLAN? A documentary comprising two sixty-minute episodes that lend themselves to leisurely storytelling, entitled *Aida Russell: Searching for Paradise.* Of all the things I have straight in my head about this concept, the clearest is that I want this show to be elevated. Inspiring. There's no place here for content that feels tawdry or shameful or ignoble.

And what could be more exalted than using Milton's epic poem, *Paradise Lost,* as the framework? Hopefully not much. I envision the first episode as framing the facts. The societal and biological and psychological challenges facing women like me. *Paradise Lost:* the story of my journey to Alchemy.

Then, *Paradise Found:* the story of my journey *at* Alchemy.

I loved this poem when I minored in English Literature. It may be a cornerstone of British literary history, but it's a lot of fun. Adam, Eve, temptation *and* Satan?

Come on. It's ripe for plundering. For modern, sexy reinterpretation.

It was Milton himself who mused: *What hath night to do with sleep?*

He sounds like he's earned a place in my narrative.

Because women my age are fabulous. So let's go celebrate them. Let's go exalt them in all their glory.

Having an audacious plan is one thing.

Acting on it—sigh—is quite another.

Since I last caught up with Gen a couple months ago, I've secured backing for this documentary. The streaming platform Azure will produce it as an Azure exclusive, and I can't deny I'm pumped. Channel 4 would have been a coup, but these folks have a higher risk tolerance.

With them at the helm, we can really turn up the heat on this thing. Take it from audacious to seriously boundary-testing.

Which is precisely why my stomach is in my mouth.

Because I've got the studio in the bag.

Now I need to come up with the goods. I need to actually fuck someone, someone I've never even met, and talk about it.

On television.

Excellent.

What seemed like a hot-as-hell concept when I hatched it alone in the bathtub with a glass of excellent Chardonnay now seems literally unhinged. I don't know what I was thinking.

Except I know that, whatever the optics, this isn't some cute little rebound stunt. This is about showing women my age that they can still own it when it comes to sex.

That they've still got it.

And if one woman gets that message, it will have been worth my while humiliating myself.

Maybe.

That's what I tell myself, anyway, as I walk up to the glossy black door of the exclusive Mayfair sex club. The club that'll host my reawakening. I've interviewed no fewer than three British Prime Ministers in my time, but the fear I had walking up the steps of Ten Downing Street has nothing on the sheer terror this place is prompting.

Alchemy.

The fabulous Georgian town house behind whose tasteful doors magic supposedly happens.

It's broad daylight, and I know—I *know*—I'm just here for a meeting. For a follow-up meeting with Gen and the opportunity to meet her business partner, Callum, who'll supposedly be my... mentor. My co-star.

If we hit it off.

Somehow, though, the stakes feel sky fucking high.

I've always gotten a rush of adrenalin ahead of a big interview. When you know you're up against someone as articulate—and slippery—as Boris Johnson, that chemical boost helps me to bring my A-game.

But right now?

How I feel doesn't even compare.

Because not one time when I've gone up against the biggest power players on our planet have I had to persuade them to fuck me.

I ring the doorbell.

4

AIDA

If I didn't know better, I'd think Gen had hired some kind of male-model-gigolo-type guy for the purposes of this meeting.

Because, come *on.*

The guy who's getting to his feet and shooting me a grin that's nothing short of appreciative is so hot he might just melt the panties right off me. I have a hazy recollection of asking Gen to come up with a Theo James clone all those weeks ago, when this felt like a pipe dream.

The Theo James thing was supposed to be a *joke.*

It looks like she took me at my word.

I'm uncharacteristically flustered, so I anchor my attention right on Gen. We've exchanged tonnes of voice notes and a couple Zoom calls since our first meeting, to the point that I feel at ease with her.

I like her a lot, actually. She's my kind of gal. Smart. Articulate. Warm.

Badass.

I've teased her about the fact that she's now dating The Big Bad Wolff, aka Anton Wolff, billionaire extraordinaire.

I've interviewed him a couple times, and he's the real deal. It makes me happy to know the mystery guy she mentioned during our last in-person meeting is the most eligible billionaire in the UK.

She's glowing. She's tan and golden and gorgeous. Mr Wolff is clearly good for her. I wish I could fixate on her longer. I wish I could ignore the other person in this meeting—the guy who's taking up way too much oxygen in this gorgeous, airy space.

But I can't.

So after I kiss Gen on both her fragrant cheeks, I mentally pull myself the fuck together, like I've gotten accustomed to doing over the past two decades in my field, and turn to him, game face firmly on.

I've interviewed Gaddafi, for God's sake.

I'm better than this puddle of nerves I'm in danger of becoming.

'Aida,' I say, thrusting out my hand. My tone, my pose, my demeanour, are all those of a woman who's used to battling for power with alpha males as soon as she walks into an interview room. It's essential, I've found, to make it immediately clear to these guys which of us will be calling the shots for the next thirty minutes.

My interviewees may be the most powerful people in the world, but when I've got them in the chair, I'm the boss.

This guy isn't biting, though.

'Cal,' he says, reaching for my hand and swallowing it up in his. His grip is firm, but his demeanour is relaxed. The way that mouth of his curves up at the corners makes him look amused, like he finds it funny that I'm attempting to rut horns right out of the gate.

But there's nothing amused in those deep brown eyes of his. I always thought the concept of bedroom eyes was some lame cliché, but clearly I was suffering under a misapprehension. Because the lazy, appreciative way those thick-lashed eyes flicker down my body before landing back on my mouth should be fucking illegal.

Before I know what I'm doing, I run my tongue along my lower lip.

He smirks.

I hate myself.

'It's a pleasure to meet you, Aida,' he says. 'I'm looking forward to working together.'

His voice is deep. Smooth. Cultured. It's what I've come to recognise as that perfect public-schoolboy drawl (because of course the Brits call their fanciest, most revoltingly elite private schools *public schools*). It's not quite as posh as my ex-husband's, but it's perfect in its studied casualness. Think Prince Harry. His voice says *I'm old money but I don't live in a total ivory tower.*

A decade or more of observing this particular subset of British male tells me that, usually, it also says *I'm a dirty bastard.*

(Case in point: my ex-husband.)

I absorb all this information in the blink of an eye or, more accurately, the swipe of a tongue. I'm used to sizing up my prey in milliseconds.

Because you can research a subject till you're blue in the face, but you can't actually size them up for real until they're shaking your hand and looking you in the eye.

Or, in this case, looking at your mouth.

'You two finally meet,' Gen says. 'I'm sorry we couldn't make it happen sooner.'

'Gen's been *busy*,' Callum—I'm not sure I'm ready for *Cal* yet—says. He releases my hand and shoots her what I instantly identify as a pesky-little-brother smirk. It puts me at ease, and I allow myself a smile.

'So I heard,' I say.

'Fuck off, Cal,' Gen says airily. I bet she swats him away all day long like a motherfucking fly.

'How is Mr Wolff?' I enquire as I take the seat Gen waves me to on the huge grey multi-sectional couch that monopolises the room. I'll do anything to delay the inevitable turn of the conversation towards this documentary. Besides, I'm excited for her. I want dirt.

Gen takes a seat across the big glass coffee table, while Callum sits adjacent to me. I don't miss the way his gaze roves over my bare legs, and, honestly? It gives me a thrill. My reputation is based on my brain, but sometimes it feels really fucking good to be objectified.

Especially after the public humiliation John's put me through this past year.

'He's amazing,' Gen says simply. She shrugs. 'Absolutely amazing.'

I smile. 'That's so fantastic. He's definitely one of the most impressive people I've interviewed. Super smart.'

'He's terrifyingly smart,' she says, reaching for the bottle of rosé chilling in a silver ice bucket on the coffee table. It suddenly seems an excellent idea. 'But he's a bit of a teddy bear when you get to know him.'

'Man, he must have fallen hard. I've never heard anyone refer to the Big Bad Wolff as a teddy bear.'

Callum slides the wineglasses towards us by their stems. 'Gen's tamed him good and proper. Glass of rosé?'

'Sure.' I feign nonchalance. 'Why not?' It's five o'clock, after all, and I'll take whatever help I can get for this conversation.

'I've briefed Cal, obviously,' Gen says once she's poured

the wine and Callum has handed me a glass with a charming grin. 'But I think he should hear it from you. Your vision for this series, that is.'

Oh, boy.

I take a fortifying sip of wine and set it down on the glass surface. When I look up, Callum's eyes are on me, dark and intense. The grin's gone.

'Tell me how you see it,' he says softly. 'Gen's told me the bare bones, obviously. But it sounds like you have a fire in your belly for this, so I want to know what you need this piece of filmmaking to do for women. And I want to know how I can help you get there.'

I take him in. He's truly gorgeous. Like, hot as fuck. His dark hair is raked off his forehead. His brows are thick. Defined. His mouth firm and sensual. Nose a little bent—looks like our boy got himself a break or two over the years. High school brawls? Rugby injuries?

He looks like he could have been a rugby player. He's a big guy. Strong, bronzed forearms under the rolled-up sleeves of his crisp white shirt. Those thighs look rock-solid.

He's the full package, and he's also *young*. Gen's already told me he's ten years younger than me, and right now I'm feeling every day of that decade-sized age gap.

Because what I'm about to propose—what I've gotten myself into—feels like some kind of cruel joke.

5

CAL

"But fondly overcome with female charm"
—Milton, *Paradise Lost*

From the waist up, she's all business.

Sensible white t-shirt under a navy blazer that's so impeccably cut it's probably Balmain or something similar.

Chunky gold jewellery.

Scarlet-painted lips that threaten to distract from her astonishing, almost-black eyes. Her hair is an immaculate long bob in shades of chocolate.

She's chic. Classic.

Below the waist, though, it's another matter altogether. Those endless legs, so famous they've probably got their own Instagram account, are bronzed and glossy and positively edible in sky-high navy stilettos.

But the best bit?

The best bit is undoubtedly the pair of fire-engine-red

shorts she's wearing in a leather that looks so buttery I can imagine how soft it would feel under my fingertips.

They're not hot-pants, more's the pity. They're—I dunno —tailored work shorts that hit around mid-thigh when she's standing. City shorts, maybe? But they ride up when she takes her seat and crosses one long leg elegantly over the other.

She's spectacular.

I've brushed shoulders with celebrities plenty of times. Partied with models and actors, even fucked a few. But Aida Russell differs from them. She's a face—and body—that belongs squarely in the respectable milieu of the evening news.

It never occurred to me, until Gen said her name, that she belonged here.

At Alchemy.

Aida may be wearing fuck-me shorts in fuck-me red with fuck-me heels, but she's clearly channelling her waist-up vibe. This woman is in business mode. Her armour's on, guns blazing. I knew it the second she gave me her best don't-fuck-with-me handshake. The one I bet she reserves for the sleaziest or the most arrogant politicians.

She surveys me now, setting her wineglass down before she speaks.

'The premise is to showcase the sexual identity crisis hitting women in their forties and fifties,' she says. 'It's a horrible combination of divorce rates peaking when kids go off to college, perimenopause, and this societal failure to not only value these women but to *see* us. We're an invisible stratum of society. And that's not right.'

Someone would have to be legally blind to find the smoke show that is Aida Russell invisible, but I keep my mouth shut.

'Agreed,' Gen murmurs.

I take a sip of my rosé as I await what is surely more detail. Because the picture she's painted so far is as dry as it is problematic. Nevertheless, I want to hear more. I want to be privy to whatever her brilliant brain is concocting, and I want to keep listening to her talking in that sexy, regionless American accent she's got. Her delivery is the clipped eloquence of a skilled orator, but there's a hint of huskiness to her voice that has driven many a red-blooded British male crazy—in a good way.

'My proposal is to tackle each of these problems, one by one,' she says. She's using her hand to gesticulate. Her movements are tight. Controlled. 'We can bring in experts, and I can talk to what I believe the issues are.'

Gen clears her throat tactfully, and I turn to look at her, because right now I'm so lost that I may have wandered into the wrong meeting.

'When we met up, back in June,' she begins delicately, 'you were pretty pissed off, and rightly so. You sold me a concept, and while all the issues you've raised just now are incredibly worthwhile, your elevator pitch back then was far more simple.'

She pauses, but Aida stays silent. She reaches for her wineglass again, molten eyes wide. She's a deer caught in the headlights, and my heart goes out to her. She's supposed to walk in here and spill her sexual vulnerabilities and desires to a random guy she's never met, in broad daylight? That's shit for her.

'You told me,' Gen continues softly, 'that you'd had years and years of totally crap marital sex, and you weren't going to stand there and take it while your husband buggered off with some young trollop—not your words—and that you wanted to show the world that women like you weren't damaged goods.'

She leans forward, and I can tell she's about to deliver the mic-drop moment. Fuck, I love Gen when she gets like this.

'You told me you wanted to experience really great sex, and you wanted to use the power of your platform to show other woman that they have value. That they're not damaged goods. And I for one thought that was fan-fucking-tastic.'

I haven't taken my eyes off Aida. She's clutching her wineglass like it's a security blanket. But she nods at Gen's words.

'Yeah,' she says slowly. 'You're right. I did. And that's what I want—that's what should be at the centre of all that. I don't want to tell people how it should be. I want to *show* them. I know that's by far the most powerful part of my whole plan for this thing. I want to show them in a way that's aspirational and thought-provoking and super inspiring. I know some women will get on board—they'll appreciate what I'm trying to achieve. And I know others will judge me and slut-shame me the whole way through.'

She pauses dramatically, and I'm reminded of quite how adept she is at holding an audience. 'And then I want those judgy ones to turn off their TV at the end,' she says drily, 'and be like "lucky *bitch*".'

That earns her a guffaw from me.

'God, I would love that,' Gen says, shaking her head.

Aida turns her attention to me. 'I'll be honest, though. I have lists of sexperts to feature, but the actual, you know, sex part is very, very unclear in my mind. And I'm so far out of my comfort zone right now that I'm losing my mind. I don't think I've ever been so under-prepared for a meeting in my life. I—'

I hold up a hand to stop her before she gets a chance to beat herself up any further.

'Aida. If I may. Of course it's weird for you. I completely get that.' I pause, trying to find the right words. 'And this isn't the right format to discuss that, because of course you don't feel remotely comfortable discussing this stuff in a meeting environment.'

I smile at her, and I hope it comes across as sincere. Open. 'If I'm going to have any value for you in this entire process, you'll have to learn to trust me. And, for that to happen, we'll have to get to know each other a lot better.'

She nods curtly, but she looks relieved. 'Yes. I agree.'

'Excellent,' I say. 'In that case, we're going to need a date. Somewhere dark and fun and sexy. And we'll need some cocktails.'

6

AIDA

In the corner of my production company's spacious and achingly hip East London converted warehouse offices, there's a small room that makes me happy. My production team and I have named it the Paradise Room.

I deal mainly in information. My brain is obsessed with joining the dots until I see the patterns. It's its own kind of creativity, and it is, of course, storytelling. Because, despite my reliance on facts as the foundations of my reporting, I can't kid myself that the narratives I present are anything other than just that. *Narratives.*

If words are my paintbrushes, then the faces of the people I meet are my canvases, and that's as true for a terror attack survivor as it is for a politician. This is all to say I don't deal in actual *pictures* very often. And, while I see beauty in life, my job is more often concerned with discussing the darkness.

So it's with genuine pleasure that I stand in front of the so-called Paradise Wall in the Paradise Room, arms crossed and fingers curved around opposite elbows as I take it in.

The team at Creatrix Productions has added a few

details since I was here last week, and the cohesive whole of this giant collage does what I needed it to do since my shit show of a meeting at Alchemy yesterday and *get my head back in the fucking game.*

This is how my programme whispers to me in my head. Especially the second episode, *Paradise Found*, which will be the racier, more hopeful, more celebratory of the two. Carnal accents of crimson and maroon and blood red amid tasteful black-and-white photos of beautiful people getting it on. Black lace lingerie and intricate eye masks are pinned to the cork-board, too, as are PR shots of Alchemy's interior and exterior... and ones of me and Cal.

I try not to linger on those too much, because he's grinning and gorgeous in his headshot, and I now possess the unfortunate knowledge that he's even more glorious in the flesh.

Fuck my life.

A production company of my own may lie somewhere in my future, but for this project I'm outsourcing to the best. Creatrix is the brainchild of two female founders, and, by a mix of accident and design, the senior members of the *Paradise* team are female, too.

There's Cate, the show's Executive Producer. It was she who believed in my fledgling vision enough to take me and my show on, and she who closed the deal with Azure. She's one of those rare people who makes combining details with big-picture genius look easy. She'll take a step back now that the show is in production, but she's here today.

Then there's our director, Lizzy, whose creative vision will inform the final product, just as it's informed the wall I'm staring at. If this brain dump is any reflection of how the finished article will be, then I approve.

Our producer, Darika, is female, too, which works well

for me, because her role will undoubtedly involve coordinating "stuff" at Alchemy—stuff I'll probably feel more comfortable liaising with a woman about.

There's a whole team at Azure on this, too, from their commissioners to their marketing people. And when you have this many people on a project, let me tell you it makes for a lot of agendas.

Most align with mine; some don't—or won't, by the time this process ends. The audience for this programme certainly isn't the only stakeholder here.

And, just in case I'm not already feeling the pressure from a million directions, least of all from myself, we have Mara.

Mara is my newish publicist. I hired her in haste earlier this year at the insistence of a good friend of mine: the skincare entrepreneur and former TV presenter, Honor Chapman.

Mara has form in helping high profile women navigate the public trauma of having shitty husbands, you see. When Honor's movie star ex-husband's cheating ways were dominating the tabloids, Mara helped her turn things around. She's also been by the side of Oscar-winning actor Elle Hart for years, since before Elle's ex dumped her on Twitter (he came crawling back five years later after doing a lot of work on himself).

So her résumé is flawless, mainly because she's so fucking terrifying. She rides an enormous motorcycle, wears brands so cool I'd be scared to touch them, and always has her clients' best interests at heart.

Even when—or *especially when*—we don't actually know what our best interests are. But we usually fall into line. We're too scared not to.

Thanks to a panicked voice message from me yesterday,

Mara's invited herself to today's meeting. It was supposed to be a quick catch-up to get everyone on the same page post my sit-down with Gen and Callum, but I suspect it may end up being a therapy session.

Suddenly, the lack of penises in the room feels extremely reassuring.

'So, how'd it go yesterday?' Lizzy asks with a huge smile once we've all taken our seats around the glossy white table. Her vision is crystal clear, but she understands that the camera is essentially a pair of eyes observing my very personal journey, and that none of us can really have any clue what's going to happen along the way.

All of which makes her flexible as hell and a dream to work with.

'I bombed.' Mara may know this, but it's news to Lizzy and Cate. So I give it to them straight.

'Here we go,' Mara groans, scooting her chair back so she can put her Off White-clad feet on the table.

Cate shoots her a stern look before turning back to me. 'How bad was it?'

I straighten my shoulders. I'm not in the habit of making excuses for myself. Years of live reporting have taught me to own my fuckups.

'I froze, I guess. I sat down with Gen and this super-hot guy who I'm supposed to be fucking sometime soon, and I totally lost my mojo. I gave him the worst pitch of my entire career and made *Paradise* sound like the driest, dullest old-lady show ever.

'Gen had to step in and remind me, basically, that when I met her in the spring, I was full of bravado. I was all like *I want great sex!* Fast forward to yesterday and I could barely mention the S-word, let alone look this guy in the eye.'

Silence.

I glance around the table. Mara's rolling her eyes at me —she's already told me, in an *animated* voice message, that she thinks I'm being pathetic.

Lizzy's processing, and I can see conflict written all over Cate's face: sympathy warring with the knowledge of how hard she pushed on my behalf to get this off the ground. While I approached Alchemy myself, and Gen was the one who suggested Callum, it'll be a real pain in the ass if things don't work well between me and the guy who's supposed to be my sexy mentor, for want of a less horrifying term.

'How'd you leave it?' Cate enquires calmly. She has one of those fabulously authoritative voices that don't need to be raised to get attention.

I sigh. 'Callum kind of saved me, I guess. He suggested that a daytime meeting with someone I'd just met wasn't the best format for me to feel comfortable sharing my sexual desires, so he's taking me out—tonight. He said we needed a date and some liquor so we could get to know each other better.'

Relief floods Cate's patrician features. 'Excellent. That sounds very sensible. I don't disagree with him—it was always going to be excruciating.'

'But first impressions are that you're attracted to him?' Lizzy asks, pointing at the wall. We all turn to gaze appreciatively at Callum.

I swallow. 'Yeah. Of course. I mean, that's part of the problem. I think it all hit me yesterday, you know? *Oh, hey, insanely hot young guy. Nice to meet you. Can't wait to fuck you. And sure, let's sit here and talk about all the ways I want that to happen. Fun!*'

'The feeling is mutual,' Mara points out. 'Gen told you how up for it he was when she pitched it to him.'

Oh God, it feels like I'm back at high school and my

friends are whispering to a guy's friends that I like him, and then it comes back along the grapevine that he might like me too, but it's never a hundred percent trustworthy.

Kill me now.

'Jesus, I don't know,' I protest. Sure, he seemed very interested in my legs, but this is all feeling far too real for me right now.

'In case this focuses the mind...' Mara says. She pulls her feet off the table and stands with a pained sigh, like she really resents that I've put her in this position. From her gorgeous, buttery Loewe backpack, she pulls an envelope that looks like it's from a printing shop and stalks over to the cork-board. I crane my neck, but I can't see what she's pinning there.

She turns with another sigh and steps aside, rapping her knuckles against the board. 'From *that* to *this.* That is what we're dealing with, love. And don't you fucking forget it.

That is a paparazzi photo of my ex-husband that I recognise from the media onslaught on our family after his women kissed and told. He was sleeping on the couch in the basement at the time. In the shot he looks exhausted, haggard, and over one hundred years old. It's an unfairly unflattering photo of a still-arresting man.

Mara's pinned him right next to Callum who, by contrast, is glowing and dripping sex appeal and looks positively lickable.

It's official.

The woman is the devil.

But she's *my* devil.

I giggle despite myself. 'Wow, that's harsh. Remind me never to piss you off.'

'You won't piss me off because you're *you.* This guy'—she jabs her fingertip at John's face—'betrayed your trust and fucked over the mother of his children. The very hot, very amazing mother of his children. And this guy'—she strokes Callum's square, bearded jaw—'wants to fuck you. That is literally the issue here. Nothing else.

'So you, my friend, are going to get your head back in the fucking game, and you're going to let Sex Master McHottie take you out tonight, and you are going to pull that stick out of your vagina and think about all the lovely things he could put up there instead.

Are you with me?'

7

CAL

I'm a little ashamed of just how big an ego boost it is to watch Aida Russell walk into a club and know she's here to see *me*. Ashamed partly because it's a pretty adolescent reaction to being the target of a hot woman's attention, and partly because this entire *thing*—however nebulous, however tantalising in its very nebulousness—is about her, not me.

Heads turn as she approaches, because her face is part of the very fabric of British culture. Or maybe they turn because she's a fucking knockout in a little black dress that shows off her spectacular tan. Her lean, toned limbs. She's wearing sky-high, bondage-style heels I bet Maddy would kill for, and her mouth is painted its customary scarlet.

I watch her visibly relax as she locates me. *Relax* is probably the wrong word. There's a palpable flash of relief followed by a pressing together of her lips like she's bracing for what lies ahead.

Smart girl.

She may be a seasoned reporter and interviewer, used to

a camera trained on her face, but one of the most charming facets of this undeniably charismatic woman is that she's never been one to hold back her reactions under a mask of implacability.

Quite the opposite.

She's made a career out of letting her facial expressions speak volumes. Aida Russell does not hold back, and if you're unfortunate enough that your answers to her probing questions disappoint her live on camera, you'll know about it.

You and the millions of viewers watching you get eviscerated by the disapproving purse of her lips. The cynical rise of her eyebrows. And, worst, the pissed-off eye roll.

You don't want to be on the end of the eye rolls that have launched a thousand memes. I imagine it's enough to crush a man, or at least to shrivel his balls.

Right now, she's wary, and it shows. You'd think someone who's achieved what she's achieved in her lifetime would be way too confident to feel any level of vulnerability walking into a crowded club.

But maybe it's her very profile that makes her vulnerable. She's gone from famous to infamous this year, despite not putting a foot wrong. She's been tabloid fodder for months now, and it must be exhausting to always be on your guard. To know the public is watching for any sign that you're not coping.

That you're human.

I raise my glass of scotch in a cheerful acknowledgement, pleasure coursing through me as she gets close enough for me to place a palm lightly on her bare arm as I kiss her on both cheeks. Yesterday's ball-breaker handshake didn't do much to establish an intimate vibe between us, and I'm determined to start things off on a better note tonight.

To that end, I've chosen an exclusive but fun supper club located in a large basement in SoHo. It's decorated like an old speakeasy, and what my stunning dinner companion doesn't yet know is that there'll be some light burlesque later to get the party started. Nothing as overtly provocative as the performances we have at Alchemy, but titillating in its own right.

I know Ms Aida Russell wants to seek refuge inside that giant brain of hers and avoid the prospect of pursuing any kind of baser activities, and I consider it my duty to coax out of her the carnal, pleasure-seeking creature I know is hidden in there.

Even if she's buried it deep.

That she arches into me ever so slightly as I bestow my chaste kisses is the first, tiniest sign that she's softening towards me, and I'll take it.

Besides. There's no way she'd wear a dress this sexy if she was trying to hold me at arm's length tonight.

Would she?

~

'To sinning and winning,' I announce with a wink at Aida. Our booth is perfect: a plush semi-circular bench behind a round, white-clothed table. We're on the raised dais at the back of the room. We can look out at the stage, where an ensemble is currently playing some light dinner jazz, but we're relatively secluded and dimly lit.

Bang in line with my evil plan.

I want this to feel like a date.

I want her to feel sexy. Uninhibited.

Brave.

I want to get that adrenalin coursing through her veins, heady and emboldening and naughty.

I want her to feel as though we're partners in crime.

In sin.

I want her to feel as though, together, we're capable of anything.

She raises an eyebrow at my choice of toast, and I think she'll protest, but she clinks her glass against mine. 'Bring it.'

Then she takes a sailor-sized glug of her dirty martini and sets it down before picking up her olive-laden cocktail stick.

I swivel on the padded velvet bench so I'm facing her as she brings the stick to that scarlet mouth of hers. She snags the first olive lightly between her teeth, and I catch a swirl of tongue as she tugs it off the stick.

She's not doing it to be provocative. She's not even looking at me—her gaze is taking in the room as she plays with the olives—but I catch that glimpse of tongue, I catch the flash of her white front teeth, and it strikes me that it's the most seductive thing I've seen in a while.

And when she shunts her gaze back to me by virtue of some serious side-eye, it's almost jarring. You don't want Aida Russell's black eyes on you, assessing you, while she drags olives off their stick with her teeth.

I'm telling you, it's unhelpful.

I shift on the bench.

And it's even less helpful when she cocks her head, glossy bob swinging as she does so, and holds the cocktail stick aloft.

'Sex club owner, huh?' she asks.

I grin. 'Yep.'

She rolls the stick and its last remaining olive between her fingers, assessing me, and I find myself tensing as I await the killer blow.

'So, tell me. What's the largest number of people you've ever banged in a single evening?'

8

AIDA

He shrugs. Grins. 'I couldn't say.'

'Seriously?' I get ahold of my inner judgemental bitch and rein her the hell in. 'How can that be?'

'You really want to know?'

I lick my lips. 'I can take it.' Of course I can. I've interviewed people about genocide. Mass graves. Paedophilia. I can handle a few tales from a sex club.

Besides, it seems a good way to break the ice. You know, talking about the elephant in the room.

Sex.

Because we've got to get to it somehow. At some point we've got to circle back to the fact that I'm supposed to get naked with this god and have him do fuck knows what kind of things to me. And while I get casual sex, theoretically speaking, and while he's one of the hottest guys I've ever seen in the flesh, the idea of it is so *freaking* bizarre. So improbable.

'Orgies,' he says now. 'You know, dim room, pulsing music, maybe a smoke machine or two. Naked bodies everywhere. Writhing, bent over, lying down. You put your dick wherever you want, basically. So, I dunno. Ten, twenty women at one party?'

I suspect, judging from his amused expression, that my eyes are widening, even though I'm trying my damnedest to keep my shit together. To act cool, when really I want to giggle like a schoolgirl.

'You're shocked.' He brings his tumbler of scotch to his mouth, watching me.

I narrow my eyes as I try to articulate how I'm feeling. 'Not shocked. More like I can't even imagine that scenario. But it feels like there's a law of diminishing returns. Like, you describing that is less shocking than you describing a threesome. Probably because it's harder to visualise.' I hold up a hand. 'I should be clear. I am absolutely not trying to visualise either of those things.'

He laughs. 'You tell yourself that.'

'I'm mainly impressed and horrified that you can come twenty times in one night,' is what I choose to follow up with, and he nearly spits out the drink he's just sipped.

'Nope—definitely not. I've had no complaints, but I don't want to mis-sell anything here. I don't finish inside each person. I try them out for size, pull out, change my condom, then try someone else.' He smirks. 'That said, my refractory period is pretty short.'

'Would you like a gold star for that?'

He shakes his head. 'Tough customer.'

'Believe it.'

'Kinkiest thing you've ever done.'

He's silent.

'You okay?' I ask, nervous that I've overstepped.

'Yeah, I'm fine. Just thinking. I wanked a husband and wife off at the same time in the back seat of their Range

Rover while pretending to be a policeman who'd pulled them over for speeding. That was interesting—and cramped.

'I've tried a bit of blood play—this summer in France. Not a huge fan. I've put my dick in every orifice, in every way—I've rubbed up against other dicks while I've done it. I've fucked a nurse over the nurse's station while she was on duty on the geriatric ward when I went to visit my grandpa. I mean, I've done it absolutely everywhere. And, it's not particularly kinky, but this one was boundary-pushing for me. I let a very scary Domme put a gimp mask on me and stick a gigantic butt-plug up my arse and spank me.'

The casual nature with which he's reeling off this endless fuck-list is terrifying in itself. And that last one sounded pretty kinky to me. I press my lips together. 'And you liked that?' I ask when I've recovered.

'Nope. Did absolutely nothing for me, but I thought I should try it. I'd much rather be in control—except with you,' he adds hurriedly. 'This is your shindig. You call the shots. You want to stick a dildo up my arse? Just say so and I'll bend right over.'

He slaps the table, and I jump. I have literally no interest in doing that to him or anyone else, which is one of the many reasons my marriage failed, but I'm not ready to divulge any of that shit to a guy I've only just met. I stay in interview mode.

'Not my thing,' I tell him curtly. 'You're safe. Now, have you ever had feelings for anyone you've fucked at the club?'

'Nope,' he says easily. 'You don't need to worry about that, I promise. I'm not going to fall in love with you and stalk you.'

All right, then. He was pretty unequivocal about that.

'Got it,' I say. Our eyes lock, and I mentally congratulate

Gen, because it looks like she found me the perfect guy. If I can view the fact that he's got three zillion times the sexual experience I have as beneficial rather than intimidating, then I can't fault him.

Of course, I don't actually *know* him, but Gen trusts him, which is good enough for me. And I can't deny he's gorgeous.

Like, dreamy, movie-star gorgeous, with a face that belongs on posters on teenage girls' bedrooms (if teens these days do anything as uncool as hanging posters). He's pretty but masculine, the long lashes and floppy dark hair beautifully balanced by the broken nose. The manicured beard.

The hand holding his tumbler is hot, too. Short, square nails. Shapely fingers. That grip looks strong. There's a smattering of dark hair on the back of his hand. He's not caveman-level hairy. He's perfect. The small V of his open shirt hints at the same. Black hair on tanned skin. The hint of his clavicle, the shadowy indent above it that I bet feels so soft against one's lips.

This guy should have some hot, willowy twenty-something hanging off him. Some girl who goes braless just because she can. Who can bend herself into a pretzel for him. In fact, the single fact I'm clinging onto, as if it's a frayed, inadequate lifeline and I'm over the cliff edge, is that any guy who can stick his dick in twenty women in a single night can't be that fussy.

Like, maybe his magical penis with its boast-worthy refractory period, is capable of banging women senseless even if they're not his type.

Even if they're forty-six and their body is the product of two pregnancies. Even if they have the banged-up vagina from one so-called natural childbirth *and* the C-section scar from the other one that didn't go as planned.

Even then.

And another thread frays on my lifeline as he sets down his drink, leans forward and bats the ball I've been volleying right back at me.

'If you're quite finished'

I grin. 'Shoot.'

'I have a question for you.' He grins sexily before reaching over and closing his warm hand over mine on the table.

'Okay,' I say nervously, trying not to wriggle my fingers under his.

'What do you want?'

'What do I want?' I repeat, mainly to buy time.

'Come on. You know the spotlight will be on you for this, not me. And while I'm an open book—I'm happy to answer any questions you have—I have a feeling this is less about you getting to know me and more about you deflecting. Am I right?'

Dammit.

Rather than answer, I give him a churlish roll of my eyes.

His grin gets wider. 'Wow. I just got my very own sexy-as-fuck Aida Russell eye roll.'

'When you ask what I want…' I prompt, playing for time.

'You gave us your spiel at Alchemy yesterday about changing the narrative. It's valid. More than valid—it's great. I'm sold.' He rubs a thumb over my fingers. 'But this isn't purely some altruistic exercise for you. It's personal. You know, we see all sorts at Alchemy. And *coming of age* is usually associated with young adults, but really, it can apply to anyone. You've identified Unfurl as a structure to help you come of age now, to help you come into the woman you should be today, but you feel like you aren't. Probably on account of your shitty husband. Am I warm?'

'Yes.' My voice is flat.

'Good. Not good—I'm sorry it's been like that for you. But it's good because now you get to do whatever you like. Fuck your ex. Fuck the press. Fuck everyone else. You are about to be let loose in a self-indulgent paradise. Consider me your sexual Willy Wonka. Christ, that sounds creepy.'

His grin has me barking out a laugh.

'Just think of yourself for a second, Aida. This whole project is about you, and your desires, and your needs. I want you to take, take, take. But Gen's been very silent on exactly what shape that'll take. And so have you, so far.

'So I'm asking you.' His hand slides up to encircle my wrist. He does it easily, and his grip feels solid. Safe. Even if it also feels a little presumptuous, in a way I shouldn't like, but do. 'What. Do. You. Want?'

9

AIDA

"The Tempter"
—Milton, *Paradise Lost*

I let my eyes flicker closed, because I can't say these things to him while I'm looking at him, and because shutting off my sight focuses the mind.

And I inhale through my nose, steadying myself.

'I want to make up for lost time,' I begin.

His fingers flex reassuringly around my wrist, his warm skin a kind of security blanket. As if he's drawn some magic circle around us in this dim club, declaring this little booth a safe space for confessions. In lieu of any spoken encouragement, his thumb strokes my pulse point.

'My marriage was decent,' I continue. 'But it was pretty underwhelming in bed. Perfunctory, I suppose. And I had needs that weren't being met, but I didn't think about that too much, because my life was pretty full with work and the kids. And John was—we had a good relationship, you know?

He's a super smart, interesting guy. Very eloquent. He stimulated me intellectually. We were great buddies. So I wasn't about to upset the apple cart over one missing piece of the pie.'

I open my eyes, weirdly surprised to see Callum's dark gaze on me. He's quieter, steadier, than I would've imagined him being. He strikes me as an energetic guy, someone who's always in motion. Always talking. Joking. But not right now.

'So, the marriage was fine, but it turns out John felt that missing piece too, and he did something about it. And I'm kind of impressed that he did, in an odd way. I just feel stupid that I never got the memo. He was having his cake and eating it, all over Westminster, it turns out. And I... wasn't. I was putting up and shutting up, which isn't my MO at all, usually.'

I chew on the inside of my gum for a second, then lick my lips. I need to say it, and I don't even think I need to shut my eyes. Avert my gaze. Because Callum is my confessor right now. An unlikely one, sure, but a kind one, I think. The read I've gotten on him so far tells me he is.

'I want to know what I've been missing,' I tell him in my Aida Russell voice. The voice that tells its listeners I'm not messing around. 'I'm forty-six, I'm still—I still have needs. I want to feel attractive and sexy, and not like damaged goods —not like I'm someone's leftovers.'

'Good,' Callum says emphatically, his thumb still tracing those tiny veins over my pulse point. 'And.'

It's not a question.

I exhale. 'I want someone to take me in hand and make me feel hot and fuck me into fucking oblivion. I want them to give me so many orgasms that I don't know which way is up and I don't care what day of the week it is because I'm so brain-dead from too much sex, and it's so good that it feels like nothing else at all matters.

'I want this particular phase of my life to be marked by indulgence, and—and *debauchery*, and filth. I'm in my sexual prime, and I don't want to waste this window before I'm totally invisible.'

The most gorgeous grin has spread across Callum's face as I've articulated that last part.

'That's my girl,' he says. 'I knew she was in there somewhere.' He slides his hand up my bare forearm. I like this kind of arm seduction he's got going on. It's hot.

'Yeah,' I say softly, holding his gaze.

'And let me tell you.' He smooths his palm back down my arm. 'You are *nobody's* leftovers, and I'm going to give you every single orgasm you desire, okay? When I've finished with you, you'll be so fucking ruined. Got it?'

I barely have time to flush at such an audacious promise, because he's reminded me of something I have to say to him.

Something very, very important.

'Hey.' I clear my throat. 'I appreciate that this is a kind of... chemistry meeting for us, I guess. But I want to be very clear. If this—if I'm not—if you're not attracted to me, then we'll find someone else. I refuse to be anyone's pity-fuck. And I could never prevail on anyone to—'

'Woah.' He lets go of my arm and grabs both my hands, clasping them tightly. His face is so close to mine now in this busy bar. 'Aida. Look at me. That's it. Good girl.'

I swallow and force myself not to look away, though fuck knows this is excruciating. I focus on his mouth, because it's easier and also because it makes for a very gratifying sight. I watch his sensual lips move.

'I know you haven't been made to feel desired in a while, and shame on your husband for that. But you need to know this. You're beautiful. You're a bloody icon, and you're so ridiculously fuckable that, if this was Alchemy, I'd have you bent over this table in seconds. Okay?'

My eyes go wide, and I nod, because this is a little more of an extreme reaction than I bargained on.

'The only thing you need to focus on tonight is whether you want me to do all those things to you—whether you want me to give you all those orgasms you need.' His thumbs are brushing over the backs of my hands, and his voice is low and caressing and full of filthy promises.

Boy, this guy is good, and my body is responding. We're in a busy bar, but the timbre of his voice makes it feel like we're in bed. 'Because,' he continues, tilting his head so his lips are drawing closer to my ear, 'I'm so fucking in it's not funny. I was like a schoolboy when Gen mentioned your name. I've always had a thing for you. You are sexy as fuck, and you're even sexier sitting here, next to me.'

I give a little laugh. He's sweet. I appreciate his reassurance, and I want to believe him. But I still think a guy like him should be out with some young yoga-teacher-slash-influencer so they can be all smooth-skinned and limber and sex-positive together.

He sighs against my ear, his breath warm on the side of my neck. 'Okay. I can tell you don't believe me. I didn't want to corrupt you yet, but here. Get a load of this.'

Before I can register what he's doing, he's tugging my hand under the starched white tablecloth and putting it on—

Oh my fucking God.

My hand's on his dick.

And it's hard and fucking *huge*.

Jesus Christ.

My heart rate goes through the roof, and I start laughing

for real—nervous, disbelieving laughter. 'Fuck,' I say, my fingers flexing around it of their own accord. Holy. Fucking. Shit.

He pulls back so I can see his smirk. 'Yeah. Fuck. You've done that. That's all for you, sweetheart, and you can have as much of it as you want, whenever you want.'

My eyes must look like saucers. I'm not easily surprised, but I'm, to use one of my favourite British expressions, gobsmacked.

Shit just got real.

10

CAL

'I'm holding back here,' I promise her as I take pity on her and reluctantly guide her hand off my dick and onto my thigh, where I keep it pressed under my palm. 'I promise. Give me the nod and I'll be unleashed. But it's got to be what you want. This attraction has to run both ways. There are a million guys at Alchemy who'd love to give you every inch of what you need, so if you want a full audition, let's go. I'll line them up for you.'

I pause to let her catch her breath, because this is a lot. I'm a lot, especially for a woman who's been with one guy for years and years. A woman who's feeling disconnected, through no fault of her own, with her sexuality and her power.

I meant what I said. The most important thing is that Aida finds someone she's attracted to, as well as someone she trusts. She's skittish as hell, but I'd put money on her being into me. That's not arrogance—that's me priding myself on having a pretty good read on women.

She's stunning. Not just stunning, but sexy, with those mesmerising eyes and that plump red mouth. And, thank fuck, her ex hasn't fully destroyed her confidence, because she's still Aida Fucking Russell and she's still got the star quality, the gravitas, that made her famous and that keeps people coming back for more.

I wait.

'You're—I find you very attractive,' she says now. Her tone is stiff, haughty even, like she's trying to impart her views of me in a businesslike way.

Like she's trying to hold herself together after I basically made her touch my dick.

She gives a nervous little laugh. 'Believe me, my attraction to you is not a problem. You're hot—totally gorgeous.' She waves the hand not pinned to my thigh in my general direction.

'I'm glad it's not one-sided,' I tell her. And I am. Really fucking glad. That would have been gutting, handing her off to someone better suited to the job.

I can tell you right now, no one is better suited to the job of transforming this spectacular woman into a whimpering, blissed-out, well-fucked, post-orgasmic puddle.

No one.

What she can't possibly know is quite how honest my confession just now was.

I'm holding back here.

Because I know exactly what she wants from me. I know what Gen wants from me, too. Believe me, I understand the assignment. The service that's required of me will be a *dirty-lite* one, if you like.

You know. Dirty, but not too depraved. Rough, but not too rough. Dark, but not too dark.

A little *good girl* here.

Some *open your legs* there.

Perhaps even the occasional *hands on the wall* or *show me how well you take my cock.*

Vanilla with a bite.

And that's absolutely fine. I can deliver that low-kink smorgasbord in my sleep. I can turn on the charm, and seduce her, and relax her, and make it feel like I'm coaxing, pushing, a little too hard when, really, it's exactly what she wants.

She's beautiful, and she's had her needs neglected to an extent that's pretty fucking criminal. She wants to be corrupted just the right amount, until she feels wanton and audacious and red blooded.

Quite right. And I'm absolutely the man for the job. I'll do it with a cock of steel and a smile on my face, because it will be my privilege to bring this woman back to life.

Still, I'll be holding back. Holding back the predator, the marauder within. The one who lurks in the shadows, scrupulously tethered in his cage as he bides his time.

Because this is about her and her needs and not about me or mine. She's a classy, sophisticated woman who deserves a classy, sophisticated dalliance.

And that's exactly what I'll give her.

By my standards, anyway.

~

We eat light—dips and chips and antipasti—and the cocktails keep on coming. As they do, she relaxes before my eyes. I suspect it's the alcohol, but hopefully my little dick-trick icebreaker played its part. I understand she's nervous about what lies ahead, but I won't tolerate her being nervous because she doubts my level of interest.

In her or this project.

We've spent the majority of the meal grazing on delicious bites and discussing the logistics of the documentary. I didn't fully grasp until now how much leeway she has with it. Azure has agreed to a two-part series with her, with a loosely articulated format (mainly to-camera interviews), but the content is at her discretion, and apparently the folks at Azure are excited to see the series 'unfold organically' as she takes her journey.

It sounds like a tonne of artistic licence and probably the exact format she needs to explore this path. I suspect they don't hand that level of ownership to just anyone. But when you've stunned audiences with the artistry, the insight, of your reporting for decades, like she has, I suppose you've earned the right to latitude.

Hearing her talk about her plans for the programme, her hopes, is fascinating. But she's still skirting around the meat of the issue to an extent I find highly amusing.

We've edged closer to each other. The bar's got even busier, but our vantage point allows us a clear view to the burlesque-slash-cabaret that's kicked off on stage. Right now, a guy who I think is supposed to be channeling Sexy Jesus is writhing on a pole in a loincloth. Fair play to him—his abs must be made of steel.

The music is sultry and loud enough to justify my putting my mouth closer to her ear as I trail the arm nearest to her along the back of the bench.

'Have you thought about how you want to kick things off?' I murmur in her ear.

She stiffens, the edge of her glass tugging deliciously at her bottom lip. I gently remove the glass from her grip and put it on the table. There's a droplet of liquid where the glass was, and I brush my thumb over it before sucking said thumb into my mouth as I await her response.

'Kind of,' she says. 'I mean, obviously. But I'm not sure I've gotten it straight in my head yet.'

'Hmm,' I say. 'Because I have.'

She turns her head sharply towards me. 'You have?'

'Mmm-hmm.'

It's true. I have. I've given it a lot of thought. I've thought of little else, in fact, since Gen casually dropped the bombshell that I'd be schooling one of the most spectacular women on this country's television screens.

And I have a tentative plan.

A plan that's heavy on caregiving and taking it slow and pampering her with just the right amount of debauchery.

A plan that's the perfect definition of *dirty-lite.*

A plan I have no intention of divulging to her at this time.

Instead, I intend to fuck with her, in the best possible way, for as long as I can get away with.

11

AIDA

'I'm not telling you my idea just yet,' Cal says, his lips practically brushing my earlobe as he leans back in. He inhales my skin, then lets his teeth clink against the diamante of my chunky double-C Chanel earring.

I'm sharply aware of the heat of his body as he crowds me. Of the fabric of his shirtsleeve against my bare upper back.

'You realise I have full creative licence here,' I say in an attempt to retain control of this situation.

'Yep,' he murmurs. 'And I'll never put you in a position you're not comfortable with. In fact, the scene I came up with is something I'm pretty sure will get you as relaxed as possible.'

I swallow. I could not be less relaxed about the prospect of going into some sexual liaison with Mr I've-Fucked-Twenty-Women-in-a-Night after a year of celibacy and fifteen more of monogamy (at my end, anyway).

'I need all the details up front,' I insist. 'I have veto rights. It's gotta be right for me—it's gotta be in my comfort zone.'

His fingers toy with the thin strap on my shoulder. I bet

he'd be so good in bed. So incredibly skilful. So confident. Confidence has to be the hottest trait in a guy.

'Of course you do,' he says soothingly in my ear. 'And you'll get them. But humour me for a minute, and let me tell you about one of the women who came through the Unfurl programme last year. Did Gen mention any case-studies?'

I attempt to clear the static in my head that his proximity is causing. We both have our heads bent, and he's shielding my face from the rest of the bar. Despite the pulsating music and the thrum of voices, it feels even more cocoon-like.

'I'm not sure,' I admit. 'I don't remember anything specific.'

'Not a problem.' He trails his fingers down my arm and burrows under the tablecloth to settle his hand on my thigh. 'This okay?'

'Yeah.' It feels great. His hand is warm, his touch anchoring.

'Good. Say *stop* if you want me to take my hand off you.'

'Okay.'

'So, this woman was—is—young. Early twenties.' His voice is light, easy to listen to, like he's lulling me into a state of relaxation with a nice story. He strokes the skin of my thigh with his thumb, but his hand stays where it is, which is right above my knee.

'Uh-huh,' I say.

'She hadn't slept with anyone, because her dad was a total religious nut, so she'd always been told it was wrong.'

Ugh. A few of my friends at college were brought up in the Bible Belt, and I know how much work they had to do on themselves to get rid of that purity culture bullshit. 'God, that makes me so mad,' I huff.

'Me too.' Callum splays his fingers on my thigh. 'So this woman—she decided to really go for it. Like, she was ready.

More than ready. And she had a lot of desires and fantasies, and she just wanted to unleash them. Now, obviously, she was a virgin, so we had to tread carefully—we weren't just going to fuck her in her first session. But we could still make it fun for her.'

I swallow. *We?* What the fuck?

'We got her in one of the rooms with a big leather chair,' he continues, his voice sensuous. Hypnotic. 'She had instructions. She put on some completely sheer underwear with a silk robe on top, and she had a sleep mask too. And when the three of us showed up, that's how we found her. This sweet little virgin, all innocent and nervous, but so fucking ready to be defiled, because she was so sick of not doing whatever the fuck she wanted with her body.'

He slides his hand up my thigh a little, under the silk hem of my flirty little dress, before sliding it back into position. But it's his words that are getting me hot, because a sharp pang of envy stabs me. Envy for this unknown woman, who was less experienced than I am but far braver. Envy that she had the guts to put herself in these men's hands and let them show her what she was made of.

'What do you think about that?' he whispers. 'Would you like that? Does it get you off, thinking about being blindfolded while all these guys crawl all over you, and play with you, and tease you?'

It really fucking does get me off. Jesus Christ. This guy is like audio porn. Maybe I should record this and play it back to myself later, when I'm alone in bed with my vibrator.

'What did you do to her?' I whisper, which is basically more of an answer than the big fat *yes* he's chasing.

Emboldened by the fact that he's still got his nose buried in my hair, his lips grazing my ear, that he can't see the effect he's having on me, I slide my hand up his arm, enjoying the sensation of hard muscle wrapped in crisp cotton as I do.

I'd like to say I rest it on his shoulder, but it's really more of a grip.

He wafts the tablecloth a little so it's covering our laps, before his hand resumes its journey up my thigh.

'Let's see,' he says conversationally. 'We got the robe open pretty damn quick. The underwear was a joke—she was completely on display for us. My mate got her legs open, and I started teasing her nipples through the mesh. I remember they were so fucking hard.'

He runs his free hand down the side of my neck, and I shiver. He doesn't stop. His fingers trace my collarbone before he turns his hand and presses his knuckles against my nipple. Through the fabric of my strapless bra, the pressure is heavenly. Fleeting, and totally fucking unexpected, but still heavenly. I inhale sharply.

'Hmm,' he says, like he's interested in my reaction. Like he's noting it. And also like he *approves* of it. Then his hand is burrowing under my hair again, cradling my jaw, holding me closer against his ear. I keep ahold of his shoulder and shift on my seat, my bare thigh brushing his jeans as I do.

'Then we got the ice cubes out,' he continues. 'And'—he gives a low, sexy laugh—'you could say they were a success. Imagine, sweetheart, three guys tending to you with ice cubes. You're not sure where they'll hit next, but they're swiping at your tits with them, and the cold feels so. Fucking. Good. Because you're too hot—you're desperate for something. *Anything*. You just need to come.'

'Mmm hmm,' I say dreamily, because this guy has me in a trance with his warm hands and his dirty words. The scent of him is so heady. He's wearing some kind of cologne, but it's super faint. He probably put it on this morning, and now it's just base notes that are woodsy and musky as fuck. Not that he needs it, because his skin smells incredible. He probably pumps out pheromones at a rate of knots.

'One of my mates, the one kneeling between her legs, gets an ice cube in his mouth and starts running it over the scrappy thong covering that pretty little cunt of hers,' he says. He's got his mouth pressed to my neck, so his filthy words vibrate against my skin when he speaks them. 'Doesn't that sound good? Are you getting wet down there, just thinking about surrendering like that?'

'Yeah,' I confess. The confession shouldn't feel as awkward as it does, because he's got me so turned on. My clit's now actually pulsing as bad as hers must have. God, having three guys as debauched as Callum touching you would send a girl through the fucking roof.

His hand leaves my thigh, and I'm instantly bereft. But the carnal sensation of his lips dragging down the sensitive skin of my neck is distracting. There's the tinkling of ice cubes, and, before I can react, he's holding an ice cube to my inner thigh. I jump at the cold. At the shock of it.

'Can I show you what we did to her?' he whispers against my neck. 'I want to show you how good we made her feel—I can make it just as good for you right now, if you let me.'

12

AIDA

Years in the field have honed the skill of split-second decision making. Of assessing risk-reward. Right now is no different.

I shouldn't be doing this. Not like this—not here, in a crowded club, before Callum and I have even worked out the parameters of this arrangement. Even through my fog of arousal, I know that much.

That said, I've been over-thinking this, spiralling about it, for months now, and I barely slept last night for worrying about how it would be with him. Whether he'd want it. Whether I'd freeze. Whether I'd be able to come up with the goods.

And here we are, and he's hot as fuck, and he's done a good job of convincing me he's attracted to me. And I am so fucking turned on. I'm so close to coming up with the goods as he slides the ice cube up and down my inner thigh.

Up and down.

This is the perfect opportunity to push through the huge barrier I've erected in my head and just get back on that sex horse, for want of a better metaphor.

Besides, I want it. He's gotten me all hot and bothered, and I'm ready to come. I *need* it.

'Show me,' I manage, and he lets out a low, rough noise in my ear that sounds like he's struggling with his own levels of restraint.

'That's my girl,' he groans. 'Open wide for me. I know how badly you need it. Trust me—I'm gonna show you the tiniest glimpse of what I've got in store for you.'

I manoeuvre my legs as far apart as I can get them, tugging blindly at the tablecloth to ensure we're still fully concealed. Callum's kissing my neck, licking it, his beard a dangerously good combination of soft and scratchy. I arch my neck sideways to give him more room.

'You smell incredible,' he murmurs, sliding the melting ice cube up my inner thigh in a glacial trail. He swirls it right at the top of my thigh, and I dig my fingers into his shoulder in anticipation, and then it's right *there*. Holy fuck—he's swiping it through my centre, and the flash of cold through the ineffectual fabric of the thong I've already soaked through is like nothing else.

'Holy shit,' I say in a strangled voice, digging my fingernails into his shoulder.

'If I thought I could get away with it, I'd get under that fucking tablecloth and tongue-fuck you with it, like he did,' he tells me. His tone is heated. *Intentional*. There is no doubt in my mind that he'd do it, too. An image of Callum under the table, eating me, brands my brain, but it's way too risky. Way too exhibitionist for my liking.

Besides, I need his huge body here, blocking me from these nice people enjoying their evening while I lose my fucking mind here on this bench.

Although—if he's this good with his hands, imagine

what the man can do with his tongue. My brain's practically exploding just thinking of it.

He doesn't seem to expect a response from me, which is good, because I'm out of practice where dirty talk is concerned. Instead, he resumes his commentary as he uses his cold, slippery little toy to wreak havoc on my lady parts. He hasn't touched my clit with it yet, and it's throbbing with need. There's no way I'm comfortable telling this guy what I need yet, but I'm confident he'll get to it when he's done teasing.

I already know for sure Callum Sinclair doesn't leave women unsatisfied.

'So, get this: my other mate is kissing her, and I'm playing with her tits,' he continues. He languidly rolls the ice cube over my swollen clit as he whispers in my ear, and I jolt at the freezing flash of pleasure, opening my legs even wider for him. 'It's so fucking full-on for her. Can you imagine, sweetheart? We're crawling all over her, and we're so desperate to get closer, but we have to keep her underwear on so we don't freak her out.'

Out of sight of the rest of the patrons, he lets the hand on my neck trail back to my breast, flicking my taut nipple with his fingertip, and I groan as much at the pleasure of it as at his words.

His mouth moves, beard tickling, kissing a line along my jaw as he puts a finger to the side of my thong. 'But you're not scared, are you?' he murmurs. 'Because you're a beautiful, carnal woman who knows what the fuck she needs. Right? Are you going to let me in?'

'God—yes,' I pant. He can have whatever he wants, because I'm gonna take as much as I can get from him. I'll take whatever he's offering—ice cubes. Fingers. The lot.

Then he's hooking the scrap of fabric to one side, and it

feels like he's ditched the ice cube, because all I can sense are his ice-cold fingers, and god, are they better.

'Fucking hell, sweetheart,' he groans. 'You are slippery as fuck for me. Bloody hell, you feel amazing.'

As does he. Those icy fingers slide and probe. They part my soaking flesh, and I arch my back to give them as much access as possible. Then he sinks two fingers deep inside me as his thumb finds my clit, and he practically detonates me like that. Yeah, I'm slippery, like he said, but his fingers are calloused, and his strokes are deliberately rough, and the friction and the cold are such an excellent combination that I might shoot off this bench in pleasure.

I turn my head right as his mouth leaves my jaw to search for mine, and then he's kissing me. He's kissing me hard, hand abandoning my breast so he can shove his fingers through my hair and grab roughly at my neck. His tongue is just as decisive and probing as his fingers. He tastes like the Old Fashioned he's drinking, smoky and aromatic, and he may just be the best thing I've ever tasted. I writhe in his arms, both my hands going to that thick, glorious hair of his as I hold him as close to me as I can.

And still, he works me. He ramps up the pace. The pressure. The friction. I'm in a total state from his dirty storytelling, but in this moment I'm not thinking of that mystery virgin and her three admirers, because this reality I've found myself in is so fucking glorious that I wouldn't be anywhere else.

God, I've *missed* this. I can't recall a time I felt like this. I can't recall it being so heady, so urgent, so carnal. Like I'll die if this guy stops. Like I want him to swallow me whole.

I wish I were in a bed with him. I wish we were naked, and those epic fucking shoulders of his were bare, his biceps flexing as he ranged that huge body over me and fucked me into oblivion. His kisses are that of a man who's desperate, and I wish I could undo him right here, like he's undoing me.

Our teeth crash. Our lips slide. His tongue rampages, and I hang on for dear life. His magical fingers thrust and rub and twist until I don't know which way is up. Until I don't know my own name, conscious only of my orgasm building in me like the sweetest swell of heat. He seems to tell I'm close—probably because I'm pushing against his fingers and moaning into his sinful mouth—because he kisses harder. Rubs harder. Thrusts harder.

As he holds my head in a vice and tongue-fucks me like an animal, the heat grows molten, and I break. I come shockingly hard, violently even, bucking against the protective shield of his body and grinding my greedy pussy against his fingers to take every last drop.

And he kisses me through it all.

13

CAL

'So.' Gen narrows her eyes at me across the large glass coffee table. 'How did last night go?'

I plaster on my signature cocky grin. 'Piece of cake.'

'Seriously?'

'Yeah. We're full steam ahead,' I tell her, crossing one ankle over the opposite knee and allowing myself a sip of my Americano while I enjoy the look of surprise on her face.

I could tell after our meeting with Aida that Gen was concerned. Concerned we wouldn't hit it off. That I wouldn't be able to thaw Aida out. Well, she has absolutely nothing to worry about on that front.

I should know.

The others are watching me, hoping for a juicy tidbit to spice up our morning meeting, no doubt. They won't get it from me.

'Well?' Rafe demands. 'Spill.'

He's a bossy bastard. He should know that shit doesn't work with me.

'Nothing to tell,' I lie smoothly. 'We had a few drinks and a good chat, and that's that. We ironed out some details, brainstormed a few ideas. She's going to get cracking on the format for the original interviews with Simone Salem, so I'm assuming we'll hear from her when they've banged out a strategy.'

Simone Salem, another household name, is Aida's colleague from the BBC and, apparently, her best mate. She'll be in charge of interviewing Aida for the show, though Aida will interview most of the experts they bring on.

'So nothing happened.' He's like a dog with a bone.

'Nothing happened.' I produce my trump card. 'I came here afterwards, for fuck's sake. Check the logs if you don't believe me.'

These guys don't need to know that the reason I shot over here like a scalded cat after putting Ms Russell—or is it still Lady Russell?—in a cab was precisely because something happened.

She happened.

Sucking her scarlet lower lip into my mouth.

Burrowing under that glossy, dark swing of hair to the sleek neck below.

The slippery heat of her under my fingers. Around my fingers.

Her little mewl of surprise against my mouth when she reached her violent, shuddering climax.

Sharp nails digging into my shoulder like spurs against the flanks of her favourite racehorse, driving him on towards the finish line.

The memories accost me—a glorious carousel of images that sear into my consciousness, despite my desperate rampage at Alchemy afterwards.

So fucking responsive.

She was a little beauty.

My evil plan for our 'date' may have included the intention of creating some ice-breaking mischief if I saw an opening, but even I didn't see that one coming: Aida Russell hurtling towards orgasm in my arms as I finger-fucked her in the depths of a club.

I have an Aida-shaped hangover this morning. I was tickled, for want of a better word, when Gen pitched this documentary to me. Tickled. Intrigued. In my head, she wasn't a real person. More a celebrity trophy to smash and grab, if I'm completely honest with myself.

But she's fucking real, all right. My formless, harmless schoolboy-level crush on her is taking shape. It's growing substance, a little kernel of desire building inside me. Because we'd be good together. We *are* good together, even if our antics were positively chaste as far as my standards go. For a hookup where I didn't even get off, its memories have teeth. Teeth far sharper than the memories of the women inside whose bodies I got my end away afterwards.

I certainly delivered a killer audition. I suspect I did her a favour last night by blindsiding her into third base before she had time to get nervous.

But it didn't feel like a favour.

Nope.

Her sharp intake of breath as I slid my lips along her jaw and an ice cube up her leg?

That was nothing short of typical Callum-Sinclair-level self-indulgence.

~

'I NEED to chat to Cal about the Masked Ball,' Maddy announces as our morning meeting draws to an anticlimactic close. She gets up from her cosy spot beside Zach, where she's been surreptitiously holding his hand for the past twenty minutes, and plumps herself down next to me.

My mate shoots me a suspicious look before Maddy blows him a kiss. 'Put the kettle on, babes? I'll be through in five,' she tells him, which seems to pacify him somewhat, and he trails forlornly towards the open double doors that separate this meeting room from our desk area at the rear of the fuck-off Georgian mansion that houses Alchemy.

His black lab, Norm, looks at his master and then back at Maddy before plodding towards us and dropping at her feet.

Poor bastard.

Zach, not Norm.

I adore the relationship I have with Mads. I'm pretty sure she adores it too. The only person who doesn't adore it is Zach, because I may have fucked her in the club after a particularly hot Unfurl session with Rafe and his now-girlfriend, Belle (who, incidentally, was the mystery virgin in last night's little bedtime story).

Yeah.

Told you the women I fool around with end up with my mates.

Anyway, that time with Mads was a one-off, and it happened way before my grieving, walled-up best friend was ready to admit to himself or anyone else that he had feelings for her.

Boy, did those feelings turn out to be big ones.

I'm also pretty sure that ninety-nine-point-nine percent of the time Zach knows he's won the lottery with her and is equally confident of her love for him. You only have to look at the two of them together to see her adoration. The girl's in deep.

But it's sweet that he feels so possessive of her, and no wonder. She is, objectively speaking, a knockout, especially in today's combo of killer heels and a clingy black dress that leaves little to the imagination.

My mate's a lucky man these days, and, God knows, no one deserves luck more than him. Together, he and Maddy are the most farfetched, and yet perfect, combination I can imagine.

Maddy's best asset, though, is her dazzling smile and cheery personality. No wonder she coaxed the grief-stricken shell that was my friend back to life, and for that we'll always be grateful. She may have been a fantastic fuck—she's one of the most sexually liberated women I've ever met, and that's saying something—but these days we have a brother-sister relationship, and it really, really works.

She twists her body towards me, one elbow propped up on the back of the sofa so she can cradle her face in her hand and the other dangling by her side, a welcome licky-toy for Norm's enormous tongue.

'So,' she says as soon as Rafe's pulled the doors closed behind him. 'Shoot.' She wiggles her eyebrows, and I can't help but laugh.

'Shoot what?' I ask her, though I know what she's angling at.

'Tell me. Aida. What's she like?' She sighs. 'Is she as sexy as she looks on TV?'

'Definitely sexier,' I say.

Scarlet mouth.

Hard nipples.

Long nails.

Jesus.

'I knew it.' Her glossy pink mouth curves into a self-satisfied smile.

'That she was sexier in real life?'

'That something happened.'

'Nothing happened.'

She tuts. *'Cal.'*

'Mads.'

'We can go through the motions for the rest of the day, or you can just dish the dirt. We both know I'll win.'

I sigh. Maddy's particular blend of cheeriness and relentless persistence is fucking lethal, and we both know it. But she knows when to be discreet, and I trust her with my confidences.

'Okay, okay.' I let my head fall back against the sofa, lolling it to one side so I can see her. 'I may have given her a sneak preview.'

She does a little full-body shimmy. 'I knew it! She got a dick preview.'

'No,' I correct her, deciding not to mention that I made Aida feel my boner. 'No dick. It was all about her.'

Maddy purses her lips. 'Impressive.'

'I aim to please.'

'And did you? Please her?'

I scoff. 'Come on. Course I did.' *Dirty-lite, right? A bit of audio porn in her ear. An ice cube against her cunt. Easy peasy.*

'Where'd you do the deed?'

I shift self-consciously, though Mads is the least judgemental person I know. 'Under the tablecloth in a booth at the Zebra Club.'

She spits out a gratified laugh. 'Good work. Lucky Aida. So it's all systems go after your little—what are we calling it—elevator pitch?'

'Nice. And yeah. I feel good about it, actually.' I roll my shoulders back and stare at the ceiling. I feel really fucking good about it.

'Do you like her?' Maddy persists. She may be a sex-positive goddess, but she's also a hopeless romantic, God bless her.

'She's hot as fuck and impressive as shit,' I say. 'What's not to like?'

'Hmm. Interesting.'

'What does that mean?'

'Nothing. Just... interesting.'

'She's far too smart for me, so don't get any ideas about us,' I warn her.

'Nobody buys that act for a second, Cal, so don't even try,' she says. 'I know you think it's not cool to show your nerdy side, but you're wrong. And you made a career for yourself trading weird stuff with scary, mysterious acronyms, so don't give me that *my brains are in my biceps* bullshit. I bet you and Aida will have a lot more in common than just chemistry.'

'You're a pain in the arse, you know that?' I tell her. I aim for a weary tone, but it comes out affectionate. Dammit.

'I know.' She pats the palm that's resting on my thigh. Her hand is that particular kind of moistly sticky that can only come from Labrador saliva.

I jerk my head up. 'Fuck—that's revolting.'

'Don't hurt his feelings.'

'Get out of here. Go deal with Zach's abandonment issues.'

She sighs. 'This conversation isn't over. I'll be watching you two with *a lot of interest*.'

'You and the rest of the country,' I say with a groan.

'Come on, Norm.' She stands. 'Let's go find Daddy.'

'For fuck's—'

'He's Norm's daddy. Not mine. I don't call him that. Well, only—'

I put my hands over my ears in defeat and cut her off before she can violate my brain any further. 'I don't want to know.'

14

AIDA

It's a crushing disappointment to the British tabloid press that Simone Salem and I aren't mortal enemies. God knows, they've pitted us against each other from the outset. Two confident, glamorous, ambitious news anchors, vying for the same top spots at the BBC? It was the stuff their particular brand of poison was made of. Especially when I went on my first maternity leave and Simone, who's publicly declared her horror at the mere thought of having children, took my place.

Sadly for them, and happily for us, their toxic little shenanigans didn't work, because I fucking love that woman. And I'm pretty confident it's mutual, too. When Simone Salem dislikes you, you're gonna know about it.

Believe me.

I waggle my fingers at her as she sweeps into the White City outpost of Soho House, conveniently located in the Television Centre, where the BBC still films the occasional programme. In her cream silk jumpsuit, immaculate blowout and chunky gold jewellery, she's the epitome of late-summer chic.

Simone speaks like the late Queen and, even on the home stretch to fifty, looks like a Valentino runway model. Case in point: the enormous gold V on her wide belt that catches the sun as she struts over to my poolside table on the tenth-floor rooftop, revelling in the discreetly curious glances from nearby tables.

The daughter of an outrageously successful Lebanese businessman, she married another outrageously successful, French-born Lebanese businessman. Her multi-millionaire husband, Karim, is short on height, long on Big Dick Energy, and his fabulous wife's most adoring fan.

She may have three inches on Karim when barefoot, but do you think she ever forgoes the heels when he's around? No, sir. My absolute favourite thing about my absolute favourite woman is her outright refusal to compromise. On anything.

'Darling,' she drawls, swooping down to kiss me on both cheeks and leaving a trail of Le Labo as she collapses into the chair across from me. 'How goes it?'

I lower my sunglasses and shoot her a coquettish smile. 'It goes great.'

She arches a perfect eyebrow. 'Really? Do tell. Fun and games with your new boy toy?'

I smirk. God knows, it's rare that I've had much to be smug about this past year.

But today?

Basking in the golden aftermath of my unexpected orgasm at the capable hands of a sinful man?

You could say I'm smug as fuck.

Glasses back in place, I smooth my palms over my cute Dolce shift. I always dress up for Simone—she both expects and appreciates it—and there's something in my Italian blood that goes feral over the colours, the opulence, of Dolce and Gabbana's dresses.

You could say they're my weakness. My mom is first-generation Italian, and those guys dress women the way Mom always said we should dress. Colour. Flair. And, above all?

Flaunt those curves.

Even when they do an LBD, it's sensuously feminine and made to stop traffic. Or so my little experiment last night suggested, anyway...

'Holy fuck.' Simone's posh curse interrupts my little daydream. 'Did you shag him?'

I roll my eyes with the moral outrage of someone who absolutely did not make out—and more—in a club last night. 'Shh! No. Course not. How's Karim?'

She gives that lame attempt at deflection the disgusted scowl it deserves. 'Don't bullshit me, darling.' Reaching over, she grabs the bottle of Pellegrino and pours herself a glass. 'Spill. I want details. Full details. Salacious details. Go.'

I sigh. My friendship with Simone runs deep. She knows all the nasty ins and outs of my marriage and divorce. I know all the less nasty ins and outs of hers. But we were both married when we met, so swapping hot gossip about guys was definitely not on the agenda. Not unless said gossip pertained to who was fucking who at work.

Because I'm a badass, hard-hitting, award-winning reporter and not some bashful teenager, I cut to the chase.

'He ended up dirty-talking me into an orgasm while he finger-fucked me under the table at the Zebra Club.'

If it wasn't for this place's no-phones policy, I'd take a snap of Simone's face, because it's a picture.

She sucks in a breath. 'Dirty *bastard.*'

'Yep.'

'I fucking love it. Tell me more.'

I let out a resigned sigh. 'He was telling me about one of the Unfurl sessions last year where it was three of them and some young woman, who was a virgin. A virgin with a *lot* of balls, because the stuff she let them do to her sounded hot as fuck. Anyway, there was an ice cube involved, and he kind of... reenacted it. He got one from his drink and slid it up my leg, and...' I shrug, attempting nonchalance. 'I kinda went with it.'

Simone's staring at me in a *who the heck is this creature* way. 'Bravo, darling. Bravo. So the boy toy knows what he's doing, yes?'

I press my fingertips to my brow. 'Oh, God, please don't call him that. It's so objectifying.'

'And I'm sure you haven't objectified him at all,' she drawls.

I sigh again. 'Okay, fine. Of course I have. He's fucking delicious. But you make him sound so young.'

Her face softens, and she reaches across the table to squeeze my hand. 'He's ten years younger than you, isn't he? You're hardly a cradle snatcher. If John can fuck women less than half his age, you can certainly take some pleasure—pleasure you absolutely deserve—at the hands of some delicious fuckboy. It sounds like the guy has experience, darling. Bucketloads of it. So *use* it, for Christ's sake. That's precisely why you approached Alchemy.'

'I guess,' I say. She's right, obviously. And last night was as enjoyable as it was unexpected. But Simone's use of the term *fuckboy,* while definitely sexier than *boy toy*, only underlines the shitty feeling that underscores all the post-orgasmic smugness.

'And it was a good orgasm?' she persists.

'Fucking amazing.' It really was. It was so *hot*. So dirty

and carnal—like I couldn't help myself. I couldn't have stopped him if I tried, because his filthy mouth and magic fingers had me spiralling into another version of myself so quick I didn't know which way was up.

It wasn't just coming at someone else's hands which, given the year I've had, was, in a word, delightful. Having someone else take control of my body. Drive it. Own it.

It was *him*. It was the overwhelming masculinity of his huge body. His absolute confidence in his own attractiveness, in his ability to work a woman's body. The way he managed to be so smutty and intense without letting go of that light humour of his. The way he spoke to me, like I was a dirty, dirty girl and he knew just how to wring me out.

I've only been waiting for someone to speak to me like that my whole married life.

'Good.' She gives an approving nod. 'How did you leave things?'

I shoot her a rueful smile. 'And here's the rub.'

'Go on.' She sits, ramrod straight, and waits.

It wasn't awkward at all after I came all over his fingers. He held me there, his arm in a vice-like grip around my back, as we made out like teenagers. I was all gooey and limp, my entire nervous system rewired in the best possible way. And I suspected, from the hungry way he kissed me, that he was still hard. Something I felt awful about, but I wasn't about to jerk him off under the table. *That* was a step too far.

But, after we finished our drinks and exchanged numbers and he'd presumably talked his boner down, he called for the cheque and walked me outside before flagging down a black cab.

'Where do you live?' I asked him, thinking I could drop him off if we were close by each other.

'Knightsbridge,' he said, stroking a warm palm down my bare arm. 'But, uh, I'm heading back to work.'

And that was it.

That was the moment the penny belatedly dropped for me.

'He put me in a cab and went back to Alchemy,' I tell Simone, and her eyes widen in understanding.

'Ah.'

'Yeah. Ah.' I press my lips together.

'Were you okay with that? *Are* you okay?'

I cock my head. 'I don't have any right not to be. I mean, we both know what this is. He owns a literal sex club. That's why we're hooking up—not because I met him somewhere and he asked me out. It's a commercial partnership, right?'

Simone merely waits for me to answer my own rhetorical question. Around us, servers in immaculate white polo shirts and navy shorts tend to the glamorous guests and the sunlight puts on a blinding, fizzling dance on the surface of the turquoise water.

'Anyway, I got off and he didn't, so he was totally justified in going back and getting laid the way he needed to. I guess I should take it as a compliment that he was so turned on he needed to go fuck someone else.'

'That's fair,' she says in a tone that suggests she's holding back.

'What.'

'There's a difference between an act being justified and it being upsetting. You're correct in that he hasn't done anything wrong. I mean, you'll hopefully be getting the full benefit of this guy's skills over the next couple of months. But you're allowed to feel upset about it, too. This is a massive step for you, darling. You're getting back out there in what will be a very public way. It's fucking terrifying.'

'I guess.' I allow my gaze to drift once again to the dancing sunlight on the water as I attempt to articulate my thoughts, to sift and weigh the confusing tangle of emotions. 'I don't think I'm upset, exactly. Nor is my ego bruised—if anything, last night was absolutely the confidence boost I needed.

'I think it's more that it made me feel a little... grubby, maybe? I'd just had this very sexy moment with a hot guy, and it felt pretty intimate by my standards, so it was a stark reminder that I'm one of god knows how many women for him. It probably wasn't even memorable for him.'

'And you're absolutely allowed to feel like that,' Simone tells me. 'Have you heard from him today?'

'Yeah.' I pick up my phone and unlock it, sliding it over to her. 'I had a message from him as I was dropping the boys at school.'

> How are you doing today? If last night was anything to go by, I'm going to enjoy our little project VERY much x

'Well, that's sweet of him,' she says, handing my phone back to me. 'He's got good manners, at least.'

'That, or aftercare is part of the service,' I say. 'But yeah, it was sweet.'

The knowledge that he'd slunk away from me last night and into the warm, eager pussy of some woman who wasn't afraid of putting out had me typing out a reply that was an exercise in restraint.

> Thank you for such a fun night. I'm doing good, thanks. Look forward to catching up soon. X

'For what it's worth,' Simone says, picking up the lunch

menu and removing her oversized sunglasses, 'I think it's brave and fabulous what you're doing. Last night was a major first step for you, and it sounds like it was a huge success. So when we do the kick-off interview next week, you'll have to pretend to be all nervous and apprehensive about letting a big, bad man get anywhere near you. Got it, you dirty little slut?'

I laugh, momentarily comforted. 'Got it.'

'Excellent.' She holds up her Pellegrino, menu still in her other hand. 'Here's to you getting schooled.'

15

AIDA

'Okay, yeah, I'm ready.'

SIMONE (OFF-CAMERA): I've known you for over a decade, darling, and admired you greatly as a journalist and reporter. *And* I've had a front-row seat to the media shit storm you've been publicly dragged into this past year. All of which leads me to ask you why the actual fuck you're putting yourself up for this?

ME: [Laughs] I've asked myself that question at least fifty times a day since I concocted this idea in my head, and the most accurate answer I can give you is that I honestly feel like I have no choice.

If I thought this was just an altruistic project, then I probably wouldn't have the guts to see it through. And if I thought it was just a passion project for me, then I'd probably see it as too self-indulgent to justify.

But, the truth is, it's both.

I've seen things in my time as a reporter and newsreader that I can never un-see—things that haunt my dreams. And I've feared for my safety and the safety of my crew far more than I would have liked. But I can sit here and tell you as a friend that I have never, ever felt more terrified about anything in my professional life than I do now.

SIMONE: [Softly] And why is that, do you think?

ME: Because of everything. Because of how shitty the past year of being hounded by the press has been—and I mean the tabloids *and* the broadsheets. Because of my reputation as a sensible, trusted newsreader who's known for shooting her mouth off, sure, but who's always carried herself with professionalism. I hope, anyway.

But most of all because I'm a forty-six-year-old woman, and our society as a whole isn't interested in the sex lives of perimenopausal or menopausal women. It's more than that —we're not even supposed to have sex lives.

To address the elephant in the room up front, my ex-husband is probably being slapped on the back by his cronies in the House of Lords for having been outed as fucking countless women, women far younger than him. And the press excoriated him, sure, but they didn't condemn his sexuality. Just his infidelity. I, on the other hand, am not deemed by society to have a sex life worth taking an interest in.

Don't get me wrong, I'm coming at this whole thing from a place of exceptional privilege. I'm a wealthy white woman who can technically still call herself Lady Aida Russell. I'm not complaining because the press isn't speculating about whether I'm getting any.

But don't you think it's interesting?

Of all the thousands of articles my research team has collated over the past year, I haven't seen one speculating over whether I'll take a lover. Because it doesn't even occur to anyone to wonder.

So, to answer your question, I'm doing this for myself and for every other women out there in their forties and fifties or beyond, who's been written off as having no sex life and certainly no sexual identity.

My identity has been tied up for so long with my career and my marriage, and shame on me for letting it take a divorce to kindle that spark of interest in who I really am beyond all that. This is my chance to untether myself from that very limited picture of who I am, and I hope it gives other women my age pause for thought.

I hope it gives them any extra courage or confidence they may need to examine the desires and needs and even kinks that make them fully rounded, flesh and blood humans who choose to live the fullest expression of their human experience.

I've never shied away from thorough research or tough reporting, but digging into and reporting on my own desires is going to be the toughest challenge I've ever faced, hands down.

16

CAL

'Stop it, for fuck's sake,' I tell Maddy. I swear to God, she's like an annoying little sister. She's far more annoying than I ever remember my actual sister being.

'What?' she asks, giving me her best innocent, doe-eyed look. 'Belle and I are just excited about meeting your girlfriend, that's all.'

'You know damn well she's not my girlfriend,' I say through clenched teeth. 'She's my... business associate.'

'Of course she is.' Maddy narrows her eyes at me slyly. 'And you're going to work her so hard, aren't you?'

'Zach,' I grit out, turning to him in frustration, but he just laughs.

'If you think I have an ounce of influence over her, you're deluded,' he tells me with a worshipful look at his girlfriend, and I sigh, because Maddy does whatever the fuck she wants and none of us can do anything about it.

I have to admit, she and Belle both look incredible in the perfectly dim light of Alchemy's bar. Unlike The Playroom next door, which is a writhing, pulsing mass of bodies on any given night, our bar is a sophisticated hangout for members and their friends.

The vibe on this side of the heavy double doors that separate socialising from sin is fully clothed and refined. The main focal point is the huge bar that stretches almost the length of the room. It's crafted from pink onyx that's luminous in the glow of its backlights. The crowd is every inch as refined, as expensive, as the decor, but even in a Thursday-night sea of beautiful people, Belle and Maddy are the true pearls.

They're on low bar stools next to each other, thick as thieves and complementary as fuck. Belle sits erect, skin and hair and aura all pure gold after summering with Rafe in Cap Ferrat. She's in a black jumpsuit that consists, as far as I can work out, of swishy black trousers and two elongated triangles that cover her perfect tits and tie at the back of her neck. Modest it's not, but her sheer allure, and the beauty of her figure, makes it classy.

Maddy has darker hair and paler, if equally flawless skin. Her glossy brown mane is in long, tumbling curls tonight, and she's in a cream mini dress that shows off her killer legs. Zach has a hand firmly clamped on one thigh, while Rafe is draped around Belle like a scarf.

It makes me laugh.

My friends are hopelessly besotted, poor fuckers. I should take a photo and show them how pathetic they look.

Not that a single person here would spare them a second of pity. Not with their much hotter, much younger girlfriends.

Maybe that's unfair. Both my mates are decent looking.

The tantalising prospect of having drinks with Aida tonight really has brought out the crowds. Gen's here too, with her boyfriend, Anton. Or should I call him her partner? He's getting on a bit—fifty-two, I think—though I suspect he could have any woman he wanted in this place. Is fifty-two too old to be called someone's boyfriend?

I'd be horrified at the thought of turning fifty if Anton Wolff wasn't a poster boy for how fucking good life can be in one's sixth decade. Tall, outrageously good-looking, seemingly in rude health, a billionaire God knows how many times over, fuck knows how many homes and yachts, and a kinky fuckboy until he fell hopelessly, irrevocably in love with our beautiful friend.

I have to admit, he's nailed this aging thing.

Several women come over to say hi, introduce themselves or wave their tits in his face, which is equally rude and stupid given he's quite clearly with the woman who could revoke their membership with a wave of her hand. But, to his credit, Anton treats each of his unwelcome admirers with a brusqueness bordering on rudeness.

Gen's the only woman he's got eyes for. Tonight she looks as flawless as ever, in a golden dress that makes her look like a goddess and a choker around her neck that glitters with diamonds—a choker that's a gift from her besotted Anton.

I sigh and subtly check my watch. Aida said she'd be here at nine, and it's ten past. Not that I'm keeping track.

'He's pining.' Zach nudges Maddy, who has to smack a hand over her mouth to stop herself from spitting out her champagne. 'Do you think she's stood him up?'

'Grow a pair,' I growl at him. I don't give a shit if she turns up on time, or late, or not at all. It just seemed like a convenient time to get her to meet the rest of the Alchemy crew, given the documentary team will do some filming inside the club when empty and she'll eventually be interviewing all four of us co-founders.

'She's here,' Gen says a moment later, the warning to us all to behave evident in the pointed tone of her voice.

'Yes she is,' I mutter, shooting to my feet, because even in a club that houses the elite of London's financial and political sectors, Aida Russell stands apart.

Her dress is long. Cream. Floaty. I couldn't tell you much about it except that it has a high collar that lies flat around her neck, while the armholes are cut all the way up to intersect with it. The pleasing effect of this cutaway design is that her toned, bronzed shoulders are fully on display, as are her bare arms, cuffed halfway up each forearm with a huge gold bangle thingy.

It's perfect. She's perfect, her posture statuesque, her poise faultless. That mouth I sucked on last week is its trademark scarlet. Full. Glossy. The kind of highly pigmented fire-engine red that I just know would leave a gratifying ring around my cock.

Several seconds pass before I notice she has her friend with her, seconds during which I hasten over to her so she's not left standing on the periphery of the merry-making. Her friend, Simone, needs no introduction. She's another household name, a newsreader I've watched since my uni days.

Gen reaches them before me. Of course she does. The three women exchange noisy greetings and effusive kisses before Aida turns to Anton, who's also beaten me to it, kissing him with what looks like genuine pleasure and affection.

I roll my eyes. Of course all these heavy-hitters, these grownups, know each other. And, even though Gen and I are the same age, I have the uncomfortable feeling that she belongs effortlessly at the grownups' table by virtue not only of her relationship with The Big Bad Wolff but of her innate, undeniable gravitas.

I'll probably spend the evening at the equivalent of the kiddies' table, lobbing metaphorical cocktail sausages and Hula Hoops at Maddy and Belle while the grownups chat nicely in the corner, discussing Ukraine and The Booker Prize and rising mortgage rates.

For some reason, the thought pisses me off, which is probably why I call, more loudly than I mean to, *Aida,* while, behind me, Rafe openly sniggers.

17

AIDA

Simone seems as happy as a pig in shit.

'It's such a shame I'm completely in love with my husband,' she mutters, while shooting some guy a flirtatious grin. 'The guys here are hot as fuck.'

We've had a few smiles, and nods, and whisky tumblers raised in greeting. I guess it tickles guys to see two news-readers in a sex club, even if we're just in the bar area. I take another peek at the heavy wooden double doors I'm told lead through to The Playroom.

It's a horrifying thought, and I can't stop craning my neck every time someone walks in their direction, because there's no escaping the fact that they're sauntering in there, casual as you like, to *fuck*.

We're standing in little clusters around the table Cal and Gen and their friends were at when we walked in. It seems more sociable than everyone sitting around on stools. Easier to mix conversations. The reporter in me is loving it. I'm observing. Analysing. Interpreting. Drinking in the well-heeled patrons and their dynamics.

It's a fabulous atmosphere—buzzing and super fun—

and I remind myself I'm in a sex club. There's no room here for inhibitions. So why do I feel almost bashful that the gorgeous guy standing next to me is the same guy who finger-fucked me to a messy, moaning climax last week?

He looks fine. So fine. Tall and broad-shouldered in a black dress shirt and black pants that showcase what great shape he's in. He's a slightly bigger build than his cofounders, Zach and Rafe, who are leaner, rangier, and it's clear he works out. A lot. Those pants highlight his trim, tapered waist and his fantastic ass.

His dark hair is raked off his face a little messily, a look that absolutely works for me. His skin is fucking gorgeous. Golden and flawless and glowing with health. Beard immaculate. But it's his eyes that really get me, because they're warm and dark and molten, and they crinkle whenever he smiles at me, which is a lot.

He stays close while we all chat. Like, shoulder to shoulder close, the heavy cotton of his dress shirt brushing the bare skin of my arm. And when he's explaining something about how the club works, or pointing someone out to me, he inclines his head and touches me lightly with his fingertips on my low back.

I like that a lot.

I mean, who wouldn't like being gently, respectfully flirted with by a crazy hot younger guy who smells insane and seems determined to ensure you're having a good time?

Simone and I had a quick catch-up with Anton Wolff, who we've both interviewed before. Seeing him so transfixed by my new friend Gen is a lot of fun. He's one of the most devastatingly smart, cut-throat business moguls I've ever sat down with, but around Gen the guy is a drooling mess, and I love it.

We're now chatting with Cal's coworker Maddy, who I

understand is also Zach's girlfriend, and her friend Belle, Rafe's girlfriend. I say *I understand*, but it's pretty obvious, because Zach is just as worshipful of her as Rafe is of Belle. I wasn't expecting all these sex club owners to be so infatuated with one woman, but who can blame them?

Belle and Maddy are young as fuck and outrageously hot. I eye Belle's practically naked upper half with a mix of admiration and regret that my skin hasn't looked that dewy or smooth for half a lifetime. Because these young women are literally half my age.

'I'm obsessed with your cuffs,' Belle says now, pointing to the chunky jewellery punctuating my forearms. They're matching Chanel cuffs bearing bejewelled Maltese crosses, and they're fucking fabulous.

'Thanks.' I shoot her a grin and hold out an arm to admire one. 'A little divorce present to myself,' I tell her and watch a pleased smile spread across her beautiful face. She has Rafe standing right behind her, pressed up against her, his arm banded around her waist, holding her to him. His dark head keeps dipping to her bare shoulder, his nose and lips tracing devoted lines to her neck and back.

I wonder how it feels to be so desired. So adored.

'I love that,' Maddy says, stepping forward and holding my arm lightly so she can see the detail. 'Ugh. They're amazing. You two are so chic.'

'I'm pretty sure I wasn't as chic as you when I was your age,' Simone tells her.

'So true,' I muse. 'Those Brooks Brothers suits I wore every fucking day at CNN. God. And so much Ann Taylor. Jesus.'

'I hope you burnt them all,' Simone drawls.

'Well, I think you're both fabulous,' Maddy pronounces. 'And we're all so excited about your documentary.'

I risk a sideways glance up at Cal, who gives me a grin that's the perfect mix of boyish and wolfish. It's a grin that says *I've got you* but also *I'm gonna show you a good time*, and I'm here for it. He slides an arm around my waist and tugs me even closer towards him. I nestle into his side, self-consciousness fluttering at the edges of the warm glow his gesture gives me.

After all, we're not a couple. Not in the slightest.

But, equally, he'll be fucking me six ways to Sunday if everything goes to plan, so what's a little cuddle?

'No one's more excited than I am,' Cal says in a tone just menacing enough to send a delicious shiver floating through my body, despite the heat of him at my side.

Maddy and Belle turn to each other and do that excited kind of smile where they beam and widen their eyes.

'Listen,' Maddy says, holding up her hand. 'Girl to girl.' She glances up at Zach, who has his arm slung around her shoulder as he converses with Anton and Gen, before continuing in a stage whisper. 'You're in good hands with this one. Belle and I can both vouch for that. You get me?'

Her meaning hits me loud and clear, a punch to the stomach, as my brain takes in everyone else's reaction. Cal's grip on my waist tightens as his body stiffens. Zach's head whips around, and he presses his lips together in a thin, grim line. And Rafe raises his head from Belle's shoulder long enough to say, 'No. No, no, no.'

Cal's fucked these women? These girls? Because that's what they are. They're young and perfect and so *fucking* gorgeous.

I know he gets around. He's told me in detail. I know he's had sex with zillions of women, and I've been trying not to get intimidated by that while recognising his experience as a gift.

But that's different from having someone hit you over the head with it. If Maddy and Belle reflect his usual standard of women, then I am in deep shit.

I attempt to laugh her comment off, because this is super awkward, and also because it looks like Zach and Rafe do not appreciate this history lesson. Not one little bit.

'Good to know,' I say lightly before burying my face in my champagne coupe. Nothing to see here.

Then Cal's arm leaves my waist and he grabs my upper arms, turning me where I stand. 'Bar. Now,' he growls.

18

CAL

Fucking Maddy.

She doesn't realise what she said, but I do. She doesn't think sometimes. She meant well just then—meant to reassure Aida that she was in for a fun ride with me—but every one of my instincts tells me that coming face to face with two of my previous sexual partners will not help her apprehension levels at what lies ahead of her.

Particularly when said sexual partners look like Maddy and Belle.

I steer Aida through the throng—or maybe *frogmarch* is more accurate. As I do, I enjoy her spectacular rear view. Her dress is equally cutaway at the back, exposing her shoulder blades, and the cream silk drapes subtly, sensually, over her gorgeous arse.

When we hit the glowing pink bar, I turn her and press her up against it, stepping forward so I'm crowding her a bit and waiting till she raises those dark eyes to mine.

'I'm sorry Maddy said that,' I begin. 'It wasn't helpful.'

'It's okay,' she says unconvincingly. She shrugs, and the move is chic and almost European.

I slide my hands up her arms till they reach her shoulders and roll my palms over them.

'I haven't fucked Belle,' I say, 'for what it's worth. I was with Maddy once, and I did a couple of Belle's Unfurl sessions, but Rafe commandeered those pretty quickly.'

She arches her eyebrows. '*The* Unfurl session?'

'I can't tell you that,' I say quickly. 'But it's water under the bridge. Believe me, we all try to pretend it never happened. The guys would have my balls otherwise. And Maddy's become a really good mate, actually. There's nothing there at all.'

She gives a stoic little nod. 'Thank you. And I know that.'

I watch her face. Watch the troubled thoughts that flit across it as plainly as clouds across a summer sky. 'So what's the problem?' I say. I let one hand skate along the crest of her shoulder, under the glossy comma of her hair and up her neck. As my thumb drags along her jaw, she lets out a tiny sigh and moves her head almost imperceptibly into my touch. I can see the moment she decides to downplay what's bothering her.

'There's no problem. It's obviously slightly jarring to be confronted with the reality of you and your lifestyle. Those women are incredibly beautiful, and they're half my age. Yeah, it's triggered my insecurities over getting naked with you, but I'll put on my big-girl pants and deal with it. End of story.'

So this is what it's like to have a conversation with an actual adult. No acting out. No giving me a hard time. No projecting her shit onto me. No passive-aggressive *I'm fine* when she means the opposite.

It's refreshing.

It's also kind of heartbreaking.

'You absolutely don't need to feel insecure,' I tell her,

sliding my other hand along her shoulder and under her hair so I'm cradling her face. So she can't look away. 'I don't pursue women based on age, the younger the better. I pursue them based on how sexy they are and how alluring I find them. And right now, God bless them, they don't hold a candle to you. Because you're the most captivating woman in this building tonight. I have no fucking interest in anyone else.'

Her eyes, almost black in this light, flicker over my face like candlelight in danger of being extinguished. Like they're searching for a kernel of honesty to latch onto. I smile down at her, stroking my thumbs along her jaw. My feet are planted firmly on either side of hers so she can't escape.

'I'm so ready to go it's not funny,' I tell her, pressing my body against her so she can see how serious I am. Her eyes widen, and she drops her gaze to where our bodies are flush. 'We can get started right now if you want.' I jerk my head towards the doors to The Playroom. 'But we're doing this at your pace, not mine. And I promise, your first proper session will be right up your street.'

'You still haven't told me what you'll be doing to me,' she says, eyes narrowing.

'I'll be doing plenty to you,' I tell her. 'I'll tell you about it on camera.'

And then, because I don't want her pestering me for clues and because that scarlet mouth of hers is twisting deliciously as I grind my erection against her, I lower my face to hers and take those lips in a scorching kiss.

19

CAL

'Why are you calling me?' my little sister asks. At least, I think that's what she asks. It's not one hundred percent intelligible over the din of toddler shrieks.

They're happy shrieks, at least.

I think?

It sounds like carnage over there. I glance around my gorgeous, minimalist penthouse flat and inwardly congratulate myself on my life choices so far.

Annabel is married to a fund manager called Giles. They live in Fulham and own way too many Cath Kidston tea towels and have popped out two babies, twenty months apart, which is incidentally the same age gap as between me and her. Obviously, Annabel is my parents' favourite because she's produced grandkids and at least pretends to conduct herself like a responsible adult.

She and Giles are indescribably sensible and boring, and if I didn't adore my sister so much, I'd despise them.

'Just calling to check in,' I say, my nonchalance belying

the fact that she rarely hears from me, WhatsApps and drunken voice notes aside.

'Bollocks,' she says. 'Are you in trouble?'

'No! Course not. How are Gracie and Harry?'

The kids favour Giles' thin blonde hair and ruddy cheeks. Happily, his unfortunate genetics look fucking adorable on them.

'Alive, as you can hear,' my sister says drily.

There's a clatter of what sounds like lots of dishes and pans being piled into the sink, and I grimace and lower the volume on my AirPods. 'Is this a bad time?'

'I have two kids under three. It's always a bad time.' She sighs. 'Sorry. No, it's fine. They've just had their tea. They're all good. Just a bit lively.'

My heart gives a tug. My sister is a saint. A living saint. I make a mental note to treat her to a day at a spa and rope Mum in to babysit. Writing a cheque I can handle. Offering myself up for childcare I cannot.

'Okay, well…' I say. 'I'll just cut to the chase, shall I? I need some advice.'

'Dating advice?' She says it with a hopeful lilt to her tone that tugs at my conscience.

'No. Sex advice.'

'Jesus, Cal!' she splutters. 'Warn a girl.'

'Sorry.'

'Why the hell are you calling me? You know a million times more about… that stuff than me. Besides, you're my brother. That whole topic should be off limits. I try to tell myself you're just a nice, mercenary hedge fund manager.'

I laugh. Rafe, Zach and I run a small investment vehicle, Cerulean, with some of our other mates from the City. It's a hedge fund that mainly manages our own money, and it makes us all enough that we can enjoy Alchemy without ever worrying about paying the bills. Everyone pitches in and trades their own area of expertise, mine being corporate debt and related instruments. I spend one day a week there, but I enjoy Alchemy far more.

'Still a sex club owner. Sorry to disappoint.'

'So why are you calling me?'

I hesitate. 'There's a woman. She's come to our club—she's recently divorced. Her husband cheated on her and she needs some TLC. I'm going to be, um, looking after her.' I clear my throat. This is awkward as fuck, because Annabel's under no illusions as to what *looking after her* means.

'Go on,' she says through gritted teeth that suggest she's regretting everything about this.

'Um. Well, she's gorgeous. Absolutely gorgeous. I'll tell you more about her a bit down the line, because it's going to be, um, public knowledge, but let's come back to that. For now, just know she's had a really shitty time of it, and she's a few years older than me, and I think she's a bit… apprehensive. About what, you know, lies ahead.'

'Don't blame her in the slightest.'

'Yeah. Well, I had an idea for our first session, and I wanted to run it past you, and—'

She groans so loudly that she almost misses me say, 'Massage.'

'What?' she says. 'Did you say *massage*?'

'Yeah,' I say again. 'Like, if I set it up a bit like a role play. You know, she comes in for a massage and—'

'—you go in deep with your very own Hitachi wand?' Annabel says through a fit of giggles.

'No,' I protest loudly. 'Not at all. I probably wouldn't even shag her the first time. I just want to make her comfortable.'

'Sorry,' she says. 'Honestly, this conversation is beyond horrifying, but I think a massage is a great idea.'

'Do you?' I'm genuinely surprised.

'I do. It's Giles' favourite way to get me in the mood for, you know...'

Now it's my turn to groan, and I do. Loudly.

'Look, do you want my advice or not?' Annabel says. 'Gracie, give that back to your brother. *Now.*'

'Yeah,' I say sheepishly. 'Sorry.' I take a swig of my protein shake and pause to admire myself in the large mirror in my living room. I'm sweaty as fuck after that Peloton arms and legs ride, but I'm looking good. Really good. I run a hand through my sweat-soaked hair, tousling it just the way I like it, and wink at myself for good measure.

Still got it.

I'm not sure how my younger sister manages to make me feel like a badly behaved child, but this little preen is enough to take the edge off it.

'You might hate hearing about the fact that Giles and I have S-E-X,' she tells me now in her Mummy Is Pissed Off voice, 'but not as much as I hate knowing that you're F-U-C-K-I-N-G everything that moves. Got it?'

'Got it,' I mumble.

'Good. As I was saying, *in response for your request for advice*, massage is a lovely segue into intimacy. For me, anyway, but for a lot of women, I think. I can't just go to bed and turn into an S-E-X goddess when I've still got bits of alphabet pasta in my hair, can I? The massage kind of relaxes me, I suppose. It gives me time to transition, and it brings my nervous system down, and it also feels like care-giving. Like Giles is making me feel so loved and cared for that I'm less likely to try to kick him in the P-E-N-I-S, you know?'

I do not know, but I can imagine that if someone had put two little humans inside my body, I might feel tempted to kick them in the D-I-C-K from time to time. I make a non-committal murmur that hopefully sounds vaguely sympathetic.

'And it also allows me to get more present in my body,' my sister muses. 'Just having skin on skin. I'm sure there's some magical nervous system explanation for it, but really, it's nice. Relaxing. It feels so indulgent. So yeah, usually by the time he's finished giving me a good rubdown, I'm more than ready for him to slip a hand—'

Yep.

We're done here.

20

AIDA

I got the house.

When we divorced, that is.

Thank God.

It would've been different if we would have lived in one of the vast houses in Cadogan Square John's family had owned for generations, thanks to some nebulous gifting arrangement involving a former Lord Russell and a former Duke of Westminster, but I put my foot down when I married him.

Those garden squares in Belgravia are stunning, but they're stuffy as fuck, and there was no way I was living there. If I had, I would have gotten kicked out by the family estate as soon as I'd quit being Lord John Henry Russell's wife.

Instead, thank God, I dug my heels in and we bought a nice little townhouse off High Street Kensington, which we upgraded to a spectacular villa in Notting Hill after Kit was born. I've been okay with the breakdown of my marriage, but I would not have been okay with losing this place.

This is my home. I've poured my heart and soul into it,

far more than John has. He kept our country place in Norfolk, and rightly so. It's a Russell family property, and God knows I have no need for a shooting estate. That house is etched onto his heart, and this house is etched onto mine.

It's a classic pale pink stucco Notting Hill villa on a gorgeous crescent. It took me ages after we moved in not to feel like I was walking in Julia Roberts' footprints in the movie every day. While this particular London village no longer feels otherworldly, it'll always retain its magic for me.

I adore the artisanal cheese stores and chocolate stores and the fancy delis where you can 'pop in' for kombucha or homemade red lentil soup. I love the people—the combination of well-heeled locals and wide-eyed tourists. I love the pretty, colourful streets and the cafe society. I love that even going out for a loaf of bread feels like a treat.

And, most of all, I adore coming home and shutting my glossy slate-grey front door behind me and feeling instantly cocooned in my carefully crafted sanctuary. It being Notting Hill, you pay a small fortune for a townhouse with a postage-stamp-sized backyard, but no matter.

There's a private residents' garden over the road—not dissimilar to the one in the movie—and the tiny courtyard out the back of our house features whitewashed walls and lots of trailing star of jasmine and a floor of the prettiest grey and white tiles. It's more like an outdoor room than a backyard.

Up one flight of stairs are our formal reception rooms, papered in a green-and-white leaf print and lined with bookshelves that heave with a mixture of political biographies and romances. John's Cold War thrillers are gone from the shelves, but you'd hardly notice given the shit-tonne of books I have.

Down here in the kitchen, however, is where I spend most of my time, sitting at our island with a cup of tea or coffee. No matter that the island is cluttered with unopened mail and the boys' pencil cases and a pile of cook books that I leafed through and bookmarked earlier this week in a fit of productivity that hasn't actually resulted in any recipe-based cooking on my part.

Yet.

None of it matters, because the clutter is a sign of a happy, if messy, life, and I value that, I cling to that, even more now that I have a failed marriage behind me.

I sit on my favourite barstool, and I swirl a ginger and turmeric tea bag around in my mug as the boys dash around the island. If someone were to take a slow lens shot of us right now, I'd be the sole identifiable subject, Pip and Kit nothing more substantive than a blur of colour and movement.

'Did you pack your cricket whites?' I ask. With these two, it's always a matter of walking the tightrope between ensuring they have the basics while trying not to foster total helplessness. It would be cruel to send them off for a weekend in Norfolk without checking they at least had clean underwear and their plush cuddly toys, but I'm conscious that the more I pick up after them, the less independent they'll be.

And, given they have a father who's intent on them following in the Russell family tradition of attending Eton when they hit thirteen, that gives Pip and Kit two and four years respectively to get their shit together before they hit boarding school.

'It's not cricket season anymore, Mum,' Kit points out. 'It's football.' At nine, he's pure lean muscle, slim and wiry and perpetually in motion. He's correct, technically, but while the new academic year has started at school, this September is still mild enough for cricket.

'Daddy told me to tell you he'll get the wickets out given the weather,' I tell him now, wincing as they emit a delighted roar in unison. They're still little boys, but they're so *male* sometimes, and it's as unnerving as it is endearing. 'Go get your whites. He's bringing your pads and helmets.'

'Did you pack my Alex Rider book?' Pip wants to know. He's more bookish, less naturally athletic than his little brother, but *God* does he try with every fibre of his being. It breaks my heart a little.

I give him a mom-like eyebrow wiggle. 'I did not. Basics only, remember? Did *you* pack Alex Rider?'

He huffs and rolls his eyes like I'm a giant pain in his backside, and I laugh. 'Go on. Go get your stuff.'

They race upstairs. My little British boys. Whatever his faults as a husband, John's a great dad, even if his idea of fathering is a little more old-school British than might be healthy. You know, the whole Eton thing. Being intent on ensuring they can hunt and fish and ride a horse and bowl a cricket ball and nail all those activities that made his exclusive English upbringing so fun for him.

To be fair to him, the upper classes in this country haven't exactly moved on from those pursuits, so maybe he's got a point. I knew how traditional he was when I married him.

I just forgot that one of the English nobility's favourite time-honoured traditions was keeping a bunch of mistresses.

The doorbell rings.

Speak of the devil.

21

AIDA

"All is not lost—the unconquerable will, and study of revenge, immortal hate, and courage never to submit or yield."
—Milton, *Paradise Lost*

When you're CNN's royal correspondent, and you've only actually been in London for a year, and most of your corresponding has been done standing outside the railings of Buckingham Palace or in the huge press pits they shove you into for royal appearances, you're going to be pretty desperate for some insider access.

Even if you know that, as an American, any chance of insider access is very limited.

So when you get invited to a fancy birthday party at the RAC Club for a royal, you don't just jump at the chance. You pretty much hyperventilate, and read Debrett's in the restroom, and bother all of your British coworkers for etiquette advice.

The party was for Peter Phillips, Princess Anne's son. The invitation was kind of a date, and that's the part I felt bad about. A nice-looking researcher in the newsroom who'd attended Gordonstoun with Peter asked me along as his plus-one, and I delightedly accepted, mainly because I was hoping to rub shoulders with Prince William and his then-girlfriend, Catherine.

I did not meet Wills and Kate.

I did, however, meet a very posh, very articulate, very charming guy named John who proceeded to get me drunk on Old Fashioneds as he whispered filthy insider gossip—off the record, naturally—about the great and good of the British aristocracy surrounding us.

He was handsome in that sleek, thoroughbred English way. Older than my twenty-nine years—early forties at least. Super smart. Sarcastic and witty in that drawling, devastating manner that Stephen Fry and Hugh Grant share.

It wasn't until the end of the night, when he asked if he could call me and we swapped cards before he bundled me into a cab, that I discovered his more formal moniker was Lord John Russell.

But by then I was already gone.

~

OURS HAS NOT BEEN a change-the-locks type of divorce. It makes my life a lot easier, in fact, if John still has a set of keys to his family home. But he would never dream of using the keys outside of an emergency, so I'm not surprised when the doorbell rings.

'Hey,' I say tiredly, leaning against the doorjamb to let him pass through.

'Hi,' he says in that serious manner that used to get me so hot, bending down to kiss me on the cheek. He'll be sixty next year, but he's still a good-looking guy. And he absolutely still has that gravitas that women seem to love. 'You're looking well. How are things?'

'Good. Busy. You?'

I shut the front door and head down the hall to the kitchen as John stands back and waits for me to pass. He would never walk in front of a lady. Those superficial manners of his are far too deeply engrained.

'Yeah, it's a little frantic at the moment,' he agrees, and I mentally ratchet that feedback up to understand that things are pretty crazy for him, too. My ex-husband is the master of understatement.

'The boys are grabbing their cricket whites,' I tell him as we enter the kitchen. 'They were so pumped when I told them to bring them. It was adorable.'

'It's perfect weather for it,' John observes. 'And there should be a good gang up there. The Kingsmill-Browns are coming along, and the Spencers. And I think some of the locals will join if we have a match.'

'Oh, fun,' I say absently. 'They'll love that.'

By *locals*, he almost certainly means the landed families in his vicinity rather than any of the regular people in North Norfolk who would have served John's family a couple centuries ago.

Nevertheless, I'm equally thrilled that the boys have a busy weekend ahead with their friends and that I no longer have to be a part of it. I always felt on the outskirts of John's social circle. The guys were charming, of course, but most of their wives were older than me and, though nice, firmly in their own bubble in the vaguely self-satisfied way most members of his class are.

It's a relief to be out of it, to be honest. Even if it means a weekend alone, catching up on research for my day job and admin for *Paradise.*

Speaking of:

'I need to update you on something while I have you here,' I say as I pour him a glass of water and slide it across the island. 'Just as a courtesy, really.'

'Of course,' he says smoothly, pulling out a bar stool and taking a seat. He prides himself on having the perfect, polite response to every situation. I think it mortified him even more than me when his exploits were splashed across every front page in the country. I still can't tell if he's a genuinely decent guy who made a few spectacular errors of judgement or a total dick whose facade got shattered.

I think it's the former, but I'm not one hundred percent sure.

'I'm producing a new documentary,' I tell him. I stay standing. I feel more in control this way.

'Good for you.'

'Thanks. I'm excited about it. The thing you should know is, it's about me. And sex.'

He frowns. 'I'm sorry. I don't quite understand.'

'I'm exploring the relationship women my age and older have with their sexuality. It's still an area that doesn't receive enough profile, and I want to use my platform to bring in experts and shine a light on the whole topic, from desires to menopause to divorce.'

He flinches almost imperceptibly then, and I know what his question will be.

'It's not about our marriage,' I say quickly. 'Not overtly. I intend to mention it as little as possible.'

'Right,' he says in a tone that tells me he's reserving judgement until he's heard more.

'But there will be a… practical aspect. I'm the conduit for this entire discussion. I embody many of the challenges we'll raise. Divorced, perimenopausal, sexually conservative.'

He looks down at his glass of water and runs his thumb over the condensation.

'And I'm partnering with a very high-end sex club,' I continue before I lose my nerve. John doesn't have a leg to stand on here, but that doesn't make it easier. That said, discussing this with the man who used to share my bed should be a drop in the ocean compared to the kind of confrontations I'll find myself in when this thing goes public.

He wrinkles his nose. 'A *sex* club?'

'Yeah. I'm being mentored by a guy there. He'll be putting me through my paces so I can gain some new experiences. It's the only real way for me to explore what my sexuality should and can look like now, in my forties.'

I pause so I can get a read on his reaction, because John is nothing if not circumspect.

'He's "putting you through your paces".'

'That's correct.'

'So you're fucking some guy on camera to provide content for a documentary about sex.'

'No. I'm not fucking him on camera. I'll fuck him in private and discuss it on camera.'

His jaw twists. 'A bit vulgar for you, isn't it?'

'I'd argue not. To me, *vulgar* is having your whores kiss and tell in the *Daily Mirror*.'

'Look, Aida. I get that you're still angry, and you have every right to be. But if you're so disgusted by my behaviour, why on earth you'd want to stoop to my level is beyond my comprehension.'

He's unwittingly hit on the very crux of our problems, and that crux, surprisingly enough, is not the fact that he slept around while we were married.

Not even close.

Our true dirty little secret is that, in our marriage, sex and shame were far too closely intertwined. More closely than certainly I realised. So closely that those toxic intertwined tendrils wound their way more and more tightly around our relationship, not content until they suffocated us both.

And, while I maintain that John bears the brunt of the blame for that, I had my part to play, too.

I allowed him to sit in that shame.

I allowed it to fester.

I allowed it to isolate him to the extent that he felt compelled to look outside our relationship for the validation and release he needed.

I can't condone his methods, but I can sympathise with the cracks in our relationship, with the absence of support, dialogue, that made him a man desperate for an outlet.

Even if that outlet was unethical and ill-judged.

'It's precisely the opposite, actually. It's not about stooping at all. It's about normalising. I plan on standing in front of a camera and shining a spotlight on myself—on my desires, but also on what about me causes those desires. And that's fucking terrifying, but I'm gonna do it anyway.

'Because when you don't normalise things that are, in fact, normal, you're really opening them up to shame and fear and hiding, which is basically what you—we—fell victim to.'

He raises his eyebrows, seemingly unconvinced, and

opens his mouth to speak, but I keep going before he can get a word out.

'Your needs never disgusted me, John, and it's my bad that I ever let you think they did. I sincerely regret that I didn't hold more space for us to be fully honest with each other. The way you went behind my back and made me a national laughingstock disgusted me far more. But, honestly, it's a good life lesson. Get this shit out in the open. Tell people it's okay to feel what they feel and want what they want.'

He shakes his head. 'I just can't imagine this is what you really want, Aida. I worry it's a knee-jerk reaction. You told me you wanted to, and I quote, "go live in the Sahara and never see another human being again".'

He's right.

I did.

I felt like that for weeks afterward.

'That was the knee-jerk reaction,' I explain. 'Not this. I know you don't get this, but I promise you I'm doing this for noble reasons. This feels like a healthy, positive outcome for what was a pretty shitty episode. I know it'll be positive for me and for other women my age. It's something I have to do. But I wanted to do you the courtesy of making you aware that, over the coming weeks, it'll be my sex life plastered all over the front pages. Even if I'm setting the agenda to a far greater extent this time.'

My reserved British husband is far less advanced on his journey than I am, which is ironic given he's the one who's been outed as a serial philanderer. But the way he's been vilified and shamed and ridiculed by the press has only underscored in his head that airing your sexual laundry in public is tawdry and distasteful and to be avoided at all costs.

I get that. I really do.

But, right or wrong, he didn't get a chance to control his narrative. I have a pretty full understanding of his story these days, and it's not what the press or the British public would imagine it being.

But I get a chance to control my narrative.

And I damn well plan on using it.

22

CAL

AIDA (OFF-CAMERA): Why don't you introduce yourself, just to get yourself comfortable talking to the camera?

ME: [Gives what I hope is a devastating grin] Yeah. Hi. I'm Callum Sinclair. Fuck, I can't believe I just waved.

AIDA: It's okay. We won't use any of this part anyway—it'll be very tightly edited. And we can also put B-roll over some of your content.

ME: Like the wave?

AIDA: Like the wave.

LIZZY THE DIRECTOR: [Sniggers audibly]

ME: I heard that, Lizzy.

LIZZY: Yeah. Sorry.

ME: Okay ladies, prepare to be dazzled. I'm really ready now. Hang on. [Rakes hand through hair] Okay. Ready.

AIDA: From the top. Just try introducing yourself again.

ME: [Grins] I'm Callum Sinclair, and I'm a co-owner of Alchemy, which is an exclusive sex club in London.

AIDA: I can't imagine the stories you could tell. Do you have a lot of high profile members?

ME: We do now, baby.

AIDA: Yeah, well. I'm gonna keep a *very* low profile. Anyway. Sex club owner. What did you do before?

ME: I traded credit instruments for a large investment bank. Mainly credit default swaps.

AIDA: Nice. So once you'd brought down the US housing market, you thought you'd try your hand at selling sex?

ME: [Laughs] Wow. Tough crowd. Something like that, I suppose, though I was way too junior to blame the Financial Crisis on. I founded the club with three good mates from uni—two guys and one woman. We dreamed the concept up over too much wine one night, but weirdly we were still into the idea the next morning.

AIDA: What was it about the idea of a sex club that made you tick?

ME: Is that a trick question?

AIDA: [Laughs] Aside from the obvious, that is.

ME: [Sighs] I think it felt... honest. That might sound odd, but we were all playing the same game. Work hard in the City by day, fuck hard by night. We were hooking up in bars and clubs. It was a lot of fun, but it was messy and exhausting.

You'd end up drinking too much and going home with a stranger and staggering into work the next day and changing your shirt at the office. It wasn't sustainable.

AIDA: So Alchemy is a more sustainable choice?

ME: It's more of an intentional choice, I would say. You go there and you know everyone else is there for the same reason. Even more importantly, they've all been vetted. They've had background and health checks done and signed ironclad NDAs. Plus, we have an extremely strict no-drug policy and a two-drink maximum. So it's a far safer place to find a sexual partner than out on the town or on a dating app.

AIDA: Now, the mere concept of a sex club will be absolutely terrifying for a lot of women. I know it is for me. How do you think women in particular can benefit from putting their sex lives into the hands of a place like Alchemy?

ME: I can't tell women—or men, even—how to feel about sex, because those attitudes will be a melting pot of absolutely everything they've absorbed throughout their life, from religion, to culture, to their parents' attitude toward sex. But one thing we really stand by here at Alchemy is that most of the shame and guilt we feel around sex is in our heads.

It's not real.

The whole point of the club is to create a shame-free, sex-positive environment for consenting adults to experiment for their own gratification and that of their fellow members. End of story. There is nothing about seeking and taking pleasure that should make you feel guilty in that context. And if that's a principle anyone takes away in the broader context of their sex lives, then I'll be thrilled.

AIDA: What kind of people would you say you attract to the club?

ME: A lot of them are time-poor, so it appeals for reasons I've just explained. You can have a great time and then head home alone and get a good night's sleep. Obviously, most of the people who apply are sexually curious and adventurous. They come because we can cater to their needs without them lifting a finger—all they have to do is show up. It pushes their boundaries—they might come to us for X and end up trying and loving Y.

AIDA: But not everyone who comes to you is necessarily that experienced, right?

ME: Right. That's really important. It's far more about mindset than experience. We have people come to us who have no experience at all, and we have a programme that caters specifically for these people in a very tailored, very safe framework if they don't want to jump in at the deep end.

AIDA: Tell us more about that programme, will you?

ME: [Leans forward] It's called Unfurl, and we gave it that name because we believe the blossoming of your sexuality is a beautiful, natural process and very much part of the human experience.

I know even among us four co-founders, at the time when we were dreaming up Alchemy, we'd all heard stories of people not enjoying their first time, especially if they were women. It was either traumatic, or uncomfortable, or just plain unrewarding.

So we thought, 'Let's design a framework where people can sign up and expand their sexual horizons at their pace, on their terms, according to their, I suppose, risk appetites and kinks'.

AIDA: And it's not just for virgins. Because that's the programme I've signed up for.

ME: [Shoots her a sexy grin] Yes you have. And, if I understand it correctly, it's because you've come out of a monogamous relationship with the intention of reactivating your sex life with other people, but you'd like things to be more structured, for you, and also more private, because the last thing you need in your position is to be with people who don't prioritise your wellbeing or who might betray your confidence.

AIDA: Exactly. But I'd like everyone watching to know that you haven't actually told me yet what the first session will be. Which is incredibly rude, because I'm supposed to be calling the shots here. This is my show.

ME: I'll tell you when you're on this sofa next to me. And remember, when you're at the club with me, it's my show, baby.

AIDA: Dear God.

ME: I promise you, I will do everything in my power to make it an amazing experience for you. The only thing that matters is that you come out of that first session feeling like the beautiful, powerful goddess you are. *The only thing.*

23

AIDA

This hot-non-boyfriend thing is pretty addictive. There's a gorgeous guy who's brought me to orgasm in a club, and pinned me up against a bar and kissed me, and whose way with words is apparently as dirty on camera as it is when his mouth is brushing my ear.

I have to admit, the dynamic is a little like being back in high school. When will I see him? Is he thinking about me? Will he send me a dirty text this evening?

(Okay, I'm way too old to have had a cellphone in high school, but you get the picture.)

It's exciting. Distracting.

Especially given how great he did on camera this morning. I could tell he was, by Cal standards, a little nervous, but he was perfect. There's no way a guy can be that smooth talking in real life and not deliver some great banter to the camera, but he smashed my expectations.

I tell myself the reason for my pleasure is purely professional. This is my show. My name on the title. My reputation on the line. It's *personal.* I want it to inspire people, to make them uncomfortable, to pose questions they'd rather not think about. I want it to stretch them and, maybe, even alter their worldview a teeny bit.

So when Cal sits in front of me and Lizzy and delivers his lines like he's been writing TV soundbites all his life, it's a good thing. It bodes well for the success of the programme and for its uptake on social, especially TikTok and Twitter. If we're all to be reduced to a meme, if the documentary of my heart will live and die by a one-liner on social, then those soundbites may as well be good.

But he nailed it. I snicker to myself as I recall his answer to my jokey question about whether Alchemy has celebrity members.

We do now, baby.

The killer moment, though, the part that gave me purely professional goosebumps, was what he said to me at the end.

The only thing that matters is that you come out of that first session feeling like the beautiful, powerful goddess you are. The only thing.

Yeah.

That'll get a girl all types of flustered, because come *on.*

I already know the nation will fall hard for Callum Sinclair and his ridiculous good looks and ability to speak straight to a woman's vagina.

No judgement here, ladies.

We're shooting the interviews in the drawing room of a suite at the gorgeous Lanesborough Hotel by Hyde Park. The location is in keeping with the aspirational vibe of the programme, and the hotel has agreed a sensible rate for the suite when we need it, which will be once a week for the next eight weeks.

Because if I'm gonna sit next to a relative stranger and calmly discuss why I intend to let him fuck me in a totally premeditated, almost choreographed way, then I'm sure as hell gonna do it on a fancy couch in a four-figures-per-night hotel with a crystal glass in my hand.

And the suite is gorgeous. There's a bookshelf behind us with old leather-bound books and an oil painting of some lady with a powdered wig and a virginal blush on her cheeks. It's there non-ironically, too. It's like we're hoping that if we make our surroundings as elevated as possible, our viewers will forget to sex-shame us. Sex-shame *me*. I doubt Cal cares. And men don't get sex-shamed, anyway. Not as much as we do.

The major risk, obviously, is that all these attempts to elevate our subject matter makes the programme feel elitist and out of touch. And it probably is. After all, Alchemy membership is affordable for only a fortunate few in our society. The entire creative team and I are well aware of that, and we've made peace with it.

Our lengthy, circular dialogue on the topic has converged to a level of agreement on one thing: that this peek into the world of elite sex clubs will be as alluring for many as the discourse around female sexuality itself. I've compromised; I've made concessions. But I've stayed unwavering on one thing.

We have this single window of opportunity to reframe our society's attitude towards going after sexual gratification in a self-loving and self-indulgent manner. I absolutely will not have the backdrop for that search for pleasure painted as an underworld.

I'm not interested in shining a furtive flashlight on dark, seedy corners and darker, seedier secrets.

I'm throwing a switch and shining a fucking floodlight on the glorious, carnal circus that awaits people who are ready to grab their sexual birthright with both hands.

And this world that my floodlight will bathe in gorgeous, dazzling light? It'll be as luxurious and fabulous and aspirational as a Gatsby party.

It'll be unapologetic as fuck, because there's nothing to apologise for here.

I feel like Hemingway would've approved of this sumptuous suite. It's so divine, so opulent, that I find myself wishing I could stay here after the crew has packed up and spend a night here, alone with a good romance novel. There's a marble tub in the bathroom that has my name written all over it. Though Cal has already suggested in a low, sexy voice that we should make use of this suite together when we're further along in the process, which is also, you know, not a bad call.

I've directed myself so many times in the field that I'm wearing my director's hat and my editor's hat and my interviewer's hat all piled on top of the only hat I'm *supposed* to be wearing right now—that of an interviewee.

When you're put on a last-minute flight to DC or Eurostar to Paris to report on breaking news or a catastrophic bombing, you often end up doing everything. I can't count the number of times it's been me and a hastily-arranged camera operator from wherever the BBC could pull one.

Often, there is no producer. Even more often, there's no time for editing, because if we're not broadcasting live then we may only have an hour or two to get our footage to London in time for the news.

In these situations, I'm my own editor. Every line I spout, every question I ask, is with the hyper-focused goal of achieving our objective from this broadcast.

What is happening here, at its very essence?

What is the the most important message the public needs to hear?

And, if my broadcast involves an interviewee: *What is the message I want to have this person say?*

I'm editing as I speak. As I question. As I listen. *Is this useful? Is this just filler? Have we gotten to the crux of the matter yet? Has this person said what I want them to say? Have they divulged anything new or interesting? Have they clarified their position? Given their agenda away? Have I been too tough on them? Tough enough? Have I been too conciliatory? Why aren't they sweating as much as I am right now?*

And always, always: *Have I gotten the soundbite yet?*

It sounds like that last question risks the temptation of encouraging salacious reporting. Oversimplifying staggeringly complex issues. But it's less about finding a salacious headline and more about achieving clarity. About distilling an event to its essence.

I always know when I've gotten it. My body tells me. The goosebumps that race over my skin, under however many layers of clothes I'm wearing. The quickening of my heartbeat.

And I can never relax in a field broadcast until I know we've gotten that soundbite.

Today's interview isn't live, obviously. And yet, my editor's brain is working. Whirring. It's taking in every optic of every detail in a way that I hope will preempt how the viewers perceive us. It's assessing this set. The proximity of my and Cal's chairs to each other. Our body language. It's doing all this when, really, it should just be focusing on answering the damn questions.

I'm glad we're in chairs. A couch would have been awkward. Cal's relaxed, back straight but legs at ease. I'm the one who has to remind myself to chill the fuck out. I'm fresh out of hair and makeup, my shoulder-length bob immaculately curled under and my makeup perfect. To differentiate from Newsroom Aida, I've opted to go heavier, smokier, on the eyes. I'm in a red sheath dress that matches my lips and heels. It's long enough to be classy, short enough to show off my legs in the chair.

'So.' Finished with her warmup, Simone turns to me. 'Tomorrow is your first session with Callum, correct?'

She emphasises *session* slightly in a way that acknowledges what an inadequate word it is for what lies ahead.

I nod and make myself smile. 'Yep.'

'How are you feeling about it?'

'Terrified.' I bark out a laugh as I glance over at Callum. He's grinning at me, and, God bless him, his smile is sexy and fond and perfect, and I mentally note that we should focus in on that smile in the edits.

He leans sideways on his chair and grabs my hand. 'You're allowed to be terrified. But I've got you.'

Even as I smile gratefully at him, I'm noting how our body contact in this moment will go over on camera. His touch is spontaneous. Warm, friendly, almost brotherly. Not flirtatious, even though he's running his thumb over my knuckles.

'You're going to be great,' he says. I lay our joined hands on my thigh. It's part calculated move and part driven by the comfort I get from his touch. Obviously what the good folks watching at home won't know is that we've already been intimate. He's already made me come.

And while I don't want to suggest to our viewers that our relationship is further along than it's supposed to be, I do want to demonstrate a level of connection. Of chemistry, though it's more than that. I want heat, yeah. I want tension.

If I'm being honest, I want everyone urging us on to fuck right out of the gate.

But, more than that, I want to show a human connection. I want to show that this isn't calculated or awkward or excruciating. It's okay for me to show vulnerability. To show how nervous I am. More than okay—it's crucial to the authenticity I'm trying to bring to this programme. But I don't want anyone thinking that the idea of Cal and me fucking is weird or uncomfortable.

His hand stays on my thigh. There's something familiar about this touchy-feely dynamic between us. It's right there at the back of my mind, bothering me, evading me.

Until it isn't.

Of course! The way we are together reminds me a little of the relationships between the professional dancers and the celebrity contestants on *Strictly Come Dancing.* It's something that's always given me a kick, seeing how physical those relationships get.

I'm not the only one—the British tabloids are always rife with speculation about which couples are fucking for the entire three months each year that the show airs. And, while dancing Argentine tangos with someone day in, day out is entirely likely to make you more likely to want to fuck them, the intensive daily dance practices tends to make every single couple physically relaxed with each other to an extent that's pretty extreme.

These guys know their way around each others' bodies, they *trust* each other with their bodies, and it shows more and more as the competition goes on. Which leads me to wonder if Cal and I will be openly making out in a few weeks from now, having ditched these chairs for a two-seater couch.

'You still don't know what Callum has in store for you tomorrow, is that right?' Simone is asking me now.

'That's right.' I squeeze his hand playfully. 'He's been playing his cards close to his chest.'

'Okay, Callum,' Simone says. 'Time for the big reveal.'

When she says that, like a *Strictly* host, I have the most uncharacteristic urge to giggle right there. Because instead of saying, *well, Simone, next week we'll be performing the foxtrot,* what can he possibly say?

Well, Simone. Tomorrow we'll be exploring the reverse cowgirl style. This is a tough one. Aida's going to need to work on her rhythm, as well as all the quad work that style involves.

Oh my fucking God.

Thankfully, Cal doesn't say any of that. He takes a deep breath and smiles straight at me, and I realise that even if he's not exactly nervous, he's hoping that what he says next will please me.

'Tomorrow's all about Aida,' he says. 'Obviously, this entire process is all about Aida. So you're welcome to veto this, sweetheart. But it's really important that we start slow. I actually got some advice from a pretty stressed-out mum I know who gave this idea a big thumbs up, so I'm hoping it'll sound good to you.'

He asked a female friend? My nervous system floods with some kind of feel-good hormone as I realise how intent he is on making this a positive experience for me.

'Go on,' I prompt, grinning goofily at him.

'Tomorrow I'll be giving Aida a full-body massage,' he says, glancing to the camera before turning his attention right back to me. He shifts in his seat so his body is facing me. 'It can be as clean or dirty as you want to make it. I'll be led by you. Tomorrow is about you getting used to me touching you. It's about you relaxing, and feeling indulged and cared for, and it's about getting you to trust me. You'll call all the shots.'

He clears his throat and places his other hand under mine so he has my hand in a kind of sandwich between his palms.

'It's about making you feel great, and getting you to be present in that gorgeous body of yours, and—this is very important—it's about showing you exactly how much I'll enjoy touching you. Because I know I will.'

His face is so intense now, those huge, dark eyes fixed on mine. His expression is as genuine as his tone, and I drink it in. I drink it all in.

'How do you think that sounds, sweetheart?' he asks.

I don't think it's just the recognition that this is TV gold that has me swallowing before I can answer him.

My daily experience throughout my career has been of shouty white men. Of entitled guys ignoring me. Talking over me. Talking over *each other* around newsroom desks or across political debates. Intent on making their own voice heard, on furthering their own agenda.

But this guy listens. He's listened to everything I've told him. And while that may seem like a low bar, it's everything to me.

'It sounds perfect,' I tell him, and I don't need to fake my smile.

24

CAL

We've arranged to do all of the sex stuff at Alchemy. It makes sense. After all, I have an entire sex club at my disposal and it lies empty until its doors open to our ravenous members at eight o'clock each night.

That's the good part.

The less good part is that, to accommodate this and Aida's desire to do the school pickup, our rendezvous will take place while her sons are at school. It's fine with me—I can fuck anytime, anywhere—but I'm conscious that ten-thirty in the morning isn't exactly sexy o'clock for her.

She's getting ready in a bathroom down the hall. All our rooms are ensuite, but I wanted her away from this room to maximise the impact when she sees it for the first time. Besides, she's recording some candid to-camera stuff on her phone. It'll be rough and ready, but she hopes it'll give her viewers a good idea of how she's feeling in this moment.

I haven't seen her since yesterday, and the parallel I could draw with a groom not seeing his bride until the Big

Moment is too fucking weird. What's even weirder is that we'll be filmed, for this first bit, at least. The camera and lighting setup is as basic as the production team could make it, the crew as skeleton.

The idea, apparently, is to capture the tension and anticipation that many women would feel when walking into a sex club to have some form of sexual relations. It's also to showcase Alchemy. We've had a camera crew in several days this week, getting B-roll of the club's layout, but the viewers are bound to be curious.

They'll want to see this den of sin. They're sure as hell not going to get any footage of me and Aida doing anything intimate, so these initial moments will need to provide a frisson all by themselves. As soon as that's covered off, as efficiently and candidly as possible, the crew will dismantle the two sets of lights currently ruining my carefully created vibe in the room and get the hell out of there.

Lights aside, it's looking good, I think. We opted to use one of our largest rooms and we've hidden all clues of kink. Alchemy's an upmarket place with a luxury vibe that's all the more alluring for its subtlety, but still. The hanging cuffs have been unscrewed from the ceiling for today's purposes, the bowls of condoms and lube removed.

The huge bed with its black satin sheets is gone, in its place a professional massage table, complete with white terry towelling fitted sheet, making the place look positively spa-like and giving us some much-needed space to accommodate these fucking lights.

There are candles everywhere—scented ones, filling the room with neroli and geranium and whatever else Gen said would be relaxing. Instead of the sexy, sultry bass that usually plays, we've hooked the sound system up with that pan-pipe type of yogi crap. A marble tray stands in the place of the usual condom bowl, laden with luxurious body oils and creams.

And yeah, there's a tube of lube, too. I wouldn't be a good Boy Scout if I didn't cover all eventualities.

All this is to say that the space looks like a spa, it smells like a spa, it sounds like a spa, and it'll hopefully say *spa* and not *kinky den of fuckery* to Aida when she walks in. I've gone for black fitted pants and a tight black crewneck t-shirt, which I think makes me look professional but also makes my arms and pecs look fucking *huge* as I surreptitiously flex them in the massive mirror that's a staple in all our private rooms. Watch and weep, Henry Cavill.

The entire crew for this production is female, and I'm the only bloke here today aside from Zach and Rafe, who are safely locked away upstairs in the office. There are two camera operators, the lighting person, Lizzy, and Darika, the producer, who's promised to stay back. This is a documentary, not a reality TV show. We're not scripted.

We're just us.

'She's coming,' Temi, one of the camera operators says, and I stand in the doorway with Temi behind me, shooting over my shoulder as Aida pads down the corridor. The other camera is trailing her. She's in white slippers and a fluffy white robe, and that bloody bridal analogy hits me again as she comes towards me.

Fuck's sake.

I stick my hands in my pockets and grin at her. 'Ah, Ms Russell,' I say, watching with gratification as she takes me in and gives me that signature move of hers. That sensual swipe of her tongue along her bottom lip. 'Ready for a good pummelling?' I ask with a smirk.

As I've intended, she laughs. 'Nice.' She stops in front of me, and we size each other up in front of the camera. She's holding the robe's lapels tightly closed with one hand.

No matter.

I'll get it off her soon enough.

'I'm Callum, and I'll be your masseur today,' I tell her. We absolutely didn't plan to do this as a role play, but I'm up for having fun with this and I'm definitely up for making her feel as relaxed as possible. 'Happy ending optional. Come on through.'

She wisely ignores my comment and sweeps through the doorframe far more imperiously than anyone should be able to do in a robe and slippers. Once the cameras are in, I stand behind her and put my hands on her shoulders. Fuck, they're stiff. I pull her back against me.

'What do you think?'

'It feels like a real spa,' she says, sounding faintly surprised. She inhales deeply, her lungs filling up against my chest. 'It smells amazing.'

'Good.' I kiss the top of her head. 'I want this to be somewhere you can relax and let go.' I slide my hands along her shoulders, over soft cotton waffle and fine bones, and squeeze her biceps.

'What do you say we kick the cameras out and we find out exactly how relaxed I can make you?'

She twists her head, looking up at me, and I hope the cameras catch her facial expression, because there's already a levity to it. She trusts me, I think, and she's actually up for this. She seems more anticipatory than scared.

'I'm down with that,' she murmurs.

'That's my girl.' I squeeze her arms again without letting go and stand back so Temi and her colleague can get past.

Temi backs out, and I lean against the doorframe, grinning straight at the lens.

'See you later,' I tell the camera. 'I've got this.'

And I wink.

25

AIDA

"The Serpent, subtlest beast of all the field."
—Milton, *Paradise Lost*

I heard what Cal said to the camera, and my always-on editor brain does a little happy dance at what will probably have women all over the nation reaching for their vibes before I forcibly shut down that part of my consciousness.

I'm not here to edit.

I'm here to be undone.

After a five-minute wrangle between the crew and the lights, the door clicks softly shut and Cal and I are alone. I can appreciate, now, the overall effect he's created with the candles. The music. The massage table. The space is dim and womblike and serene—not at all like a sex club and exactly like a high-end spa. Except I've never been to a spa where the masseurs are this hot.

He stands in front of me, impossibly gorgeous, his fitted

black clothes showing off that gym-honed bulk. He's made everything all about me, so far, but *he's* the most important part of this entire experience. Which is a vague way of articulating the fact that I can't wait to get his clothes off at some point.

I can't wait to see that body. Feel those muscles.

The idea of lying naked under *that* is so insane that it makes me feel a little woozy if I dwell on it too much.

'You doing okay?' he asks softly.

'Yeah,' I tell him. I mean it.

'Good.' He pats the bed. 'Take the robe off and get yourself on the bed, face down, under the towel. The eye mask is up to you, but I thought it might help to cut out stimuli. I'll turn around.'

I have to stop myself from smiling, because he sounds exactly like a professional masseur, and I can't help but find it adorable that he's trying so hard to put me at ease. I do as he says, laying my robe on a chair and sliding my naked body between the fluffy towel and the heated bed. I even put the sleep mask on, though I suspect his reasons for suggesting it have less to do with stimuli and more to do with removing some layers of self-consciousness.

He's a sweetie.

And this is already heaven.

Believe me when I say that as a single mom, I find even getting a bikini wax relaxing. Lying on a bed in relative silence for twenty minutes? I'll take it. But, as Callum moves around the bed, tugging the heavy towel upwards so it covers my shoulders and smoothing firm hands over it, I feel cared for in a way that I haven't since my last facial. I get daily, nightly cuddles from my boys, of course, but caregivers they are not. So having a guy who's slowly becoming a friend perform this simple ritual for me is as touching as it is intimate. I cradle my head in my arms and let out a contented sigh as my eyes drift closed.

'I'm going to go slowly,' Cal says. 'I want this to feel as much like a regular massage as possible. I meant what I said out there—there's a happy ending if you want it, but it's optional. Let's see how we go. Today's about getting you used to me touching you and letting you see how much I like it. Okay?'

'Okay,' I echo easily, because I'm on board, and the tension is already leaving my body.

'Good.' He's bending over, his breath warm on my ear. 'Because I can't wait to get my hands on every inch of your gorgeous body.'

I make a nervous, high-pitched noise at the back of my throat that I'm not proud of, but I sense him moving away and hear the clink of bottles. I adjust my head so I'm face-down in the bed's padded hole. Then he's back, and I'm hit with the most wonderful scent. It's similar to whatever candles are burning in the room—heady and rich and rounded, and I sniff appreciatively.

'Here are a couple of options for your massage oil,' he says. 'This one is the restorative one, and this one is more energising.'

He waves another scent under my nose. He's right. It's fresh and zingy—grapefruit, maybe? It's lovely, but I'm not here to be energised.

I'm here to be restored.

'The first one.' I wonder if he did that masseur thing where he dabbed a little of each oil on a cotton pad? It almost makes my heart hurt to think about it.

'Great. I'm going to start with your legs. If you want me to stop at any time, I will. Just say so.'

I hum my acknowledgement, and he's off, lifting a

corner of the towel to expose one calf and foot. I'm momentarily chilly, but then his big hands are on me, smoothing warm oil down my leg and rubbing at the arch of my foot with thumbs so strong I practically moan with pleasure.

'Pressure okay?' he asks.

'Perfect,' I mumble. I'm in a darkened, sightless cocoon, my front warmed by this fantastic heated bed and my left leg in sensory heaven. And, right here and now, I decide to take this moment for what it is. It's not some intimidating gateway leading to a terrifying path of debauchery. It's a massage. A free one. And mothers do not turn down free massages, period. Nor do they fail to wring every last drop of pleasure from them.

Cal finds his rhythm, and he's so convincing, so sure of himself, that I almost forget who he is and why I'm here. I allow myself to be lulled into a state that's fifty percent contented sleepiness and fifty percent awareness that having this gorgeous man's hands commanding my body like this feels seriously great.

After he's worked my calf and foot until I'm practically purring with pleasure, he lifts the towel higher, so it's grazing the crease where my ass meets my thigh. More oil goes on, and his strokes grow longer, more decadent, sweeping easily down my lubricated thighs and calves. His large hands cover their ground easily, his thumbs dragging down my inner thighs.

The overall sensation is so wonderful that I have to remind myself that this is okay. That the warmth spreading through my lower half at his touch is allowed. He's not some poor random guy. If I start to fantasise about those hands of his moving higher, that's okay. I'm not violating him.

In fact, I'm starting to realise that he's edging me in the most effective way. He's giving me just enough to build the desire in my body. To build the suggestion in my mind that I want more. The *more* won't come from him—it'll come from me.

Clever guy.

He's playing me like an instrument.

With that in mind, I shift a little on the bed, emboldened to nudge my legs farther apart. A moment later, he folds the towel back further, exposing one butt cheek before sliding his hand over it. The move is decisive, almost proprietorial, and I shiver inwardly.

'So fucking gorgeous,' he murmurs softly, and then his hands knead. They knead my butt, my thigh, my calf, my foot, until my entire left side is a mass of sensation. He squeezes the very top of my thigh, his fingers digging into my inner thigh near to where I'm starting to crave them. They're so close. This massage was the best idea ever. To know that he'll work me up, wind me higher, until those magic fingers of his are sliding between my legs, sliding inside my body just how I need them? It's sublime.

I allow myself to arch into his touch, my ass lifting slightly into the air. His pace is still as slow as when he started out, but the strokes are rougher. Deeper. His hands are higher, fingers growing closer to my pussy.

'Feels good, does it?' he asks through what sounds like gritted teeth.

'So good,' I hiss.

'Glad to hear it,' he says softly.

Then his hands leave my skin and the towel comes down to cover it.

What the actual fuck?

26

CAL

We haven't even got to the *dirty-lite* bit, and I can already tell I've warmed this beautiful creature up as much on the inside as I have on the outside. Her skin is supple, soft, and these famous legs of hers feel even better than they look. Toned and shapely. I bet they could hold on tight if she wrapped them around my waist.

As I cover her leg with the towel and smooth my hands over it, I allow myself to enjoy the sharp stab of pleasure that hits me at knowing I'm affecting her. My—so far, relatively innocent—touch is arousing her. I'll have her writhing on this massage table before too long, but right now I'm content just to know she feels amazing.

I uncover her other leg and proceed to repeat my actions: warming the unctuous oil between my hands, placing my palms on her skin and oiling it up, working my fingers into those tight muscles in her calves, rolling my thumbs back and forth over the arch of her foot.

This time, there's no surprised hitch in her breath when I bare her gorgeous arse cheek to me.

This time, I allow my fingertips to graze further around, till they're at the very top of her inner thigh.

I drag my thumb along the crease of her arse.

I knead that toned cheek just a little harder than the other one.

And I even permit myself to bend and press a kiss right in the middle of it as my fingertips trail so lightly along her inner thigh that I know it must tickle.

She lets out a surprised little moan at the kiss, and I smile to myself. 'Delicious,' I mutter against her skin. And she is. It takes every ounce of self-control I have not to sink my teeth into it.

All in good time.

I straighten up, my rock-hard cock complaining silently to me, and dutifully fold the towel back down to cover her leg. This time, when I run my hands up both towel-covered legs, I allow my thumbs to press right in between her thighs. Right where that fleeting pressure of terry towelling must feel the most torturous. Sure enough, the moan she makes this time is a little more frustrated.

'Is my warmup working?' I enquire idly as I circle the bed, coming to stand at its head.

'You know it is.' Her response is muffled, but her tone is clear.

She's getting pissed off.

'Good.' I lean forward and fold the towel away from me so it exposes her entire back, right to the curve of her ass. Fuck, her back is beautiful. Flawless skin, bronzed to perfection aside from a sweet little white bikini strap mark. I trail a fingertip across it. 'No topless sunbathing for you this summer, sweetheart?'

'I may be Italian, but I'm way too anglicised for that,' she says drily. 'My sons would've killed me.'

'Shame,' I say. 'You're not the only one who's turned on, you know.'

'Seriously?' She lifts her head slightly, even though she's still blindfolded.

'Seriously. I'm hard as fuck touching this beautiful body of yours. But I'm dealing with it. So be a good girl, and be patient, and I'll reward you. Okay?'

I take her frustrated groan as acquiescence and get to work, warming more oil before sliding my palms down her back. Her muscles are tense, but the skin covering them is pure silk. She's fine-boned and slim, the arms I've already seen on display the feminine kind of toned that a conscientious gym or yoga routine creates.

'You are beautiful,' I tell her, my hands doing lazy laps of her body. 'Just beautiful.' I spend a few minutes working on her shoulders and upper back, because they really do feel stiff. Then I let myself have a bit more fun. I bend right over her body, my hands digging under the towel to grab that arse again, fingers grazing her crack before I drag them back upwards along her sides. I push them under her body so I can cup her tits, and she lets out a surprised, happy gasp that goes straight to my dick.

'Fuck,' I say, finding her nipples and rolling them around as best I can with barely any space. 'I want to play with these properly. What do you say you turn over and we lose the towel so I can make you feel good?'

'God, yes,' she gasps.

'That's my girl. Keep the mask on.'

I have the towel on the floor with a single tug, and then she's fully, gloriously naked in front of me. I get a fleeting glimpse of the perfect violin shape of her arse and hips and waist before she's flipping over onto her back, dark hair falling over her face and sleep mask as she does, and holy *fuck*.

'Oh, yeah,' I growl, raking my fingers through her hair to get it off her face. 'You are fucking *perfect*.'

She really is. Jesus Christ. The way she's been carrying on about her age, you'd think she was wrinkled and decrepit. She's a fucking smoke show. I can't wait to see her tits when she's upright, but they're perfect and plump with taut, dark pink nipples. Her stomach is flat, smooth, and the landing strip of dark hair has my name on it. I can't wait to slide my fingers and tongue into her wet heat, but it'll have to wait.

First, I bend and cup her upside-down face. 'You're so sexy,' I say. 'Gimme your hand.'

She raises one arm over her head and I pull it backwards to cup my very hard, very angry cock.

'Feel that?'

'Fuck,' she says. 'Yes.'

'Good. That's what you do to me. Now, you lie here like a good girl while I enjoy you. Got it?'

'Yes,' she says, back arching involuntarily.

'Good,' I repeat, my gaze sweeping over her body. I love having my women blindfolded. Love the control it gives me, love the dampener it puts on their insecurities, the way it dials down their self-consciousness and dials up their anticipation. Right now, the famous, dazzling Aida Russell is naked and blindfolded and fucking dying for my touch, and *Jesus*, the things I could do to her—

Dirty-lite, I remind myself sternly. *Get a grip, you horny fucker.*

She's laid out like a feast, and I barely know where to begin. But this isn't about me, it's about her, so I begin where I think she'd like it. I keep her jaw cupped and lean down to kiss her, tugging at her plump lower lip with my teeth when she opens her mouth. I release it, gripping her face harder as I invade her mouth with my tongue, and fuck, it feels so carnal having her spread out like this for me.

I enjoy her mouth for a few more seconds before releasing her jaw and straightening up. 'Don't move,' I warn her as I tip more oil into my hand and warm it up. Then I'm back at the head of the table, sliding my palms over her soft tits and hard, needy nipples and all the way down to her stomach before I drag them back up.

The sound she makes when I brush over her nipples is a thing of great wonder. Her lips part involuntarily, and I admire the pretty way she arches her back, needing more of my touch.

'Aren't you responsive,' I mutter. 'More?'

'*Yes.*' It's a prayer.

'I'm here to serve,' I tell her, and I make another lavish sweep of her torso. Fuck me, I could do this all day. This time, I linger on her tits on my way back up, kneading them and weighing them, flicking those little nipples of hers till she's wriggling on the bed and inhaling sharply.

'That feel good?' I ask, my extreme arousal making my tone more brusque than I intended.

'Yes—don't stop,' she begs.

'You need more?'

'Yes.'

'Where?'

She hesitates, though her body is still moving. Writhing. Chasing sensation.

I tweak both her nipples with my slippery fingers, and she bucks. 'You're the client. This is your massage. Tell me where you want my fingers.'

27

CAL

"Carnal desire enflaming; he on Eve
Began to cast lascivious eyes, she him
As wantonly repaid; in lust they burn"
—Milton, *Paradise Lost*

'Inside me,' she admits, sounding defeated.

'Inside where? Your mouth? Your arse?'

'Inside my—pussy.'

'Yes, you do. You know it. Permission to switch to lube.'

She laugh-groans her assent.

I release her nipples. 'What a good, dirty girl for me. Stay exactly where you are.'

I'm washing my hands as fast as I can in the ensuite bathroom, soaping them up because I suspect this scented oil is not pussy-friendly and I don't want to mess with her lady garden. You work with Gen long enough, you become a reluctant expert in the wonders of the vaginal microbiome.

I've got lube if she needs it, but I bet she fucking doesn't.

In the minute I've been gone, Aida's drawn her feet up flat on the massage table, shapely legs moving restlessly, oiled skin lustrous in this dim lighting. I stand beside her and smooth a palm down her breastbone so I can splay my fingers over her stomach. Making her orgasm spontaneously in the Zebra Club was a lot of fun, but having her naked and worked up and all to myself is a whole other stratosphere.

With my other hand, I graze the silky length of her thigh before stopping just shy of where I know she needs me. I brush the backs of my knuckles over the soft skin there.

'Tell me what you can feel here,' I say. My fingers splay wider, more possessively, across her stomach.

She exhales softly. 'Your hand on my stomach.'

'And how does it feel?'

'Like... you're grounding me. It's a really good weight. I feel safe.'

'Good,' I say gruffly. 'It'll feel even better in a sec when I'm massaging you from the inside. And here?' My knuckles continue to tease her nerve endings.

'Your hand about three inches from where I actually need it,' she retorts, and I snort. This woman.

'Patience is a virtue,' I say patronisingly, 'and frankly, it's the only kind of virtue I'm interested in. How do you want the rest of your massage—you want me to take it slow? Go lightly? Wind you more and more tightly? Or you want me to let rip, show you what I'm really capable of when no one else is around?'

'Oh God,' she groans. 'Sometime I'd like you go to slow, but not now. You've gotten me too hot already.'

'I can see that.' I drop a kiss to her knee before pulling it towards me so her leg drops open. Even in the relative dark, her cunt is glistening so prettily. She's fucking soaking, and I haven't even touched her there. I could—Jesus fuck, I could climb up and sink so deep inside her she wouldn't know which way was up.

But not today.

Today is about her. About ensuring she knows she's squarely in the driving seat. About responding to her needs rather than asserting mine.

Inflicting mine.

'So what you're saying,' I continue slowly, my fingers now teasing the soft pad of waxed skin inside her thigh crease, 'is you need me to fuck you as hard as I can with my tongue and my fingers.'

'Uh, yes,' she pants out, her desire warring with what's clearly an unease with advocating for her needs.

I'll soon fuck the latter out of her.

'That's lucky,' I tell her, 'because I've been wanting to spread you out, and taste you, and suck on your clit very badly indeed since you walked into my club in those red fucking leather shorts, and in a lower-key way for a long, long time, baby.'

Without further preamble, I push two fingers hard inside her and seal my thumb to her clit. It's a good thing I'm holding her down with my other hand, because she practically shoots off the bed.

'Fucking hell,' I say. 'No lube needed here. You are fucking drenched, my darling. Have you been lying here this whole time, getting wetter and wetter and just waiting for my hands?'

'Yeah,' she moans.

'Damn right you have.' I release her clit and crook my fingers inside her, and she inhales sharply.

'Jesus, Cal.'

'Jesus is right. Right now I'm your saviour. I'm here to

bring you back to life, you know? Because no one, and I mean no one'—I bend and press a kiss to her inner thigh—'is allowed to let you feel like you're anything other than the glorious, sexy as fuck, *sexual* being you are.'

I can't hold off anymore. With my head bent, I can smell the unmistakable musk of her need. I need to bury my face right there.

In nirvana.

'Hold on,' I grunt, moving to the table. 'Shuffle down a bit.' I preempt this by grabbing her under her thighs and pulling her down a few inches by the arse so I can go to town on her more easily.

'Oh, baby,' I say, both hands massaging her oil-slicked tits before I drag them south and spread her thighs. I hold her like that, wide open and glistening just for me, before I lower my head to sample her.

Fuck. I love eating pussy. I love everything about it. Love how filthy it feels to bury my nose and mouth in a warm, wet cunt. How carnal. I love the power it gives me. Love how mutually beneficial it is—how wet and wanton it gets the women I tend to and how hard it gets me.

But let's face it. Most of the women I eat are Alchemy regulars: beautiful creatures who know what they want and shove their pussies in my face and rub them against my tongue. They're old hands.

This is different. Aida is different. There's no doubt she wants this—badly—but she's fragile. This is a very conscious act for her. It's a big fucking deal for her and a big responsibility for me, and the sense of wonder I feel that it's me she's entrusted to do this washes over me afresh as I bend my head, and breathe in her scent, and run my tongue upwards from her entrance to her clit in the longest, roughest lick I can give her.

28

AIDA

The moment his mouth connects with my flesh, I'm done for. Gone. I arch right into that strong hand. The one that's splayed across my stomach, holding me down protectively.

Like he knew I'd be at risk of falling off the fucking table and he preempted me.

As his tongue hits my pussy, he makes this earthy kind of groan that's just so *male*. My erudite, well-bred husband was many things, but he wasn't the animal I would've liked. Not with me, anyway.

But Cal sounds unleashed. And I fucking love it. It's a selfish sound, a carnal one, like right now he's looking after his own needs as much as mine, and it gets me even hotter. God knows, this guy is good at working women up. And when he touched me at that club it was incredible. But being alone with him? Being spread out for him, blindfolded and naked and wanton and willing for him to do absolutely anything he wants right now?

It's the hottest experience of my life. This guy is a prophet, it seems, because he was right. Massaging me, having him touch me and stroke me and loosen me up like this, was the most sensual, pleasurable experience I could have asked for. The sensation of his huge hands roaming over my skin was almost worshipful. It seems like he enjoyed it too—I hope he did—but right now I'm so far gone I don't give a fuck.

'Mmm,' he says, voice muffled, the sound vibrating against my flesh. 'Fuck. God, that's good.'

I wish I could see him. Wish I could watch as that dark head of hair dips between my legs and samples me. Wish I could see his fingers white-knuckling my thighs. His tongue sweeping through my centre.

But I can't, and whatever I'm missing out on in terms of otherworldly visuals, I'm making up for in sensation, my lack of sight ratcheting up the intensity of his touch.

And then he really begins to eat me.

He licks me from my entrance to my clit one more time before my legs are forced even further apart, like he would climb inside my body if he could.

'Hold it like that,' he orders, before releasing one leg. He's got the other one pried open against the forearm of the hand he's holding me down with. A second later, two of his thick fingers are shoving back in inside my pussy so hard that my body doesn't know whether to brace or celebrate. All I know is I feel full and invaded and it's fucking amazing. Then his tongue is back on me, but this time it's right where I need it.

Right on my clit.

I don't even try to hold back, because the pleasure rolling through me in huge waves is so strong, so completely *right*, that it's all I can do to go with it.

His mouth on my pussy is life-altering. He's sucking my clit, then licking it, those lips of his dragging over the surrounding flesh as he goes, like he wants to cover every inch of my most intimate areas.

His fingers stretch me open. They twist. They crook. He adds another as the hand on my stomach presses down even harder, and my entire pelvic region fills with gorgeous, molten heat. He's still working my clit with that lascivious mouth and its filthy licks. This might be the most sexually satisfying moment of my life.

I feel blindly for his head and grab at a handful of his thick hair. I don't need to tug him closer to where I need him because this guy is *everywhere.* He's devouring my pussy like a starving man, his sounds of satisfaction now almost as primal, as hungry as the moans I'm making.

'God,' I grit out, but it's more of a pant than a blasphemy, because I'm so close I can barely get myself to sound human. I'm bucking against his hand, fucking his fingers, grinding against his tongue like the most shameless, desperate whore who's ever lived, and I love it. I fucking *love* it. It seems I've embraced Cal's confidence, his enthusiasm, and his general dirtiness, which I guess was the idea.

But this is better than I could ever, *ever* have conceived of. This is who I am. This is what I was put on this earth to do. It's primordial. Elemental. It's—

I explode.

Over and over, heat racing through my nervous system like a fire through gasoline, relentless and all-consuming, so intense that it obliterates my consciousness and sends me hurtling into transcendence. I lie there, writhing blindly and abandoning myself to this unearthly pleasure as Cal continues to eat, lick, suck, finger-fuck, and groan his way through my orgasm.

It subsides gently, almost as if it's conscious of not leaving me too bereft. Too hollowed out. It ebbs away like the gauziest, the frothiest, of waves on the shore, leaving not a void in its wake but a beautiful, shimmering completeness.

Cal is still touching me. His hand strokes over my stomach. He's scattering kisses over my thighs. I tug off my sleep mask and raise myself up onto my elbows with difficulty, and he looks up.

Jesus. He looks as just-fucked as I do. Hair mussed. Dark eyes glassy. Even in the dim light, his mouth looks swollen, wet, like his assault on my pussy was as wonderfully rough on him as it was on me.

He relinquishes the pressure on my stomach, his hand sliding around my waist to help me sit up. I brace myself with a hand behind me, but before I can make some inelegant attempt at articulating my appreciation, he's wrapping his other hand around my neck and sealing his mouth to mine.

He tastes like me. It's jarring and arousing. He has me in his arms now, even as I sit up on the bed. His kisses are hard and fevered and demanding, and I meet them with the blissed-out sensuality of a woman whose orgasm has just torn her apart, my hands stroking languorously up his mostly bare arms and over the taut musculature of his back as his fingers weave through my hair.

I'm suspended, my earlier nerves subsumed and my consciousness shot through with halcyon details: the press of his pecs against my breasts and the taut probing of his tongue and the smoothness of the skin at the nape of his neck.

Eventually, he breaks our kiss and presses his forehead to mine.

'How do you feel after that?' he asks softly.

'More amazing than I've felt in a very long time,' I confess. 'I don't know how to describe it.'

'Good,' he murmurs, pulling away. 'Jesus, look at these. They're even more perfect like this.'

These are my breasts, and a flicker of self-consciousness hits me as I remember that Cal's fully dressed and I'm sitting here, stark naked. But the way he's backing away so he can look at them properly tamps that unease down, and I straighten up so I'm sitting upright on the bed, legs dangling over the edge in front of him.

'I don't think they're perfect,' I demur, but he tuts.

'Nope. None of that bullshit with me, sweetheart. Cup them for me. And open your legs while you're at it.'

It's super dim in here, but still. It's not like I'm used to a man commanding me like I'm here for his pleasure. Like this sight of my forty-six-year-old body, with its crepey tummy and C-section scar and mom-thighs could actually bring him pleasure.

But it seems to.

He's telling me with his words, but also with his eyes. With the teeth that tug on his full bottom lip as I cup my breasts like he asks and basically put them on a platter for him. And most definitely with the unmistakable bulge in his trousers. The one he's—

Oh.

My.

God.

He's palming his cock, rubbing at it absentmindedly, like he doesn't even know he's doing it.

'Look at you,' he says, and even his voice is absent-minded, like he's talking to himself and not to me. 'Look how flushed and beautiful you look after you come. That pussy is just... and those fucking *tits*. Jesus.'

'Hey,' I tell him, reaching out for him. 'Come here.'

He takes a step towards me like he's sleepwalking, his

eyes still trained on my body, his hand still palming that erection.

I hook my arm around his neck and cover his hand with mine. 'Let me… I want to take care of you.'

That seems to jerk him out of whatever aroused stupor he's in. 'Nope. Not today. This was about you.'

'Yeah. And you did a great job on that,' I tell him. 'And now I want to make you come.'

'Aida.' It sounds like he's pleading with himself, with his self-control, more than with me. 'Another time. You don't need to.'

'*Cal.* This isn't about reciprocation, or manners. This is about me wanting to get my hands on that gorgeous dick of yours.' I smooth my fingers over the hand that's standing between me and said dick.

He makes a pained sound. 'How do you know it's gorgeous?'

'Are you seriously going to tell me it isn't?' I bend my head and drag my lips over his beard, gratified at the shiver I feel in response.

'Well, obviously not.'

'I need it, Cal.' I shimmy to one side and push off the bed, dropping straight to my oiled-up knees beside him. I can tell he's trying to be noble. Professional, even. And it breaks my heart. Hopefully, actions will speak louder than words.

He turns so his hand-covered cock is level with my mouth and gazes down at me, conflict written all over his face.

'Aida,' he says through clenched teeth. 'I'm just—it's better if I take care of this myself.'

'I want your dick in my mouth,' I tell him in my most imperious newsreader voice. 'I'm not messing around here. Seriously, just fuck my mouth. Show me you want me.'

It's always struck me that giving someone a blowjob and having them fuck your mouth are two eminently different things, the latter involving head-grabbing and thrusting, and while my experience of this more aggressive form of fellatio is limited to dark romance books with morally grey, oversexed antiheroes, I know I need it from Cal.

Because it's been a long time since a man has looked at me like my very presence is a threat to the layers of self-control that house his inner beast, and it's even longer since I've met a man so beautiful. So unashamedly sexual. And so generous with his skills.

In any case, it seems like my slutty little plea works, because he chokes out a strangled *fuck* and lets his hand drop, defeated, to his side.

'You sure?' he whispers hoarsely.

'I'm certain,' I whisper back, looking up at him and placing my palms flat on his thighs. His quads contract as soon as I make contact. His eyes are dark, impenetrable, their thick lashes casting a fan of shadows over each cheek as he looks down at me on my knees before him. His hand cups my jaw before sliding around to entangle its fingers in my hair.

'Okay then,' he manages. 'Take it out, sweetheart.'

29

CAL

"To do aught good never will be our task, but ever to do ill our sole delight."
—Milton, *Paradise Lost*

Fantasising about someone is a poor man's game, but you never quite realise it until they're right there in front of you.

Warm flesh and hot blood.

Wet cunt and willing mouth.

Golden limbs and chocolate eyes.

Hair to pull and tits to suck and skin to inhale.

This is Aida. Not the Aida of my shower fantasies, but the living, breathing woman who lets me massage every inch of her glorious body and hold her down and eat her out. Who comes like a champ on my tongue and then slides to her knees and begs me to fuck her mouth.

Begs me to show her I want her.

Obviously, I'm in over my head. This woman uses her brains and charm to manipulate the most powerful men on the planet. And by *manipulate* I mean that she makes them do or say or react exactly what or how she wants, even if they don't realise it.

I realise it. I know exactly what she's doing. But when she plays her trump card and insinuates that I'm doing her a favour, that I'm building her confidence?

So help me God, I'm too weak a man to call her out on her bullshit.

Because I want her scarlet, sinful fucking mouth sealed around my cock like I want nothing else on God's green earth, and a naked, sated, slippery Aida, the most alluring of supplicants, on her knees in front of me is a force so powerful I'll give her anything she wants.

'Take it out, sweetheart,' I grunt. I'm sweating with the effort it's costing me not to shoot my load. Not to push her onto all fours and slide home. My entire consciousness has narrowed to a singular focus, the way it does in any situation that requires extreme physical willpower. The next step on a marathon. The next downward push of the pedal on an uphill bike ride.

Dirty-lite.

Dirty-lite.

I repeat my ridiculous, condescending, made-up phrase like a mantra. *This* should be my singular focus. My reminder of my duty of care to Aida. I think I acquitted myself pretty perfectly just now, given the constant pulse of my raging hard-on. I don't want to fuck it up now.

She thinks she wants me to fuck her mouth.

She has no fucking clue.

But ensuring today goes perfectly for her is the most

important thing. It's definitely more important—and more valid—than my right to fuck every hole in her body, hard as I like.

Unfortunately for her, I'm a man pushed to the brink of desire, and I'll do anything to come.

She smiles at my order like I've pleased her, her hands moving to my flies. As soon as she has them undone, my cock surges forward, still encased in the black jersey of my boxer briefs. She glances up at me briefly through her eyelashes, as if checking I'm still on board, before pushing my trousers down and wrangling the elastic waistband of my underwear over my aching, weeping cock.

'Fuck,' she murmurs as soon as she sees it. It's a reaction I get a lot, and the awe never stops being gratifying. I don't respond—mainly because I'm channelling all my executive function into fending off my inner caveman—but the trembling in my legs grows a little more intense.

She gets my underwear down properly and wraps a slim hand around me, her other hand going to cup my balls, and the feel of it, the warm, slick, pressure of her skin against mine is enough to draw a shuddery exhale from me, because Lord above.

'Jesus Christ, Cal,' she mutters. 'You've got a lot more dick here than I know what to do with.' But even as she says it, she's running the pad of her thumb experimentally over my weeping slit, smearing my precum around my crown and down to my frenulum.

I close my eyes and let out a low, anguished hiss as I reach for her face. It's taking all my self control not to clamp a palm on either side of her head and slam my dick into her mouth.

Again: this is about her. Not me.

'God, you're *so* hard,' she says in awe, running her hand up my impossibly stiff shaft, and then she's licking my crown like an ice cream, that mouth of hers so soft and wet and perfect.

I drag my thumbs along her jaw, my fingers under her ears, cradling her head with the painfully jerky, careful movements of a man walking through landmines. Because, in this moment, all bets are off. I have zero confidence in my ability to acquit myself well here. One false move, and I'm finished.

'Fuck, that feels good, baby,' I tell her shakily. 'I've dreamt of your mouth on my cock—*fuuuck*.' My anguished curse comes as a result of her taking me in deep, so a good amount of my length is sheathed in wet, silky heaven. 'Look at you,' I rasp. 'Fuck, yeah.'

I stand there, pleasure swirling viscerally through me, around me, as she lavishes her perfect licks and sucks upon my cock, her teasing fingers feathering over my sac. It's sublime and hellish; it's too much and nowhere near enough.

She gives a low moan of pleasure and then pops her mouth off my cock. 'Fuck my mouth.'

'Er, no, sweetheart.' I laugh nervously, unsure of my ability to maintain my current Herculean levels of self-control. I tighten my grip on her neck, my fingers tangling in her glossy hair. 'You're doing so fucking well,' I say through gritted teeth. 'It's perfect.'

She in turn tightens her grip on my shaft and glares up at me, her dark eyes glittering. 'Cal. I mean it. Show me. I want you to show me how you are with those women at the club.'

Nope.

Nope.

Nope.

That kind of behaviour has absolutely no part to play in this little scene. The side of myself I let loose in The Playroom has no business showing his ugly face when I'm in instructor mode. Mentor mode. I'm here to teach Aida the art of pleasure, the pleasure that's evaded her for too long. I'm categorically not here to untether the beast within.

'No,' I gabble. 'That's not—this is amazing. This is great. It's so—*shit*.'

This last part is in response to Aida licking a rough line all the way down the vein on the underside of my cock.

'I want you to show me,' she says against my balls before licking back up again. 'Come on, Cal. For fuck's sake. I'll slap your thigh or something if I can't take it.'

With that little announcement, she takes my cock so deep she gags a little before making a pleased noise in the back of her throat that vibrates around my crown.

She's doing it again. Masterminding things. She's bewitching my cock, and therefore my mind, and manipulating the outcome. Turns out her deep-throating abilities are just as deadly as her skill at debating immigration policy and knife crime.

Who the fuck is this woman, and what is she doing to me?

I'm barely capable of anything right now. Every ounce of blood, every last vestige of self-control, has gone straight to my dick. Consciousness is the warm, wet slide of Aida's mouth and tongue, the grip of her fingers. Callum Sinclair, patient teacher, is disappearing out the door and in his place is the beast. The predator who thinks only of conquering. Of coming.

Fuck.

Fine.

'Slap my thigh if you need to, okay?' I tell her in a voice I barely recognise, my breath coming in harsh spurts from my flared nostrils.

It's the extent of the nobility I'm capable of.

And as soon as I hear her garbled *okay* I'm clamping my hands around her head so fucking tight and letting rip, volleying my hips in a series of thrusts that jam my dick so far down her throat that I hit soft tissue over and over.

Fuck me.

Fuck *me*.

This is... I'm lightheaded. Reeling. Sensation has me in a chokehold as I grip her head between my hands, watching in wonder at the sight of her sucking and writhing, at her attempts to override her most basic instincts and slap my thighs so she can get my cock the fuck out of her mouth.

But she doesn't. One hand is still on my balls, though her other is on my bare arse, holding me against her, as if the grip I have on her head isn't enough. I can tell from her flailing, jerky movements and little noises that she's in panic mode, but she doesn't stop. She digs her nails into my arse, she massages my balls, she sucks her little heart out with strangled moans, and she takes. Every. Inch.

I'm gonna come. Hard. White-hot pleasure is racing through my balls, down my cock, spreading all over my body. I drive into her mouth over and over like a man possessed, holding onto her face for dear life, and then I stiffen. Still. And I erupt, rutting violently against her face, shooting my load into her mouth and it's fucking—it's fucking *amazing*.

My climax tears through me, wiping out everything that is not it. My body is a circuit, and she's lit me the fuck up. This orgasm is a glowing, pulsing thing. And as it courses through me, this miraculous, life-affirming release, it relaxes every bone in my body.

I realise I'm holding her face so tightly I might squeeze her brains out, and I let go, hauling her up by her armpits before she's done sucking me clean and crushing her blessed nakedness against my body.

'Fuck,' I mutter into her hair, the fog of pleasure dissipating and leaving patchy, but appalled, awareness in its wake. 'That was *not* the way that was supposed to go, but Jesus *Christ*, baby.'

She allows me to hold her, her laugh tinkling, her breath warm against my neck.

'Are you okay?' I ask her, pulling my head away so I can see her face. 'I didn't mean—I went at you far too hard. I'm so, so sorry.'

'Are you kidding me?' she asks. Her eye makeup is smudged, her cheeks wet with the tears that fell when I choked her with my dick. Her lipstick is mostly gone, though I hope she left a ring around my dick.

Property of Aida Russell.

I blink.

'That was awesome,' she says against my mouth. 'That's what I wanted you to do. You're so sexy—I didn't want you to go easy on me like I was some little snowflake. I wanted you to show me what I've been missing.'

I give a humourless little laugh. 'I'm not sure you've been missing *that*.'

'A super hot guy suggesting he can't get enough of me?' she asks softly. 'Yes, I have.'

There's only one way to respond to that. So I kiss her heatedly, thoroughly, to demonstrate how much she blows me away. I kiss her until I'm sinking gracelessly to my knees, cock twitching and trousers halfway down my legs. Until I'm lying down, my head hitting the hard floor with a dull thud, and tugging her on top of me, my hands roving all over her sensational, oiled-up, naked body.

I kiss her until I feel confident I've proven to her that I cannot, indeed, get enough of her.

30

AIDA

SIMONE: Sooo...

ME: [Giggles and looks at the ceiling] Yeah.

SIMONE: You did the dirty deed?

ME: [Another far too high-pitched giggle] We did... some dirty deeds.

SIMONE: You realise you can tell us as much or as little as you like, right? Because, obviously, if you don't feel comfortable sharing much on air then I'll just drag you off and get you drunk later so you spill the beans. But, my darling, one of the reasons you asked me to interview you is because you knew I'd push you.

This is your show. You can fuck behind closed doors and stay quiet about it like everyone else, or you can use your platform to vocalise your experiences, and your reactions in the moment, and your feelings after the fact. So which will it be?

ME: Remind me why we're friends?

SIMONE: Because I'm fabulous, and because I don't blow smoke up that tiny little arse of yours like everyone else. Spill it, Russell. And don't play coy with me. You have never once sat down in front of a camera without knowing exactly what message you want to impart. So I'm asking you now. What's your message after Round One of kinky fuckery?

ME: [Sighs] You're right, naturally. And I know exactly what I want to say. Of course I do. That doesn't preclude me from being all sorts of nervous and exposed and horrified, but neither do those feelings preclude me from sharing my message. And I guess it's this. I'd put it up there with jumping out of a plane: it was the most terrifying, exhilarating experience of my life.

SIMONE: How so?

ME: Because every single thing about the way we're bred as a certain type of woman—the good girl who goes to college and works in the corporate world and keeps her head down and gets on with it? All those things tend to intersect with a certain approach to sex.

I'm generalising here, but it's a generalisation that feels valid when I put it like this: nobody would expect a woman like me or you, who operates within those blurred boundaries of whatever 'The Establishment' is, to appear on television and talk about how hard they came the previous day.

SIMONE: I'm sorry. Were you trying to say something smart about our culture? Because I didn't hear anything except that last sentence.

ME: Yeah. Well.

SIMONE: Can you tell us more? Or is your brain still too orgasm-addled?

ME: Definitely the latter. But I'll try, because it's important. Look. Nobody should judge anyone else's sexual appetites. Right? But they do. We all do. I know I do, and it's something I want to change about myself.

But I'm coming at this as someone who thought being

able to say she'd never had a one-night stand was some kind of badge of honour. I mean, how ridiculous is that? That's purity culture at its most insidious, because we let it inform how we judge ourselves and how we think others judge us. And all I can say now is *what a load of bullshit*.

I think the thing about doing this *thing* at this point in my life is that I'm old enough to regret those little life rules I carried around with me, and I'm old enough to regret what they led me to miss out on. Do I regret not having had more great sex before I got married? Hell, yes! I mean, come on.

So I'm making up for lost time here. I'm finally in a place where I've made peace with myself and the public's perception of me sufficiently to go and take that pleasure. Just *take* it.

SIMONE: So tell us how you took it.

ME: Well—I had my massage, and it was glorious. He did it at his club, Alchemy, when it was empty, but he had this room set out exactly like a spa, you know? There was a full-on massage table, and candles everywhere, and it even smelled like a spa... and he was super professional. At the beginning, anyway. [Giggles]

But, you know, he got it completely right. He called it. Because I know a lot of women out there will empathise when I say so much of the female orgasm is in our heads, right, and it's not even how we feel about the person we're with. It's how we feel about ourselves, our bodies, whether we're stressed, or exhausted, or our brains just won't shut the fuck up.

So his massage was exactly what I needed. It gave me a chance to unwind, it got me used to having his hands on me, it was an act of caregiving and service, I would say, as much as it was a roundabout form of foreplay. Doing what he did made me feel far more sensual than if I'd had to get down to action at eleven o'clock in the morning.

SIMONE: I totally agree. So, can I ask, how did the massage segue into the rest of it?

ME: [Blows out a breath] Oh God. I cannot believe I'm discussing this on camera. I guess I should have mentioned that he was looking super hot when I showed up. Like, he's a seriously attractive guy, right? That's not up for debate.

SIMONE: Nope. No debate needed on that front.

ME: So there was that. Obviously, I'm attracted to him—I personally couldn't do this if the chemistry wasn't there. But then I put a sleep mask on and that helped too, I think. It helped me get out of my head and into my body. So by the time he'd finished doing my back, I was pretty worked up.

SIMONE: That's my girl. And?

ME: And, I guess... when he suggested I should roll over onto my back and lose the towel, I was very much on board with that. And then he gave me a... happy ending, I guess.

SIMONE: Did you guys have sex?

ME: Nope.

SIMONE: Did you, you know, reciprocate?

ME: Um, maybe. [Giggles way too coyly for a forty-six-year-old woman]

SIMONE: Look, I'm not here to ask you how you feel about this guy or get into the nitty gritty of what you got down to, but I am interested in how you feel. You just came out of a fifteen-year marriage. By your own admission, you didn't get around too much before your marriage. You went to a sex club and got on a massage table for a guy you don't know particularly well, a guy who is *very* experienced in this stuff. And you guys indulged in some mutual pleasure-giving.

I'm so proud of you for doing this that I could burst, but I want to know *how you feel*, twenty-four hours on.

ME: I feel fantastic, and not just because I had an earth-shattering orgasm at the hands of someone else. Although that was definitely the biggest part of it.

I guess I feel liberated, like I've come through the other side of something I was super scared to do, and I have zero regrets about doing it. But obviously you get that feeling whenever you face down a fear and realise there's nothing on the other side but good things.

It's more specific than that, I think. It's that I faced down years upon years of self-judgement, and judgement of others, and preconceptions about what sex was, and what was okay, and what was not okay. Right? Sex was this *whole, huge thing* in my head, and sure, I totally bypassed the Tinder generation because I was married.

So I get that I'm late to this party, but I suspect a lot of women my age are. And what yesterday really, viscerally *proved* to me was that sex can exist on its own. Outside of a relationship, outside of judgement, outside of shame.

I had one of *the* best orgasms of my life with a guy I'm not in a relationship with, who has such a different outlook from me, who was super considerate and super hot... and it was a one hundred percent positive experience. And now I'm kicking myself that I haven't done it more often, because this whole no-strings, hot sex thing?

It's really, really phenomenal.

31

CAL

'I absolutely reject your premise,' Aida is telling Richard Dowling, our current Health Secretary, live on TV. 'Come on. We both know it's a house of cards. So why don't you quit trying to sell the public on this strategy of yours once and for all and focus your attention on creating a premise we can actually buy into?'

She glares at him and re-crosses her legs as he haltingly, and foolishly, attempts to bring the conversation back to his plans for more NHS cuts.

I'm not listening to a word he's saying.

Nope, I'm gazing instead at the woman who, two days ago, was naked and on her knees, sucking my dick, and is now eviscerating a senior member of our cabinet with her trademark aplomb and no mercy whatsoever.

Poor bastard, I think, taking a leisurely swig of IPA. I've done a weights session and eaten a chicken salad, and this is my reward. *This* being an ice-cold beer and a chance to perv freely at one of Britain's best imports.

Tonight's programme, *Centre Stage*, is a BBC flagship that Aida's hosted since she left her regular evening news slot a few years ago. It focuses squarely on the most pressing current affairs—the ones that warrant more attention than a five-minute news slot can give them.

The armchair format, which allows Aida to lull her guests into a false sense of security before publicly tearing them to shreds, has the added bonus of giving the viewer a cracking view of her spectacular legs. She's wearing a fitted black dress with short sleeves and those chunky gold bracelets I recognise from her visit to the club.

It makes my blood boil to think about how many men are perving over Aida's legs right this second. Obviously, it's different when I do it, because, come on. She came on my fucking tongue. I don't think she'd mind me looking at her legs.

The woman on my screen is the real deal. She's stunningly beautiful, glamorous, educated as fuck, and impeccably prepared for this interview—far better prepared, it seems, than the spineless wanker whose actual job it is to run our National Health Service.

She holds up her prompt cards—which I haven't seen her glance at once tonight—as she lays into him again. Fuck. No wonder she and Gen have hit it off. They're both terrifying when they want to be.

To my shame, I'm watching her scarlet lips enunciate, and I'm watching that body of hers twist in her chair, such is her level of moral outrage, but I'm zoning out the actual debate they're having, because my dick is getting hard and my brain is merging the woman on my huge TV screen with the woman whose epic blowjob is living rent-free in my brain.

I palm my cock lazily through the heavy jersey of my jogging bottoms. Fuck, that feels good. That poor sap, Dowling, is going to crawl out of there a broken man, the latest casualty of my victorious queen. She's so sure of herself. So crushingly confident.

But earlier this week she was putty in my hands. Moaning and writhing and begging for my tongue. My fingers. My cock. Seeing her excoriate him, flay him with her words till he's a ravaged carcass fit only for the papers to finish off tomorrow, is doing magical things to my ego and my cock. Because this woman doesn't roll over for anyone.

Except me.

When I told her quite literally to roll over and lose her towel, she did.

I'm fully hard now. Need to come. But not while Richard bloody Dowling is jabbering on. I turn the TV off and pull up TikTok on my phone, typing in *Aida Russell edit* as I tug the elastic on my jogging bottoms down far enough to free my cock.

Part of me considers jumping in a cab to Alchemy, but I can't be arsed to put on a smart outfit. Besides, I don't really want to fuck anyone else in this moment. This is an itch only Ms Russell can scratch.

My phone's propped up on my bathroom shelf as I liberally apply lube to my palm and begin to stroke myself with long, indulgent strokes. Fuck, yeah. This is what I needed.

On my screen, a fast-moving edit plays to Ariana Grande's *Dangerous Woman*: Aida striding across various newsroom sets in sky-high heels, Aida rolling her eyes, Aida giving death stares, Aida licking her scarlet-painted lips. Over, and over, and over. A million different times.

Lick.

Lick.

Lick.

Fuck, that mouth of hers should be illegal.

Jesus, the feel of it around my cock was un-fucking-real.

Look at those legs. I want them wrapped around me. Why have we not fucked yet?

The edit plays over and over.

My strokes get faster. Harder. More desperate.

And then I'm coming, my grunts harsh and the pumps of my fist punishing, shooting my load all over the marble basin.

ME: I watched you annihilate Dowling and you were so sexy I just wanked into my washbasin.

It's called aftercare. You know, checking in after a big moment for her this week. Letting her know I'm thinking of her.

She responds an hour later.

AIDA: How charming.

I groan as I flop down on my bed.

Dowling's not the only guy she's capable of roasting.

32

CAL

I'm serenading the beautiful woman in front of me, and I think she's into it.

Sure, we're standing by the fireplace in Alchemy's main reception room, waiting for the others to get their shit together so we can all sit down.

It also may be eleven o'clock in the morning, but she's into it.

I can tell.

I have my head bent so my mouth is right by her ear and only she is privy to my sweet, sweet words.

I'm gonna fuck you, I croon to the tune of *You are my Sunshine.*

I'm gonna fuck you,

I'm gonna fuck you till you're sore.

And when I fuck you,

Oh, when I fuck you,

The only word you'll scream is 'more'.

She's pinching the bridge of her nose hard, her entire body shaking with laughter. I drop a kiss on her bare shoulder and take a big inhale before launching into the second verse with gusto.

I'm gonna eat you—

'Please stop,' she kind of laugh-sobs, her palm going to my chest. 'I can't take it.'

Her touch against my heart feels great, even through my shirt, and I'm reminded once more of exactly how keen I am for one hundred percent nudity between us.

'But I have so many more verses,' I say, my voice filled with mock hurt. '*You're gonna blow me, I'm gonna rail you...* I was planning on finishing with *You love my di-ick.*'

She snorts and lets her forehead drop to my shoulder, and I use the opportunity to snake my arm around her waist and pull her a little closer. We're not a couple—obviously—but we've been intimate enough that touching her feels natural. That she looks and smells sexy AF only helps.

Besides, I like making her laugh. It's not like I can deliver some intelligent commentary on her attack on Dowling the other night. Comedy's more my niche than political insight, so I'll stay in my lane. And if playing the fool helps build our working relationship and her comfort levels with me, then all the better.

Because I meant it.

I'm gonna fuck her.

Aida's come here this morning not, astonishingly enough, for my cock or my vocal cords, but for a sit-down with all of us to discuss the progress of the documentary. She's looking sleek and professional in a fine-knit sleeveless camel turtleneck-thingy with cream trousers and killer heels.

All I know is that this power player vibe she has going on makes me feral. And when I pull back enough to look at her, those dark eyes of hers are amused and interested in equal measure.

'I think it's too early to say the L-word,' she says drily, 'but I'm definitely into your dick, if you couldn't tell the other day.'

I smirk, my fingers flexing on the indent of her waist. 'I could tell, baby.'

'You two look cosy,' Gen remarks, bustling in through the double doors. She's particularly bright-eyed and bushy-tailed today—she's been like this all morning. The Big Bad Wolff must have given her a particularly good seeing-to last night. When she's like this I tend to piss her off by referring to it as her BCE—Big Clipboard Energy. If she didn't enjoy fucking so much she'd have made a great headmistress.

I ignore her comment, but Aida springs away from me as if we're two teenagers sprung behind the bike sheds and goes to hug her.

~

IT APPEARS THAT, despite not having had my cock properly yet, Aida is also full of Big Clipboard Energy, because she has a *lot* of updates for us. I have no clue how she's juggling all this documentary stuff with mothering two boys, preparing for her weekly *Centre Stage* interviews and all the other pop-ups she does on various BBC news and current affairs shows during the week. She may not be one of the main anchors anymore, but she's heavily involved.

Her life makes me feel exhausted and also lazy, because I have a pretty nice gig with my little financial side hustle at Cerulean one day a week, organising events for Alchemy by day, and participating in them by night. I've always considered myself an ambitious, successful guy, but it's a bit lame when I put it in the context of Aida's calendar.

As the creative vision behind the documentary, she's appointed herself as the primary liaison between the Azure, Creatrix—the production company—and Alchemy. The programme is scheduled to drop on two consecutive Thursdays in January, with the intention of blowing everyone's New Year blues out of the water with our salacious (by Azure's standards) content.

That's under four months from now, but the trailer is slated for two weeks' time and will inevitably prompt an avalanche of press and social media interest and a torrent of requests.

Aida and I have already shot some footage for the trailer —far more for her than me. Mine mainly involved me sitting in a chair in the suite at the Lanesborough, dramatically lit and sexily satanic (Aida's brief to me) in all-black, while spouting various provocative soundbites that she and the Creatrix team concocted to ignite curiosity. I'm sure it will also ignite plenty of judgement and slut-shaming, the brunt of which she will undoubtedly bear.

The thought makes me fucking furious.

Still, I'm sure I'll be in for my fair share of ribbing from my mates when they see me intone such pearls of wisdom as *all women deserve to know mind-bending pleasure. And I'm the man to give it to them.*

Even I baulked at that one. But I understand I'm playing a part here. I represent an opportunity, a truth that can liberate. I'm a unicorn, an enigma. The skilled sex club owner whose ultimate act of altruism is helping women discover the power that lies within their own bodies. They're painting me as some kind of sex maestro, and I'm not exactly complaining.

Possibly the strangest part of the whole charade is that I've spent far less time obsessing over how much more pussy I'll get after it airs than I thought I would.

I mean, come on. I'll be chest-deep in pussy for the foreseeable future. I'll be a sex celebrity. A sex-lebrity, even? Women will stop me in the street and beg me to fuck them, to "teach" them, or so I imagine. Gen, devious little witch that she is, even threw that visual out there when she was getting me over the finish line on signing up for this.

You won't just have a reputation at Alchemy, she purred. *You'll have a national, or probably international, reputation for being the man to see when women want to be fucked back to life. Surely that's your life's goal?*

I confess she wasn't far wrong. I should be high-fiving myself in the bathroom mirror each morning in anticipation, but I'm far too caught up in wondering just how much I can blow Aida's lights out to give much bandwidth to those faceless women.

In any case, the programme will be controversial.

The woman fronting it will be even more so.

The trailer will probably break the internet.

So I understand why an intense and intricate PR and social media plan is so necessary for proactive and reactive reasons alike.

Maddy's in her element. Azure has fancy people doing fancy campaigns, but Alchemy will be playing its part, disseminating the official graphics and leveraging the likely uptick in profile while also reassuring its members that their privacy is still of the upmost importance.

It's also a superb opportunity to tie the main message of the documentary in with our own ongoing educational content and hopefully attract more women of Aida's age as members. It's been bothering us for a while that our over-forty members skew far more towards men. Hopefully this platform will give us the power to change that.

Aida runs us through the lineup from now till mid November, when filming is due to draw to a close, aside from pickups and concluding segments. While the interviewing timetable is a scheduling masterpiece, the fucking timetable, for want of a more technical term, is the absolute opposite.

There are a few reasons for this. First, very little footage of us fucking will actually be captured. This isn't a porno. Any preambles or post-hookup interviews can, worst case, be filmed on different occasions.

A far more important reason is that, when she embarked on this project, Aida and her production team decided unanimously that putting deadlines to these very personal, very intimate milestones would make them far too daunting. The poor woman didn't want to have to fuck to a schedule.

But the final reason is the one most exciting one for me personally. And that is that Aida's journey of self-discovery should be fluid. She couldn't possibly know at the outset of this adventure how her tastes, her appetites, would change.

She still doesn't know.

Every time she steps foot in the sultry confines of Alchemy, she should feel as though she has a carte blanche for whatever filth she'd like to get up to. Everything should feel possible. And that delicious sense of possibility is what'll make for TV magic as a national treasure explores limits she may not have been aware of before.

33

CAL

All this is a roundabout way of saying that she and I have yet to fuck, that we have not yet conceived of a concrete plan of action for when and how to fuck, and that, despite my best efforts at guarding Aida's privacy from even my team, everyone in this room knows we haven't yet fucked.

Gen, bless her, tries to find the most discreet way to raise the issue. 'Do you guys have a date yet for the next, um, instalment?'

We glance at each other from our places side by side on the sofa. 'Probably next week,' Aida says. 'I have the PM on *Centre Stage* this week, so I'm pretty jammed till Wednesday.'

She has our Prime Minister lined up for the hot seat, and all I've got lined up on Wednesday is my after-work battle ropes session with Rafe.

Jesus fuck.

'Not sure you can compete with the PM,' Rafe quips in my direction.

'Ha fucking ha,' I say.

'Unless I come in Thursday?' Aida suggests. 'I could probably use some relaxation after wringing him dry over why the fuck he doesn't fire his fascist Home Secretary.'

'No can do,' Gen points out. 'It's the party on Thursday night—the whole place will be chaos that day.'

'What party?' Aida asks.

'One of our semi-annual themed nights,' I tell her. 'It's the Masked Ball. It's a lot of fun, but the ballgowns are a lot less obligatory than the masks, if you catch my drift.'

It's actually up there with Slave Night as one of my favourite events. There's something about those lavish masks that makes our members even more feral than usual. They lower inhibitions and ratchet the debauchery right up.

Aida shrugs. 'That sounds fun. I could... come along?'

It does not sound like fun. It sounds like a bloody nightmare. The place will be heaving. I'll be in Events Manager mode while also being in a constant state of arousal. This is precisely the kind of event where I unleash my inner beast and allow him to play.

I'd mount that woman so fast and so hard she wouldn't know what had hit her.

There'd be no warming her up.

No aftercare.

To say one of our most popular themed nights would be a baptism of fire for a woman who's just come out of a monogamous relationship is like saying I like women. The understatement of the fucking century.

'Not a good idea,' I tell her with a quick shake of my head. 'Let's do it the following week.'

She twiddles her pen between her fingers so it drums a steady beat against her notepad. The interviewer with a nose for the barest hint of a redirect. 'And why not?'

'Because it's a fuck-fest. It's basically one giant orgy, and no offence, but you'd be way out of your depth.'

She cocks her head. 'Is that so? What if the reporter in me wants to see the club in full swing?'

'You can see the club in full swing anytime you want,' I tell her. 'Just say the word. But if you're suggesting we should be… together that evening, then I promise you, that's a terrible idea.'

'It really is an amazing evening, though,' Maddy chips in unhelpfully. 'The masks are sooo gorgeous. And no one's allowed to take them off in the main Playroom, so it's really hot. You should definitely come and see it—I for one think it'd be a great first experience at the club.'

'I agree with Mads,' Gen says before I can reiterate my utter opposition to this crazy idea. 'It really is spectacular—like a carnal Cirque de Soleil, if you like. We have amazing performers, too. It always feels quite magical.'

'Could we film the performances?' Aida asks.

'Possibly,' Gen muses at the same time as I say, 'Categorically not.'

'We might be able to get a small crew in before the doors open to everyone else,' Rafe suggests. 'Presumably you only need some brief footage to set the scene.'

'Exactly,' Aida says. She shifts on the sofa and turns her body towards me, her hand going to rest on my forearm. 'Think of it with a producer's hat on, Cal. If it really is this carnal circus, like Gen says, then what a perfect way to introduce Alchemy in full swing.

'And if it's a daunting atmosphere, then all the better. It'll seriously amp up the tension for the audience if they feel like I'm being let loose at a total meat market. They'll feel like I'm the gladiator and they're the crowd, baying for my blood.'

'Jesus Christ,' I say, feeling the blood drain from my face. 'That all sounds a bit extreme. I can't protect you properly in that scenario.' I lower my voice so the entire room isn't privy to my plans for our first proper fuck. 'I want this to be relaxing for you, you know? I want us to be able to take it slow if you need that.'

'You're so sweet,' she says, and I could swear I see amusement in those dark, expressive eyes, 'but we did relaxation already. And it was wonderful. You're right, obviously. It sounds like a lot, but I can't turn down the chance for that sense of theatre. Put it this way: it'll make for far better television than me "popping in" for a cosy mid-morning fuck. It'll probably be far sexier, too. And you and I both know it.'

34

AIDA

"Better to reign in hell than serve in heaven."
—Milton, *Paradise Lost*

Okay, so I am fucking terrified.

I committed a huge own goal when I put my producer hat on over my real hat, which is that of a forty-something woman who's seriously out of practice. I chose theatre over security.

The problem is, I couldn't resist the lure of the spectacle that is the Alchemy Masked Ball. If we can pull off the footage we need in the crazy tight time constraints we have, it'll provide the perfect carnal backdrop for my coming of age story.

It could be the high point in my on-camera story arc.

Because what could be more alluring than this intrepid middle-aged adventurer stumbling upon the ultimate bacchanalian orgy? *Paradise Found*, indeed. It's the mic-drop moment the production team and I have been searching for, and it's fallen into our laps.

I partnered with Alchemy for a reason that had less to do with its overall offering and more to do with the seemingly safe confines of the Unfurl programme. But the deeper I get, the more the filmmaker in me wants to push the boundaries.

If we're pursuing a story about sexuality, doesn't it follow that Alchemy is a natural climax for that story?

And if I'm exploring my sexual hopes and dreams and possibly, just possibly, giving air to my darkest, most carefully hidden fantasies, doesn't it follow that keeping things nice and safe and choreographed with Cal might not be the apex of my adventure? That participating, even in the most marginal way, in a full-on orgy might?

I always knew my story would unfold chapter by chapter as I set out to tell it. I was aware that I didn't know the ending. I still don't, obviously.

But I know a damn good climax when I see one. Pun intended. And if I'm gonna do this insane thing and put myself out there on television, I'm gonna fucking *do* it.

I stand by all of the above. Unfortunately, none of it does anything to make me feel like less of a sacrificial lamb. Weirdly, the only thing that really gives me courage is Cal. The same Cal who's asked me a couple times since that team meeting to reconsider. The Cal who seems stressed as hell that our first time naked together will be at the kind of event he clearly lives for.

Because I have a feeling about this guy. About this beautiful, funny, generous, thoughtful man who I know is only showing me a part of himself. He's been in mentor mode, and he's smashed it, and I'm deeply grateful for the care and consideration he's shown me so far.

But I don't want to be a pity fuck for him. He tells me he's attracted to me, and it seems to be true. We get along great, and the chemistry between us is smoking. But I can't shake the sense that the only time I've really seen behind his charming, comedic persona is during those few minutes when he held my head and fucked my mouth with the anguished desperation of a man on the brink.

That's the guy I want to see more of. *That's* what I want for the first time I get fully naked with someone new and let them fuck me. I don't want polite, considerate, careful sex. Jesus, no. I want to put myself in Cal's hands and *I want him to show me what I've been missing.* But based on the amount of times he's apologised for the face fucking he gave me, I'm guessing that's not what he has in store for me.

Tough shit, because that's what I want.

~

MY DRESS IS RED.

My lips are red.

And I'm ready for whatever tonight brings.

Don't get me wrong. I'm terrified. Far more terrified than I was of the PM yesterday (though arguably less terrified than he was of me by the end of our half hour together). But I have my eye on the prize, and the prize is Cal in a room, naked on top of me, and I'd say that's a dazzling enough prize to justify the quest.

His texts this week have been less filthy and more logistical than I would've liked. He'll remember something, and start to panic, and shoot me a message when he's out and about.

Exhibit A:

There's a cloakroom just inside The Playroom so people can leave their clothes if they want to take anything off

Because they have to be fully clothed in the bar beforehand

And we don't want anyone's Chanel or Gucci going missing when it's been stripped off them

Not that you should remotely expect to take off any of your clothes in The Playroom

I just wanted to mention it in case you were bringing a coat or something

OK I'll shut up now xx

See what I mean?

He's been in major Mother Hen mode all week, and I actually feel bad for inflicting this on him, because he has enough on his plate orchestrating this party without me commandeering it for filming purposes.

I console myself with the thought that I'll have to ensure I make it worth his while.

~

When I show up at the club, the bar is already pumping. The music is louder than last time I was here, every single person is masked, and the dress code is far higher octane. The men are mainly in black tie or all black, allowing the women to shine.

And shine they do.

There are sequins everywhere, glorious dresses in silver and gold and red and purple, micro minis and full-length gowns slashed to the navel and the thigh. Other women are wearing tuxes or corsets with leather pants. But the real focal point comes from the masks, because they are simply beautiful. Stunning, intricate, and beguiling.

I cast my eyes around the room. Disco balls hang from the chandeliers, casting the room in a constantly rotating glitter bath that bedazzles everyone's skin. While some of the masks are classic Venetian in style, others are more modern. More abstract. Then there are the guys who've gone full Ghost Face, which is far hotter than it should be, and even a couple in full-on balaclavas.

Jesus fucking Christ.

I guess I shouldn't be at all surprised that Alchemy's guests have interpreted what sounds like a glamorous but innocuous theme in a super kinky way, but I am. I surreptitiously eye up one of the balaclava guys. He has a similar build to Cal and is wearing fitted black dress pants with an equally fitted black dress shirt that's tucked in but opened almost the whole way, revealing a ripped chest.

Jeez, I wonder what kind of stuff Balaclava Guy is planning on getting up to tonight. He probably has kinks I've never even heard of. Kinks I can't conceive of. The thought should make me run a mile. Instead, my skin flushes with heat and a staccato pulse begins to thrum insistently between my legs.

Hold on a sec—he's coming over.

What—?

Oh, Jesus fuck.

I think it's Cal.

I'm frozen to the spot, but he keeps coming, walking towards me with what is definitely Cal's swagger. He has a crystal tumbler of scotch in one hand, and the grotesque mouth hole in his balaclava is large enough to show his lips curving into a smile.

That's definitely Cal's smile.

Shit.

He stops in front of me and looks me up and down, openly appraising my body.

'Well, you look good enough to eat,' he drawls.

I swallow. *Get your shit together, Aida.* 'I thought you said you were wearing a Phantom mask,' is what I come out with.

'Changed my mind.'

No shit.

'Mmm-hmm. I see you've gone for terrorist chic instead.'

He grins broadly, and it's disarming to see his gorgeous smile and crinkling brown eyes under a mask I associate with hardened criminals. 'I'm not planning on terrorising you tonight. Unless you want me to. Your tits look amazing. That dress is fucking stunning.'

'I—thank you.'

'I like your mask. Glad you've left your mouth free.' He dips his head and kisses my jaw, his warm skin brushing mine as the cheap, nasty fabric of the balaclava scratches me lightly in a way that should be fucking creepy and instead, it seems, is quite the opposite. It sends delicious danger signals scattering over my skin in the guise of goosebumps.

It sends equally delicious visuals stampeding through my brain.

Cal in that thuggish mask, pushing me to my knees.

Cal, shoving the sumptuous crimson silk of my two-thousand-pound dress around my waist as he forces my legs apart and eats me through that hole.

Fucking *hell.*

I tilt my head, affording him more access. 'Looks like

you've kept your mouth free, too,' I tell him as he kisses down my neck.

'Certainly have.' He nips lightly. 'Want a drink before we go through?'

Definitely.

I *need* a drink before we go through.

35

CAL

I'm not sure what the fuck I think I'm playing at, wearing this mask when I'm supposed to be maintaining very clear boundaries around Aida tonight.

Those boundaries are, in a nutshell, not to behave like a fucking animal.

I had the Phantom mask all ready to go. It's a winner—the previous times I've worn it to this event, women have gone feral for it. I suppose the Phantom was a dirty, repressed bastard with a kidnapping kink, so I get it.

But yesterday, on a whim, I Amazon Primed a shitty ten quid polyester balaclava, and when I tried it on this evening, it felt *right*. I can't say why. It felt... freeing. I'm not sure that's a good thing when I'm supposed to be on my best behaviour, but when I saw Aida clock me, I knew it was the right call.

'Did you recognise me?' I asked her as I drew her over to the bar to get her a sharpener.

'Not immediately, no,' she admitted. Just as I suspected. I, of course, recognised her at once. The gorgeous red dress that showed off her curves. The killer legs. Strappy heels.

That fucking mouth. She looked expensive and classy and fuckable as hell. But her expression didn't change behind that intricate, red-feathered mask until I approached her, and I knew she was ogling my sexy Organised Crime persona and not Cal.

I still have major misgivings about her coming along to this fuck-fest, but I'll admit the masked dress code is great for her. She doesn't have to worry about everyone recognising her. When we go through, she'll realise how liberating it is to hide behind a mask. How refreshing.

'You ready?' I whisper in her ear. We've finished our first drink and caught up with Gen and Anton, who look like they've just stepped off a fucking gondola or escaped from a Ferrero Rocher ad. Both are groomed and glossy and dripping in designer threads with proper old-school Venetian masks on that Anton probably had flown over from a Venetian artisan on his jet.

There's no sign of the others yet, but I like it that way. I want tonight to feel anonymous for Aida when we head next door. Having the place thronged with my mates won't help.

'Ready as I'll ever be,' she murmurs, and I watch those red lips move. Christ, she's sexy. I take hold of her hand and brush my thumb over her knuckles.

'I'll be right there with you the whole time,' I say. 'We won't get our room for another thirty minutes, but if you don't like it next door we can come back out here till then, okay?'

'Okay.' She gives a curt little *let's do this* nod.

'You need a safe word,' I blurt out. I should have thought of it earlier, because she definitely fucking needs one with me in this mood.

'A safe word,' she repeats. 'Um, all right then. Shit, I can't think of one.'

'Don't overthink it. It just needs to be something you wouldn't usually say in bed.'

She purses her lips before answering. 'Huh, that's a pretty long list. Um, fine, what about… parliament.'

I laugh. 'Parliament?'

'Sure. I don't plan on talking about our government institutions while we're, you know.'

'I should fucking hope not,' I mutter. 'Parliament it is. Nice job. That'll definitely stop me in action if you say it.'

And with that, I lead her to the huge double doors of The Playroom.

36

AIDA

"The Infernal Serpent"
—Milton, *Paradise Lost*

As soon as the bulky security guy opens the door for us, it's like I'm stepping through a portal onto a different planet.

Holy fuck.

I don't even know how to process what's in front of me other than sensory overload. My first impressions? Smoke. Dim lighting overall, flashing lights coming from one side where it looks like someone is performing on stage. People, or more accurately, bodies, intertwined. Writhing. Loud music—far louder than in the bar—that's a well-known aria I can't currently place overlaid with some hypnotic techno beat.

Chunky white pillars punctuate the room, white drapes flowing between them. I'm taking everything in while trying not to look at anything too closely, because I still don't know how I feel about seeing other people having sex. The idea of it still kinda gives me the ick, so I'm grateful all this smoke and darkness is muddying the picture to the point that I see skin and grinding but not the raw details. Not yet.

'Cloakroom,' my very own thug says against my ear, tugging me to one side, and I nearly laugh, because he made a big fucking deal of this feature via text. I have nothing to check, but I follow him over to the kiosk.

He stops and turns to me. 'Take off my shirt, baby,' he says, and I widen my eyes in surprise. Not that him taking off his dress shirt in the middle of a sex party is weird in itself, but because I wasn't expecting it just yet. But who am I kidding? I suspect this gorgeous former rugby player is a total exhibitionist. I bet he was one of those guys at college who always took his shirt off on the dance floor after a few beers.

'Sure,' I say, and my fingers go to his buttons. He has most of them undone already, anyway, so it's not exactly a tough job. I tug his shirt tails out of his pants and undo the bottom few buttons so it swings open. Even in the dim light, his stomach is clearly flat and toned with a dark trail of hair leading south that looks so insanely *male* it has me salivating.

He holds out his wrists and I unbutton one cuff and then the other.

'Take it off,' he says above the music. I look up at my masked man and snag my lower lip between my teeth, because I've been wanting to get my hands on his skin so badly. I reach up and glide my palms over his chest, pushing the shirt further open. *Mmm*. His skin is warm, and smooth, and gorgeous, the smattering of dark hair soft beneath my fingertips and the curve of his pecs perfectly firm.

I slide his shirt over his shoulders, down his arms,

exposing a body so beautiful and male and *young* it's frankly ridiculous. God, he's in great shape. Like, ridiculous, Magic Mike shape. He's fucking huge on the shoulders and arms, like I knew he would be, but seeing the definition of his muscles is a whole different thing from feeling them through his clothes.

The lights dance over his skin, throwing his sculpted, gym-honed physique into sharp relief.

But best of all?

He has a tattoo.

A huge one down one side of his abdomen. A thick, twisting, intricate serpent.

I didn't expect that at all, but now I've seen it I realise I shouldn't have been surprised. And if I've known since I met him that he was a naughty boy, then seeing him like this, shirtless and masked and tattooed, has that understanding ramping up to a whole other level.

I'm out of my depth here, that much is clear. In this place. With him. But as I take in his sheer beauty, he slips his shirt the rest of the way off his wrists and catches it in one hand, holding his arms out in a *look your fill* kind of way.

'Touch me, baby,' he says, and I step forward, because there's nothing I want more. I lay my hands on his chest again and let them wander over his soft skin. I trail them down his arms, skating over the ridges of his triceps. I bend my head and kiss a line across his pecs. And when I look back up at him, he's quiet. Watchful. The single eyehole is large enough for me to see his eyes clearly. They're impossibly dark, his lashes long.

He is the most sinful looking man I've ever laid eyes on. He's a fucking fantasy come to life. He's ridiculous, frankly. He's—

Two women interrupt my ogling. They flank Cal, and

even though they're in masks, their lithe figures and long, blonde hair and teeny, flimsy dresses and perfect skin suggest they're seriously young. Belle and Maddy's age, probably. I don't hear what they say to him, because they're each whispering in an ear, but they're handsy as fuck.

I back away, suddenly reminded that we're standing at the outskirts of an orgy. This is a free-for-all. Normal night-club etiquette absolutely does not apply. Cal gives them a tight smile and takes a step back so he can shrug them off before holding up his hands. He shakes his head, and it's pretty clear he's telling them *no.*

They turn to go, pouting as they do, and Cal reaches for me and pulls me roughly against his body. As I inhale the gorgeous, masculine scent of his skin, a thought hits me, so horrifying it knocks the breath right out of me.

Because I am *so fucking stupid.* Stupid and naive and rusty and unable to read the fucking room.

This should be Cal's big night.

Maddy said so. Cal said so. It's a major staple in Alchemy's calendar. An orgy of more dramatic and epic proportions than any other night at the club. So it stands to reason that on occasions like this, he lets loose.

I mean, look at the guy. He could fuck every single woman in here if he wanted to. That night he told me about —the orgy where he put his dick inside something like twenty different women in one night—was probably one exactly like this.

Jesus. I've waltzed in and hijacked his big night of fuckery, and now he's stuck babysitting some middle-aged woman when he should be showing off that gorgeous body and capitalising on all the women he can get.

I lift my head, aligning my mouth with the bump in his

mask that denotes his ear. I know what I want to tell him, but I have no idea how to articulate him.

'I can—' I begin. 'Look, I'm sorry. It hadn't occurred to me that you'd probably want to fuck around tonight. I didn't —I can go. Or we can, like, do this quickly, and then I'll leave you to it.' I stop, embarrassed.

He grabs ahold of my biceps so he can hold me at arm's length. The look he shoots me is one of total bewilderment before he leans back in toward my ear. 'What the hell are you talking about?'

'I'm cramping your style,' I say. 'I railroaded you into making tonight about us, but this is your party. You should be having fun and fucking whomever you like.'

He releases one arm and hauls me over to a huge pillar which he uses his body to press me up against. Then he bends his face towards mine. I watch his lips move through the hole in his mask.

'Do you want to fuck me tonight, Aida? Because if you've got cold feet, no hard feelings.'

'I do,' I protest, squirming at the sensations his proximity is giving me.

'Good,' he says. His eyes look so much more intense surrounded by the menace of his mask. 'Because I want to fuck you, too. Do you know why I didn't want to do this with you tonight?'

I stay silent.

'Because I knew that if I got you in here like this, with our masks on and everyone fucking around us, I'd be so fucking wound up that I wouldn't trust myself to take it easy on you. Do you understand?'

'Yes,' I say meekly.

'It's not because you're cramping my style. Jesus, I haven't even been in here since before your massage.'

'What?' I ask. Surely that can't be true. I thought he'd be in here every night—I've just tried not to think about it.

'Seriously. The only woman I want to fuck is you.' He's speaking through gritted teeth, like I'm really driving him to the brink.

He steps closer, pinning me against the pillar with his hips, and I suddenly understand why he's on the brink, because his dick is like a damn baton inside those fitted black pants.

His lips go to my ear again. 'The only thing I can think about is fucking you every which way, and my only concern right now is that I'll go so hard on you you'll run for the hills. It is *not* whether I can have a piece of those vapid blondes or their little friends tonight. *Got it?*'

'Got it,' I say. My breath is coming fast now. This is a *lot*. The mask. The erection. The soaring opera and its pulsing techno beat. The bodies writhing around us. Cal's words. His intensity. And, above all, the feeling I can't shift that he's a different version of himself tonight.

A hungrier one.

My smiley, jokey, good-time-guy Cal is gone and in his place is this ridiculous, hulking masked man who seems unsure of whether he can control himself around me.

That makes two of us, buddy.

That desire to please him is back, because he's extraordinary. And if this thing began as a polite, professional agreement for him to fuck me and show me a good time, then it's quickly spiralling out of control.

I've gotten us here. I sensed a better story than the one I was writing in my head, I put my hand up for more, I insinuated my way into tonight's debauched circus, and I can feel said circus weaving its twisted magic around me.

If our masks are the starting point—the props that allow

us to shelve our usual personas and assume darker, more daring, more carnal ones—then the sensory alchemy this place is creating around us will take us the rest of the way.

Cal keeps me pinned to the pillar. His head is still bent. His lips brush the skin of my neck and I shiver. The touch is light, but I wouldn't call it gentle. I'd call it threatening. He puts his hands on my hips, his fingers digging into the flesh there, and I allow myself to touch him, too. To trail my fingertips up his impossibly smooth back. To learn the curves of his muscles.

'I know you're a woman who needs hard evidence,' he says, and I'd giggle at his unintentional pun if I wasn't so fucking turned on. 'We'll get our room shortly, but how about you let me show you how much I want you in here?'

His thumbs squeeze between our bodies and press into the skin in front of my hip bones, a possessive gesture that has me grinding against him. This wasn't the plan, but I blew the plan to smithereens when I moved our little rendezvous to the scene of an orgy.

Besides. The vibe in here is getting to me. Over Cal's shoulder, a guy wearing just tight boxer briefs and an eye mask is tugging the dress off a woman and bending to take her nipple into his mouth. Cal has me facing away from most of the action, but just seeing that is making me feel wanton.

And don't get me started on Cal himself. This mask of his is making me feral, as is the fact that we haven't kissed properly this evening, and I want his tongue in my mouth so badly I can barely think straight.

Strike that. I want all of him. I want us both naked. I want him ranging over me, bearing down on me, thrusting inside me. I want his tongue and his fingers and his dick.

And in this brief, heady moment of insanity, I want it so much that I'll do whatever he wants right here.

Because tonight I'm not a mom or a news anchor or a divorcee. I'm a masked, incognito woman in the arms of a man who looks like the sexiest serial killer I have ever seen, and I am all in.

'You can show me however you want,' I tell him.

37

AIDA

"What in me is dark illumine, what is low raise and support."
—Milton, *Paradise Lost*

That earns me a kiss.

He releases one hip, grips my jaw, and parts my lips with his tongue.

Sweet Jesus.

I open for him immediately. When his tongue finally drives into my mouth, it's intoxicating. Hot and hard and male. Probing. Invading. His grip on my jaw is almost painful; his cock is grinding against my silk-covered pelvic bone. The feathery, bejewelled intricacy of my mask grates against the rough fabric of his face covering, but I couldn't give a shit.

He can ruin my mask and grind me to dust against this pillar for all I care.

He releases my mouth and takes a step back from me,

hooking a hand under my knee and pulling my leg up. The flowing silk of my dress bunches at my hip and that mouth of his curves into a satisfied smile as he glances down and sees my bare leg lifted for him.

I drop my head back so the pillar's taking all my weight, and gaze up at him. My hands go to the gorgeous bare domes of his shoulders, and I tell myself I'm digging my fingertips into his skin so I don't fall over.

'I think you like my mask,' he says. Watching his mouth enunciate over the music, watching his lips move in isolation, is nothing short of mesmerising.

I swallow. 'I like it a lot.'

'Good.' He has my leg hanging over his arm still. With his free hand, he burrows under the silk of my dress and brushes his knuckles over the scrap of lace covering my pussy, and holy fucking Lord. I suck in a sharp breath through my teeth as he watches me intently.

'You're a very reckless girl, taking me on tonight,' he says. He hooks a finger under the lace and pulls my thong aside, and the brief chafe of the fabric as he displaces it is enough to have me shivering with need. 'You told me when you blew me that you wanted me to show you how I am with women I fuck at the club. Now you're that woman, and I'm in serious danger of fucking you up so badly you won't want anything more to do with me.'

It's warm in here. Still, my pussy feels exposed. He has my thong pulled fully aside, but he's not touching me, and I need him to. I need him to touch me really, really badly.

Maybe I need to provoke him. Poke the bear.

'You won't fuck me up,' I tell him. 'And you won't scare me off.'

'You have no idea what I'm capable of,' he says right as he pushes two thick fingers inside me, and my mouth opens in a silent scream. I can't take my eyes off him, can't get enough of those dark eyes boring through his mask. Of that sensuous mouth on show.

He twists his fingers, and I'm wet, but it stings a little. I want to flinch, but I also want him to never, never stop doing this.

'Keep your eyes on me,' he mouths, dragging a thumb over my swollen clit. Jesus Christ, that's *so good*. I push my pelvis into his touch, and he sinks his teeth into the pillowy softness of his lower lip as he pulls his fingers out and shoves them back in hard. His thumb's on my clit, but it's not moving like I need it to. I need it to rub me. I start rocking my hips in search of the missing friction.

His huge chest is heaving. His shoulder is working as he works me, his bicep straining as he crooks his fingers deep inside my body. I don't take my gaze off that mouth. Those eyes.

'Like being finger fucked up against a wall at an orgy, do you?' he asks, his tone deceptively idle.

'Yes,' I moan.

'Course you do,' he says, and it sounds approving rather than taunting. 'Hold this.'

This is the bunched up silk of my skirt.

'Hold it up,' he says, releasing my leg. I put my foot down on the floor. 'High. I don't want anything keeping me from this pretty cunt.'

Oh my God.

I throw the fabric over one arm and stand there as Cal proceeds to get to his knees in front of me and tug my thong down. I step obediently out of it, and he tucks it into the pocket of his pants.

I'm standing in a room full of people, naked from the waist down, and at my feet kneels a gorgeous guy, masked and bare-chested, a perfect sculpture. Seeing the hooded crown of his head, all that gorgeous dark hair concealed under the most menacing of disguises, makes me fucking feral. And that's before he takes the leg I've been balancing on and drapes it over his enormous shoulder.

I am hypnotised. Frozen. I grip the pillar ineffectually with my free hand for balance and watch from my vantage point as he slides a hand between my legs and parts my lips. Then he presses his forehead to my pelvic bone and licks me hard where he's holding me open.

If I was primed before, I'm transformed now. I don't care where we are. I don't care who sees us. Who recognises me. The only thing I care about in this moment is the next perfect, rough lick from Cal, because my entire consciousness has shrunk to my clit.

From this angle, I can't tell it's him. When I look down, all I can see is a guy in a black mask kneeling before me, his head buried between my legs as he licks me, and it is the single hottest moment of my life. Mozart's hypnotic *Lacrimosa* is playing now: the soaring of a woman's voice overlaid with a thrumming techno beat that's building in time with the beautiful, ageless melody and, it seems, in time with my arousal. The celestial sound muddies my senses even more.

Cal shifts a little, tugging my leg a little further over his shoulder and using calloused fingertips to open me up more for him, so that his next lick hits even harder. I shudder at the sheer delight of his tongue on my flesh and then stiffen as he jams a couple fingers back inside me, filling me up just how I need.

Pleasure, hot and pure, is coursing through my entire body. He's really fucking going for it now. There's no strategic targeting. He's licking me roughly, using his tongue as a weapon, and finger fucking me in hard, fast shoves just the right side of painful.

His movements feel selfish and thuggish and unhinged, like he's violating my body for his own depraved needs. Like any pleasure I may glean from this is incidental. For some reason, that knowledge has me soaring even higher, has my greedy pussy clenching around him as he continues his onslaught.

Because we're both being selfish here. We're both taking. There are no manners or polite considerations. There's just Cal holding me wide open for him while his mouth and fingers fuck me as aggressively as they can, and me leaning into his filthy onslaught.

The way he's behaving makes the anticipation of how he'll be when he gets me in that room almost unbearable. This gangster-like persona he's adopted tonight is more than just a mask. It's an MO, and I'm willing to bet he'll carry that through to our room when he's got me behind closed doors.

If this spree is anything to go by, I know he'll take everything from me when he gets the opportunity to rampage all over my naked body.

That thought—the thought of him naked and masked and fucking huge, using my body how he wants—has the heat his mouth and his fingers have built in my pussy igniting into a fire far, far beyond my control.

Right there, arching away from the pillar and into his touch, I combust into flames around him.

38

CAL

"Him the Almighty Power hurled headlong flaming from the ethereal sky, with hideous ruin and combustion, down to bottomless perdition, there to dwell in adamantine chains and penal fire."
—Milton, *Paradise Lost*

I haul myself up her body, dragging my fabric-covered face, my arousal-covered lips, over silk. She looks and smells and tastes expensive, which makes the satisfaction of defiling her and tearing her apart all the sweeter.

I'm oblivious to the people fucking around us, because a single thought is burning through my brain and ringing in my ears.

I.

Need.

To.

Get.

Her.

On.

A.

Fucking.

Bed.

I'm shaking with the need to shoot my load. Inside her. All over her. I don't fucking care at this point. I'm an animal, my fancy education and usually polished social skills shot to hell in the face of one woman's exquisite cunt.

She still looks far too together for someone who just came as hard on my tongue as she did, beautiful mask and immaculate hair and perfect, scarlet lipstick still intact.

We'll have to do something about that.

Won't we?

As soon as I'm fully standing, I kiss her hard, my tongue still ravenous for more of her holes. I want her to taste herself on me. I thrust my dick against the silk that's covering her up again. It's both a threat and a promise.

She wraps one hand around the back of my neck, her other clawing at my back as she lets me invade her, explore her with my tongue.

'We need to find our room,' I tell her, barely able to hear my own voice above this insane music. There's just enough blood flow left in my brain to recognise that what we just did is a step far enough towards exhibitionism for now. She'll need privacy for the next part.

Besides. I don't want to be an exhibitionist for once. I need a bed and some cuffs and Aida all to myself. I'm the only lucky fucker who gets to see her laid out and begging for it tonight.

I tug her into my arms and turn her around, my hands roaming over her hips, her arse, as I direct her towards the corridor bearing the private rooms as gently as I'm capable of.

Our room is ready, and I utter a quick prayer of thanks to a god I almost certainly don't believe in.

And then we're in.

I'm turning the lock.

I'm pulling down the blind on the window that lets voyeurs see what people are getting up to if all parties are up for it.

No fucking way.

I lean back against the door, my head hitting the wood with a dull thud, and survey her. She's standing in the middle of the room, right in front of the foot of the bed, surveying her surroundings. It must look a bit different from when she was at Alchemy for her massage. She's a lobster in a pot who's realised too late she's fucking boiling.

I take her in. Silk—blood red in this perfectly dim light—pouring over her curves. The slender lines of her arms and throat illuminated in gold. The gleam of her dark hair. The slash of crimson at her mouth. When she moves, her reflection glitters and shimmers above us in the darkened mirror that dominates the ceiling.

The ache I have for her is so extreme that I'm not far off being a danger to her and to myself. This need is burning every last binding that tethers the beast within, and I can practically smell the acrid smoke as they blaze.

'Aida,' I say in as normal a voice as I can muster. 'You don't have to—you can get out of here right now.'

She smiles at that and comes towards me. She doesn't hesitate, though she should. Her hands go to my shoulders and she glances down at my torso. I'm too far gone to even remember to contract my abs like I usually would if a woman was checking me out.

'No fucking way,' she says. That glorious music is playing through the speakers, but at a much lower volume, and it's fucking with my head. It's classy and decadent and sophisticated and insidious and sensual and dangerous.

Just like her.

'Safe word,' I say weakly, because there's no way a safe word is an adequate substitute for her running for the hills.

'Parliament,' she says, before running her tongue over her lower lip in her trademark style. Her perfume tonight is rich and musky and floral and I can't. I just can't anymore.

'Remember it,' I bark. 'If you're in pain. If anything hurts. If you don't like any of it.' Then: 'Mask off.'

She reaches up and tugs it off, and there she is. Beautiful, but a shade more vulnerable without her mask, if I'm not mistaken. A shade less certain.

Good.

'Turn around,' I grit out. I'm unzipping the back of her dress before she's fully turned, yanking the zip down her back as urgently as I can, until it's falling in a pool of luxurious silk at her feet. I grab both cheeks and squeeze as I bend and put my lips against her ear.

'I'm going to keep my mask on, and I'm going to cuff you and fuck you harder than you could ever imagine being fucked when you were married to that pathetic piece of shit,' I say. 'And the only way you're getting out of those cuffs is your safe word.'

She moans and rubs her arse against my cock. 'God, yes please.'

I release her cheeks. 'Bend over and take your shoes off.'

She bends over like the obedient girl she is. Mmm. I run a few possessive fingers over her cunt as she fiddles with her buckles, enjoying her wetness and anticipating the moment I'll be balls deep in her.

But first:

'Get on the bed,' I say as I pull her back upright. I suck my fingers into my mouth. Fucking delicious.

She walks over to the bed and I follow her, because the sooner I get her restrained, the sooner I can shoot my load. When she's lying back on the black satin sheets, her head propped on a couple of big pillows, I put a knee on the bed and grab at the nearest cuff. It's a standard metal one on a chain that's affixed to the wall, and I make quick work of snapping it closed around her wrist before doing the same on the other side.

Only then do I allow myself to stand and take her in properly. I've seen her naked before, but this is different. The massage was fun, but a massage table isn't exactly a suitable base for fucking on.

Besides, I was behaving myself then.

Things are very different now.

She's lying flat on the bed, her arms outstretched, those liquid black eyes of hers watchful. Anticipatory. Her body is beautiful: tanned and taut with those tantalising paler bikini lines on her tits and her arse. I see her taking me in, and I glance up at the mirror on the opposite wall.

Jesus Christ.

For a second, I see myself how she sees me: an anonymous, hooded, ripped thug, muscles flexing and tat on show and dick threatening to tear through the tent in my trousers.

I look fucking terrifying.

And I love it. Because this feels right. This is who I want to be in this moment. My reflection is just that. A *reflection* of how I feel, of the kind of rough sex I want to have tonight. And if this beautiful, intelligent, spectacular woman is happy for me to cuff her to this bed and unleash my need on her in her like an animal, then fucking *bring it on.*

39

AIDA

"T' explore the secrets of the hoary deep, a dark, illimitable ocean without bound."
—Milton, *Paradise Lost*

Cal watches me as he undoes his belt. His movements are hurried, jerky. Desperate, even. But he doesn't take his eyes off me. My gaze, however, flickers up and down his body, because he's so freaking hot I can't bear it. The bottom of his hood kisses his collarbones, and then it's skin. Muscle. Hair. Even a little ink: that serpent hugging his tapered waist.

His hands are large and male and strong.

Why is watching a man undoing his belt buckle and zipper so incredibly hot?

Probably because it's so intentional. He's getting his dick out. For *me*. And yeah, I've seen it, sucked it, but this is different, because we'll both be naked. I'm so transfixed by the show before me I almost forget to feel self-conscious, even though I'm butt naked and trussed up in chains as though I'm in some kind of porno.

He gets his zipper open and shoves his pants down, hopping a little in his haste to get them off. But when he straightens up, his crown is actually poking out of the top of his snug black boxer briefs, and it looks angry.

Holy *fuck*.

He rubs his hand over his length and then tugs his underwear down so he's naked in front of me, and I swallow. Shit—I'm way, way out of my depth here. I have this beautiful, beautiful man in front of me, and he's fisting his enormous erection and pointing it straight at me, and his gorgeous face is covered like he's a common fucking criminal.

Seriously, he looks like he belongs in a supermax prison, and it's making me so fucking wet. I blame my *Starred Up* obsession.

He comes right to the edge of the bed.

'Legs up,' he barks. I obey right away, sliding them up and open so my feet are flat on the sheets. He pumps some lube from the dispenser on the nightstand into his hand and climbs between my legs so he's raised up on his knees. He's shaking, I realise. My beautiful man is pointing his dick at me and shaking with the effort of holding himself back, and it makes my heart twinge.

'I can't wait,' he shudders out, giving his cock a single pump with his lubed-up hand. 'Have to take the edge off before I fuck you like you need. And it's about time I covered your tits in my cum.'

His pump is slow, but he's white-knuckling the damn organ like touching himself is the only thing keeping him from crashing through the sanity threshold and into the darkness. He runs his free hand up my inner thigh before dragging a thumb through my wet pussy and groaning.

I watch, transfixed, as he kneels there and jerks himself off. His strokes are so slow and long and fucking powerful. This may just be the most hypnotic thing I've ever seen. John wasn't—

Nope.

There's no room for John here. Not when Cal's in his Felon Era. Not when he's giving me the private show of a lifetime. I'm totally conflicted, because being cuffed and helpless is really doing it for me, but I've never wanted anything like I want to get my hands on his dick.

'You're so fucking sexy,' he pants as his hand moves up and down. Up and down. He's so rough with himself—rougher than I'd dare to be with a guy. 'Jesus *fuck*, the way you tasted... look at your tits. Look at them. So fucking soft. I'm gonna come all over them. Legs *down*.'

He removes his hand from my core and I lower my legs so he can step his knees over them. He's straddling my hips now, looming over me, this great, hulking man, his mouth parting in a combination of anguish and ecstasy as he fucks his hand hard.

'Fuck, I'm close,' he grits out. 'Need to blow. *Fuck* —I'm—'

His hand speeds up. The way he's working his dick is almost violent. He throws his hooded head back and really lets himself have it, his hand a blur of movement, his entire being a vision of hyper-masculinity. In this moment, he epitomises the staggering beauty of the male form.

And then he roars like he's in so much pain, and ropes of hot cum hit my body like lashes. My stomach. My breasts. My neck. My jaw.

Branding me as his in the most primeval way there is.

40

CAL

Jesus fucking Christ.

Holy *shit*.

I come in endless hot jets that paint Aida's beautiful body, the ropes of my cum glistening on her skin in this dim light. The sense of release is stupendous, but that's all it is.

Release.

My infamous refractory period will be non-existent tonight. This was just the warm-up: my way of working the worst of my animalistic urges off so I can give her the thorough fucking she needs and deserves.

She's gazing up at me, still strung out on the bed, and the sight of my spectacular, sophisticated little protégée in chains, trapped between my thighs and covered with my cum, is so fucking gratifying I can barely breathe.

Protégée literally means *protected*. I quickly shove the unwelcome thought that I'm making a mockery of our intended relationship back down into the darkness from where it came, because she doesn't look upset or offended or violated right now.

She looks transfixed. Aroused.

The little beauty.

I plant a hand on the bed, next to her ribcage, so it can take my weight. My cock's still semi-hard. I release it and, breathing heavily, lean forward.

'You are insane,' I tell her. 'You're so fucking sexy you blow my mind.' I run a finger through my cum and trace a meandering line over her stomach. Up between her tits. I circle a stiff little nipple, and she sucks in a breath.

'That was the best show I've ever seen in my life,' she tells me, her scarlet lips curving up into a smile that has my ego inflating to epic proportions.

'You have no fucking clue,' I tell her, my voice low and filled with menace. '*You're* the show. You're gonna put on a show for me while I fuck you into this fucking mattress. Got it?'

Her expression is defiant. 'Bring it.'

'You're hardcore,' I say. I pause and exhale sharply, nostrils flaring, as I smear more cum over her tits, paying special attention to her nipples. They're so slippery. So hard.

Her breath is coming in short, shallow bursts. Her tits are heaving under my touch. She's so fucking gorgeous.

'What would they all say if they could see you now?' I muse aloud. I've got my palm flat on her skin, rubbing my cum all over her chest and stomach. 'Everyone's precious Aida, slayer of politicians, chained up and naked and gagging to be fucked by a thug?'

'I don't give a flying fuck what they'd say,' she spits.

So help me God, I believe her.

'Stay there,' I order ineffectually, because she's not going anywhere, and I hop off the bed. In the ensuite bathroom, I run the tap until the water's warm, then soak and wring out a washcloth. I take great pleasure in wiping it gently over her captive body.

My dick is hard again. I give it a quick once-over with the washcloth before chucking it in the direction of the bathroom. It hits the doorframe with a wet slap and slips to the floor.

Whatever.

I bound onto the bed and straddle her shoulders, putting most of my weight on her chest. I stare down at her, and she gazes up at me, her eyes huge. Before she has time to react, I fist my cock and drag it over her bottom lip. The one that makes me crazy. It drags at her mouth, and that sensation of her skin brushing along my crown has me shivering.

'Cal,' she begins. 'Do you—'

'Shut the fuck up,' I say. 'Fucking take it.' Then I'm shoving my hard cock down her open throat, and she gags as soon I hit the back of her throat.

Jesus fucking Christ, that feeling. It's like nothing else. I stare down at her and grit my teeth together as I slap a palm to the headboard, because the thrill of dominating her, of sitting on her chest, and feeding her my dick, and watching as her eyes sparkle with unshed tears and her hands tug at their cuffs and her head attempts to thrash from side to side, has adrenalin coursing through my veins, hot and sick and impossible not to act on.

I fuck her mouth for a couple of minutes, noting with satisfaction how my girl finds a rhythm. Finds a way to take me, to overcome her gag reflex.

'There you go,' I tell her, thrusting back into the warm, wet oblivion of her open mouth. It is fucking nirvana. 'Knew you could do it.'

I allow myself a few more drives, because she's taking me

like a fucking champ, and gazing into her watering eyes, seeing her struggle turn to surrender, is hypnotic.

I can sense her lower body moving. I reach one hand behind me, trailing my fingertips down her stomach until they find her cunt. Jesus.

'You're fucking soaked,' I tell her, allowing myself to jam a couple of fingers inside her satiny wetness. She instantly tilts her pelvis so she's grinding into them. 'What a greedy little whore you are for my cock. Is choking on my dick turning you on?'

She attempts to nod, her eyes wide.

'Better fill you up then,' I grit out. I'm back on the knife edge of desire so strong I'm barely functioning. My entire awareness has narrowed to Aida's mouth around my dick and the prospect of burying myself inside her cunt. Of fucking into her over and over so hard we both explode.

'You don't get to speak,' I tell her. 'You can say your safe word, and you can moan and scream and show me how much you love being fucked, but you don't get to speak. You're mine to play with tonight. I don't need your smart mouth.'

I rear up slightly, pulling my dick out of her mouth and replacing it with my fingers. She sucks her own arousal off them obediently.

What a good girl she can be when she wants to be.

As I get off the bed and grab a condom from the bowl, I ask her, 'Anything you want to say to me?'

She raises her eyebrows at me but shakes her head.

'Fine,' I say. 'Don't say I didn't warn you.'

This woman is a piece of work. She wants a baptism of fire, she'll get one. She's so much more impressive, more accomplished than me in every way, and I couldn't find that more of a turn-on.

But this, right here, is where I'm as accomplished as they fucking come. This is my kingdom, and this is where I'll make Aida Russell lose her power of speech.

I roll the condom on as she watches with hungry eyes and get back between her long, shapely legs. Another quick glance in the mirror, and I still fucking like what I see. I jerk my head towards our reflections.

'Look.'

She looks and sees what I see.

Her, chained to the bed and spread out for me. Arms up. Back arched.

Me, hooligan mask on and muscles flexing as I lean over her. I hope she sees how big I look on top of her. How much more powerful than her.

I hope it feeds her desire as much as it feeds mine.

I lower myself over her and notch my dick at her entrance as I bend my head and invade her mouth with my tongue. I'm sweating hard under this fucking mask, but I'm damn well letting my inner thug play the rest of this out.

He's who I want her to see ranged over her.

He's who I want her to see when she's stretched so far around my cock she can barely draw breath.

He's who I want her to see when she fights to get free from her chains and can't.

'So wet,' I groan as I slide my latex-covered crown through her wetness. 'God, you love it, don't you? Love me tying you up. You love knowing you're my little fucktoy tonight and I can do whatever I like to you?'

I swallow her moan of agreement with a deep kiss, my tongue probing and devouring and taking as I massage one perfect tit, palming her nipple. She's panting into my mouth and squirming beneath me, trying to grind against my cock, so I'll give it to her.

Let's see if she can take me without lube. It'll be a tight fit, but she's wet enough. I raise myself back up onto one elbow and she opens her legs wider to accommodate me as I thrust forward, wedging the first inch or two inside her.

Her moan is guttural. Almost primal. I swear it makes me harder, because feeding my cock into the body of a woman who's desperate for it is the best fucking feeling in the world.

It has me driving forward more savagely than I mean to and shunting a couple more inches inside her. The snugness of the fit has her mouth opening in a silent scream and my skin pricking with fresh sweat. Fuck me, it's going to be tight. I pull out and crouch between her legs, putting my hands on her knees to pull them apart as I take aim and spit.

Bullseye. It hits her right on the clit, and I don't miss her sharp, involuntary gasp of surprise. I smear it over her entrance, and then I'm scrabbling up her body and driving back in.

Driving home.

The moment I'm fully inside her, that expressive face of hers contorts in rapture.

'Fuck,' I tell her. 'You are so fucking full of my dick right now.'

It hits me afresh that she's seriously out of practice and seriously neglected on this front. I'm going to pump her so full of my cock she won't remember her own name. I'll fill her, and fuck her, and own her body so completely she'll leave this room a different woman.

I start to move, my dick dragging out of her before driving forward and filling her up. A glance down at our joined bodies shows me her tits jiggling as I find my stride and start to pummel her. She's meeting me thrust for thrust like she can't get enough, like she's savouring every single inch I'm giving her.

I love looking down at her like this. The characteristic scowls and eye-rolls are gone, and instead she's showing me, with every emotion that passes over her beautiful face, how much she loves this.

How much she loves me filling her up and, it seems, how much she enjoys being told to shut the fuck up and take my dick like a good girl.

When an entire nation consistently projects its sky-high expectations onto you and your intellect, maybe sometimes you just want to be fucked into next week.

Yeah. I adore being on top like the untamed beast that I am, railing her into the bed. But she forwent my offer of a nice afternoon fuck with Regular Cal and opted for the Full Monty, so that's what she's gonna get. I'll show her no mercy. I'll give her everything I've got, but I'll fucking well take everything she has to give, too.

I pull out and flip her over without warning. 'Elbows and knees,' I grunt, hauling her arse up in the air with an arm around her waist. Her chains are crossed, but there's plenty of latitude in those things for a bit of variety.

Yesss. She's gorgeous like this, head down, arse in the air for me, holes on display. I slide my dick back in again, and she shudders out a loud moan when I'm fully in. Fuck, yeah. I grip her hips and roll mine against her so she feels every single millimetre of me in this position.

'See, sweetheart,' I say conversationally. 'You came to me because you needed a really good fucking, and you were a clever girl, because you knew my dick was what you needed. And now you have me stuffed inside your pretty, wet cunt.'

She lets out a strangled whimper. I like that. I like that a lot. I roll my hips again. 'I'm gonna fuck you harder and deeper and rougher than you've ever been fucked before. Ever. Because I know that's what my dirty girl needs. A seriously good fucking.'

I bend and give her arse cheek a good bite, because, fuck me, it's too plump, too smooth not to mark. It's asking to be marked.

And then I let her have it.

I fucking *go* for it.

I tug off this sweaty fucking mask, and I drag my dick out, and I ram it home. My fingertips dig into her hips as I hold her in place for me so she has nowhere to go, no way to alleviate the onslaught. I want her to take everything. Savour every sensation. I want her to allow my dick to hit every fucking nerve ending in her body and light her on fire.

Every hour of pain I endure in the gym pays off in these moments, because my stamina is second to none, and I can fuck this beautiful, sensual, responsive woman into next week if that's what she wants.

In. Out. In. Out. I thrust and thrust and thrust, and every time my angry, engorged cock disappears inside Aida's body I want to cheer. Because I've wanted to do this to her, for her, since she walked into our offices, but now I'm bottoming out in her, over and over, and it feels like nothing else on earth.

She's taking me like a champ, the noises she's making getting more and more desperate, more hungry, as I wind her higher and higher. I treat every drive as a move to master. I want every single second to give her pleasure. By the sounds of it, they are.

'You're going to come for me, baby,' I tell her, releasing one hip so I can run a hand up the delicate curve of her spine. 'I can feel it. You're going to come so fucking hard around my cock.'

She moans, breathing heavily. I don't think she could

speak if she wanted to. I drag myself out and then plunge back in. She actually screams, one of her hands shooting forward to claw at the sheets as she twists her head to one side and lets it collapse against the mattress. She's full-on convulsing, her beautiful body jerking as I fuck her through her violent orgasm, ramming home inside her over and over.

It's the perfect contractions of her cunt around my dick that finish me off. As her deepest internal muscles milk me, the heat that's been building and building races through my balls and down my dick, and I let out a roar that's nothing short of utterly fucking victorious as I erupt.

41

AIDA

I'm slumped against Cal like a goddamn rag doll. He practically had to carry me into the bathroom, and he held me against him, his arm a vice around my waist, as he waited for the shower to run hot.

That arm is still around me, holding me up as we stand under the spray together. My arms are clasped behind his neck, and I'm drinking in the view. Because that mask was fucking hot, but his face is better. Especially when he's smiling his beautiful smile at me.

This is so crazy. My little boys are tucked up at home under the care of their favourite sitter, and I'm standing under a shower in a sex club with the sexiest guy I have ever met in my life, feeling sore and used and just-fucked and more alive, more sated, than I can ever remember feeling.

We just blew way through our first-fuck plan and then some. That was the most insane, out-there thing I've ever done. The thought makes me giggle.

'I'm so proud of you,' Cal says, dipping his head so he can rub his nose against mine. 'I had no idea you were such a greedy little slut for my dick.' He backs up his comment with a slap on my ass.

'I had no idea either,' I tell him honestly, watching with pleasure as those warm brown eyes crinkle at my response. 'And I *definitely* had no idea you were such a depraved motherfucking thug.'

The smile disappears. He tugs me more tightly into his arms and buries his face in my neck. My fingers trail through his wet hair. He's so huge, and so strong, and so overly virile in so many ways, and yet he still has this boyish quality that I find totally unfamiliar and extremely charming.

He ghosts light kisses down my neck. 'Yeah,' he mutters against my skin. 'You're absolutely right. That wasn't what you signed up for. I feel like we vaulted over about a million steps in our programme. I really pushed you hard in there, and I am so incredibly sorry. That was pretty fucking intense, even by my standards. I was a fucking animal, no two ways about it.'

I pull away a little so I can see his face. I have no idea how I'll feel about all this tomorrow, when the orgasm fog has lifted and I'm reviewing our actions in the cold light of day. Especially when I review them with my producer hat on. But right now, in this steamy shower with Cal's arms around me, I'm flying high.

'Hey,' I tell him. 'I'm *great*. It was amazing. You got me so worked up. I didn't know I could be that... feral.'

His smile returns, more rueful now. 'We were both feral.'

'So you roughed me up a little. I loved it. You blissed me out. We're all good.' I slide my hands over the gorgeous planes of his damp skin so I can cup his face. 'I'm still processing, but I know for sure that was the most intense, amazing sexual experience of my entire life. The only regret

I have is that I'm forty-six and I wish this would have happened earlier.'

And I wish it would have happened with a man I chose to spend the rest of my life with instead of a beautiful, devastating sex club owner who'll be giving another woman that same treatment before I can say parliament.

Only I don't say that part, because he's erasing my regrets the best way he knows how, with his mouth on mine as he strokes a firm hand down my wet hair, smoothing it over my scalp, my neck.

There's something about his gentleness in this moment after his roughness just now that my soul craves as much as my body does. The same parts of me that needed him to cuff me and flip me over and spit on me and fuck me now desire his kisses. His praise. His tender touches.

Maybe it's closure. Maybe it's a validation of sorts. A way for his body to tell mine that everything's okay. That I could get off on a masked man ravaging me, because it wasn't real, and now he's confirming that through what is basically a very sexy cuddle.

Being in the shower with him, though, and having his wet, strong body pressed against mine? That feels dangerous in a whole other way from his masked persona. Because just as I've been sexually frustrated, this past year—and longer—I've been lonely, too.

I've been lonely in my divorce, and I was a lot lonelier than I realised in my marriage, too. I'm not ready to walk away from Cal's orgasms yet. Nowhere near ready. But a pang of wistfulness hits me as Cal's tongue sucks on mine, as his fingers trace the bumps of my spinal column with something approaching reverence. Almost as if I'm missing this easy intimacy already, even when I'm right in the middle of it.

He releases me to pump some body wash into his hands, and the entire stall fills with a gorgeous botanical scent as he rubs his palms together. Then he's smoothing his hands over my body with a light, sensual touch. He frowns a little, intently focused on his task, before raising his head to shoot me a grin that's devastating in its boyish sincerity.

I turn away and grab some body wash so I can soap him right back.

Because that pang just got a whole lot worse.

42

CAL

"I made him just and right, sufficient to have stood, though free to fall."
—Milton, *Paradise Lost*

D*irty-lite.*

It wasn't such a difficult mandate. Not such a difficult concept to grasp. I show Aida a good time within the clear boundaries that this documentary—and her personal situation—dictates.

I charm her.

Make her feel like the amazing, sexy woman she is.

I fuck her, giving her just enough kink to show her what she's been missing, but not too much.

That's it.

Instead, I slipped a mask on last night, and chained her to a bed, and came all over her tits, and shoved my dick down her throat, and unleashed a torrent of verbal filth, and flipped her over, and *spat on her fucking cunt, for fuck's sake,* and railed her as hard as I've ever railed anyone in my life.

Nice, Cal. Really nice.

Jesus fucking Christ.

I'm not hungover, which is one of the best things about Alchemy—you never get drunk on alcohol there. You just get drunk on pussy. Still, I'm exhausted. My body's tired despite spending six or seven hours comatose. And I can't shake the weighty feeling that I did really, really badly.

When I get to work just in time for our morning meeting, everyone else looks knackered, too, even Gen, which is vaguely reassuring.

'Hi,' I say, flopping onto the sofa and stretching my legs out in front of me. I look around. 'Where's Mads?'

'She's not feeling great,' Zach says. 'We didn't actually make it last night—she's a bit fluey.'

'Ah, shame,' I say. I know how much Mads loves the Masked Ball. Almost as much as she loves Slave Night, which is saying something. 'Is she staying home?'

'Yeah, she's in bed,' he says. 'I got her a hot water bottle and some ginger tea before I left. I'll text her shortly to make sure she's okay.'

I smirk. He's so pussy-whipped it's not funny. I go to open my mouth, but Rafe beats me to it.

'You're so caring,' he croons in a piss-taking voice. 'Did you put some Vick's Vaporub on her too, before you left? Give her a good chest rub?'

'Fuck off,' Zach says as Gen and I snigger.

'No offence, but I'm glad she's not here,' Rafe says. 'There's something I want to talk to you guys about, and I don't want her to know.'

'Jesus, me too,' I say, resting my elbows on my thighs and

rubbing my eyes with the heels of my hands. 'I seriously fucked up last night. But you go first, mate.'

'No, you,' he says. 'Honestly. Sounds serious.'

'Yep.' I drag my hands down my face and survey them. 'Got a bit carried away with Aida.'

'I'm not surprised, wearing that thing,' Gen scoffs. 'You looked utterly terrifying. What on earth possessed you?'

'Dunno,' I say, just as Zach asks, 'What was he wearing?'

'Full-on balaclava,' Rafe tells him. 'He looked like a fucking rapist.'

Zach raises his eyebrows. 'Ah,' is all he says, but the way he says it speaks volumes.

'Is she okay?' Gen asks, leaning forward. 'That's the most important thing.'

I think of Aida screaming as I shattered her with my turbo dick. The way she wrapped herself around me in the shower. The kiss we shared in the cab when I dropped her at her front door.

'She was a lot more than fine last night,' I say. 'She was very happy indeed. But I want to check in on her today, because it was a lot.'

'Define *a lot*,' Gen says in her most terrifying voice.

'Um.' Shit, she makes me nervous when she takes that tone, and I know how protective she feels of Aida. At least Aida has one responsible adult looking out for her. I shift uncomfortably. 'Let's just say I got into character. It was pretty... intense. She had a safe word, and she was definitely on board. It was just a lot rougher than I intended. I won't go into details out of respect for her.'

And out of respect for my balls. Gen might actually chop them off if she gets wind of exactly what went down. She's glaring at me as if she's mentally sourcing a pair of rusty gardening shears for the job right now.

'This is why I didn't want her to come,' I protest childishly. 'You and Maddy were the ones who persuaded her it would be like *Cirque de Soleil*. If we'd done it in a more private setting, I wouldn't have got so carried away.'

'Come on, mate,' Rafe scoffs. 'A little accountability, please.'

I sigh. 'You're right, obviously. And, look, a good time was had by all. She was a very happy girl afterwards. I gave her plenty of aftercare, okay? I know how this works. I just hope I didn't push her too hard, too fast.'

Pun intended.

The aftercare wasn't purely altruistic, even though it's an integral part of the Unfurl programme now. We learnt that lesson the hard way when Rafe had Belle in tears after a scene during her programme. Our intention with the Unfurl sessions was previously to keep them short and sweet. Clear boundaries, you know?

But poor old Belle was overwrought after Rafe kicked me out of a particularly kinky priest role play and proceeded to bestow the mother of all pearl necklaces on her, and I know for a fact that the way he cared for her afterwards proved to be a massive turning point in their relationship.

They basically became a couple after that night.

And that should probably be ringing alarm bells for me right now, because my memories of Aida and I soaping each other up in the shower, of the pleased little smirk on her face as she lavished particular care on my dick, are making me feel all sorts of warm and cosy. Yeah, she was in an orgasm cloud—we both were—but knowing we had that time together helps to assuage my guilt over being Mask Guy.

'The only way to know is to talk to her, mate,' Rafe says.

'At the end of the day, we can sit here and give you a hard time, but it's really between you and Aida. I know you well enough to be confident you read the room last night. You've got really good judgement when it comes to this stuff—that's why Gen chose you.'

'Yeah.' I rub my forehead. 'Thanks. I'm—there was communication, you know? I'm just freaking out a bit because I usually keep myself under control pretty well but last night was...' I blow out a breath. 'I was really in it.'

'Interesting,' Gen muses aloud, but when I jerk my head in her direction she doesn't look pissed off. Instead, she's smiling her signature cat-like smile, like she has a delicious secret.

I can't be arsed with analysing the enigma that is Genevieve Carew today, so I strategically ignore her. Instead I ask, 'Have you guys ever woken up and sex-shamed yourself? Or had, like, sex anxiety, where you're not sure if you went too far the night before?'

'Well, obviously,' Zach says, and we all fall about laughing. I suspect that guy wakes up most mornings with Maddy and wonders what the fuck went down.

That woman is *wild*.

He's a lucky guy, but not as lucky as her.

'Remember the first Slave Night?' Zach says sheepishly. 'I was so freaked out I'd unleashed the beast that I actually went and saw John for confession the next day.'

Rafe is now laughing so hard he can barely breathe. Even Gen's shaking.

'You muppet,' I say affectionately. John was at school with us, a seriously good guy who Zach was always very close with. He's now a priest and still provides Zach with counsel, mostly of the friendly kind rather than the priestly kind. Obviously,

Zach was dealing with a whole other level of sex-shaming himself, because that Slave Night event was the first time he allowed himself to really go for it with Maddy and, in doing so, take a huge first step in moving on from his late wife.

Zach's laughing too. 'I know. She wound me up for so long beforehand, and I was so worried I'd disappoint her. Anyway, clearly I *didn't* disappoint her, but I really struggled to make peace with how far I'd taken it. Like, I really scared myself. Then John told me to get my head out of my arse and go have some fun with her, and'—he shrugs—'I got out of my own way.'

'When an actual *priest* tells you to loosen up, you know you're uptight as fuck,' I say.

'Seriously,' he agrees.

'I don't sex-shame myself, but it's a very conscious decision,' Gen says. 'As in, I have to give myself a talking to and tell myself that if all the parties were consenting adults and everyone was happy, then no harm was done. It's different for women, possibly. My chats with myself—before Anton, obviously—have always been more along the lines of whether I'm happy with the things I've let other people do to me. Whereas I'm guessing what's bothering you is whether you pushed Aida too far, rather than pushing yourself?'

'Of course,' I say. 'And clearly, most of the time when we're here at night people are pretty experienced. But you gave me a clear mandate for a very special woman, and I want to make sure I don't fuck her up. I only want to be a force for good in her life.

'That said, she's been pretty clear about keeping the majority of this documentary unscripted for the exact reason that she wants to do this at her own pace. So I'm hoping I read her cues right, and she was happy to up the pace last night.'

The faces around me are sympathetic, thoughtful.

'What's done is done, mate,' Rafe says. 'Go and see her. Check in with her, make sure she's feeling okay about it all. That's all you can do.'

I nod, feeling better about all this. 'Yeah. Will do. And Gen, I'll suggest a chat with you if she needs a woman's perspective?'

'Absolutely,' Gen says.

'Okay.' I blow out a breath. I feel a bit fragile, almost teary, which is seriously fucking weird. I'll go see her. I'll bring her some flowers, and I'll make sure she knows how much I admire and respect her.

It'll all be fine.

'What was it you wanted to talk about while Maddy's not here, mate?' I ask Rafe, mentally shrugging off my Aida concerns until I can devote myself to her in person.

'Oh, yeah.' He shifts a bit and rubs his palms on his thighs. He looks flustered, which isn't Rafe's style at all. He's a cool customer. 'Well, I wanted to tell you guys first. I'm going to propose to Belle this weekend.'

43

CAL

Gen's hand flies to her mouth as she gasps loudly.

I slap my thigh in delight. 'Fuck, *yes*, mate.'

'Ah, that's amazing,' Zach says, reaching over to slap Rafe heartily on the back. 'I'm so happy for you both.'

'She hasn't said yes yet,' Rafe reminds us.

We all scoff, because the idea of Belle turning him down is frankly ridiculous, and he knows it.

'Done deal,' I tell him.

'I hope so. Obviously, I couldn't have told you with Maddy around.'

'Um, nope,' Zach deadpans. No one knows better than him that his girlfriend is as indiscreet as she is effusive. 'I'll have to pretend I didn't know. She'll be furious if she thinks I knew before her.'

'Tell us the plan,' Gen demands, clasping her hands over her crossed legs.

He clears his throat. 'I was going to take her abroad, but I couldn't work out how to get the ring through security at the airport without her spotting it.'

'Valid point,' I say, nodding. I love that my ex-playboy mate has himself tied up in knots over proposing to his girlfriend.

'So I've hired out the Wallace Collection for next Friday evening,' he says, 'and I've got a string quartet booked. We'll have a stroll around, and I'll propose in one of the rooms, and hopefully she'll say yes, and then we'll stroll some more, I suppose. Enjoy some champagne. Just... let it sink in. I dunno.'

We're all quiet as we take in his plan. I can't say I've ever been to the Wallace Collection, but I know it's a small, private art gallery in a gorgeous mansion near Marylebone. It's presumably the perfect place to propose to Belle, who's an art dealer and very passionate about her field.

'It's bloody perfect,' Gen says, and I don't miss the catch in her voice. 'Oh, wow. Well done you. She's going to love it.'

'You think?' Rafe asks, scratching at his stubble.

'Absolutely, mate,' Zach tells him as I say, 'She'll be in pieces. Like Gen said, it's perfect.'

'God, I really hope so,' Rafe says. 'I think it's what she wants—marriage, I mean. We've discussed it, you know? In an abstract way. It's just—she's so young. Part of me feels guilty about tying her down so early. I've sown my oats, and then some. Marriage is so final for her. Maybe it's selfish, but I can't wait.'

Jesus, what the fuck is wrong with me this morning? There's a prickling at the back of my eyes, and I blink it away in a panic.

'It's not selfish,' I tell him. I feel strongly about this. 'It's wonderful, and it's exactly what Belle wants. You know she's never had this inclination to play the field. She adores you. You're her entire world, and her future, too. So what if she's young? I say you're both lucky. You get plenty of time together.'

'Maybe,' he says. 'I just—fuck. I can't wait to start a family with her. But I'm so conscious that we'll be on my timeline, because I'd love at least one kid before I'm forty. Whereas she could easily wait another decade if she wasn't with me.'

'I hear you, mate,' Zach says, exhaling heavily. 'I feel so guilty about that too. It tears me apart, actually. I mean, Maddy's living with me and the girls so she ends up acting like a de facto stepmum, and it kills me. As you say, they're so young. I kick her out the door to go and have fun as much as I can, but she says it's what she wants, and she talks about babies incessantly. I just hope I haven't totally ruined her youth. But I get it, I really do.'

'Stop it, you two, you hear me?' Gen says. 'I have never seen two young women more in love than Maddy and Belle are with you two old fools. So, for God's sake, stop worrying and give them a little credit to know what they want. I agree with Cal. They're lucky to have found such happiness so early on. Anton tells me his biggest regret is that he didn't meet me earlier, and I honestly feel the same. So go forth and marry them, and knock them up, and build beautiful families with them, and for fuck's sake allow yourselves to be happy.'

'Hear, hear,' I echo emotionally. 'You've got this, mate. She loves you. She wants this. Go and woo your girl.'

'Right,' he mutters. 'I've got this. Fuck, I'm terrified.'

'You'll all drop like flies,' I predict. 'This time next year, all three of you will be married.'

'And Gen will have four step kids,' Zach says with a cheeky side eye at Gen. We all giggle like schoolboys, because Gen's never made any secret of her total lack of interest in ever having children.

She doesn't deny that marriage is on the cards. I suspect the Big Bad Wolff has made his intentions clear already. When he wants something, Anton Wolff does not mess about. Instead she says, 'Well, at least they're all sixteen and over. And the Terrible Twins live with their mother, so it could be worse.'

'God help them, getting landed with a wicked stepmother,' Rafe drawls, and I snigger.

'She'll be the wickedest.'

Gen glares at me. 'You. Don't you have some fuckboy grovelling to do? Get out of here. And you'd better take your best flower game, too.'

I don't need to be told twice.

44

AIDA

My attempt at shifting into BBC mode isn't exactly helped by the tenderness between my legs. I can barely sit down—I feel like I cycled the entire Tour de France.

Is it weird that I don't hate it? That it feels like a badge of honour? The same goes for the red lines on my wrists where I pulled a little too hard on my cuffs in the throes of passion.

I'm in a meeting with my *Centre Stage* producer, Rory, talking on Zoom with two of our researchers who are based at our headquarters in Manchester about a special programme on immigration we're planning for next month. It'll be a panel discussion, and our researchers are busy vetting the participants. It happens more often than I'd like that people with inflammatory social media profiles slip through the net. I don't want to give a national platform to anyone who doesn't merit it.

My phone pings quietly on the table, and I glance down.

It's from Cal.

CAL: Hi. Can we talk? Any chance I can come see you?

I close my eyes for a moment, which is a mistake,

because it gives the filthy montage that's been haunting me all day a blank screen to play on.

That fucking mask.

It was just a goddamn mask! Why the hell did it make me so feral? I'm a grown woman who has won actual prizes for her reportage, but put a ripped as fuck guy with a cheap-ass face covering on his knees in front of me and I am a total fucking disaster.

My poor, swollen pussy pulses at the memory of his head between my legs against that pillar, and I don't hate the pain. Jesus fuck, that was hot.

As was every single thing he did after he made me see stars.

'Excuse me a moment,' I tell Rory and the guys on Zoom and pick up my phone.

ME: Hey. I'm at the BBC for most of the day but if you can swing by the Television Centre we can talk. I'll be free in an hour.

He replies immediately.

CAL: Great. I'll swing by at 11 xx

ME: OK x

I put my phone face down and attempt to refocus my brain on how the fuck this country can do right by the people who are seeking refuge on our shores every day.

I FIND Cal waiting by the front reception desk, looking like every woman's fantasy in a crisp white dress shirt and black pants with a lightweight jacket slung on top. His hair is styled artfully off his face. He's every inch the City playboy. If I didn't know him, I'd guess he was some flash trader or hedge fund manager.

He's also holding an enormous bouquet of velvety dark-red roses.

I go in for a double kiss, but he grabs me after the first one and swallows me in a hug, holding the flowers away from his body. Geez, this guy can hug. He feels and smells as amazing as he looks.

'These are for you,' he says, shoving the bouquet awkwardly at me.

'Thank you,' I say as I accept them, cradling them in one arm like a baby. I lean forward to inhale their fragrant scent. 'They're so beautiful.'

He shoves his hands in the pockets of his pants. 'I wanted to... well. I respect you so much and—um, anyway. You deserve them.'

Okay. So they're guilt flowers. I'll let it lie—the poor guy's already gotten himself tied up in knots.

'Who are you, and what did you do with my favourite felon?' I ask him, pointing at his smart attire as I lead the way to the elevator. It might be a joke, but it's hard to believe this is the same tatted, masked guy who chained me up and did all sorts of wicked things to me last night.

He flashes me a huge smile designed to devastate vaginas everywhere.

Hmm.

On second thoughts, maybe it's not so much of a stretch.

'He's serving extra time for bad behaviour,' he says with a self-deprecating grimace, and I try to hide my smile.

'Ah,' I say sagely. 'Makes sense.'

Yep. He's definitely feeling guilty.

I lead him upstairs and sequester us in an empty meeting room off to one side. It'll be a lot more difficult to smuggle Cal in here next week, when the trailer's aired and everyone knows our faces, but I still don't want any questions.

We take our seats at one corner of the conference table and I place the flowers down on the shiny surface, facing me so I can enjoy them. They really are sumptuous. I can't remember the last time a guy bought me flowers for non-professional reasons.

Cal shrugs off his jacket, muscles flexing beneath the thick, expensive weave of his dress shirt and reaches over to take my hand across the table. 'I wanted to come and see you'—he clears his throat—'and, you know, check in. See how you're doing this morning.'

'I'm great,' I say automatically, though that's a gross simplification of my tangled mess of feelings this morning. Physically I'm sore, yeah. Tired. My body's still wrung out from last night's exertions. But boy, did those orgasms take the edge off. They were a reset.

That said, I'd be lying to myself if I didn't silently admit it was a lot. What I did with Cal not only went way beyond anything I've ever experienced with a partner, but vaulted over any fantasies I've ever let myself have into territory I've never even let myself explore in my head.

I met him there, though.

Somehow, despite my not really understanding what I was signing up for when I insisted on attending the party, my needs met Cal's needs in that room. Perhaps it's more accurate to say my needs *caught up with* his. He was way ahead of me, but it terrifies me how easily I went along for the ride.

I trusted him.

I wanted him.

My thought process wasn't much more complex than that.

If we hadn't had that time together in the shower afterward, where he washed me and kissed me and dried me in that wonderfully unhurried manner, I'd probably be spiralling more right now.

But that time gave me what I needed. It made me feel like we were co-conspirators, for want of a better term. We came down off our highs together. He checked in with me then. He cared for me.

So he really doesn't need to be here with his gorgeous big puppy-dog eyes and his well-meaning roses, because it honestly makes everything more complicated.

He frowns at my *I'm great* response and strokes a thumb over my hand.

'I pushed you really hard last night,' he says slowly, like he's trying to find the words. 'And it was amazing, but it was selfish. I didn't do that for you—I did it for me. And that was not how this partnership was supposed to go between us. I totally lost control, and it was unacceptable, frankly. So if you're feeling a little, I dunno, fragile, or even used, then I'd like to know.'

He swallows. There's an ominous sting behind my eyes, because I'd prefer to have left things with the memory of relaxed, post-orgasm Cal than with this officious, concerned version of him.

'I'm not feeling fragile at all,' I tell him. *I wasn't until you showed up, anyway.* I pull myself up straighter in my chair, wishing I was wearing my professional armour instead of head-to-toe Sweaty Betty for my casual research day. This is my turf, dammit, and I'm a grown woman who refuses to let men's behaviour influence her emotions or reactions on a daily basis, in a vast public arena.

So I refuse to let Cal come in here and make me feel shitty, even if he means to do the opposite.

I take a deep breath before I continue, pulling my hand away. 'Look,' I say to the beautiful man sitting across from me. 'First, I had an incredible time. I think that was pretty obvious. Second, I signed up for this. I railroaded you into letting me come to the party.'

I pause as I select my next words. 'You run a sex club. I'd be stupidly naive not to understand that that's the kind of kink you get up to when you're there with more experienced women. Right? I didn't want you going easy on me. I wanted you to do the exact stuff you would have done if I hadn't been there. I told you, I didn't want to cramp your style. So you got in the zone, and it turns out I loved everything we did, so we're all good.'

He glares at me. 'Jesus Christ, Aida. I thought we went through this last night. Is this your way of saying you think I fucked you like that because I was up for behaving like a thug and you were the person I was stuck with for the night?'

I'm silent, because that's exactly what I think. He's as good as admitted it. *I didn't do that for you—I did it for me.* His words make me feel like I was collateral damage, some anonymous woman to be used and fucked. And while that got me off in the moment, it's not exactly comforting now. I'm vaguely aware of running my tongue over my lower lip as I sit and stare at him.

He groans and closes his eyes for a second. 'Fuck's sake. When you do that... Look, baby. I thought I'd spelt it out last night, but clearly I need to repeat myself, which is fine, because I'll say it as many times as I need to.' He tugs his chair forward until we're knee to knee at the corner of the table.

'I was out of control last night *because of you*. I was selfish and fucked you way harder than I should've *because of you*.

Not because I was in a wild mood and I'd signed up to fuck you. Not even remotely. It was because you turned up, and you looked so fucking ravishing, and yeah, I was in the zone.

'But I wanted you so badly I had tunnel vision, and I took and took and took, and you were a fucking champ. I never wanted another woman last night—not for a second. All I could think about was pushing you as hard as I could physically get away with, and that was really wrong of me. I didn't make it about you, and I should have. But honestly? If I could drag you back in there right now and push you even harder, then I'd do it again in a fucking flash, because you drive me nuts in the best possible way. Are you with me?'

I gaze at him, momentarily speechless. My stomach is a butterfly net; my sore pussy is clenching at his words. At the heat in those gorgeous dark eyes of his. At the intensity of his expression, because my sweet, light-hearted Cal has vanished, and feral, all-consuming Cal is back.

And this version of him pulls me under into a swirling vortex of want and need every time.

He leans forward and gets my jaw in a strong grip. 'I said, *are you with me*?'

I nod as much as I can in his vice. My breath is coming hard. 'Yes.'

'About fucking time,' he says, and he crashes his lips to mine.

45

CAL

This woman will be the death of me.

I can't kiss her properly like this. I release her jaw after a moment and pull us both to our feet before I walk us over to the side of the room. Her head hits the wall, and I slap a palm next to it, taking a second to enjoy the surprise on her face before I dive back in.

I slide my mouth against hers. When she responds, I waste no time licking at her lips until she opens for me. My hungry tongue is in there immediately, entangling with hers. I have her pressed to the wall with my hips. She's not going anywhere, and it seems she's getting the message, because one of her hands comes up to my shoulder and the other is in my hair, clawing at it.

That's more like it. I drag my thumb down her neck and encircle it lightly with my fingers as I use all my tongue skills to show her exactly who's boss. Her face might have been plastered all over the reception area when I came in—queen of the BBC's Hall of Fame—but right now she's in my arms, pliant as a doll, and last night she answered only to me.

Damn right.

As I kiss her, she makes these breathy little noises that go straight to my cock, and I grind harder against her. Just reminding her what she's missing every minute I'm not inside her.

Why is every single thing this woman does so fucking sexy? Aside from the fact that she's beautiful and smart and sophisticated and well educated and articulate as fuck, that is. She's a bombshell, a siren, whose intoxicating looks have nothing on her ability to silence the most powerful men in the world.

I find it so incredibly hot that she gives me the time of day, never mind shutting up and letting me effectively gag her with a single order.

Shut the fuck up. Fucking take it.

I meant what I said last night. The basic little blondes pawing at me did nothing for me. But when Aida Russell looks at you with awe and desire in those huge black eyes, you're a goner.

And when she tells you to show her how much you want her, you get on your fucking knees and you serve her.

I don't think I could have been clearer how much I needed her last night. For someone so sharp, she has a short fucking memory when it comes to the stuff that counts, and it tells me the killer confidence she brings on screen doesn't necessarily find its way into the bedroom. Not unless she's riding high on sex hormones, that is.

We'll need to do something about that.

I kiss her for a little longer, both to ram my point home and because she's fucking delicious. When I come up for air and pull my face away, I plant my other palm on the wall, effectively caging her in.

'Still with me, gorgeous?' I ask, attempting to keep my voice level.

Her tits heave in her gym gear as she catches her breath. 'Yeah,' she says with a little laugh, like she's gathering her wits.

'Good.' I glance between our bodies and back up. She's in tight yoga pants that show off her toned arse and legs, and a snug-fitting zip-up thingy. 'You look beautiful today.'

That's met with a classic Aida Russell eye roll. 'Please. I look like shit.'

'You look hot as fuck. And I can see your nipples.' I tut. 'Think it's appropriate to bring your nipples to the BBC, Ms Russell?'

'They weren't a problem until you showed up and kissed me,' she retorts.

Fuck, I'm basic, because that pleases me enormously. 'How's your cunt?' I ask softly. 'You sore today?'

Another eye roll. 'Very, thank you for asking. I can barely sit down.'

I can't help it. I smirk.

'Jesus Christ, your ego is massive. And here I thought you were concerned.'

She's not wrong. 'I'm very concerned,' I protest. 'If you'd like to bend over the table for me, I'll kiss it all better.'

She shivers, and I'm pretty sure it's a good shiver. 'I bet you would.'

'What are you doing later?' I ask, lifting a hand off the wall so I can slide it over her jaw.

She tilts her head a little, leaning into my touch. 'Probably bingeing *Young Sheldon*. It's my weekend with the boys.'

'Oh, yeah. Of course.' Stupid fucker, Cal. Of course she's with her kids.

'Yeah. So no orgies for me tonight,' she adds in a teasing voice.

I frown. It doesn't come as a surprise that she assumes the worst of me, but I'm not going to lie—it stings a little. 'I didn't mean that. I was going to see if you'd like to come over and let me cook for you.'

Her eyes widen. She wasn't expecting that. 'Cal...' She slips out of the space where my hand was and spins around. 'Going to your house feels like a...'

'Date,' I supply, turning to face her.

'I was going to say *blurring of boundaries*, but sure. Date works. Look. I appreciate how sweet and attentive you're being, and before you ask, I understand that you're telling me the attraction is real and you're not humouring me. I appreciate that. I really do.'

She takes a deep breath. 'But I'm a single mom, and I got burned pretty badly by my ex-husband, and the last thing I need'—she holds my gaze steadily—'is for some crazy hot sex club owner who's way younger than me and way more experienced to start blurring lines and sweeping me off my feet.

'Because you, my friend, are a very charismatic guy. And when you turn on the charm like this, it's a *lot*. I'm only human, and I'm lonely, and I enjoy basking in the warmth of your attention way too much. Like, I enjoy it so much it's problematic. So I need you to keep things clear between us, okay?'

She holds out her hands, palms up, as if warning me to keep my distance. 'You've already ruined my entire sex life for the rest of my life. I mean, how the fuck am I supposed to find a guy who can rival the way you made me feel last night? So when you start kissing me in broad daylight at my *workplace* and asking if you can cook for me? You're gonna wreck me. I can't do that stuff with you and not fall like a tonne of fucking bricks. I won't survive it.'

She's slaying me. I feel like I'm dying, like she's ripping my heart out of my chest. And then she looks at me with those huge eyes and delivers her parting shot in a whisper.

'Are you with me?'

Oh my good Lord. How a woman this smart can be so fucking obtuse is beyond me.

I take a step towards her and put my palms to hers before interlacing our fingers.

'I hear what you've said,' I say carefully, because no, I'm not with her. Not at all. Clearly, I need to spell this out for her in terms so simple she can't possibly fail to understand. 'But you don't get it. I'm not trying to blur lines. I'm trying to take the next step with you. I *want* this to be more than what it was when we started out. Let me put it in black and white. You're Taylor Swift in this scenario, and I'm Travis fucking Kelce. You understand?'

Her eyes widen before she kicks into a mouth purse and an eye roll. She's dismissing me again.

Nope.

'No,' I say sternly. 'Don't do that. Sure, I have no problems getting women. I'm adorable.' I flash her a cheesy smile. 'But you, baby, are a fucking superstar, and you have no idea how much you blow me away. You're so far out of my league it's crazy, but I don't care. I probably should, but I don't.

'Call me cocky, but it seems to me I make you happy—just a little bit? So I'm going to forge on ahead here, and, just like last night, I'm going to be the cheeky fucker who takes as much as he can get from you.'

She's staring at me like I've lost my damn mind, so I close the gap between us and drop a tender kiss on her lips.

'Now, let me ask you again,' I murmur against her mouth. 'When are you next kid-free, and can I cook you dinner?'

46

AIDA

'Well?' Simone says, dropping her enormous Bottega Veneta tote on the soft carpet of the Lanesborough's drawing room with what some might say is excessive drama. 'You can't leave me hanging like you did.'

I sigh and settle onto the overstuffed couch. We're having a quick coffee while the crew gets our suite upstairs prepped for our latest interview. 'Yeah. Sorry.'

'I don't want sorry. I want details. *Omit nothing*.'

I roll my eyes at her. One of Britain's finest newsreaders is, in fact, a dirty little ho for other people's gossip, especially when it involves sex.

'It got out of hand,' I say matter-of-factly.

She leans forward. 'In a good way or a bad way?'

'In a great way, I guess.'

'And who let it get out of hand?'

I consider. 'I insisted on going to this party I knew would be wild. He turned up in a full balaclava like he was gonna commit an armed robbery, and I went along with every single thing he suggested.'

She arches her perfect eyebrows. 'Willingly?'

'I was the most enthusiastic consenter in the history of consent.'

We pause and smile politely at the fresh-faced server who comes to take our coffee order. Nothing to see here. Just two household names discussing kinky sex.

'Hmm. How extreme are we talking?' she asks when our server has trotted off.

I roll my tongue over my bottom lip while mentally preparing a litany. 'Let's see. Exhibitionism, I guess. I let him go down on me against a pillar in the middle of what was basically an orgy.'

She spits out a shocked laugh. 'No.'

'Yes. In my mind, I had a mask on, so that was ample protection.'

'Right. Good logic. And it was hot?'

I run a hand over my fabric-covered thigh. I'm in a black jumpsuit for today's interview. It's tailored, extremely chic, but deliberately edgier than my *Centre Stage* wardrobe.

My monkey brain dives back of its own accord to the other night. The dim, smoke-filled room. The pulsing, soaring music. Cal, mask on and shirt off, on his knees in front of me, his skilled tongue working my pleasure centres until I went up in flames around him. *Fuck*.

'It was extremely hot,' I say shakily.

'I bet it was, you dirty little bitch,' she says, and I laugh. 'Fuck. Good for you. Seriously. Then what?'

'Oh, God.' I bend my head and press my fingertips to my temples—lightly, so as not to ruin my immaculate makeup.

'Hey. Don't get bashful now, darling. You've got to go upstairs in a few minutes and confess on camera, remember?'

I laugh. 'The camera's getting an abridged version for sure. Azure would pull that contract so fast.'

But I tell her.

I give my dear friend a blow-by-blow account.

Literally.

The cuffing, the pearl necklace, the choking me with his dick, the flipping me over and, yep, *spitting* on my pussy and taking me from behind, all while he was in character as some dangerous, hooded thug whose commands were terse and whose moves were rough.

Then, when it looks like she might have an actual heart attack, I tell her about the shower. How sweet he was. How careful. How tenderly he looked after me.

But I don't tell her about him coming to see me on Friday, because that episode is a shiny, fragile bauble, a secret so delicious and so new I want to wrap it in cotton wool and warm it next to my beating heart.

The things he said.

The kisses he gave me.

The way he was with me.

Or the way I've been feeling all weekend: a pot-pourri of precarious and hopeful and incredulous and dreamy and perplexed.

Because the public doesn't get to consume or enjoy or dismiss or mock or excoriate those intrepid new seedlings.

Only Cal and I get to do that.

47

AIDA

SIMONE: What did you get up to late last week, Aida?

ME: In a nutshell, I had sex with Callum.

SIMONE: To recap. He's the first person you've had any sexual relations with since your divorce, correct?

ME: Exactly.

SIMONE: So last time we sat down, you'd had your massage, which had a very happy ending for you. And it sounded like that was a heavily planned, highly choreographed event?

ME: It was. Well, the ending wasn't. [Laughs] But the overall concept was, yes.

SIMONE: And did you go with the same route for the next step in, for want of a better word, unfurling yourself?

ME: I didn't. I've been fortunate to have a lot of creative licence with this production, and that's something I pushed for, because there was no way I was cramming my sexual reawakening into someone else's schedule.

SIMONE: Quite right. So how did you approach the next step?

ME: We had a tentative plan to meet up at Alchemy, Callum's club, when it was empty. But I found out they were hosting a big masked ball there last week, and I guess the same side of me that's dragged me into the middle of riots and terror attacks and even war zones smelt a story.

SIMONE: Yeah, you've never had much of a survival instinct.

ME: [Laughs] Right?

SIMONE: So you signed yourself up for this masked ball. And I'm guessing *masked ball* is a polite term for a sex party?

ME: It was an orgy, yes. [Licks bottom lip nervously] So there were a lot of firsts for me that night.

SIMONE: You're telling me. Wow. [Looks around comedically] Okay, no one from your production company has pulled the plug on your mic yet, so I suppose you'd better keep going with your fabulous adventure. Can I ask, was this just your nose for a good story driving you? Or was it something deeper?

ME: It was both. I instinctively knew a party would make for better TV. We got some early footage of the setup and the performers before the guests showed up. I wanted it to be immersive for the viewers.

That said, it was more about me pushing my boundaries, going to places I'm not necessarily comfortable. As you say, I've always done that in my career, so why not my sex life? This show is called *Searching for Paradise*, and the masked ball idea sat so well with that. If my current journey is a quest for pleasure on my terms, then perhaps this is what finding paradise looks like for me.

SIMONE: It seems like you're taking that idea of what you want and what you deserve up an entire notch from where you started out, and I love seeing this organic shift in your expectations.

ME: Thank you. It's definitely a realignment, but it really does feel organic. This is an adaptive experience for me. I'm recalibrating as I go along, working out what feels right for me. And I'm partnering with a sex club, for God's sake. So I may as well provide myself and our viewers with something a little more boundary-pushing than some very safe, very vanilla, choreographed sex. Right?

SIMONE: Amen to that. Now, I despise myself for being so utterly predictable, but did you, ahem, find paradise last week?

ME: [Laughs] I did, thank you for asking. And then some.

SIMONE: Lucky girl. You've already told us you had sex with the divine Callum, and I'm sure every woman and a decent number of the men watching are jealous as hell of you right now. But what else can you tell us?

ME: I will say this. Pretty much everything I did that night was outside of my physical comfort zone, and a lot of it was outside my mental comfort zone, even. We all have fantasies, really dark ones, that live in our heads but that we don't suffer too often. We don't give them oxygen, and we often shame ourselves for having them, even when simply imagining something harms absolutely nobody.

A big part of my journey to where I am now has been unlearning a lot of the damaging rhetoric that we, especially women, have been told is damaged or perverted or even, if you've been brought up religious, sinful. But putting those fantasies into practice last week in a safe space, with a sexual partner who I trust implicitly, was simply incredible.

And I'll also say this. When you act on your fantasies with other consenting adults, the sky does not fall. I haven't been struck by lightning or burst into flames. It's all good. The experience was so liberating. It was scary and unfamiliar and *fun*. So much fun. Kind of like going on a roller-coaster ride. It's a wonderful human experience when you feel endangered but you know deep down you're safe. This was similar.

SIMONE: You mentioned how important it is to have a partner you can trust. How much did Callum play into this whole experience?

ME: He was integral, absolutely. I know he was doubtful ahead of the event that it was the right format for our next step, but we both came away very happy. I find him incredibly attractive, obviously, because I have a pulse. [Laughs] He's caring, and I trust him with my wellbeing. We communicate.

And I know I'm in safe hands, because he's far more experienced than me. And believe me, putting yourself in the hands of someone who knows exactly what they're doing is very, very rewarding.

SIMONE: You're several weeks into this journey. How are you feeling at this point? Do you feel different?

ME: Yeah, I do. First, I feel extremely proud of myself for doing this, because as I've said, I push myself for stories, so why not push myself for my own wellbeing? I want to know what I've been missing by adhering to deeply ingrained, hetero-normative, monogamous, and you could say, patriarchal, cultural norms. I want to be the so-called bad girl for once, and I'm thrilled to confirm that there's nothing bad about what I've been doing.

I'm also happier. Lighter, I guess. I'm a pretty intense person, and I'm a working single mom, which means duty always comes first. These past few weeks have shown me a whole other side of myself. I'd go so far as to say I like myself better. It seems I'm a nicer person when I'm having regular orgasms.

[Both laugh]

SIMONE: Hallelujah. So, my overachieving angel. You've shot the lights out on your last mandate. You were supposed to go off and get laid, but Aida Russell has, of course, to take it one step further and get stuck into an orgy. All that remains, then, is to ask what the utter fuck is next?

ME: [Smiles] Ask me in a week or two when I've worked it out.

48

AIDA

God knows, I've been intimate with Cal.

I know the guttural roar he makes when he comes. I've seen how black that trail of dark hair leading south from his navel to his penis gets when soaked by the shower. I've let him inside my goddamn body.

I've given him my fear and my vulnerability; I've bitten down on my safe word because I trust him to know how far he can push me; I've come undone as he's performed acts on my body even I didn't know I wanted or needed.

We've gotten hot and oiled-up and sweaty and cum-covered.

We've been *close*.

But going to someone's home is a whole other level of intimacy. A less breathless, gasping, desperate one, sure, but a form of intimacy it is.

On the face of it, Cal's as accessible as they come. His grin is as readily available as his one-liners. He's a talker, without much of a filter. I suspect he tends towards being emotionally slutty, spilling out effusive declarations with childlike, unguarded joy and an equally childlike lack of regard for consequences.

(That last one doesn't bode well for me, given what he said to me at the BBC a week ago.)

Still, it's all those factors that make me wonder how well I've really gotten to know him. That happy-go-lucky persona is as effective a defence as a squad of linebackers. If anything, the closest I've been to the real Cal is those unguarded moments where he's tugging on my hair as I kneel before him or straddling me, glassy-eyed and desperate, jerking himself off on my breasts.

That's not to say the nice guy act is just that, or the beast he unleashes in those brief, unwary glimpses is the real Cal. I don't believe that for a second. But I do believe there's far more to him than meets the eye.

As a journalist, you always seize the opportunity to interview someone in their home. While they gain from being on their own turf, you gain, too. Because their home will almost always yield clues about them.

Unless you're Emily Maitlis, performing *that* interview of Prince Andrew at Buckingham Palace. The royal family probably had a different agenda there.

So when I say I've spent the past week impatient to get inside Cal's home and prowl around, that's an understatement. I have this sense that if I can see him in his natural habitat, I'll understand him better.

There may be other reasons I'm excited to spend the evening with him, too.

It's no surprise that he lives in a sleek, modern condo in Knightsbridge. I'm tempted to laugh at myself as I exit the elevator straight into the penthouse, no less, because what the hell am I doing? Going for Friday evening dinner at the pimped-up bachelor pad of a guy ten years my junior, who also happens to own a sex club, that's what.

It's almost like I've forgotten I'm a middle-aged divorcée.

Well, I don't care.

Not tonight, anyway. God knows, I could use some fun. And if I want some fun, Cal's definitely the man for the job.

His apartment is stunning on first impression. Huge and uncluttered, which is what every mom fantasises about. No toys or letters from school, crinkled from having been stuffed at the bottom of book bags. Nope. Just polished concrete floors, oversized furniture that works well with the surplus of space, and windows for days.

The vibe is warmer than I expected, too, with a kind of deep taupe on the walls and pendant lamps casting a rosy glow over the spots they hang above. The island. The huge rough wood table.

But none of it can compete with the guy standing in the middle of the space, damp-haired and barefoot and smiling at me like I'm the most delicious thing his elevator ever spat out. He's wearing a navy polo shirt that hugs his pecs and strains against his biceps, and old, worn jeans that angels must've sewn to his legs. It really, really works.

'I've got Aida Russell in my flat, finally,' he says, prowling towards me. 'Welcome to the lion's den.' And then he's tugging me against him with an arm around my waist, and relieving me of the bottle of wine I've brought, and kissing me. His lips are soft, so soft, and his tongue is cool, like he's been drinking a cold drink, and God, this feels easy.

It feels easy to wind my arms around his neck and kiss him back. To melt against his hard, warm body. It feels easy because Cal makes it effortless. There's no over-thinking, no strategising. There's just his beautiful smile and his natural affection and his seemingly genuine happiness at seeing me.

He holds the cold bottle of wine against my butt as he slides his other hand under my hair so he can grip my neck. His mouth moves against mine, his jaw working as he explores my mouth with his dangerous tongue.

I am a badass grown woman who may actually melt in his arms.

49

CAL

I can't believe she's here.

I keep sneaking sideways glances at her as I busy myself with pouring her a glass of perfectly chilled Chassagne Montrachet from my wine fridge. I told her to keep it casual, and she arrived wrapped up in a Burberry trench that made her look like a very sexy spy.

She's lost the coat, and now she's floating around my flat in an olive-coloured longish, silky dress that's belted at the waist and has buttons the entire way down the front. She's left the buttons undone from mid thigh downwards and from just above where her bra begins.

All this makes me extremely happy and also a little hard.

When I think about the women I've fucked in my lifetime, they're this faceless blur of hair and limbs, which is awful, I know. But Aida is so unforgettable in every way. She's searing herself onto my consciousness so sharply I may not survive it.

I have to confess, I've fallen down a major Aida Russell rabbit hole online. Not just to be stalky, which I am. Not just to jerk off to, which I do, especially because I haven't seen her in person for exactly a week. But also because I want to understand this woman more fully—this woman who's let me into her body and her confidence. Who's entrusted me with rebuilding her sexuality, in a way.

I watch interview after interview with everyone from Barack Obama to Russell Brand to Jane bloody Fonda, which is epic in itself. The size of her brain makes my own little brain hurt. Her ability to think on her feet, to pivot, to ask exactly the right question at exactly the right time in order to eviscerate her interviewee is simply staggering.

It's like watching Nadal play some fifteen-year-old amateur. Total fucking annihilation, every time.

Don't get me wrong. I know she has a huge team of people researching on her behalf, and briefing her, and even role-playing to prepare her for big events like the debate she chaired for prime ministerial candidates.

But none of that should take away from her ability to rhapsodise live from the Paris terror attacks or to land exactly the right question at the right time or to perceive, uncannily and seemingly effortlessly, the exact heart of any issue she's addressing.

She makes it all look easy, and that makes my head spin.

Not to mention, she's beautiful. So beautiful, it hurts my heart. She's grown into her bone structure. Her cheekbones are more pronounced than they were even a decade ago. Her huge dark eyes are more hooded, more dramatic. She's svelte and toned, and I can safely say, with my wealth of experience at hand, that she has the body of a woman ten years younger.

I've built her up in my mind into the icon that she is. You'd think, having fucked her, that feeling would fade with the relative familiarity and intimacy we've enjoyed. But it hasn't. If anything, it's grown. I idolise her, and that sense of wonder, of worship, even, grows every time she lets me get close. And with that sense of wonder comes the responsibility for the wellbeing of a woman the nation adores.

She's in my flat, and she's strolling around, admiring the huge abstract oils on the walls and teasing me about my bookshelves—I'm big on sports biographies. I reckon I'd outperform her at interviewing any Premier League manager or England cricket team captain, past or present.

'You really like Spurs,' she observes.

'Yep,' I tell her. 'London boy, born and bred.'

'Hmm,' she says. 'Interesting. And you *really* like cricket.'

'I fucking love it. I've played for a club every summer except this one—we opened Alchemy in Cannes so I spent most of the summer down there.'

'I bet you did, you dirty boy,' she says, pulling out my Alastair Cook memoir. 'But I wish I'd had you around this summer. Kit and Pip are obsessed with cricket.'

'I wish I'd been there, too,' I tell her softly, and something in my voice makes her turn and give me a once-over. 'Nah,' she says, sliding the book back into place. 'Orgies in the South of France or bowling endless balls to my kids? You don't fool me for a second, Sinclair.'

~

I KNOW two things to be true.

Whatever Aida needs, I'll give to her.

Whatever she'll let me have, I'll take from her.

Need has been building throughout the meal I cooked us—seared fillet on a bed of julienned vegetables if you must know. I have her in my *home*. We're less than ten metres from my fucking *bed*. And all the heady insanity of last week at the masked ball couldn't make up for what we have now.

Privacy and time.

And I'm a master at availing of both.

But first, when you have the most fascinating woman you've ever met to yourself, you listen.

Like I said, we've got time.

I resist the urge to ask her what Obama was like in person—because everyone does that, right? Instead I ask, 'Have you ever had brain freeze live on air?'

She gives a little laugh. 'All the fucking time.'

'No way. I don't buy that for a second. You always seem so terrifyingly on the ball—your mental gymnastics are insane. It's one of the absolutely most impressive things about you.' I take a leisurely sip of the very smooth Pomerol I decanted to complement the steak.

'They *were* insane. They're not anymore.'

'What do you mean?'

She sighs. 'It's—not embarrassing, but it's awkward.'

'Okay…' I say. I wait and swill my wine.

'You won't know anything about this, because you're thirty-freaking-six, but I've been perimenopausal for the last couple years. That's the period before you hit actual menopause, and it can last years and years.'

I make a sympathetic moue with my mouth and reach over to take her hand, but I don't say anything, because I have nothing intelligent or helpful to contribute at this point. So I stroke her thumb instead.

'Anyway, there are a lot of insidious symptoms that creep up on you, and you don't realise what's causing them, and you chalk it up to losing your goddamn mind. And brain fog was one of those for me.'

She pauses. 'It's a stupidly inadequate term for having

absolutely no brain function. I kept losing my train of thought when I was talking. I found myself trailing off at the end of sentences a lot, and I couldn't hold a question in my head, you know? I'd be interviewing someone and mentally queuing my next question while I listened to them speak, and when I cut in it was like *poof!* My question had just vanished. It started happening on air more and more. There were a couple times my producers had to rescue me through my earpiece.'

I'm staring at her in horror. 'Jesus,' I say, squeezing her hand. 'I can't imagine how bloody terrifying that is.'

'Terrifying and humiliating. I felt like such a cliché—that middle-aged woman who's losing her mind, or losing the plot, as you guys say. There are some very nasty TikTok montages of it.'

'Seriously? That's so fucking rude.'

'Uh huh. People are shitty. I haven't watched them, obviously. But it was one of the reasons I stepped down from the nightly news. It really dented my confidence—I'd panic right before I was due to go on air. You know those dreams where you're on stage and you don't know your lines, and then you realise you're actually naked, too? Oh, and the play is in Japanese?'

'Yeah. They're the worst.'

'They really are. But it felt like that was happening all the time, just in real life and live on air in front of millions of people. So I pulled back. The BBC was amazing about it, and they supported my decision.'

'I read a book about a guy who that happened to.' I attempt to wrack my brain for the name. 'He had a full-blown panic attack live on air. It sounded horrifying. He was a US news anchor, but think it was drugs-related.'

'Yeah, Dan Harris. I read that too. *10% Happier*. It's a great book—hilarious in some ways.'

'He was funny as fuck,' I agree. 'But you're always incredible on *Centre Stage*. You always seem so on it.'

'Aww, thanks. Well, I've been on hormones for a few months now, and they've helped me get some of that clarity back, thank God. It's also easier on that show than on the news—I'm way more in the zone, I'm better prepped, and there's less chance of being blindsided, I guess. And, obviously, it's recorded a few hours in advance, which makes all the difference in my head.'

'I'm sorry you've had a tough time of it, though,' I tell her. I really am. She's so smart, so able. Her brain is her thing: she's known for her lucidity, her razor-sharp mind. For her to have felt like she was losing her mind must have been nothing short of terrifying. 'That and the whole divorce—what a fucking year.'

She laughs. 'What a *fucking* year. Amen to that. I was struggling before John's fuck-fest even went public, but when a huge crisis hits like that, you think that's to blame for everything. I couldn't see beyond it, you know?

'I thought I was depressed and weepy and preoccupied because my husband was cheating and the paparazzi was stalking me, but it turns out there were a whole host of deeper issues that made things far worse. And had I been aware of them or treated them, I could maybe have had more resilience. As it was, my capacity for dealing with that whole shit storm was pretty fucking limited.'

She wipes a tear off her cheek angrily. 'Fuck's sake. I thought I was done with my pity party. I'm so—I'm embarrassed. Sorry.'

'Hey.' I scoot my chair closer and wrap both my hands around hers. 'Why on earth would you be sorry? You're amazing—you've had the worst year ever, and you're still going strong. You're out there, building your career, nailing every sleazy politician to his own cross and holding them accountable, and you're pushing all your own boundaries with this *Paradise* stuff. You're my hero.'

She gives me a watery smile and sniffs. 'I'm sorry because we're supposed to be having fun tonight, and here I am, being Debbie Downer.'

'No you're not. You're being human, and you're letting me in, which I appreciate more than you know,' I tell her. It's true. She's a fortress, and sometimes the age gap between us feels far more than a decade when I think about how much actual adulting we both do.

Unlike when I get her on a bed, when everything feels equal and right and perfect.

'Besides,' I tell her with a trademark Cal wink, 'we're definitely going to have fun tonight, baby.'

That gets me a wider smile, one that reaches right to the stunning dark eyes that sparkle with unshed tears.

'This is why you're so good for me,' she tells me, squeezing my hands. 'Honestly, you and my little guys are by far the best things about this year.'

'Yeah?' I ask, and yes, I'm shamelessly digging. 'Why am I good for you, again?'

She runs her tongue over her lower lip in that way I love before answering. 'You make me smile,' she says. 'You lighten me up. You're such a warm, open-hearted person. It's infectious, you know that? And'—her mouth twists—'you have certain skills that, when you employ them, make me lose my fucking mind, in a *good* way, this time. Like, a really, really good way. You make me feel sexy and desirable and strong, like I'm not some broken, faded old hag. Instead, I'm this woman who's brave enough to gaze into the darkest parts of herself and trusting enough to hand the keys over to someone who can take her to places she never thought she'd visit.'

She swallows. 'Places that are more extraordinary and transformational than she could ever have imagined. I don't know who the fuck I am with you, but I like her a lot. And helping me find her is the best gift you could ever have given me.' She lowers her voice. 'So thank you.'

There are so many things I have to say. So many words I could use to describe how angry and betrayed I feel on her behalf, how brimming I am with admiration, how conflicted I've felt.

I could tell her she's simply the most incredible woman I've had the privilege of laying eyes on.

I could tell her how much my desire to take her, control her, fracture her into pieces haunts me, because it makes me wonder if I'm some kind of pathetic, misogynous monster who gets off on subduing women who are eminently more impressive than him.

But she's sitting here telling me that my twisted appetites work for her. That they help. That, by some fucked-up alchemy, the things she's let me do to her are as freeing for her as they are for me.

So, yes, there are a million things I can say in this moment.

But all I need are two words.

'Come here.'

50

AIDA

Come here.

How two simple words can scatter goosebumps over my body, I'm not sure. It's probably how he makes them positively drip with intention. Possibility. And, if I'm not mistaken, threat.

The way his sensual mouth moves when he says them may also have something to do with it.

As does the way he releases my hands and pats one toned, denim-clad thigh without breaking that dark gaze of his.

Whatever's behind the magic, I don't care. Because I've just cried and confessed my middle-aged curses to him, and he doesn't look like a man repulsed.

Quite the opposite.

I rise from my chair, a little smile playing on my lips, and go to sit sideways on his lap, but he tuts.

'Nope. Straddle me.'

It's like that.

I see.

I gather the billowy folds of my dress up a little so I can

widen my legs and lower myself onto his lap, feet planted wide. The fabric of my dress lands softly around us, the cascade of open buttons allowing a decent glimpse of my thighs.

'Closer,' he says, tugging me toward him with one hand on my ass and the other clamped to my neck. I get a second to enjoy the view of his gorgeous face so close to mine before that hand on my neck tugs me the rest of the way down and I'm falling into a kiss that's urgent and hungry, our mouths sliding together, his tongue stealing into my mouth.

I grab at the longer hair curling onto his neck with one hand as I run the fingernails of the other down the perfect scratchiness of his beard. All it takes is the rasp of it against my chin for the memory of it against my most sensitive flesh to echo deep in my core.

When I break away, he's grinning at me. It's not a boyish grin but something heavier and more carnal.

'Hey, beautiful,' he mutters lazily, his dark eyes flashing south of my face and back up. 'Lose the dress, why don't you?'

Let it be said that I have not performed a striptease for a man for many moons. If I was standing across the room from Cal I'd undoubtedly feel self-conscious, but I'm not. I'm sitting inches from him, and he's gazing at me like I'm a gift he'd like very much to unwrap, so it doesn't take much bravado to release his neck and untie the fabric belt of my dress before turning my attention to my buttons.

Geez, this guy is gratifying. A sexy striptease this is not, but he's lapping it up. He tugs his bottom lip between his teeth as he watches the suggestion of my brand-new, eye-wateringly expensive lingerie come into view.

As soon as I have the last button undone, he's pushing

the dress off my shoulders, his movements hurried. And when it slithers to the ground in a soft pool of parachute silk behind me, his dark eyes turn positively feral.

I try to enjoy having his gaze on me and not to overly fixate on tilting my pelvis to make my stomach flatter. Yeah, I'm in decent shape, but it's not like I'm twenty-five anymore, and this isn't the most flattering position. Not that Cal seems to care, because he slides one bra strap down and presses a surprisingly chaste kiss to my shoulder before straightening up.

'Time to take this very sexy bra off,' he tells me, and the low, commanding tone of his voice has something shifting inside me. He's gonna tell me what to do, *order* me what to do, more like, and all I have to do is comply.

Besides, his dominating tone has my nipples instantly tightening behind their skimpy lace. I love hanging with carefree, hilarious Cal, but dear God, I adore being fucked by intense, unleashed Cal. It won't take much more of that tone of his for me to be squirming in his lap like a kitten who adores being petted and praised.

I shoot him a slow smile and reach behind me to unclasp my bra before shimmying my shoulders so it slides off my arms and falls between us. I don't miss the hitch in his breath as he takes in the sight of my bare breasts.

'That's it,' he says, running his hands up my thighs before squeezing my waist. 'Jesus Christ, nothing, and I mean nothing, gets me off like having you do what I say.' He slides his hands further up my sides and strokes the undersides of my breasts with his thumbs. My nipples practically leap to attention at the eroticism of that simple touch.

His eyes are fixed on my bare breasts, even if his hands are not. But then they flash up to me. 'You want my hands on you, baby?'

I shiver. 'Yes, please.'

'What a good girl. So polite.' He slaps my ass. 'But I won't touch you till you're completely naked for me. So you know what to do.'

He licks his lips and gazes at me expectantly, and there's a moment where I'm suspended in time as the two sides of my personality war with each other. The Aida who's used to running the show in her interactions with the most powerful men in the world baulks at the deliberate condescension in his tone, while the Aida who needs the sweet bliss of submission to course like honey through her veins thrills at it.

The second Aida wins by a country mile.

I rise from his lap and kick my dress to one side before hooking my thumbs into the sides of my thong and tugging it down my legs. He watches me avidly, the hunger in his dark eyes belying the casual nature of the tone he's adopted so far.

'Like what you see?' I ask, attempting to shrug off my discomfort at standing here butt naked in front of this god.

'You know I do.' I swear, his voice is lower and rougher. 'Get back down here.' He slaps his thigh, and I know he wants me straddling him again. I put my hands on his shoulders and toss my hair off my face with a jerk of my head as I lower myself back down to him. He parts his thighs as I do, forcing me into an even wider stance.

The lighting in his dining area is dim. That said, I feel exposed like this. Exposed and hopelessly excited as Cal's hands roam over my skin, exploring my body, mapping its curves and indents and joints. My arms are looped loosely around his neck, so when he drags his hands up my sides, my breasts are right there for the taking.

I need his hands on me so, so badly. I need him to strum

my nipples, to pull at them with greedy tugs of his fingers. His teeth. I need him to run his knuckles through my centre and learn for himself how wet I already am. I can feel my arousal so distinctly in this position, with my legs spread open for him and my pussy on display. Even if I'm slightly more elevated than him, it still feels arousingly debased to be seated this way. I'm like a plaything spread wide for his pleasure, to toy with and tease should he be so inclined.

And if I'm the plaything, he's the young, entitled master, used to getting whatever he wants, answerable to no one, and breathtaking in his own sensual brand of arrogance.

'Cup your tits for me,' he drawls, and I do as he says, holding my breasts up on a platter, my poor, needy nipples pointing straight at him.

'Fuck, yeah,' he says, then brushes a fingertip over each of them in tandem. I jolt, because they're so sensitive already, and inhale through my teeth. I'd give anything for him to dip that dark head of his, and latch on, and suck for dear life.

'How badly do you want my mouth on them?' he asks, because clearly he's a mind-reader.

I shudder. 'So badly.'

'Hmm.' He plays with them for a moment, teasing with his fingers, rolling and pinching them into impossibly stiff little nubs. 'Your nipples are so fucking perfect. But all in good time.'

He keeps ahold of one while he trails his other hand down over my stomach. I tense with need as he nears my pussy. Then he's right there, those calloused knuckles I wished for dragging through my slickness, and it's like they ignite every single nerve ending they graze.

'Oh, God,' I say involuntarily. 'Shit, that feels amazing.'

'So fucking wet,' he says, letting his forehead drop to mine. 'Take me out, love.'

51

AIDA

"Better to reign in hell than serve in heaven."
—Milton, *Paradise Lost*

I scramble to do as he says, tugging at his belt buckle and getting the zipper of his jeans down over his huge bulge. I free his dick from above the waistband of his boxer briefs, registering how huge and hot and hard he feels.

'Okay,' he breathes against my mouth. 'Here's what we're going to do. You need to get off, dirty girl, so you're gonna use my dick to do it. I'll hold your greedy cunt wide open.'

Holy crap. I don't need to be told twice. I release my breasts and wrap an arm around his neck for stability as I nudge my body further up his thighs, lining up the engorged, weeping head of his cock with my poor clit, and holy fuck. That first slick sweep of his wet, swollen flesh against mine must be the work of angels, and the sensation of his strong fingers prising me as open as humanly possible for him feels as filthy as it does right.

I cry out and shudder, letting my head fall to the crook of his neck as I drag him greedily down to my entrance, where I let him pulse for a moment before pulling him back up to find my clit.

'That's it,' he hisses. '*Yes*. Fucking go for it. Use me like you'd use my tongue if I was down there eating you.'

And I do. I really do go for it. I slide him back and forth over my clit like the most delicious vibrator as his fingers hold me open and his other hand works my nipple with tweaks that bring pain and arousal coursing through my breast in equal measure.

God, I'm close. This feels filthy and wanton, straddling his lap and rubbing myself with his gorgeous dick. My breath gets more fevered as I grow more desperate, more greedy for my impending orgasm. But just as I'm entering the extreme pleasure zone, Cal releases the lips of my pussy and covers the hand on his dick with his own, effectively withdrawing my personal sex toy from me.

'What are you doing?' I gasp blindly, lifting my face from where it's been drooling on his shoulder so I can see him. His grin is that of a man in pain, but there's a sadistic element there that I've learnt too quickly does not bode well. Uh oh.

'Giving you a grand finale,' he says. He lifts my hand off his dick and puts it on my pussy. Even my own touch has me shivering with want. 'Feel how wet that cunt is. You need more friction.'

'No, I'm fine,' I insist. I want my magical Cal-shaped wand back, goddammit.

'Here's what you're going to do,' he says, blithely ignoring my protest. 'You're going to get on one thigh and rub yourself against my jeans, and it'll be fucking spectacular for you. Imagine how good this rough denim's gonna feel against your poor, swollen clit. And if you ride my thigh nicely like a good girl, I'll work your tits so hard you could come from that alone. Got it?'

I shoot him a look so mutinous that any self-respecting man would roll over, but he just laughs.

'You're my favourite little hellion. Come on, sweetheart. Ride me like the needy little whore you are right now.'

If I was any less turned on, I'd be second guessing myself, because this is way out of my comfort zone. But, happily for him, I need this orgasm so fucking badly I'll do anything, including give him the cheap little show he desires.

Besides. Much as I hate to admit it, he's right. Between my arousal and his, things were getting way too slick down there. I need serious friction to scratch my itch properly, and now he's made his filthy suggestion, my poor, orgasm-starved mind is singularly fixating on just how good it will feel to rub myself against that denim.

'Fine,' I say through gritted teeth, and he laughs again.

'That's my girl. And when you're doing it, know I'll be fucking you straight afterwards, okay? This is what you've got to look forward to.'

With that, he grips me hard around the forearm while jamming two fingers up inside me, and it's so brutally perfect that I let out a barely human howl.

'God, yeah,' he says, pulling his fingers out and driving them inside me hard. 'That's what I'm talking about. I'm going to fuck you on the floor so hard that big brain of yours will explode. You won't remember your *ABCs* when I'm finished with you.'

With that ominous prediction, he pulls his fingers out roughly and nods. 'Go on. Ride me.'

It would be insane to pretend I'm not loving every second of Cal toying with me and dirty-talking me and spurring me on to this shameless behaviour. I raise myself up and step between his legs before planting myself squarely on one rock hard thigh, just far enough away from his knee that I won't fall over backward.

I have my feet planted as wide as I can get them, and the second my poor pussy hits denim I practically weep with delight. 'Jesus Christ,' I say, looking between us. Cal's dick is still fully erect and weeping, but he ignores it, crossing his hands behind his head as he leans back to give me some space. His entire demeanour is that of a guy determined to enjoy the show.

'Imagine I've paid you for a lap dance,' he grits out, 'but you're such a greedy little slut that you can't help but grind against my leg and make a mess of my jeans. If you do a good job and lick it all up, I'll give you more money than you've ever dreamed of, and I'll even throw in a rough fuck, just the way I know you need it.'

Jesus Christ, I am going to hell. There's no doubt about it. His words have the desired effect, which is to cheapen me and turn me the fuck on like I didn't even know was possible. I'm showered in shame and arousal, but my hips start to move like they have a mind of their own, because my only chance of an orgasm right now is to rub my clit against this rough fabric.

And I do, like my life depends on it. God, the drag of the cotton is so fucking good. He was right. His thigh is hard, unyielding, the denim perfectly abrasive, and I'd rub myself raw if it made me see stars.

'Arms behind your head,' he barks. 'I want to see your tits.'

I drown in his black eyes as I obey, mirroring his stance, raising my arms and interlocking my fingers at the base of my skull as I find a rhythm and grind against him. I can't imagine how wanton I must look like this, but the ravenous expression on Cal's face gives me courage. That and my sheer desperation to come.

He rewards my bravery by unfolding his own hands and palming my breasts, and I swear I arch into him like the most shameless creature on earth, moaning as my nipples press against his palms.

'Ride me harder, gorgeous,' he says. 'Take everything you can, greedy girl. I want my money's worth.'

Then his palming turns to pinches as he pulls on my aching nipples like a man deranged, his nostrils flaring and teeth sinking into his bottom lip as he stares at me, spurring me on. I grind and grind and rub and rub until all I can think of is that next vicious stroke of his denim-clad thigh against the little, swollen nub of my clit.

'Harder,' he says, and I drive into him, thighs trembling as I chafe my most sensitive flesh against him. I'm a crazed, roiling mess of blind, primitive need as I rut myself headlong into the white-hot oblivion I've chased so desperately.

Every inch of Cal's own hunger is etched on his face and written into the savage movements of his hands on my breasts, into the way he's rutting himself, hips thrusting uselessly below me and his dick driving into nothingness.

Claiming my own orgasm as he sits there, servicing me and taking nothing for himself, feels awful and selfish and nasty and cheap and fucking amazing. And I let that riot of emotions cascade over me, heightening the impossible pleasure that inflames my entire body and has me bucking and crying out as my hands go to his shoulders.

His first words are compliments, lavish adulations bestowed on me alongside hungry kisses as he praises my filthiness, my cleverness. But as soon as I raise myself off his thigh, my legs shaky and my clit already feeling unnervingly like it's suffering from carpet burn, he glances down at the dark, wet patch on his jeans.

'Lick it up like a good girl,' is what he tells me next.

52

CAL

And lick it up she does.

She sinks gracefully to her knees, and bends her silky head to my thigh, and runs her little pink tongue over the wet patch she's made on my jeans. It's a fool's errand, because the thick denim has already absorbed most of her arousal, but no matter.

My poor cock stiffens impossibly at the scene. After her little leg-humping show I can think of only one thing: being balls-deep inside her.

'Very good,' I croon, combing my fingers through her dark hair and pushing it over her face. 'You are so fucking beautiful.'

She looks up at me, tongue out, black eyes gleaming, and I experience a jolt of desire and affection and pride and *rightness* so strong it has me reeling.

'Turn around and crawl away from me, baby,' I tell her, my voice hoarse with need. I drag my thumb down her temple. 'I want to torture myself with the view before I get stuck in.'

Her face, which tightened into a pissed-off grimace at

the word *crawl*, softens. 'Be my guest,' she retorts, and she turns and drops to her hands and knees.

And she crawls. She fucking crawls, just like I asked, her naked body moving sensuously across my wooden floor, her arse cheeks swaying and her beautiful pink pussy on show for me. I stand, dick still at full mast, and take a step to the side to enjoy the glorious sight of her tits hanging full and heavy beneath her.

It takes me three strides to catch up with her, then I'm dropping to my knees behind her and fishing in my back pocket for one of the condoms I stashed in there earlier. I kick her legs out so I can come in close, and then I'm sheathing myself with rushed, jerky movements, and gripping her hips so tightly I'll probably mark her, and gritting out a garbled *fuck, need to be inside you* and *I'm going in, baby*.

I thrust into her in a single desperate drive, like my cock is in full control and the rest of me is just along for the ride, and dear Lord of all that is holy, the fit is so snug and warm that my entire body sings with relief. She tenses against me, and I realise belatedly she might be a bit chafed down there after her little stunt.

If I have to spend the rest of the night tenderly rubbing aloe vera into her sore cunt, I'll do so happily.

'You okay?' I manage.

'Yeah.' She goes to roll her hips experimentally, and I loosen my grip.

'You sure?'

'Uh-huh. Come on and fuck me like you mean it, Cal.'

I bark out a surprised laugh. This baby girl is playing with fucking fire. I bend over her and grab a decent handful of her hair. It's not long enough for me to wrap around my fist, but it's long enough to grip.

'You have no fucking idea who you're messing with,' I hiss in her ear, and she gives a little shimmy.

'So show me. Fuck me like you're wearing your mask. I need you to take me to that place again.'

It's music to my ears. 'Seriously, baby?' I ask, my bottom lip brushing the velvet of her ear lobe.

'*Yes*. I need it already.'

There's no mask tonight. No sex club. No chains. Just me and her on my kitchen floor. And I will not fucking let her down.

'Fine.'

I rear back up.

'Don't say I didn't warn you.'

Then I'm slapping her arse hard and slamming into her, rough as I can, harnessing all my desperation into a single drive, her cry of surprise only spurring me on. Even through the latex she's heaven. *It's* heaven, this sensation of being embedded deep inside her beautiful body.

The arch of her back as I grip her hair, the faint illumination of her jawline under the pendant lights... She's a masterpiece of flesh and blood. I can't shake the feeling that she's this priceless, mesmerising work of art and I'm the bull in the fucking china shop, the ex-rugby-playing punk she's, for some unfathomable reason, permitting to smash her to smithereens.

That strikes me as the most wonderful dynamic I can fathom, and it fills me with awe as much as it turns me the fuck on.

She can take it.

She's told me to fuck her like I mean it.

She needs this.

This release that her ex couldn't provide.

That only I can give her.

I release her hair and drag my palm over the bumps of her spine before gripping her firmly by the hips and really letting her have it. I'm closer than I'd like to be to shooting my load, but I can't stop now. This animalistic need to bury myself as deep inside Aida as I can, to catapult her into a different stratosphere, has me in its grip.

And when the timbre of her moans changes into something deeper, more guttural, I know she's right there with me.

'Oh God.' She sucks in a breath through her teeth like she's trying to hold herself the fuck together.

'I know, baby. I know,' I manage. 'You feel so fucking good. You're so good at taking every inch of me.'

I may not be role-playing a masked thug tonight. We're here in my home, and it's just me and her, and if I want to call her my *baby* I damn well will, but that doesn't mean I'm not giving it to her.

It doesn't mean I've remotely forgotten she needs a raw, dirty fucking where her knees will scuff, and her cunt will chafe, and her soul will reach places she didn't know it could, and I'll brand her as mine, inside and out.

'Come on,' I urge, all fast, shallow breaths and fevered thrusts and jerky movements. '*Show me.* Show me how much you love taking my cock.'

'Fuck,' she lets out on a pant. Reducing this impossibly elegant, erudite angel to single-syllable expletives feels like the best form of gratification, and I grin to myself through my haze of sweat and need and tensed muscles as I bring our orgasms home.

She comes suddenly, violently, like her climax has blindsided her, her cries those of a woman who's holding nothing back. They echo around the vast space as the perfect contractions of her internal muscles obliterate the last of my thinly-held self control, and I shatter around her, pouring jet after jet of my cum into the condom as I hold onto her like she's my port in a storm.

My orgasm is a wild thing, totally fucking unhinged, rendering me blind and dumb, wringing me out until I'm an empty, well-used shell of a man capable only of collapsing over Aida and using my lips to worship the lines of her shoulder blades.

Just as it should be.

53

AIDA

'This is the best sleepover I've ever had,' I tell Cal.

I'm propped up on one elbow, feasting on the mighty fine view of him lying naked against his beautiful white sheets. We just about made it to his bed for round two—round three for me, I guess, after my little horn-dog show against his thigh. This time, we made each other come with our mouths, which I suspect was entirely for the benefit of my poor, raw pussy. Cal's wet tongue was the perfect form of aftercare.

He's also fed me ibuprofen and pretty much funnelled a pint of electrolytes down me, and now we're well-fucked and drunk on the kind of woozy contentedness only a few rounds of excellent orgasms can provide.

He's grinning up at me, and he's so smug and confident and boyishly sexy that I'm a lost cause.

'And we haven't even slept yet,' he points out.

'I think it was precisely the not-sleeping part that made it so fun,' I muse.

'Wait till you sleep with me. Are you a cuddler?'

I narrow my eyes at him. 'Not especially. Are you?'

'I don't really have the opportunity,' he says. 'I don't tend to bring women back here, unless I'm dating someone, obviously. But that hasn't happened for ages. Not since Alchemy.'

'Figures. The candy's too good at the club, right?'

'The candy's *very* good at the club.' God, his smile is lethal. Absolutely lethal. 'But it was fucking delicious just now. And I want to cuddle you. You're soft. I'm going to cuddle you all night long.'

He accompanies this statement with a brush of his knuckles over the skin of my stomach.

'Shoot me now. You can't tell a forty-six-year-old woman she's *soft*. You may as well tell me I have no muscle tone left.'

'I meant your skin is soft,' he protests. 'You know as well as I do you're in fantastic shape.'

He wraps an arm around my waist and tugs me down to him so we're lying nose to nose, and God it feels good. The simple pleasure of post-coital luxuriating in Cal's enormous bed with him is right up there. Who even am I?

'I have a secret,' he mutters against my lips.

'Oh yeah?'

'Yep. Do you want to know what it is?'

'Sure.'

'I'm going to cuddle you so much tonight, and be so adorable, and give you so many more orgasms in the morning that you'll have no choice but to make this a two-night sleepover.'

I smile against his mouth. He's the absolute sweetest when he's like this.

'Is that right?'

'It is. And don't think you can argue your way out of it, because I know for a fact your kids won't be home till Sunday afternoon.'

He's correct. They're in Norfolk again with John. They'll come home shattered, and there'll be the inevitable scramble to do homework because John won't have gotten it done while they're away, and I'll be tired and irritable and feeling guilty, and—

I stop myself. I don't need to think about it right now. It's at least forty hours away. And in the meantime...

The potential of a full weekend with Cal dangles itself before my mind's eye like the most delicious treat. Could I? Should I?

I suspect the better question is *shouldn't I?* Because why the hell not?

'I was supposed to do some work tomorrow,' I protest weakly.

'We can go and get your laptop in the morning,' he offers. 'Or we can stay at yours and I'll curl up next to you and stroke you like an adoring slave while you work.'

I laugh to hide the weird, uncomfortable thrill that courses through me at the prospect of hanging out with Cal in our family home. 'That doesn't sound distracting at all.'

'Of course it'll be distracting. Because work is boring and I'm *me*.'

He rolls me onto my back and climbs on top of me. I adore the sensation of being caged in by him far too much. He blots out everything else in life.

'I've been working on another serenade,' he says now.

I giggle. 'Oh no.'

'Oh *yes*. Would you like to hear it?'

'I'd love to.' I raise my legs up so he can settle his weight between them, anchoring me to the soft solidity of his mattress.

'Right answer.' He takes a breath.

'All I want is Aida's cunt,' he begins to the tune of

Wouldn't it be Loverly from *My Fair Lady*. His Cockney accent is as ridiculous as his lyrics—he's shot way past Audrey Hepburn and is firmly in Dick Van Dyke territory. My giggles intensify.

'Thrusting in with my crown that's blunt,
In one enormous shunt,
Oh, wouldn't it be se-exy?'

'Please, make it stop,' I mutter, before I hook an arm around his neck and pull him down for a kiss that is wholly successful in shutting him the fuck up.

54

CAL

'You sore?' I ask Aida as we lie together in my bed. I can't stop touching her, stroking her skin.

'A little,' she admits. 'The meds helped, though.'

'Good.' I hesitate. 'Can I ask you something?' It's a question that feels personal given we're not mid-fuck, and I don't want to make her uncomfortable. Add to that the dull flare of my usual post-rough-sex paranoia and self-flagellation, and it's safe to say I'm treading carefully.

'Of course,' she says, running her knuckles over my stomach with the lightest touch.

'When we go at it... rough, is that something you've always liked? Or is it my bad influence?' I hope that's ambiguous enough. I'm not asking if she credits me with uncovering her kinky side as much as I'm asking if she had this kinky side before and failed to mention it in our early chats.

She's quiet long enough that I start to panic, but I force myself to give her space.

'Put it this way,' she begins. 'It's not something I've ever had the luxury of entertaining in previous relationships, if you catch my drift.'

Got it. 'You told Gen you'd had an underwhelming sex life when you were married,' I venture. 'Is that what you mean? It was pretty vanilla? If you feel weird discussing it, that's fine,' I add hastily.

'My husband fucked around behind my back and several of his lovers sold their stories to the press. It'd be ridiculous if I had some false sense of loyalty to him after having had both our names dragged through the mud. The truth is, our sex life was very... safe. And it was safe not because we both preferred it that way, but because our preferences, I guess, weren't compatible.'

I slide my hand up her back and give her shoulder a little squeeze. 'I'm sorry.'

'Don't be. I think I mentioned that first time we went out that our marriage was super strong when it came to our intellectual relationship.' Another pause. I sense her usual eloquence has deserted her. 'But John made it clear early on that he liked being dominated. He wanted—well, he wanted all sorts of things that left me cold.

'We tried stuff once or twice—stuff I didn't love, that did nothing for me—and then we both kind of gave up and stuck to the basics, you know? I feel so stupid saying that.'

I frown. 'Why on earth do you feel stupid? None of that was your fault—of course you shouldn't have done things you weren't comfortable with.'

'I guess because you're the poster boy for sexual liberation, and making peace with your needs, and going after what you want. But when you're in a monogamous relationship with a human being you love, and your wilder sides aren't compatible, what choice do you have but to meet in the middle, for want of a better term?'

'Can I ask what kind of stuff he was into?' I ask, and she notably tenses under my hand.

'I mean, nothing crazy, just—dominatrix stuff, I guess. He wanted me to tie him up and whip him and, you know, prod him with my stiletto heels. I tried a couple times at a more basic level, but honestly, I hated it. I hated seeing him lying there, all trussed up.'

She takes a deep breath, like she's getting ready to share a fresh confidence. 'I wanted it to be me. I wanted him to tie me to the fucking bed and flip me over and just fucking *fuck* my brains out, but I never even asked him for that, because it was so obvious he wanted the same from me. He would never have done a one-eighty. And I know he felt rejected, too, because I basically rejected his kinks and shied away from giving him what he needed.' A heavy sigh. 'I let him down.'

Nope. No. Not having that. 'Hang on a sec. That's absolute bullshit. You didn't let him down. You two just weren't sexually compatible. That's the beginning and the end of it. The depressing thing is, I suppose meeting in the middle was all you could do, really, aside from walking away or having you both play roles you weren't comfortable with.'

She blows out a breath. 'Yeah. I guess.'

'You don't guess, you know,' I say, more firmly than I mean to. 'Those other women he shagged—did they dominate him?'

'Fuck knows. I'm guessing so, or maybe they were just new and young and shiny and adoring enough that he got his kicks from them anyway.'

The way her voice cracks on the word *young* has me tugging her into my arms so fucking tightly. 'Sweetheart,' I say into her hair. 'You are so fucking beautiful. So sexy. And the way you are with me—the way you let me cuff you and order you around and fuck you hard—is so utterly, unspeakably perfect I can't bear it.'

I clarify, because I need to make sure she understands this. 'Everything about the way we are together is flawless. You give me everything I crave, but I just want more, more, more, because I'm a selfish bastard and I can't get enough of you. I'm addicted to you, you understand?'

She nods into my chest and I hear a muffled *yes.*

'Are you saying,' I continue carefully, because I don't want to put words into her mouth, 'that the way we fuck is what you've been needing all this time?'

She pulls away a little so she can raise her face from under my chin and face me. And when she speaks, there's no hesitation. None at all.

'The way you fuck me, and the way you make me feel when you're doing those things to me, is so right and so elemental that it feels like every planet out there has aligned. It scares the ever-living crap out of me, because it makes me not want to come back down to earth.'

55

AIDA

Waking up with a warm, sleepy Cal next to me is pretty special. I surface on my stomach, face turned into the crook of one arm. One of his huge hands is stroking my ass slowly, which I'm pretty sure is what woke me up. And when I let my eyes flutter open, it's his face I see in the soft morning light.

'Hey,' I murmur, those first cloudy seconds of bliss yielding to an almost instant flare of panic, because I haven't woken up with a guy who is not my ex or one of my sons for a very, very long time. And I'm pretty sure my just-woke-up look isn't as cute as the ones I used to pull off.

His smile, though. His smile tells me all is well. It tells me he's pretty happy to have me in this huge, orgy-sized bed of his.

'How'd you sleep?' he whispers, his hand trailing from my ass and up my back. His touch feels so good. Casual, but sure.

'I slept great,' I tell him, curling onto my side, and it's true. I totally wiped out.

'Good,' he says. He pulls me into him, and I tuck my face

under his chin. His morning wood settles against my stomach, his hairy leg wrapping around mine. And so we remain as he falls easily back to sleep.

I guess I must drift off, too, because the next thing I know, Cal's disentangling himself from me and getting out of bed, and I groan feebly at the loss.

'Hey,' he says softly. 'Stay there. I'm getting you some coffee.'

The C-word has my eyes flying open, and he laughs. 'Yeah, baby. Give me five and I'll get you caffeinated.'

He's gone a lot longer than five minutes. I use his palatial slate-grey wet room to brush my teeth, wash my face and steal his robe, and I'm inhaling the *Washington Post* on my phone—an ancient, engrained habit—when he reenters the room.

And what a sight. I immediately forget about the op-ed that had me so engrossed, because Cal, dressed in only a pair of tighty-whity Calvins and bearing a heavily laden breakfast tray, is a sight to behold. He's so fucking gorgeous, still tan and buff as hell, that inked serpent winding down his side. He's ridiculous, and right now he looks good enough to eat.

'Well, hello there,' I say, throwing my phone onto the comforter and staring hard. 'What's all this?'

'This'—he moves around the bed towards me—'is a little breakfast for my beautiful guest.'

I pull my legs up to my body and hug my knees so he has a flat surface for the tray. When he lays it down, arm and chest muscles flexing, it's clear he's been a busy boy.

There are two huge cups of coffee with hearts drawn onto their perfect crema. I start salivating on the spot. There's also a fruit platter, the thin slices of strawberry and kiwi and cantaloupe arranged just so in sweet little fans, smoked salmon and lemon wedges, and buttered sourdough toast in all its craggy, holey glory.

I know the latter is for me because my living god right here doesn't let grains pass those gorgeous lips of his.

He places the tray toward the foot of the bed and climbs back into his spot next to me. I lean over and kiss him lightly on the lips.

'This is more than a little treat. This doesn't happen when you're a mom, so... thank you.'

'You're welcome. You deserve to be spoilt. Besides.' He pulls away and clears his throat. 'It's all part of my audition process.'

I laugh a little at the earnest look on his face. 'What audition process?'

He doesn't break eye contact. 'To be your boyfriend.'

56

AIDA

I think he just broke my brain.

I stare at him blankly, because for all the filth and jokes and ridiculous songs that come out of his mouth, the B-word was *not* one I was expecting.

Not at all.

He chuckles awkwardly and covers my hand with his. 'Abject panic. Just the reaction a guy hopes for.'

'No—of course not,.' I stumble over my words. 'I'm—where did that come from?'

He lets go of my hand and leans forward so he can lift a coffee mug from the tray and pass it to me. He doesn't speak again until he's grabbed his mug and is sitting back against his pillows. 'Is it a total surprise to you that this is where I'm going with us?'

'Um—yeah. It is,' I say flatly. 'I thought you were just—'

Humouring me. I mentally censor myself before I can say the words, because I know they'll piss him off. 'Having fun,' I finish lamely.

'I am having fun. I'm having more fun than I've ever had.

Which is why I'd like to have more and more fun with you while we give this a proper shot. Wouldn't you?'

'Sweetie.' I search in my unusually resistant brain for the right words. I blame all those orgasms. My basic powers of articulation haven't really recovered from last night, it seems.

Or maybe it's because the sweetest, hottest, funniest guy I've ever known is proposing something that sounds an awful lot like commitment.

'Absolutely nothing about my reticence has to do with what I want,' is what I settle on. I'm back in the field, processing in real time as I attempt to disseminate complexity into clarity.

'Go on,' he says, his voice gentle. He rests the hand holding his coffee mug on the comforter as he raises the other to stroke my cheek. 'You can say anything to me. I'm just sorry I blindsided you.'

'No.' I shake my head, feeling a little teary. 'This is the best blindsiding I've ever gotten, believe me.'

'So shoot. Vomit it all out. Process out loud.'

'You sure about that?' I ask with a shaky laugh.

'I'm sure. I just told you I wanted to be your boyfriend, didn't I? Even I know that involves listening and supporting as much as it involves bending you over my dining table. Come here.'

He wraps an arm around me, and I navigate the small distance between us with a butt shimmy as I keep ahold of my mug. Then I'm inclining my head to the left so I can rest it against his bare shoulder.

God, this is gorgeous. He's gorgeous. He's so insanely wonderful—way too good to be true.

'Right.' He kisses my temple and keeps his arm wrapped around my neck, hand dangling over my shoulder. I reach up with my free hand and entwine our fingers. 'Tell me why the prospect of me even trying to be your boyfriend had you acting like a rabbit in the headlights. Spit it out. I'm a big boy—I can take it. Though I'm not remotely used to dealing with rejection, so maybe go a little easy on me.'

I laugh. 'Okay. Full disclosure, seriously?'

'Full.'

'One. You run a sex club. Nothing about that says *able to commit*.'

'I give you Rafe, Zach and Gen. But okay.'

'Shh. Two. I've had it very firmly in my head that this thing of ours has a shelf life. Sure, it's gone way beyond what I hoped it would be for the purposes of the documentary, but I still thought we were just messing around.' I take a deep breath. 'So I've told myself not to get attached. I've very much told myself that all along. You know, *don't fall for the guy every woman wants.* It's cliché and pathetic.'

He doesn't say anything then, just kisses my hair and squeezes my fingers harder.

'Three. Is it three? I'm a lot older than you. Like, a lot. I'm flattered you're attracted to me, but I'll be way less attractive in ten years time and you'll be hot as fuck for decades and decades still.'

'We'll come back to that one, because I fundamentally disagree,' he says.

'Fine. Four. It's related, but I assume we want different things in our lives. I can't give you babies of your own. I have two kids, and we come as a package deal. I've already done a decade of the parenthood experience, and I'd never want to deprive you of that. I realise you're not asking me to marry you, so I'm probably overreacting, but if you're proposing a relationship, then I see that as a factor.'

'Anything else?' he asks, taking a sip of his coffee.

I sigh. 'I guess it's a general one, but it didn't occur to me that I'd get into another relationship so soon. I mean, this year has been about the very messy, very public dissolution of my marriage. I'm not saying I'm not ready, but it wasn't really on my radar, you know?'

'I get that,' he says. 'Mine neither. Are you quite done?'

'For the moment,' I say, snagging my mug between my thighs and reaching for a piece of buttery toast. I'm sure I have more incisively valid points to make, but I think those are the main ones.

'Good. Because I have to say, for someone whose profession is creating compelling arguments, that was fucking useless.'

I bark out a surprised laugh. 'What do you mean?' I ask through a mouthful of excellent toast.

'I mean those 'issues' are all lame as fuck. Honestly. Pathetic effort.'

'You're horrible,' I tell him.

'Yep. But listen to me, baby. You're fixating on the wrong stuff. I don't give a shit about our age difference, except that it makes you a hell of a lot more interesting than most of the women I've been with. I just care about how it is between us, and it's really fucking good.'

'The sex is really amazing,' I tell him carefully, because I've belatedly realised what all my objections boil down to, 'but I guess my overall worry is that you'll get bored and I'll get hurt.'

There. That's what I should have said up front, because, honestly, that's right at the heart of my reservations. And yeah, it feels humiliating to say it out loud, but if Cal can be vulnerable, then I owe it to him to share my vulnerabilities, too.

Especially if being brave now saves me from getting hurt down the line.

'Wow.' He twists to set his mug down on the nightstand before turning back to me and doing the same with mine. 'Okay. Time for some real honesty, because if that's how you're feeling, then we absolutely can't have that. Tell me something, baby. Do you think about me when we're not together?' He's twisted all the way around to face me and his hands are cupping my face.

I nod against them. 'Yes,' I whisper.

'Yep. Me too. Do you miss me when we're not together?'

'Yeah.' I swallow.

'Good girl. See how good you are at this? Me too. Now, do you find that the more time we spend together, the more you want? Like, last night just makes you want more and more? Like you can't get enough of us?'

I start to tremble. He's holding my face so I can't look away, and in the morning light his brown eyes are raw and searching and so, so profound. I'm almost afraid to answer, but I do, because this beautiful man deserves the truth. 'Yes.'

His smile is glorious then. He drops his forehead to mine. 'Me. Fucking. Too,' he whispers, and then he kisses me. It's slow and deep and intimate and perfect.

'I'm not claiming to be the expert between us on relationships,' he says, pulling away from our kiss but keeping his hands on my face. 'You've been married, I haven't.'

'After what I told you last night, I think we can agree I'm far from an expert either,' I say drily.

'Fair. But, as far as I can tell, everything we've just admitted to is as good a fucking start as any. We click. The sex is off the charts. We can't get enough of each other. We make each other happy, don't we? So far, anyway?'

I nod. 'We do.'

'Well I hate to tell you, sweetheart, but all the other shit is stuff we can work out in good time. It doesn't have to feel like falling off a cliff—we can take it day by day. But if we *want* more of each other, it sounds like you'd better agree to be my girlfriend like a good fucking girl so we can *have* more of each other. What do you think?'

'I think that sounds... sensible,' I say slowly. 'It sounds good.'

I'm still computing in real time, but this man and his proximity and his touch and his words and his eyes are conspiring to spin me into a surreal vortex of happiness and hope. Could this really be achievable? Could we really pull this off, Cal and me? This unlikely, energising, fledgling relationship?

'Promising start,' he says, shimmying down the bed and tugging me on top of him. 'We'll get there. I'll just have to overachieve on being a boyfriend like I overachieve at sex. I said it to myself when you first walked into Alchemy. You're a tough fucking customer.'

57

CAL

'You have a great voice,' Aida tells me as I lather up her hair in my cavernous shower.

I pause my exuberant rendition of *Jerusalem.* The acoustics in here are excellent, and I'm slightly addicted to the added richness the echo gives my decent baritone. 'Why, thank you. I love a good hymn. Not that this is a hymn.'

'It's not?' She tilts her head to one side so I can massage the nape of her neck.

'Nope. It's actually considered pretty blasphemous by a lot of Catholics. The priests would never have let us sing it at school, which is probably why every school mate of mine has had it at their wedding.'

She laughs. 'Such rebels.'

'Yeah. *Jerusalem* and kinky sex were our main ways of acting out. Shocking.'

'Why is it blasphemous?'

'I think because Blake based the poem on some bullshit legend made up by monks in Glastonbury about Jesus having visited Somerset when he was a kid. It was all a load of bollocks to make their mead, or ale, or whatever the fuck they were brewing, seem more authentic, basically.'

She giggles. 'Jesus at Glastonbury is a pretty trippy visual. And who knew medieval monks were into mis-selling?'

'Right? Dodgy fuckers. Anyway, Blake ran with it, and Parry put it to music, and it's a fucking good tune.' I angle her head back with my thumbs on her jaw so I can rinse her hair and resume my singing, rolling the *r* of *bring* with gusto.

'Bring me my Bow of burning gold:

Bring me my arrows of desire.'

'I don't think you need any arrows of desire,' she points out.

'*You're* my arrow of desire. You hit me, good and proper, and I'm completely fucked.' I smile down at her as I gently coax my fingers through her hair, washing out the last of the shampoo.

She smiles back at me, catlike. 'You're adorable.'

'I am. When do I get to meet your kids? Now that I'm your boyfriend.'

'Funny,' she says, 'I recall you saying you wanted to audition to be my boyfriend, but I *don't* recall me saying you'd passed.'

Tough fucking customer, this one. Aida Russell isn't the only eye-roller in town. I give her one of my best. 'Was that not an excellent breakfast in bed?'

'It was.'

'And was the orgasm that followed it not also excellent?'

'It was,' she owns.

'So...'

'Can we take it day by day?' she pleads. She runs her palms lightly up my arms before interlocking her hands behind my neck. I tug her in closer.

‘I want it,’ she admits. ‘I really do. A lot, actually. But, honestly, putting a label on us is less important to me than how we actually are together. I think we need to see how this works in practice. But yeah, I agree you should meet Pip and Kit if you’re serious about this. Even if I won’t be throwing labels around when I introduce you. Does that sound okay?’

That sounds more than okay.

58

CAL

At around the same time on Friday that I was seducing Aida in my home with my excellent skills, both culinary and sexual, Rafe was proposing to Belle. And it sounds like his skills were right up there with mine, because I've never seen my mate look so fucking perky on a Monday morning.

His perfect happiness is a welcome distraction.

The trailer for *Searching for Paradise* gets released today after a successful, and total, embargo on the show's existence, and it's fair to say I'm nervous. Not for myself so much as for Aida, who's positively bricking it. I hated letting her go yesterday afternoon, knowing how much she's steeling herself for the depressingly inevitable backlash.

A "middle-aged"woman (her term) hooking up with a younger sex club owner to rediscover her sexuality: we're both confident the tabloids will find the most judgemental, reductionist, lurid way to spin our situation and that the British public will positively rejoice in tearing her down for it. God forbid she should emerge triumphant from the farcical conclusion of her marriage.

All of which makes me even more determined to be there for her. And I will. I'll stick to her like fucking glue this week, see if I don't.

But first, we're doing a coffee toast to Rafe, our intrepid explorer and the first of our little foursome to propose life-long, till-death-do-us-part commitment to another human being. When you think about it that way, it's really something.

'Tell us everything,' Gen begs, as if three million messages weren't exchanged over the weekend on our group chat. 'So she was totally shocked, yes?'

Rafe crosses his knee over its opposite ankle and sits back, all contented ease now he's secured his future happiness. 'Totally fucking gobsmacked,' he confirms, grinning to himself at the memory. 'She kept remarking on how quiet it was. I had the string quartet set up just outside that sweet little room that's all panelled in Fragonards, and she was like "What a shame these people are playing such beautiful music and there's no one around to appreciate it." She didn't click at all, until I went down on one knee, and then... Yeah. She clicked.'

Jesus, my eyes are wet. I blink furiously as Gen lets out a squeal.

Maddy's bouncing up and down. 'She still won't tell me what you actually said to her. Even though I spent most of Saturday night begging her.'

'Yeah, we agreed we'd keep the specifics between the two of us,' Rafe says. 'It's private, you know? But thanks for coming over on Saturday,' he says to Zach and Maddy. 'She needed someone to talk it all over with—we both did.'

'You couldn't have kept me away,' Maddy retorts, and we all laugh.

'What's important is she said yes, mate, and you look

like the happiest man alive,' I tell him. Usually, I'd be tempted to take the piss a little, because I've never seen him hit over the head quite so hard with the love stick, but I can't knock a man who's this happy. Can't take away from this moment.

'Yeah.' He nods slowly, like he's trying to absorb the fact himself. 'She definitely said yes. It's odd. Obviously, I engineered the entire evening around her, and I wanted to make it as special as possible, but seeing her face when she realised what I was doing—she was so fucking ecstatic—I tell you. I'll never forget that feeling as long as I live.'

There's a silence during which Zach gives an enormous, wet-sounding sniff.

'Jesus Christ, mate,' I say, pinching the bridge of my nose in an effort to stop my own waterworks.

'So, engagement party here, I assume?' Gen asks with excellent comic timing, and we all crack up.

'Can you imagine?' Rafe asks. 'Belle's dad would cough up a bollock if we held it here. No, I think we'll aim for somewhere a bit more conservative. The Mandarin or the RAC Club.'

'Bring it,' I tell him. 'We'll all be there to embarrass you. You set a date for either?'

'Not exactly, though we spent the entire weekend talking about it,' Rafe says. 'Probably late spring for the wedding—neither of us wants to wait. And we'll get the engagement party sorted for a few weeks' time. The most important thing is that Belle's brother Dex can make it.'

'He's in New York, right?' Zach asks.

'Yeah, at Goldman Sachs.'

'Have you met him?'

'We did that trip in June, remember?' Rafe asks. 'He's a good guy. Not mad keen on London, mainly because he likes to keep as much distance between him and their dad as humanly possible. But he told us when we Face Timed him this weekend that he's considering a transfer back here, so he's going to try to tee up some meetings at the same time as the engagement party.'

'Did their dad fuck him up as much as he did Belle?' I ask, curious. That guy sounds like a religious nut-job, from what Rafe's told us.

He cocks his head, considering. 'Hard to tell. On the surface, no, because he rejected all that shit a lot earlier than Belle, and more openly, too, from what I hear. But she reckons he's fucked up in his own way. He fucks around but beats himself up for it.'

'Maybe you should put him through Unfurl,' I deadpan, and everyone laughs.

'Believe me, he's not one hundred percent convinced about me,' Rafe says. 'Not by a long shot. He warmed up over the weekend we were out there, but he's still not a massive fan.'

'You're fourteen years older than his little sister and run a sex club,' Gen points out. 'There's really nothing to like, if you're him.'

That sets us all off again.

'You are every big brother's walking nightmare,' Zach agrees, shaking his head in mock horror.

'Yeah, yeah. I get it. But he knows I love Belle, and he knows she's my whole world. I think standing up to Ben earned me some brownie points with Dex, at least. If I had to guess, I'd say he's made peace with me and her being together, but there's something about my proximity to Alchemy that has him shitting the bed.'

'You mean he doesn't trust you to be faithful?' Gen presses. 'Surely not?'

'No,' he says. 'Not that. It's more… I don't know; it's just a hunch I get. I suspect he finds the whole prospect of a sex club tantalising and morally outrageous in equal measure. Like I said, the guy has serious issues, even if he acted out earlier than Belle. There's definitely stuff he hasn't made peace with. So I suspect he feels threatened just by my ties to this world.'

'Interesting,' I muse. I'm lucky enough to have come out of my ultra-Catholic education reasonably intact. I never really allowed the doctrine we were force-fed at school to take root, unlike a huge proportion of my classmates. It helps that my parents aren't religious—Mum's Catholic and pushed for me to go to Loyola, but Dad's a Scottish Presbyterian in name only.

So I probably don't have a huge amount of sympathy for adults in their twenties or thirties who are still grappling with guilt over betraying teachings that I've only ever seen as total horseshit.

'Sounds like we need to forcibly drag him to Alchemy,' I conclude. 'A night here will sort anyone out.'

59

AIDA

"The mind and spirit remains invincible."
—Milton, *Paradise Lost*

I give the newsroom at the BBC a full three hours' notice before Azure's *Searching for Paradise* trailer is due to hit the internet at noon. In the world of breaking news, it's more than enough time for them to cobble together a response, but not enough time for anyone to leak it effectively. I'm not sure if I should be delighted or terrified that it's a slow news day—the various editorial teams shouldn't have much else on, but that means there's little to distract from the interest my latest project will undoubtedly garner.

And yes, *interest* is a euphemism for *total shit show.*

BBC News, that juggernaut responsible for presenting over six hundred hours of news each week on television and radio, holds an eight-fifty morning meeting every weekday like clockwork. The meeting is an opportunity for senior management and department heads to discuss priorities ahead of the departmental editorial meetings shortly after.

While presenters don't join these meetings as a matter of course, senior anchors will often attend to share their opinions on how the BBC communicates certain stories or issues. I probably should have gone up to our Manchester headquarters to sit in on the meeting in person, but it's a school day, so I'm making do with calling in from one of our meeting rooms. I have my *Centre Stage* editor, Rory, with me to keep him in the loop.

I'm fully armoured up this morning in my favourite Balmain blazer and a full face of makeup. When I brief management, it's how I would brief them on any story where I'm reporting live. I deal in facts and action points, nothing else.

The only person in BBC News who's aware of my creative partnership with Azure is its Director, Davina Pearce. She gave her authorisation when I signed my initial contract. But she's not present today, and it's the Deputy Director, Dave Hodgson, who gives me the green light towards the end of the meeting.

'Aida?' He looks at the camera. 'You had something?'

The people around his table swivel to take me in on their huge screen.

Here goes.

'Thanks Dave. Yes. I wanted to share that I've been working on a two-part documentary with Azure for the past couple months and the trailer is due to be released at noon today. I expect it to garner plenty of press attention. The programme is called *Aida Russell: Searching for Paradise*, and I'm producing and presenting it.'

I clear my throat. I've been practising my elevator pitch all morning, and yet I know this will be less articulate than I want. If I'm honest, I want this to be the anti-elevator pitch. I want it to sound so utterly dry that no one will ask a single follow-up question.

'The subject matter is female sexuality in one's forties and beyond, and it deals with divorce and perimenopause, around other issues.

'The main thing to be aware of is that I'm putting myself in the hot seat, as it were. Most women my age weren't brought up in an especially liberated environment, so more than anything this is a search for sexual freedom and expression after a long period of monogamy. I've partnered with an exclusive London-based sex club for the purposes of the show, and one of its founders has been...' *Showing me the ropes. Literally.* 'Mentoring me,' I conclude lamely. 'The footage will not be explicit, but the topic, and the discourse around it, will be. I have a full briefing pack ready to send out with talking points and quotes from me, Azure and some of the experts I've interviewed. Simone is also involved —she's interviewing me. Questions.'

There's a moment of silence as everyone processes my bombshell, and I feel the physical distance from the rest of the meeting participants as keenly as I feel Rory's silent judgement emanating from where he sits in my peripheral vision. I force myself not to cross my arms as I stand and await the inevitable post-processing tidal wave. I don't need to defend myself.

Besides, these guys are my colleagues. They're a downright friendly jury compared to what I'll face in, ooh, three hours.

'Let's make sure I have this straight,' Dave says. 'You're presenting a programme where you presumably bang a guy from a sex club to rediscover your sexuality?'

I can't fault his factual summary any more than I can

pretend to like it. Neither can I articulate precisely why I dislike it. I'm a big girl. I've put myself into the middle of the most heated debates imaginable with some of the scariest people to have held power on this planet. I go in, guns blazing, when a story is controversial or provocative. I am not known for holding back. Ever.

But I guess that's because I'm usually the mouthpiece. The vessel for the story.

Today *I'm the story.*

'Exactly,' I say in a tone that somehow communicates *I'm not sorry* and also *try judging me to my face, fucker.* I don't love Dave, but his judgement is usually decent.

A beat, then, 'Got it.' There's no gold star or slap on the wrist. I want neither praise nor censure from my coworkers, but I'd like more of a read on his reaction and I can't get one from here.

'This is a documentary, not reality TV, correct?' Sasha Riddell, our Head of Breakfast News asks with the habitual weariness of someone who's been at work since four o'clock this morning. 'What's the tone?'

'Correct,' I say crisply. 'There are unscripted fly-on-the-wall sections, but it's mainly interview-based. It'll be an elevated piece of film-making that examines important issues in a high-concept way while at the same time being, hopefully, very human.

'This is a sensitive and extremely personal journey for me, obviously, but my decision to share some of it on camera comes from the hope that, by doing so, it will drive curiosity and debate and allow the thematic content to resonate far more strongly.

'One of the themes we explore is women "of a certain age" not being seen as sexual beings. I'm hoping that by talking about my own sexual journey in an open and honest way, I can cast a spotlight on female sexuality in my age group and beyond while addressing some of the more taboo subject matters out there, like women using sex clubs.'

'And the timing?' Dave asks.

'Right. The first episode will stream in early January and the second one the following week. I'm expecting plenty of interest and censure from the press—I'm sure I don't need to spell out the myriad ways they could go with this—but it's not a news story per se. Most of our filming is done, so I plan on presenting *Centre Stage* as usual between now and then.'

'Did the BBC get a chance to bid on this programme?' Helen Forrester asks. She runs the research team for *Newsnight* and is a force of nature and a BBC veteran. Most people are more than a little scared of her, though she's been nothing but supportive of me in my transition from the news desk to *Centre Stage*.

I swallow a smile as I opt not to correct her. There was no auction. It turns out, a sex documentary about a forty-something woman is not television catnip, according to most of the broadcasters I met with. I had a chance to sit down with a couple of the BBC's documentary commissioners, who politely and unequivocally communicated their total lack of interest.

'They saw it, yes,' I tell Helen.

It's poor Dave who gets the full force of her glare. 'Well, shame on them,' she says. 'This is precisely the kind of content we should be prioritising, especially when the film-maker is one of our own.'

'I think the programme has the right partner,' I say gently. 'We've been able to raise the heat level—in a tasteful way, of course—far higher than the BBC's audience might have been comfortable with.'

'Well, I think it's a damned shame,' she grumbles. 'Good on you for doing it. I shall be cheering you on, as I'm sure we all will. Right, folks?'

There's a collective, embarrassed rumble of agreement through my screen that seems more reflective of everyone's fear of Helen than any genuine support for my project. It's an awkward way to wrap up the meeting, but it strikes me that perhaps I should be enjoying my colleagues' lukewarm reaction.

Because the press' reaction will be far from lukewarm, that's for sure.

60

CAL

You know in movies, when a news story hits and they do a cheesy montage of all the headlines whirling into focus and building on top of each other like a giant fucking sloppy headline pie that makes your head spin?

That's how I feel as I monitor the news sites and social media after the *Paradise* trailer drops. Aida's explained to me that the coverage will come in waves of initial knee-jerk reactions and lengthier, more thoughtful op-eds.

Today, we can expect the coarsest, most reductionist knee-jerk reactions in the shape of tweets and headlines on news sites. Tomorrow, we'll probably make the front pages, and we should see more opinion pieces popping up. Then, over the next few weeks, and especially once our show airs, the newspaper coverage will filter down to women's magazines.

A similar trend should roll out on television, too: headlines today as news outlets pick up the story, followed by the likely dissection of Aida's personal life on this week's morning shows and eventually her appearance on chat shows. Her publicist, Mara, has her confirmed for *Gordon Kay*, which is pretty fucking epic from where I'm sitting. Gordon's chat show hosts the biggest celebrities from both sides of the Atlantic.

Every news outlet I click on has the trailer playing in a pop-up box, which seems pretty good publicity from where I'm sitting. Seeing it play on every site from Sky News to the *Daily Mirror* is messing with my brain.

Just when I think I'm nailing my audition process to be with her properly, it hits me over and over like a sledgehammer: This is Aida Fucking Russell we're talking about. Her face is on every news site in the country. I mean, so is mine, but that's irrelevant. It's her they all care about. Her whose life makes national news.

I let the trailer play on mute, over and over, washing over me. I've seen it before, several times, but watching it on the BBC News homepage is a different ball game. Aida's face is one almost every adult in Britain knows, and here it stares back at me, beautiful and sexy and authoritative as her red mouth moves silently. Beguilingly.

There she is walking over the Millennium Bridge, the camera behind her, giving every perv in the country a killer shot of her cracking arse in a figure-hugging scarlet dress.

And here's a wide shot of her talking to Simone in our usual suite at the Lanesborough. She's gesticulating forcefully. Her body language is as compelling as it is every week on *Centre Stage*. The subtitle says *Enough is enough. Let's stop this ridiculous, and extremely convenient, collective pretence that women over the age of forty aren't sexual beings. I'm going to show you all that women my age think about sex as much as the rest of you, and that we want a damn sight more than a quickie in bed with the lights off.*

That's my girl. No lights off for her—that would be a

crying shame. The weirdest surge of pride and gratitude and jealousy swirls in the pit of my stomach. She's public property, and everyone with a dick will be wanking off when they see this side of her.

But I'm the *only* one who gets to do the honours. That's what's important. That's what I've got to remember. Still, it's hard to quash this panicky FOMO-type anxiety. I wish I was by her side today—it feels wrong not to be—but Simone was intent on sweeping her off for lunch at Scott's, both to celebrate the release and to keep her mind off the headlines. Then she'll be with her boys.

I'm nowhere in the picture today. I scratch frustratedly at the tiny fragment of loose lacquer on my desk. At least the rest of my team have abandoned all pretence of working, too, and are avidly scouring social media as we sit in our horseshoe-shaped configuration. Rafe's ostensibly at Cerulean today but is more likely skulking around Belle's gallery. He can't leave that poor girl alone. But Gen, Zach and Maddy are as enthralled as I am.

'How are the headlines looking?' Gen asks.

'BBC's keeping it fairly vanilla,' I say. '*Aida Russell Partners with London Sex Club in her Search for Paradise.* Let's see... The *Mail's* gone full prude—*Russell Sinks to her Husband's Level.* Jesus Christ, what a bunch of twats.'

'He's her ex-husband, you pathetic wankers,' Gen says. 'Get your fucking facts right.'

'Exactly. And a grown woman going after her own pleasure is obviously the exact same "level" as a husband cheating on his wife with his subordinates—fucking infuriating.' I hit return on my keyboard more viciously than I need to in order to make my point. 'I don't know how she deals with this shit.'

'Because she's an evolved human being who's well

versed in this game,' Gen replies smoothly, 'and she knows that pursuing her own happiness *and* blowing this debate wide open in a way that may benefit millions of women is far more important than giving a single fuck what the self-righteous white male pricks who run our national media may think.'

I blink and fight the impulse to stride over to Gen's desk and plant a smacker on her lips because Christ, I love this woman.

'What she said,' I say lamely instead, allowing myself to be mildly distracted by my own grinning face flashing up on the trailer. Fuck, they've lit me well.

A soft laugh from Zach tells me I'm not the only one Gen impresses on a daily basis.

'Twitter is the slimy shit-show you'd expect,' Maddy says now. 'Bloody hell, they've all come out to play. If I had to make a pie chart, I'd say...' She pauses. 'Let's see. Twenty percent women coming out in, like, crazy support of Aida. Forty percent *men* saying she's an old slut and the BBC should fire her. Forty percent men saying they'd do—ew—*lots* of things to her now they know how up for it she is, and probably another ten to twenty percent women saying Cal's really hot and Aida's way too old for him.'

The blood rises to my face. I want to take on each and every one of these creeps and slut shamers and the toxic fucking women who don't know how to support other women.

'Um, that's over a hundred percent all in, sweetheart,' Zach tells her. Wow, he's a braver man than me.

Maddy rises slowly from her chair. 'I'm sorry, what did you just say, Spreadsheet?'

I glance over. His face is a picture.

'Um, nothing, sweetheart.'

'Glad to hear it. Because if you want even the remotest chance of being blown again in your sad, miserable life, you do not attempt to maths-shame me. *Got it?*'

I swallow a smirk as I cast my eyes back to the trailer on my screen. Aida's talking again. I hit pause and linger on the sight of her dark, gleaming eyes. On the line of her bare throat. She is so fucking alluring. The camera loves her, but I have the privilege of knowing that what it sees doesn't come close to the truth of how captivating she is in the flesh.

'I asked her to be my girlfriend,' I say.

Maddy stops her evisceration of Zach and turns to gape at me.

'Aida?'

'Yeah.'

She lets out an excited little squeal.

'What did she say?' Gen wants to know.

'She's thinking about it.' The admission hurts. I glance back down at the paused video. I feel exactly like I did before I met her, like a schoolboy with a crush on his most incredible teacher. She's so out of my league it's not funny.

'It's high stakes for her,' Zach says softly. He'd know, even if he doesn't share Aida's celebrity. He has kids, and I know the emotional toll it took on him as he prepared to bring Maddy into his daughters' lives in a formal sense.

'I know,' I mutter.

'Zach's right,' Gen says. 'All this—it's a lot. And I know for a fact she hasn't gone into this project looking for a relationship.'

'I know,' I say again.

'I also know,' Gen continues carefully, like she's choosing her words, 'that what she's had with you has meant an enormous amount to her. You've given her a wonderful gift, Cal. And I definitely got the impression, last time I chatted with her, that what she feels for you goes beyond the physical, but it's going to be an adjustment for her. She's having a hell of a year.'

I believe Gen. I believe Aida has feelings for me. That face of hers gives her away every time.

'Maybe actions speak louder than words in this case,' Maddy suggests. 'Maybe being there for her right now is what she really needs. Help her get through this mayhem, you know? She's really cool, and I know she's a badass at this, but it can't be easy, reading this stuff about yourself. Maybe just act like a boyfriend rather than badgering her to put a label on it.'

It's so similar to what Aida told me she needed the other morning that it gives me pause, and not for the first time I'm struck with gratitude for the amazing women who surround me.

Mads is right, of course, and it's what I've already decided for myself. I'm going to be there for her so fully it's not funny.

61

AIDA

When I court controversy, it is absolutely not because I seek drama. It's because I believe the subject at hand warrants more profile. And if I can increase that profile by throwing my weight behind it, I'll do it. I'll push boundaries, question assumptions, engage in uncomfortable conversations. I will stir that shit as much as I deem it necessary.

Doesn't mean I always enjoy it. Especially when the public backlash to my actions is as downright vitriolic as it has been today.

Do I believe that my journey to "find paradise" is the right one for me and the right dialogue to raise in society more broadly?

Unequivocally yes.

Am I comfortable with my particular kind of profile shifting from that of a hardened journalist and uncompromising interviewer to a woman of a certain age putting herself out there, not on the dating market, but worse: on a journey for sexual satisfaction, pure and simple?

Fuck no.

But for the first time all day, the special kind of terror that is putting one's head above the parapet for all the world to see is dulling, easing a little. Because, for the first time all day, I have something that succeeds in distracting me where even Simone's pep talk and my boys' cuddles have partially failed.

Callum is kicking off a performance for me on my iPhone screen, and I am one lucky gal.

'When you said you wanted to be there for me today,' I remark, 'I did not expect *this*.'

'You should expect the unexpected where I'm concerned,' he shouts. The shouting is necessary, because he has Enrique Iglesias singing *Tonight (I'm Fuckin' You)* at full pelt. His shirt is already off, and his bare torso looks magnificent in the low light of his bedroom. He gets his belt unbuckled and pulls it out of its belt loops in a single smooth movement before throwing it somewhere behind him.

'I'm beginning to work that out,' I mutter as I shamelessly watch him drop his pants, but it's not totally true. Really, I've known this since Callum Sinclair rolled that ice cube over my underwear at the Zebra Club.

A second later, I'm narrowing my eyes in disbelief. 'Is that... *baby oil*?'

'You know it,' he pants, dousing his palm liberally with some Johnson & Johnson's. He sets the bottle down and rubs his hands together before smoothing the oil over his shoulders and down his biceps. I swear, this routine would not be out of place on stage at London's iconic G.A.Y. club. They'd go crazy for him with his gorgeous body, the tight little black boxer briefs with their alluring bulge, and those dangerously gyrating hips.

'If it all goes wrong at Alchemy, you could be a go-go dancer,' I tell him. 'Or even a Chippendale.'

'Nah,' he says. 'They'd probably make me wax my chest. And I'm all man, baby.'

I giggle as he smooths the oil through the dark hair on his chest. 'Yes, you are.'

Satisfied that he's oiled his chest up sufficiently, he hooks his thumbs into the waistband of his boxer briefs. 'You ready for me to be *all* man?'

I take a sip of the large glass of chardonnay on my nightstand and settle back against my pillow. 'Hell yeah,' I say with the bravado of someone who's not actually in the room with him. 'Bring it on.'

He shimmies out of them and his cock pops out. He's fully hard and fucking gorgeous. I am one lucky woman. I lie there and enjoy the view as he dances around the room, singing about motivation and reputation, turning so he can wiggle his ass at the camera.

And it is a very fine ass.

When he turns back to me, he has his dick in his hand. He comes toward the screen, which seems to be at perfect dick height, and grabs some more oil from the bottle before smoothing it liberally over his length. His crown is gleaming, and I involuntarily run my tongue over my bottom lip, which is my tic for most emotions from fascination to arousal.

'When you lick your lips like that, baby, it makes me even harder,' he tells me. The song begins again—he must have put it on repeat—but he turns the sound down.

'I wish I was there,' I confess. I really do. It's odd. I haven't known Cal long, but he knows exactly how to bring me down from wherever I'm spiralling to. He knows how to get me out of my head. Case in point: this little stripper routine. I could really use the comfort of his body and his hugs and his touch right now.

I could also really use his gorgeous dick in my mouth.

'If you were here,' he rasps, backing away from the camera so I can see him more fully, 'I'd have you on your knees so fucking fast, and I'd shove my cock past those fucking ridiculous lips of yours so hard you'd choke on me.'

'I want that,' I tell him, shifting in my bed and rubbing my thighs together. Beneath my loosely fastened robe, my body is heating.

'I bet you do, you filthy girl,' he says. 'You like it when I choke you with my dick, don't you?'

'Yes.'

'Show me your tits.'

I tug my robe open and slide it off my shoulders. His teeth catch on his lower lip as he takes me in, and I have the strongest desire to run my mouth all over his body. To snag that lower lip between my own teeth before sinking to my knees to take him in my mouth.

He's so, so hard. I'm actually jealous of his hand as it works his length. The amount of baby oil he's employed has it moving easily over his stiff column of flesh.

'Like what you see?' I ask, sinking back against my pillows.

'I like it so much I'm going to pretend I'm coming all over those gorgeous tits. Stay like that, sweetheart—actually, cup them for me.'

He steps forward again, crowding the camera so all I get on screen is his big hand working his giant dick for me with even, hypnotic thrusts.

Scratch the Chippendales. This guy would kill it on Only Fans. I can't believe this performance is just for me. The way his engorged crown is pulsating, leaking is positively pornographic. I lean forward, wineglass back in hand, because this beats *The Crown* hands down. Jesus fuck is the sight of Cal jerking himself off mesmerising.

He begins to moan, and it's so male and unrestrained that it gets me all kinds of hot.

'Show me,' I say. 'Show me how much you wish I was there on my knees for you. Pretend it's my mouth taking you.'

'Jesus, sweetheart,' he groans. His hand works faster, a blur of hungry jerks. I tilt my head to one side and watch in fascination.

Then there's the pained intake of breath through his teeth, and in the split second that follows, I don't really process what's happening until the screen goes whitish at the same time as I hear a wet *splat*.

Did he—?

Another anguished noise from him, and the screen goes even whiter. I can't see a thing.

Oh my fucking God. I think he just came all over his phone.

I can't help it. I lose my actual shit. The laughs burst out of me and I quickly set my wineglass back on the nightstand, because I'm definitely going to spill it otherwise.

'Fuck,' he says, the hunger in his voice turning to panic, and I begin to howl. I collapse forward on my bed, smacking my hand hard on the comforter.

'Oh my God,' I gasp. 'Did you just shoot all over your phone?'

'Yeah—shit, hang on...'

My forehead hits the comforter, because this is the best thing *ever* and actual tears are coming out of my eyes. I'm laughing so hard in this position my abdominal muscles are screaming, but I can't stop.

There's a scrabbling noise, and I look up in time to see something dark passing over the camera. I can make Cal out now, blurry and indistinct courtesy of a layer of remaining cum-smear. Jesus Christ. I will never get over this.

'Fuck,' he says, 'I think I need a flannel. Can I use something wet, do you think?'

'Just make sure you wring it out as hard as you can before you do it,' I advise. I raise myself up with difficulty and resume my seated position as he takes me on a little virtual trip. I recognise his bathroom floor tiles before the phone is laid flat somewhere.

There's the hiss of running water, followed by lots of drips, and then more rubbing on the screen. A blurry, fluffy towel comes towards me, turning the screen black, and then Cal's handsome face appears from above.

I grin at him, still giddy from that slapstick high. 'Hey there, stud.'

'Yeah, yeah, you're hilarious.'

'Did you get your cum out of all the *crevices*?' I manage to ask before collapsing in a fit of giggles again.

'Your concern is truly touching, but yeah, I think so.'

'Good. Because that would have been an awfully awkward conversation with the Genius Bar.'

He flashes me a cheeky grin. 'Yeah, it would. And for that, you're going to watch me wash my cock.'

He sets the phone on a ledge and gets to work rinsing the washcloth, or *flannel* (such a weird boarding school word —it gives me the ick), again before tending to his still-semi-hard dick. He's so fucking adorable in the brighter light of his bathroom, his dark hair falling over his face as he looks down, stomach flat and hard and dissected by my favourite trail of hair.

He really is a beautiful man.

Still, I have to ask. 'Did you mean to aim right for the phone?'

He gives me a sheepish grin. 'I was aiming for your tits.'

'Which were *on the screen*. So that's a yes, I guess?'

'It's a *I didn't really think through the consequences.* I got a bit carried away, as you could probably tell. Besides, I wanted you to have a bird's-eye view of the action.'

That sets me off again. 'Ohmigod, I definitely had that. That splat was hilarious. Just hilarious. It sounded like bird shit hitting a windshield, but louder.'

'Did you just compare my powerful, masculine ejaculation to a *bird shitting on a windscreen*?' he hisses.

'Yes. Yes I did. Only, you know, far more erotic, and, um, masculine.'

'Aida fucking Russell. The mouth on you. If I were there, I'd put you right over my knee.' He picks up the phone and I smirk at him as he takes me back into his bedroom.

'I'd like that,' I tell him honestly.

'I know you would, you little slut. Now, let's get you off. Maybe we can see if you can spurt all over *your* screen.'

'I'm sorry,' I tell him through my giggles, 'I think that ship has sailed tonight. But you made me laugh so hard I forgot all about the people who called me a haggard old whore and a disgrace to Britain for a few minutes, in case that makes you feel better?'

'Bullshit,' he says. I can tell he's kind of pissed, and I kind of love it. 'Open your fucking legs for me and show me how much you want me.'

62

AIDA

'Come on, sweetie,' I tell Pip. 'Just get your blazer on and it'll all be fine.'

I'm doing that thing where I'm being extra sweet and caring to compensate for how close I'm coming to losing my shit, because I have five more minutes to get the boys out the door for school and there are at least twenty reporters outside my house. While I couldn't be more pissed that they're here, my top priority right now is getting the boys to school on time and with minimal trauma to them.

Not only that, but the WhatsApp group for our street is blowing up with a combination of those who are even more pissed than me that my "headline-worthy antics" are disrupting everyone's morning and those trying to sort out a temporary guard or two from a private security firm we sometimes use, because I am by no means the only high-profile resident on this street.

Judging from the noise outside, no guard has yet materialised. Why is it that the repeated sound of my own name shouted in that cajoling, persistent manner has me itching to slap someone hard?

That itch grows worse when I look at Pip's little white face. This is a kid so wracked with anxiety that we had to tell him Santa didn't exist two years ago so he'd stop spiralling into hysterics over the idea of a random dude infiltrating our house in the dead of night. (I get it. It's a creepy concept, if you think about it too hard.)

'Why are they standing out there?' he asks as I feed his blazer up his arms and pull it over his skinny shoulders. This kid is a beanpole. 'It's rude.'

'Because they all want an exclusive with Mummy,' Kit says breezily from his squatting position as he ties his shoelaces. My youngest loves drama as much as he loves an audience, but the media's pursuit of our family during John's women's "exclusives" was hellish enough to leave all of us scarred.

'We talked about this, remember?' I tell Pip. 'Kit's right. I have a new TV show coming out, and people are interested in it, so the media has a lot of questions, and those reporters are always looking for an angle no one else has to make their coverage stand out.'

'Just like you used to do in the field, right, Mummy?' Kit asks, and I stifle a smile. This kid and his newsroom jargon.

'Exactly. But I'd like to think I was more courteous than they are, and my stories were very different from the ones they want to report on. Even so, it's easiest if you don't take it personally. They're not here to rile you. They're here to do their job. *Your* job is to ignore them, and to go to school, and to get on with your day.' I cup Pip's little face in my hands and stroke my thumbs over his silken cheeks.

'Will they be here when we get home from school?' he wants to know.

'Hopefully not, sweetie.' I sigh as I turn to the huge mirror in the hallway for one final check. I don't want any *gaunt and drawn* headlines today. Neither do I want too many people speculating that I'm way too old and haggard to be hooking up with a guy like Cal.

Hopefully, the amount of makeup I've slathered on this morning will do the trick. My lips are perfectly scarlet, and I'm wrapped up in my most gorgeous cream double-faced cashmere coat. I also spent too much time giving myself the perfect blowout this morning.

While I'm used to being judged on my face and body when I'm trying to do a job, this is the first time—my ex-husband's public philandering aside—that I've been judged as a sexual being in my own right. I grab my oversized sunglasses along with the boys' schoolbags and football kit and all the other paraphernalia they need for their day.

'I'm so sorry about this,' I tell them as I stand with one hand on the door handle and the other holding Pip tightly. 'I'm gonna get it sorted while you're at school, okay? Remember what we've talked about before? Reporters are like...'

'Puppies,' Kit finishes enthusiastically. 'If you give them a single scrap, they'll keep coming back to the dinner table for more.'

I shoot him a genuine smile. 'Right! So don't engage. Kit, stay behind me. Let's do this.'

And with that, I swing the door open and we step out into the sunlit crowd.

63

CAL

How's it going over there? Press still hanging around?

The security guy's arrived but it's still a fucking circus

You OK?

I'm pissed. I can handle it but I hate this feeling of being hounded in my own home

How's the coverage looking this morning? Saw The Times

Fucking Lorna Davison.

She's a dried-up woman-hater. The WORST kind of woman. Ignore her

I guess

IGNORE HER. Seriously. You want me to come over?

No. I'm just having a pity party. I'll be fine, honestly

I'm coming over

I don't want them getting a photo of you at my house. That would just add fuel to the flames

There are ways around that. See you in an hour

I jump on the tube from Green Park so I can head home and grab my car. We've had a few reporters sneaking around Alchemy, but nothing like what Aida's had to endure. Still, Gen had the foresight to put some of our evening doormen on a day shift, and our muscle quickly got rid of the journos. That's why she's the best COO ever.

It only takes fifteen minutes to get through the park from my place to Notting Hill. I park up on Aida's road, and pay the parking charge on my phone before reaching over to the passenger seat and grabbing the balaclava I bought for the Masked Ball. I tug it on and check in the rearview mirror that it's on straight before grabbing the man-bag I stuffed a few bits in.

Yep.

That'll do nicely.

I know exactly what she needs. In fact, I'll bet I know better than her what she needs.

I call Aida from the car. 'I'm on your street. I'm disguised. Tell your guy to let your good friend Rafe in.'

She giggles at that.

I must look fucking weird, strolling down one of Notting Hill's leafiest and most exclusive streets in a Tom Ford suit, a Dunhill man-bag and a cheapo balaclava, but I couldn't give a shit. A mother with a toddler in a stroller hurriedly crosses the road to avoid me, and I don't blame her. There's a crowd of reporters with cameras and those big fluffy mic things on the pavement outside Aida's house, but her front garden is clear and there's a massive scowling guard standing in front of her gate.

He looks like a Bratva enforcer, which pleases me enormously, because none of these parasites are getting past him. 'She's expecting me,' I tell him, pushing through the crowds. His mono brow doesn't move at the sight of me. Clearly this guy has seen it all.

'Name?' he barks.

'Rafe,' I lie smoothly.

As he stands aside, the reporters vie for the attention of the masked guy sauntering up the immaculate limestone-tiled path to Aida's swanky villa. There's the click of cameras and the inevitable cat-calling.

'Oi, mate! Who are you?'

'You a friend of Aida's, then?'

'Why you wearing a mask, mate? You going to rob 'er?'

I ignore them all and bang hard, twice as I make a fist with the other hand. I would really enjoy punching some of these wankers in the face. The door opens, the woman of the hour presumably hiding behind it, and I push through the space and slam it behind me, pulling her into my arms.

'Hey,' I croon as I stroke her hair. 'How are you holding up?'

She sags against my body, but I've got her. 'I can't believe you're wearing that. They'll have a field day.'

'Don't give a fuck. Tell the boys one of your friends from work came to see you and he disguised himself.'

'My hardened criminal in shining armour.'

'Believe it, baby.'

She pulls away a little so she can lift her face to mine. She looks tired but absolutely stunning. Her lips are my favourite red, and she's in sleek black trousers and a fine knit sweater that hugs her tits far too perfectly.

'Do you normally hang around the house looking like a supermodel?' I ask her.

'Definitely not. Knowing you're going to be splashed all over the tabloids has a motivating effect when it comes to one's morning routine, I'll tell you.' Her gaze flits over my masked face, and she licks her lips.

So she already has a Pavlovian response to my mask, does she?

Interesting.

Her dark eyes are shining as she stares up at me. She is the sexiest, most sophisticated woman I have ever, ever seen. Having her in my arms, my senses full of her, leaves me reeling.

I make a decision.

My hands on her biceps, I push off the door and march her backwards so she's up against the wall.

'Tell me,' I say in a low conversational tone, my mouth so close to hers, 'do you know what happens to rich, bored, sexy-as-fuck housewives when they're naïve enough to let a masked thug into their fancy Notting Hill home?'

This woman is no bored housewife, and I'm only a thug

some of the time. Still, I see the second she understands the game. She swallows, her bare throat a long, smooth column, eyes glittering.

'I don't.'

A step forward has me pinning her to the wall with my hips. I twist my upper body, reaching into my man-bag and pulling out a length of rope that I hold up for her to see before chucking the bag onto the glossy tiles. Only then do I lower my mouth to her ear.

'They get *exactly* what they deserve.'

64

AIDA

"His red right hand."
—Milton, *Paradise Lost*

He's crowding me in the hallway of my home. The reporters outside are still chanting my name, but his presence drowns them out, somehow. It's just me and his huge body, the gorgeous suit at odds with the mask.

Those words in my ear send a trail of instant goosebumps flitting over my body. I thought he was coming over to comfort me, but maybe discomfiting me is better. Maybe I need to surrender and let Cal do what he does best: wreak total annihilation on my body and soul.

I know he'll never hurt me.

I trust him with my life.

But the words, and the tone, and the heat of his body against mine, and his scent, *and the goddamn rope*—they're enough to flip an instant switch inside of me.

I turn my head so my cheek is brushing against his balaclava.

'And what's that, exactly?' I drawl.

If his words flipped something in me, mine do the same for him. In an instant, he has my jaw in a grip so hard it aches and his mouth millimetres from mine.

'Whatever the fuck I feel like,' he snarls. 'Got it?'

He's as good as his word, swallowing my *yes* with his mouth, his lips hard on mine, tongue sweeping in effortlessly, invading, probing, as he takes exactly what he wants, his fingertips still digging into my jaw. As he grinds his growing hardness against my stomach, I'm vaguely aware of trying to slide my feet apart, because I am clearly a total whore for this man and his filthy mouth and even filthier imagination.

And God knows, if the entirety of the UK wants to believe I'm a slut, I may as well have some fun proving them right.

~

MY BEDROOM CARPET usually feels soft underfoot, but its fibres are rough beneath my bare knees. The rope digs into my wrists and chafes against my sitz bone. Cal towers above me, as naked as I am but undeniably more powerful, feet planted wide and thighs straining and mask firmly on as I kneel before him.

I'm in a haze of desperate, roiling want as I look up at him. I hate nothing more than being without agency—this morning being a case in point. So why, when this man takes my agency from me, does it have rightness swirling through my veins as surely as if he's injected me with it?

His hand tightens in my hair, tugging painfully at my roots. 'Again.'

From beyond my bedroom windows the faint, relentless chants of reporters continue. But here, in this bright room, I am merely sunlight and sensation, chasing my next instruction.

My next taste.

My next hit.

I wonder if Cal gets off on this as much as I do. The very woman whose name they're all calling is bound and on her knees for him, staring up at him as though being his captive is her only means of escape.

I obey, turning my head and pulling at my roots so I can catch the crown of his hard, weeping dick in my mouth once more. I lick it before it bobs and evades me, precum painting a stripe along my jaw. It's like my childhood games of bobbing for apples, only *better.*

My next attempt is more successful. I get his whole crown in my mouth and swirl my tongue around it, flicking over that delicious, sensitive little notch of skin at its base before sliding it over the silky wetness of his slit. His groan is low and raw and male and confirms that the power dynamics here are absolutely not how they seem.

It's a hit to my bloodstream as I take him deeper in my mouth, shuffling my knees a little wider to feel the air on my aching pussy and flexing my hands uselessly in their bindings as he fists my hair more tightly and thrusts so I'm full of him.

My eyes fill with tears as I gag involuntarily, breathing in wildly through my nose and using every ounce of strength I have not to gag again. I can't slap his thigh like this, but I could absolutely jerk my head away enough to spit out *parliament* if I wanted to.

I don't.

I want this.

I want Cal gripping my head and fucking my mouth and making me wet as I contemplate just how sweet and rough my reward will be.

'Fuck, *yes*,' he hisses as he hits the back of my throat once again, sending my eyes rolling back in my head and tears cascading down my cheeks. I must look like a panda by now. My knees widen even further of their own accord, and he laughs harshly.

'Getting wet from choking on my cock, are you? Husband not giving you what you need? I bet he's some posh chinless wonder with a pencil dick he doesn't know how to use.' *Thrust.* 'Not like this. Take your fucking fill while you can like the little whore you know you are.'

Another vicious thrust has me flailing, my fingers fluttering behind my back as I attempt to keep up, to take his ridiculous length and girth. I'm drooling, the saliva making it easier to suck and harder to keep ahold of him. But the relentlessness of his grip on the back of my head means I'm not going anywhere.

'You're lucky I came along,' he says. His tone is a mix of conversational and menacing. 'I'll give his bored, hot little wife a good filling up while he's off doing fuck knows what. Fuck, you know how to suck dick. Come here.'

Without warning, I'm pulled slickly off his cock and tugged up with one of his hands still in my hair and the other lodged under my arm. Blood rushes to my head as he gets me on my feet, and there's a moment where our eyes connect.

His burn through the mask, eyes black, almost all pupil. He takes me in, and in them I see pride and infinite, desperate hunger until he throws me on the bed. I land face-down and am promptly dragged backwards by my ankles until I'm bent over the end of the bed, knees on the floor and my flushed cheek against my cool comforter.

'Stay,' he commands, like I'm his puppy, and then there's the sound of him rifling through clothing and the rip of a condom wrapper.

He's back behind me in seconds, sinking to his knees and kicking mine apart before his calloused fingers find my centre and begin to rub hard.

'Jesus fuck,' he says, bending over me so his breath is hot on my ear and his body a solid bulk behind me. 'You are fucking *soaking*, you shameless little whore. You like me roughing you up?'

'Yes,' I moan, shame and self-consciousness warring with brazen need. I could die like this, with Cal's hulking great body wrapped around mine like a shell as his fingers probe at the softest, neediest, most vulnerable part of me, like I'm his to do whatever the fuck he likes with.

'Fuck, yes, you do,' he rasps, jamming three fingers inside of me so suddenly that my entire body bucks against his. 'Such a needy little slut. What do you need?'

'Your—your cock,' I gabble, stuttering over my words in my desperation to have even more of him inside me. He's stretching me so well with his fingers, but it's not enough. I need more, and he knows it.

'Yes you do.' His mouth against my ear makes me shiver. 'You need my cock like you've never needed anything in your life. You needed it in your mouth, you need it in your cunt, and at some point I'll come back, when that useless husband of yours is away and you're home all alone, and I'll ram it up that tight little arsehole, too. Got it?'

I need him. I need him everywhere; I need the filth of his words in my ear and the heat of his body at my back and the entire length of him so deep inside of me I don't know my own name.

'Yes,' I gasp. 'Yes, please.'

'I'm gonna fuck you now,' he says, his voice low. His control is audibly hanging by a thread, and it makes me so hot. I'm a squirming, leaking mess, sandwiched between him and my bed like this. 'It's gonna be rough.'

'Yes,' is all I get a chance to say before he's pulling his fingers out harshly and rearing up. My back feels instantly cold, bereft, with his heat gone, but then he's splaying a hand over my face to press me to the comforter as he slaps me hard on the ass. I can't help it. I let out a surprised yelp. He pauses a second—probably to give me time to cry out my safe word—before he does it again. And again. Same cheek, so hard it stings like a motherfucker. Four. Five. And, just as suddenly, he stops and jams his dick inside of me suddenly, aggressively. My body wants to react on instinct, closing up against this perceived invasion, but he's having none of it.

Harder, his hand flattens me into the bed. Harder, his dick drives its way in. My pussy is so primed, so swollen already that the pain from his intrusion and from his spanking gives instant way to a heated glow of pure pleasure as he moves. He doesn't hold back with a single fibre of his being. Instead, he's all hot desperation and unleashed animal behind me, around me, inside me.

His unfeasibly hard dick drags against every single nerve ending I possess as he slams into me over and over. It's like unleashing your fingernails on an itch you've been told not to scratch. There's zero finesse, just crazy, crazy friction, and the build is so fucking fast and hard it feels like I'm a rocket being launched into the stratosphere.

I scrabble at the comforter for purchase as Cal rams home, the heel of his hand bruising my jaw and his dick a blunt slam as he bottoms out. The heat blooms and blooms and floods me before catapulting me over the edge into a black-red galaxy.

I fall and fall and fall through time and space, past stars and moons, taking and taking as he stiffens and roars and jerks out his own spectacular space odyssey before collapsing, spent, on top of me, his hand releasing my face so he can kiss my jaw, my cheek, over and over and over.

65

CAL

'Want to hear something funny?' I ask. In some feat of Herculean post-orgasmic strength, I managed to haul us both off the carpet and up the bed so we're curled into each other under Aida's duvet, gazing at each other like a just-fucked mutual appreciation society meeting for two, if that's a thing.

'Always.'

'You'll laugh.'

'Lorna Davison called my show "unseemly and staggeringly ill judged". I think I deserve a laugh today, don't you?'

'Fair enough.' I take a moment to run a featherlight fingertip over the shell of her ear. 'So, when Gen pitched me this—you—I had a strategy for how I was going to, you know, tackle you.'

Her eyebrows wing up in twin crescents of amusement. Here we go.

'*Tackle me*? Go on. I can't wait to hear this.'

I clear my throat. 'Yeah. I called it *dirty-lite.*'

She bursts out laughing. 'Meaning?'

'I'm sure you're smart enough to work it out.'

'I *know* I'm smart enough, but I'd enjoy hearing you explain it far more.'

'Okay, so...' I sigh. 'It means what it says. Dirty, but not too dirty, you know? A little dirty talk, a little *good girl*...' I tail off, embarrassed.

'Wow. So you blew right through that assignment, and then some.' She reaches for me under the covers and snuggles closer.

'That's a fair assessment, yeah.'

'So was showing up at my house in a mask with a *rope* and making me blow you part of the *dirty-lite* thing?'

'Erm, nope.'

'Got it. And going down on me during an orgy and then cuffing me to a bed?'

'Not quite.'

Her face lights up in a huge grin. 'Lucky I'm a good *sport*, as you guys say, right?'

'You mean, lucky you're a dirty little ho who likes it good and rough?' I grit out, rolling her onto her back and climbing on top of her.

'That too,' she concedes with a smirk.

'It's safe to say, Ms Russell, that I spectacularly underestimated you,' I tell her, pinning her arms above her head. Her dark hair is a lustrous halo on the pillow. Her eyes are shining and, for now, the faint chants outside are forgotten. It seems that, by some happy miracle, I've given her precisely what she needed this morning.

'Many a man has done that, Mr Sinclair, and none of them had a happy ending,' she tells me with a smile.

'Except for me,' I insist. 'I was stupid enough to underestimate you and I've had lots of happy endings. And, if I haven't made you too sore, I think I'm about ready for another.'

'Go for it, but none of that *dirty-lite* shit,' she tells me. 'Have a little self respect and give it to me like a man.'

I rear up above her, not missing the hitch in her breath as she drags her gaze down my body to where I'm fully hard again.

Game fucking *on.*

66

AIDA

"The mind is its own place, and in itself can make a heaven of hell, a hell of heaven."
—Milton, *Paradise Lost*

There should be no room for ego in my profession. The way I see it, it's kind of like politics. You know you need people who can serve as well as they can lead rather than being total egomaniacs, but, alas, that career path is rife with power-hungry dicks.

It's the same with the news. Disseminating the news is a service, not an ego trip. Obviously, many news broadcasters disagree. Their endgame is being a household face and name. But what I'm trying to say, very inarticulately, is that there's usually a disconnect when I see myself on camera. The stories aren't mine to tell. I'm merely a vessel whose job it is to relay other people's stories with clarity and accuracy and sensitivity.

That's it. It's never about me.

Looking at the latest draft of *Paradise Found,* the second part of my documentary, is a totally different feeling. Because, while the programme deals with some huge universal truths, the channel for those truths is not only my story but the most horrifyingly private part of that story.

Lorna Davidson's words keep running through my mind. They're a paper cut that won't heal—measly and insidious and fucking painful.

Unseemly and staggeringly ill-judged.

That she applauded the concept made it worse. Called it *beyond timely.* What she objected to was the crassness (her word) of my decision to craft such a dialogue around my own lived experience and the inevitable tabloid frenzy it would pique, undoubtedly detracting from the importance of the subject at hand.

Fuck, that hurts, and it doesn't help my PMS and insistent headache. But I'm nothing if not determined, and having one of the most overtly feminist writers among our broadsheets slam my baby right out of the gate has me determined that this will be the most beautiful, elevated, thought-provoking sex documentary ever produced.

And you know what? Watching it makes me feel better, because we've crafted something wonderful here, and nothing about what's playing out on the big screen in front of us feels crass to me.

Last week, we spent a couple days filming additional content at Alchemy. The production team felt the debauched vibe of the Masked Ball was the perfect depravity with which to end my search for paradise—on air, at least—and they hadn't gotten nearly enough footage on the evening of the actual party.

So The Playroom was re-decorated, and the on-stage acts re-hired, and God knows how many scantily clad extras employed to recreate the bacchanalia of the evening. In addition, Cal and I were drafted for reshoots, and I know instinctively as I watch the footage, edited into a riotous, trippy Baz Luhrmann-esque carnival, that this is close to being our climax.

Unfortunate pun not intended.

At the time that most civilised Britons were taking their elevenses last Wednesday, Cal and I recreated the moment he dragged me down Alchemy's main corridor for our masked tryst.

I wore my original red dress and ornate mask for the shoot. My lipstick was smudged in a far more orderly fashion than it would have been on the night, my hair mussed just so. In short, I was sexily dishevelled, my arms and chest and collarbones daubed with horrifying amounts of highlighter to achieve an alluring sheen for the cameras.

And Cal? Cal was in his trusty balaclava, shirt off, his gorgeous upper body oiled up to create a similar effect and black dress pants as well tailored as always. He looked the real deal: thuggish, terrifying, and sexy as fuck.

The only part they didn't try to recreate was his enormous hard-on.

I watch my on-screen self as Cal marches me down the corridor, his body towering behind me and his grip firm on my upper arms. The *Lacrimosa* that was playing that night haunts my ears over distorted voices shouting and laughing and making merry. The artful camera angles and sultry lighting and dramatic shadows ramp up the tension to a level that's almost foreboding.

The final frames slow right down.

Cal bends his masked head to whisper something in my ear.

My face swings to the camera, mask glittering and

smudged scarlet lips parting in slow motion in what appears to the viewer as a knowing smile.

A *carnal* smile.

I look like a woman who's well aware she's about to find paradise.

~

'HOLY FUCKING SHIT,' my publicist Mara says, which is my reaction exactly. 'That is hot as *fuck*.'

I stare at my frozen face, over which the words *Searching for Paradise* have appeared in the show's classy serif. We must have shot eight or nine takes of that scene, with Lizzy encouraging me to dig deep and recall the heady mix of apprehension and desire I felt that evening, walking to our private room.

It was she who directed Cal to bend and whisper something dirty in my ear, and it worked.

It fucking worked.

'The footage is great,' Lizzy confirms. 'What we're missing is the central message. That's what we wanted to brainstorm on today.' She pulls up a stool at the large white table dominating the room and collapses onto it. 'You started this journey with a palpable air of vulnerability and apprehension, and I really feel we've communicated that in the first episode, not to mention your extreme frustration at all of the limited thinking around female sexuality.

'Now we've upped the ante. This is the point where women start to go, *Fuck, yeah, I deserve more than this shit.* And in that shot'—she points at the screen—'you're the cat who got the cream. No doubt about it. You're Aida Russell, and you've done what you always do, which is to identify a problem and go the fuck after it and find a solution.

'But is this the story? Aida gets laid in style, Aida can have her cake and eat it, blah blah blah—is that the note you want to end on? Because we have an opportunity here to potentially overlay this with a bigger message entirely.'

She waves her hand around, and I stare at the screen.

However churlish it sounds, I really wish people would stop asking me what I want.

'I love this so much,' Mara chimes in. When I turn to her, she's rubbing her heavily ringed fingers together, and I can tell she's itching for a vape. She leans back in her chair —she has, naturally, taken the only seat in the room that actually has a back—and puts her Balenciaga-clad feet on the table.

'The whole world watched you lose your paradise. They stood by while your ex-fucking-husband turned you into a joke. And you never lost your class. You never stooped to his level. But you certainly needed to reframe the narrative.

'And now look at you. You've created a beautiful piece of filmmaking that deals with really important fucking issues, and you've done it in a seriously classy way, no matter what Lorna Dickwad Davison says, and you're having the time of your life getting fucked senseless by a guy giving serious Michele Morroni vibes right there... *You* are having the last laugh. And it's bloody wonderful.'

'I guess,' I say unconvincingly.

She swings her legs to the ground and twists her body so she can full-on glare at me. 'This is why you hired me. Rewrite the narrative.' She brushes her palms together. 'Done and dusted. Remember what you kept saying to us in pre-production? You wanted it to have the *lucky bitch* factor? That, right there, is the *lucky bitch* factor. Look at that fucking smile on your face. Even I'm jealous as fuck.'

She gives me one of her rare grins, and it has me grinning, too, because she's right. 'Yeah.' I drum my fingernails on the table in an effort to pull myself the hell together. 'I know you're right.'

'Of course I'm right. I'm always right. You've gone from *poor bitch* to *lucky bitch* in a single, perfectly executed master stroke, which was the entire fucking mandate. And you, my friend'—she points at Lizzy—'are a genius.'

'She definitely is,' I agree, more resolutely this time. Lizzy's film is everything I could have hoped for and more. She's captured the zeitgeist while elevating my storytelling to a timeless level. I don't really know how she's done it.

I swallow. 'But what if that isn't the end of the story?'

'It's never the end of the story,' Lizzy says, 'but we're always going to have to choose a note to end on. And the question is, does this ending feel representative? Does it pull the messaging together sufficiently?'

'No, I mean...' I swallow. 'Cal and I are... together, kind of.'

It's an utterly inadequate depiction of how we are.

He asked me to be his girlfriend, and I still haven't given him the courtesy of a firm *yes.*

He came over to my home the other day and flipped my mood upside down.

He occupies my thoughts and commands my body.

He's gone from being a good-time guy I was supposed to hook up with once a week to being the single most important person in my life aside from my sons.

Inadequate or not, it's enough to send Mara over the edge.

'Oh, Jesus fuck, no,' she groans, letting her forehead plant dramatically on the table. 'Mother of God, tell me you're fucking with me.'

'I'm not fucking with you,' I tell her, more firmly now. 'He wants a relationship.'

She raises her head and grimaces in distaste. 'And you?'

A beat passes, and then: 'I want one, too.'

'Fucking useless,' she mutters as Lizzy titters.

'He makes me happy,' I plead.

'Of course he makes you happy. If he put on a mask and tied me up and stuck his enormous dick inside me, he'd make me happy, too. That guy makes *everyone* happy. No wonder his Instagram following has grown by a hundred thousand since the trailer dropped.'

'It has?' Cal must be thrilled. I'm amazed he didn't wow me with the stats yesterday.

'Focus, Russell. You're not supposed to fall for the young, hot, professional shagger. What did Simone call him? Your *boy toy*. You're supposed to enjoy him, not sail off into the sunset with him.'

'Why not?' Lizzy asks, crossing her arms. 'For the sake of the messaging. Is *Aida Russell finds happiness with a hot younger guy after her un-hot, older husband fucks her over* not a compelling message?'

Mara holds up her hands in defeat. 'Honestly, you don't pay me enough to deal with this muppetry. You're both intentionally missing the point. This experiment is supposed to be about smashing stereotypes. Breaking boundaries. Doing whatever the fuck you like with a guy who's completely inappropriate and showing the beloved Great British Public that the sky does not fall when you indulge yourself once in a while.

'This Cal guy is a bloody KFC Bargain Bucket. Fucking delicious, great for the occasional treat, and fills you up good and proper, but *you're not supposed to get hooked.*'

67

AIDA

'That's a shitty analogy, and you know it,' I tell her. I'm pissed, and there's no way I'll admit her metaphor would make me laugh at any other time. The man's dick fills me up, that's for damn sure. 'I could gorge myself stupid on him and it would only do good things for me.'

'Yeah, until it all comes crashing down and it's a million times worse than it was when John fucked off, because you really gelled with this guy,' Mara says matter-of-factly.

Wow.

Even someone who I know has my back, who I'd consider a friend, sees me and Cal as a temporary fling at best. But Mara and Lizzy aren't the kind of women whose hair you braid as you all sit around and discuss feelings over milk and cookies.

Nope. They're both experts on messaging in their own ways, and it would be stupid to disregard their advice.

I lean forward and cover my face with my hands. Fuck, my head is sore. I need some painkillers. 'Sheesh. Talk me through it like I'm five. Is a Happy Ever After not an option here?' I don't need to spell out that *here* in this instance refers to the show and not my actual life.

'Lay it on her, Liz,' Mara says with the air of one who's fatigued by my obtuseness.

'This is your vision, Aida,' Lizzy tells me more gently. 'But you brought me here to keep that vision straight, and to make sure that the actual story we're telling matches that vision.

'This entire journey is about contrasts, right? Conforming to hetero-normative, patriarchal expectations of monogamy versus overturning said expectations. Responsibility versus liberty. Shame versus shamelessness. Settling for what you have versus demanding more. Keeping up appearances versus writing your own script. God, I dunno, fucking *missionary* position with your husband versus sex in a sex club with whomever the fuck you want.

'Contrast is one of the most powerful tools we've got as content creators. You don't need me to tell you that. Fuck, even the titles are contrasting. *Paradise Lost* versus *Paradise Found*. The first parts of every pair I just threw at you belong in the *Paradise Lost* episode. You know it. And you know as well as I do that when you lessen the contrast, you lessen the impact of the message.'

Silence, then Mara blows out a breath. 'What she said.'

'Old, traditional husband versus young, hot boyfriend?' I offer weakly.

Mara doesn't miss a beat. 'Heteronormative monogamy with a privately educated white male versus heteronormative monogamy with a privately educated white male.'

'Give me a break,' I say. 'You two are vicious.'

'You know I'm in the school of tough love,' she says, slapping her hand on the table so hard it makes me jump. 'You know you don't pay me to blow smoke up your arse. And

Lizzy here has what you're missing in buckets, my darling. That's perspective.'

I turn to stare blankly at the screen. At the victorious face of the woman who's made a bet and gotten one hell of a payout.

'It's not about what I want, is it?' I mutter.

'Nope,' Mara says, at the same time Lizzy says, 'Afraid not. It's about the messaging. What's the most helpful, most impactful message you can end with? What will resonate so much with the audience that you'll have women turning it over in their minds when they go to bed that night?

'That you can drop back into a relationship, even if you've gone about finding it in a slightly less orthodox one than your first one? Or that it's okay not to have answers? It's okay to have no fucking clue what the future holds—that the very uncertainty that lies before you is what puts the colour into life?

'That the stability we've been taught for so many years to strive for, in our jobs and in our family life, is often pretty fucking overrated? So, no. I'm afraid, in this instance, it's not actually about what you want. It's about using your highly visible platform and your immense privilege to send a clear message, which is exactly what you chose to do when you signed up for this gig.'

~

I CRAWL home via the school run with my head spinning. The headache is making it harder to think, and the thinking is worsening the pain. As luck would have it, Cal's coming over this evening to meet the boys. My plans to cook are rapidly dissolving into nothingness. Takeout it is.

I should probably manage Cal's expectations on my rapidly escalating personality failure.

You ok with a lowkey one tonight? I have a bad headache so I may not be much fun

oh baby. So sorry. Do you want to cancel?

No—the boys are super excited to meet my "fun friend" Cal. Come over. I'll get takeout

I'm excited to meet them too. Not as excited as I am to see you...

I sigh to myself as I pull crumpled school pants out of Kit's PE bag. He had games last period, so he's still in his sports stuff and his uniform looks awfully like King Kong has sat on it. We've had infinite conversations about this, but it always comes back to the same thing.

Officially, the teachers don't give them enough changing time to factor in the systematic folding of uniform before stuffing it in their bags.

Unofficially, Kit doesn't give a flying fuck.

When I've laid the clothes out on the back of the couch in the hope that the creases will magically drop out all on their own, I pick up my phone again.

I'm excited to see you too xx

It's true. More than true. I feel especially weepy and clingy this afternoon, a state I'm pretty sure is seventy-five percent PMS and twenty-five percent courtesy of Liz and Mara's emotional battery.

I'll sort dinner. I can pop to Sally Clarke's.
Do they eat lasagne?

He's an angel. Sally Clarke is a food writer who runs a catering business and wonderful deli in Kensington. She's a lifesaver when you're cash rich and time poor. It's pathetic how quickly I yield.

Yes and perfect thank you x

Poor Cal. Hopefully, he's not interested in me for my homemaking skills.

68

CAL

Aida still has a security guard at her door, but there are no paps when I show up. Looks like he's scared them all off.

My visit this time is a little different. No mask or rope or other kinky fuckery, just a Sally Clarke carrier bag full of comfort food and a couple of VR headsets that were a spontaneous idea and may just hold the key to this evening's success for all concerned.

She answers the door looking pale and tired and gorgeous, and the hallway is deserted enough for me to drop my things on the floor and enfold her in a huge bear hug. She looks like she could use one and, sure enough, she clings to me hard.

'How are you feeling?' I murmur, my lips moving against her glossy hair. I could happily stand with her like this all night.

'Shitty, but I'll live,' she says, her arms wrapping around my back. She smells divine. 'Sorry I won't be the life and soul of the party.'

'Actually, you're not invited to the pre-dinner party.'

'No?' She pulls away a little so she can look up at me, and I shoot her a grin.

'Nope. As soon as I've stuck the food in the oven, you are going to run yourself a bath and go have a good soak while I bond with the boys. I have just the thing.'

She eyes me suspiciously. 'Are you my fairy godmother?'

'Something like that. I definitely have the legs for a tutu. Honestly. Trust me. I've got this.'

I'm nowhere on the parenting skills scale, but I do know how to have fun with kids—mainly because I still am one, most of the time. I also have a sound understanding of the value of well-timed bribes where kids are concerned.

I pick up the bags and follow her down the hall, taking a quick break from ogling her arse to check out my reflection in the mirror. *Looking good as usual, mate.*

If Aida had daughters, I'd be bricking it, but I'm not nervous about meeting her sons. What can I say? Boys are pretty basic, and I already know they like cricket. We'll be fine.

~

THESE KIDS ARE FUNNY. As I predicted, they go fucking mental when I show them I've brought two Oculus Quest headsets with me.

'How come you have two?' Aida asks, watching in confusion as Pip and Kit tear into them. We're in the basement, which is a very nice den area and the perfect space for playing VR games. There are no stairs they can accidentally fall down while they're exploring the jungle or the forest.

'Rafe and I used to play a lot at my place before Belle came along and ruined everything,' I mutter. 'One of them's technically his.'

'I see,' she says with a knowing smirk that makes me feel about twelve years old. I can tell she's visualising me and Rafe going for it amidst the sophisticated minimalism of my flat, and I suspect whatever she's imagining, the reality was even dorkier.

Not that there's any way I'm exposing Aida's kids to Blades of Sorcery or Population One anytime soon. We'll be sticking firmly with Gorilla Tag this evening. I'm confident they'll love it. I mean, kids are basically chimps, right?

'Hang on a sec, mate,' I tell Pip. He's got his headset on, but it's way too big for his little head. 'I need to tighten this thing up. Aida, go and have a bath. Honestly. I've got this.'

'Really?' she asks in a tone that begs me to be sincere.

'Yep.' I jerk my head towards the door for good measure. 'Go.'

'Okay. Thanks.' She looks like she wants to kiss me, but a glance at her boys has her heading for the door instead. 'You don't need to tell me twice.'

I allow my gaze to linger on her retreating figure before turning back to the boys. 'Right. Now we've got rid of your mum, we can really have some fun. Ready for Gorilla Tag?'

'I am!' the little one, Kit, shouts. After only five minutes, I can tell he's basically how I was as a kid. Fearless enthusiasm. Act first, think later. Unlike his brother, who seems more circumspect. He's an observer of the world, I suspect. A thinker.

Not unlike his mother.

'My friend Milan has Gorilla Tag and he says it's the funnest game ever,' Pip chimes in. 'He hasn't got further than the Canyons, though.'

My brain glitches a little.

'Hang on—you have a friend called *Milan*?'

'Yeah.' If he thinks that's fucked up, he doesn't mention it.

Okaaay then. I'm hoping Milan's parents have a keen sense of humour, but I doubt it, somehow.

Poor little fucker.

I tighten their headsets and adjust them until both boys tell me they can see the forest around them clearly. Their noisy whoops of surprised delight tell me they like what they see. Once they've got their controllers in their hands, I begin my tutorial.

'Right. So, moving forward is called the funny run. Use your arms like this.' I grab Pip's skinny little arms and move them in a doggy-paddle motion. I suspect he'll require more tutelage than Kit who, sure enough, appears to already be funny running.

We cover off branching—jumping from branch to branch—duking, and lucio, which is running super fast. Within moments, they're writhing around on the spot, their little arms a blur of movement, their voices growing noisier as they react and interact.

I wonder if Rafe and I look quite so ludicrous when we play together.

Probably.

Still, it cracks me up watching them as they have the time of their lives.

Seems like shameless bribery and novelty factor are the perfect formula for these little guys to accept me into their lives, if only on the most superficial level.

69

CAL

'I'm going upstairs to check on dinner,' I say after about twenty minutes. The boys have the hang of the game—it's truly unbelievable how quickly kids pick these things up—and their disinterested grunts tell me their interest level in where I'm going is zero.

Excellent.

After a quick peek in the oven to confirm the lasagne is on track, I take the stairs two at a time to Aida's room. I wasn't focused on anything but her the other day, but her home is undeniably stunning: an enormous fuck-off Georgian villa with a seemingly effortless mix of style and comfort. It wouldn't look out of place on the pages of a glossy interiors magazine, but it's very much a home, too.

Once again, this formidable woman makes it look easy. And by *it* I mean juggling an insane career, single parenting, and running a household big enough to be a hotel.

'Hey,' I say softly, mainly as a warning, as I head into her ensuite bathroom. The room is dim, lit only by a scattering of candles on the shelf, the air a warm, fragrant cloud. Aida's lying in the tub, her head resting on a towel and the water level high enough that her tits are completely obscured by bubbles, more's the pity. Her collarbones and shoulders glint in the candlelight, but when I crouch down by her side and she turns her head towards me, I can see she's been crying.

She sniffs. 'Are the boys okay?'

'They're fine.' I take the hand resting on the side of the tub and run my thumb over her wet knuckles. 'They're like pigs in shit down there.'

'Thanks.' She gives me a weak smile.

'Want to tell me what's up?' I ask gently.

'I wouldn't know where to start.' She looks away and shifts below the water.

'Try me. You upset about the coverage again?'

She blows out a breath. 'No, not really. I mean, yeah, obviously I am, but I've managed to zone the majority of it out. And I can't tell you how many shitty, judgemental passive-aggressive comments I've gotten from the moms at school this week. But I can handle most of it.'

I wait, the skin of my dry hand flush against her damp one. If these are parents who think it's all right to name their sons *Milan* then I can only imagine how obnoxious they must be.

'I'm just... I dunno. I'm spiralling and being pathetic.'

In light of my observation just now, this judgement seems inaccurate at best. Aida Russell's idea of *pathetic* is what most normal people would call *crazily high-functioning.*

'I bet you're neither. But it's okay to be both. If you can't lose your shit in the bathtub, where can you?'

That earns me a weak smile. 'True.'

Again, I wait.

'People keep asking me what I want. You asked me what I wanted, that very first time.'

I frown. 'Right...'

'And I realise being asked what you want is the epitome of privilege, and—'

'Baby. You don't need caveats with me. Spit it out.'

Her expression is defeated as she turns to look at me.

'It's like they ask—other people, not you—but they're really asking what I think I should want. Or should think. The production team. Mara. Lizzy. I feel like I've created this persona of Aida Russell, progressive superwoman, who's always on message and never lets her mask slip and is, like, this paragon of perfection who gets paraded around.'

'That sounds fucking exhausting,' I say. It's true. Her accomplishments, her pace, the number of balls she has in the air at any given time... they all make me feel tired. I just didn't realise they made *her* feel tired too, and it's reassuring, somehow.

'Yeah,' she mouths, then snags her bottom lip between her teeth. She looks as though she's deliberating on something.

I brush my fingers lightly over her jaw. 'So,' I say as gently as possible, because I don't want to come at her like a bull in a china shop and risk her clamming up, 'if I was to ask you what *you* really want right now, would that be helpful or unhelpful?'

Her eyes are huge and dark, luminous with unshed tears.

She's not deliberating anymore.

She's on a fucking precipice.

'I want,' she says slowly, a tiny furrow appearing between her eyebrows, 'to find the courage to enjoy this process without feeling endlessly beholden to a million parties.'

'And what process is that?' I whisper.

She lets out a long, shuddery sigh, but her eyes don't leave mine. 'This process where I'm falling deeply, terrifyingly in love with you.'

The silence that follows her words is one that splits my heart open. If anyone is capable of delivering a mic-drop comment, it's Aida, but there's something about the simplicity of her words and her willingness to let them hover between us, in this damp, scented air, that has me reeling.

I can't stop staring. It's as if I'm terrified that, by dropping eye contact, I'll shatter the sheer magic of this moment.

But I can't leave her hanging, either.

Nor can I resist the smile that's growing, threatening to split my face in two.

'You're in love with me?'

Her eyes dart over my face. She's on the brink of reneging. Of turning and throwing herself onto solid ground, saving herself from that sheer drop. 'I know it's quick,' she gabbles, pulling her hand out from beneath mine. 'I mean—'

'No.' I grab her wrists. '*No.* I'm not going to let you ruin this with logic.' I bend further over the side of the tub so my face is inches from hers, my thumbs taking the frantic pulse beating through the thin skin of her wrist. She's a deer in the headlights, but I've got her.

'Baby,' I say, my gaze searching her face, 'are you saying you love me?'

It's the most important question I've ever asked anyone, and the way she inhales tells me she understands that.

'Yes,' she says, her voice and gaze steadying in my grip.

'*Good.*' I close the gap between us, my kiss as emphatic as my tone. I don't know how this happened; I don't know how on earth a muppet like me has caught the heart of a woman like Aida. But, as I've said before, I'll take whatever she has to give.

No qualms.

No shame.

No regrets.

Her mouth is soft, her lips tear-slicked when I suck on them. I release her wrists so I can cup her jaw. My cashmere-covered elbows hit bubbles and hot water, but I don't care, because the most captivating woman I have ever met loves me, and everything else is dust.

When I seek out her tongue, her kisses go from tentative to hungry. Then I'm invading her mouth properly, pouring my disbelief and gratitude and adoration and hope into her through the language in which I'm most conversant. She responds in kind, her body arching into me, lips and tongue sliding against mine, hands weaving through my hair.

It's heaven, this kiss. It's unconscionable, really, that flesh on flesh can feel so like soaring. But after a few moments I pull away, because it's time to try out a new language for size.

It's time to come out with a phrase I've never uttered to a woman before, in a language I'm far less fluent in.

I throw myself off the precipice to join her in the exhilaration of this free-fall.

'I'm in love with you, too,' I tell her, and I see a thousand fireworks flare in those black eyes of hers at my words.

Is this what it's like?

Quiet, simple utterances that, when whispered to another human being, can cause planets to shift and suns to rise and stars to burst?

70

AIDA

"Two hearts in love need no words."
—Milton, *Paradise Lost*

There's a tightness, an ache, in my chest at his words, but it's a good ache, I think. It's the same ache I get when I check on my sleeping boys at night. When I look down at them and wonder how the hell I got so lucky. When the rush of love is so visceral and terrifying that I have to remind myself all is good.

Nothing's wrong.

I can lean into this feeling, revel in it.

A thousand reasons to pull back are humming beneath the surface, but they can't compete with the reality of him, right here. His words. His tone. The way he's looking at me, the way his face relaxed as he told me he loved me, as if the declaration lightened his entire being. Changed him, somehow.

We stay like that for a moment, silent except for the

faintest lap of water and the sighs of our breaths. This instant is a bubble, as fragile as it is beautiful, and I sense neither of us wants to break it.

There's a smile dawning on my face, though, at the understanding that Cal is in love with me, that this gorgeous, passionate, vital man who has always struck me as an untameable beast has seen something in me that makes him whole. That his soul recognises my soul.

If that's not joyful, I don't know what is.

His smile is breathtaking. 'Beautiful Aida,' he whispers, the hand on my jaw sliding around to cup my neck so he can close the gap between us again. His kiss is worshipful and incredulous, as if kissing me now is a totally different experience from before.

I yield to the perfect fusion of our mouths. My body is tired, but my heart is hopeful.

Surely *I love you* can be a new beginning as well as an endgame?

Surely we don't have to have everything figured out right this second?

I'm not used to acting without all my ducks in the neatest little row, but if Cal and I are doing everything in the wrong order, then my only option is to trust that we can figure this shit out together.

Because we've known each other for a matter of weeks.

I've been divorced for a matter of months.

He's spent less than a half hour with the two most important people in my life.

I'm about to release a show where apparently I'm preaching to women that great sex without love is both morally acceptable and highly recommended.

In a nutshell, this entire thing is fucking insane, and my only two options are to do a one-eighty so fast I get whiplash or to lean in and trust Cal to help me build a workable, practical structure around these crazy feelings we have for each other.

Cal ends our kiss with a gentle tug on my lower lip before resting his forehead to mine. 'Can I tell you some of my wishes?'

'Sure,' I whisper, luxuriating in the feel of his thick hair between my fingers.

'They're for down the line, not tonight, so don't freak out,' he says, and I hum my acknowledgement. It seems I'm not the only one spiralling headlong into the future.

'But I wish for a time where I don't have to leave after dinner,' he says. 'I want to be able to climb into this tub with you and take you to bed afterwards. And yeah, I realise that also means I help you put the boys to bed, and that one epic game of Gorilla Tag doesn't earn me the right to do that yet, but I'd like to try to earn it.'

'I'd like that,' I murmur, my thumb stroking the skin at the back of his neck, tentative hope coursing through my veins.

'Yeah? Good,' he says softly.

I take a deep breath. 'I realise it's very early in this... relationship. And I don't want all the steps we haven't taken to detract in any way from what I just said to you. Because I mean it. But I also recognise we have a long way to go.'

'So you're basically telling me you're gagging to be my girlfriend?' he asks, and I laugh, because that's such a Cal thing to say.

'I am literally begging for it,' I say.

'Yeah, I can tell. So I passed my audition, then?'

'You nailed it so hard. Harder than anyone's ever nailed it.' I move my face so I can drag my lips over his beard.

'I'll nail *you* so hard.'

'You'd better.'

'I will. I'll come over as soon as you get those little chimps off to school tomorrow.'

'Glad to hear it.'

He pauses. 'Just so I have an idea... do you think you'll talk to them at some point? About us?'

I've been thinking about this all evening. 'Yeah. I should probably talk to them tonight, after you've gone.'

'Good idea. I'm riding high on the Gorilla Tag bribery right now. We should close the deal while the momentum is in my favour,' he says, and I laugh.

'Absolutely. Make the bribery work for us.'

'Right?' He pauses again. 'How do you think they'll take it?'

'I honestly have no idea,' I tell him, and it's true. 'I know they'll like you—how could they not? But they've also had a shitty year. That said, Pip's been pretty protective of me. So if I have a new, um, boyfriend who makes me happy, I'm hoping that's something they can get behind.'

'That's something we can all get behind,' he says. 'I don't want to rush any of you, but I also don't want to sneak around. You should know I don't give a shit who sees us or what photos they publish, but obviously I want to make sure you've had whatever chats you need to with the boys before we get outed.'

'I'll talk to them,' I promise. 'I need to talk to the *Paradise* team too and get our message straightened out.'

'What's the problem?' he asks.

I sigh. 'Messaging. They think my entering into another monogamous relationship isn't the right way to end the documentary, optically speaking. It's not... radical enough.'

His mouth twists. 'Fuck's sake. If they saw the stuff we

get up to together, they'd change their tune. So what do they want?'

'They've got the footage. I mean, those reshoots from last week look incredible—exactly what we wanted. It's more my voiceover. I need to lock myself in my study and figure it out. We've got this one opportunity to pack a punch, you know? And I don't know yet what that punch will be.'

'If they think you and I being together is too boring and predictable a note to end the show on,' he says, 'then we'd better show them they're wrong, hadn't we?'

'What do you mean?'

'Once you've spoken to Pip and Kit, we go public in a big way. I'm sorry, but there's no way the tabloids won't swallow that shit up.'

'They'll say it's a publicity stunt.'

'I don't give a flying fuck what they say.' He traces the outline of my cupid's bow with a fingertip. 'It is a publicity stunt, it's just a real one. You keep talking about changing the narrative. It's your fucking show. You should set the agenda.

'Let's see how excited we can get people about the prospect of us being together. If we play our cards right, they'll be clamouring for more of us as a couple. Then you can talk all you like at the end of the show about how much you love me, and they'll eat it up.'

He shrugs, a cocky grin on his face, and I survey him thoughtfully. He's oversimplifying, but he has a point. And much as I dislike the idea of willingly throwing us and our fledgling relationship into the spotlight, I can't deny it would be a powerful way of ensuring that the messaging in the show lines up precisely with both what I want in life *and* the kind of impact Lizzy and Mara want the show to have.

Who says the idea of my settling down with Cal is

boring? I for one know it's anything but. So maybe it's time to take a little of that heady magic that Cal Sinclair weaves upon womankind and sprinkle his fairy dust more widely.

If half the female population is in love with the idea of him, and us, before the show even airs, then I've made my point.

A relationship with Cal is *more* radical, *more* exciting, than unfettered sex at Alchemy is.

'You're a media genius,' I tell him. 'Ever considered a career as a political spin doctor?'

He grins and replaces his fingertip with his mouth for a gentle kiss. 'I'm far too morally upstanding.'

'Hmm,' is my diplomatic reply to that. I keep ahold of his shoulders while I pull myself upright. The flare of hunger in his eyes when he sees my wet breasts is unmistakable. He reaches down to weigh them in his hands, flicking a thumb over each nipple, and I shiver at the pleasure of it.

'Jesus, sweetheart,' he says reverently to my breasts, eyelashes fanning over his cheeks. 'So fucking beautiful.' He releases them and strokes my cheek with a wistful smile before getting to his feet.

'Ouch. Dead legs. You soak, okay? I'll check dinner and keep an eye on the boys.' He stoops to kiss my forehead. 'I love you. And I'm here for whatever media circus you think is necessary. Bring it on.'

71

CAL

'I have a girlfriend,' I announce to the room at large. 'And she loves me.' I pause. 'And I love her, obviously.'

Cue stunned silences all around me.

Except, that is, for Norm, who opens his jaws to emit the most enormous yawn before settling his head back on the rug.

I have no idea how I've kept this to myself all week. I wanted to wait until Aida had chatted to her boys and pitched my PR strategy to the *Paradise* team.

Suffice to say, the boys were an easier win than Lizzy and Mara, but the latter are coming around. They've reluctantly agreed to record various voiceover options for the ending and to withhold judgement until we can assess how the public responds to Aida and me. The *Paradise* trailer was hot as fuck, but that's not enough for anyone to go on.

They need to see us in action.

Which is why I'm doing the school run with Aida later and will also be an enthusiastic audience member on the *Gordon Kay* show when she makes her appearance on his sofa tonight.

Back to the stunned silences.

Gen recovers first. What a shocker. 'Wow. Well, I love this for you,' she says with her usual cat-like grin. 'Honestly. For both of you. I'm so happy for you two.'

'Thanks, babe,' I tell her.

Rafe and Zach are nodding like proud fathers. 'Didn't think we'd see the day, mate,' Zach says. 'I mean... I would never have put you two together in a million years, but like Gen says, I love it. She's...' He trails off and holds his hands up, like Aida defies description, which is a sentiment I can get behind.

'I know,' I say. 'It's crazy. She's like some kind of brainiac megastar who's also sex on legs. She's so fucking accomplished, too. The woman makes me feel simultaneously exhausted and so proud it's ridiculous.'

'She's a proper grownup,' Maddy says sagely. 'She's like Zach, but famous.'

'And a lot sexier,' I point out.

'We need to meet her again so we can see you two together properly,' Rafe says. 'Last time at the club you were both really fucking awkward.'

'No we weren't,' I lie, because that evening was pretty uncomfortable. I didn't know how to act around Aida, and Maddy shot her mouth off, which didn't help. 'But yeah, you do. You'll see her at your engagement drinks.'

Rafe rolls his eyes. 'Like I'll be able to enjoy catching up with my mates then. I'll be too busy trying to play nicely for Belle's dad and his cronies so he doesn't disown her and ruin her life because she's too good a person to cut him off like she should.'

I grimace. 'And we don't mention the A-word, right?'

'No. Alchemy doesn't exist.' He sighs. 'I dislike the lying, but there is no point in rubbing salt in the wound by telling

Belle's parents that the guy who corrupted and stole their darling daughter also runs a sex club. It would finish off their relationship once and for all.'

'I totally agree,' Maddy says. She's known Belle since their school days, so, aside from Rafe, she's probably the best qualified of us all to weigh in. 'Belle's come so far since she started dating you, Rafe. Her parents know meddling in your relationship won't get them anywhere. They're just about holding down a civilised relationship now, so for God's sake, let's try to keep it that way.'

'Agreed,' Rafe says. 'Still think Dex should swing by when he's in town. I'd like to get him on board with me and Belle properly.'

'Dex is *super* hot,' Maddy muses, earning her a scowl from Zach. 'All Belle's school friends were in love with him. And he's kind of fucked up, which is always a turn on.'

'Only if you're dysfunctional,' Zach growls.

'Alas, women always go for fucked-up guys,' she sighs, but she's too nice to make a meaningful face at her boyfriend, because he was the epitome of fucked up when they got it on.

I narrow my eyes in amused suspicion. 'Did you and Dex ever...'

'God, no,' she says. 'Not for lack of trying, though. He's six years older than us, so he had no time for Belle's silly little friends. He moved to New York when we were around sixteen, I think. More's the pity.'

'And then you went for someone properly old,' I point out, and we all laugh. We may be the same age as Rafe, but that's not the point.

'Changing the subject,' Zach says through gritted teeth, 'what's up next for you and your very hot new girlfriend?'

Rafe replies before I can. 'If you'd told me six months

ago that Cal had fallen for one of the smartest people on television, I'd have laughed in your face.'

'Same, mate,' Zach says, though he's grinning now. 'But what's even more insane is that she's fallen for our Cal. Right?'

They're right. Obviously. It hits me like a tonne of bricks over and over.

I make Aida Russell happy.

It's fucking insane.

I'd say I'm the least cerebral of the lot of us. I'm a pretty straightforward guy, and I know how to have a laugh. What you see is what you get with me.

Who knew that would be what she wanted?

'Knock it off,' Gen says sharply. 'Yeah, they're opposites, but you could say the same for all of you. And probably me and Anton, too. So be happy for them.'

'Sorry,' they murmur in unison.

'Obviously, we're thrilled for you, mate,' Zach says, looking a little stricken. 'She's one hell of a lucky woman.'

'Thanks,' I say.

'Yeah,' Rafe chimes in. 'We didn't mean—we love you, bro. She has fucking good taste, if you ask me.'

I know they're happy for me—ribbing each other relentlessly is what we do. And I get it—it's really fun to watch your friends fall head over heels for someone you would never in a million years have matched them with.

I guess that's one of the beautiful mysteries of love. Another, it seems, is thinking you're the luckiest bastard in the world. Being totally bewildered that you get to be with this unique, captivating person and—and this is the really weird bit—knowing that, by some crazy magic, they feel exactly the same about you.

What's up with that?

It blows my mind, actually.

So when Zach tells me Aida's a lucky woman, I find myself hoping that he's not just saying that as my loyal friend. I want nothing more than to make her feel like the *happiest* woman in the world every day. And if that also makes her feel *lucky*, I'll take it.

'Anyway,' I clear my throat, because I don't want Rafe, Zach and I to start hugging it out and braiding each other's hair any more than they do. 'We're about to go on a bit of a publicity spree—give people plenty of reasons to get behind us as a couple—'

'I can help!' Maddy says, bouncing a little on the sofa to make her point. 'We can definitely do some of the heavy lifting via the Alchemy socials. Ooh, I feel a few cutesy reels and TikToks coming on.'

'Honestly, I'd love that,' I tell her. 'Basically, Creatrix is giving Aida a hard time about any messaging that so much as hints at a monogamous happy ever after. They want this documentary to really pack some punches, so we need to show everyone that being with me is punchy as fuck.'

'Amen to that,' Rafe drawls, and everyone laughs.

'Why do I suspect you're far more comfortable with that than Aida is?' Gen asks.

'Because you know what an attention whore he is,' Zach points out. 'Remember that fashion show at uni when he went out on the catwalk in just a pair of too-small briefs, all oiled up with a fucking *tyre* on each arm?'

'What, a car tyre?' Maddy asks, as the rest of us fall about laughing.

'Yep,' Gen says drily. 'I can never unsee it, unfortunately.'

'I could have had any girl in the entire fucking place that night,' I protest. 'They were gagging for it. My Hot Mechanic routine was like catnip to every girl there.'

It happens to be true.

'Dear God,' Gen says.

'From Hot Mechanic to Hot Armed Robber in the *Paradise* trailer,' Maddy muses. 'It all makes *so* much more sense now.'

'Fifteen years on and he's still working the baby oil,' Zach says, and I guffaw along with the rest of them, because the guy has a point.

72

CAL

It's Gen who corners me, discreetly but deliberately, in our kitchenette a bit later.

'So,' she says, smiling down at the spoon she's using to stir her tea bag in her treasured *Wolff Holdings* mug. That woman is a total simp for her boyfriend. 'Monogamy, eh?'

Ah. So *this* is where she's going with it.

'Yep,' I say.

'I have to hand it to you.' She looks up at me through her eyelashes. 'Aida's… amazing.'

'She is.'

'I never thought, when…' She shakes her head. 'It's really fantastic, that's all. I strongly suspected you two would have chemistry, but I didn't see you falling in love. I'm thrilled to bits.'

'She's very easy to love,' I say, and she smiles.

'As are you,' she says quietly but firmly.

I smirk. 'Obviously.' I've been told I'm lovable all my life. I suppose it comes with having always been a smiley kid and then a good-natured adult—people warm to me. But that's totally different from having a beautiful, mesmerising, intellectual powerhouse of a woman fall hook, line and sinker for me.

Nope. *That's* a singular pleasure I'll wallow in for as long as Aida bestows her love upon me.

'Still,' Gen muses aloud as she squishes her tea bag at the side of the cup, 'it's a big change in lifestyle for you. Going from Alchemy to a monogamous relationship.' She fixes her big blue eyes back on me once she's disposed of the tea bag, and I feel the weight of her scrutiny.

This is the part where I could get defensive. Where I could say *Well, I've managed so far* or *You guys did it. Why not me?* But I don't, because I know exactly how she means it. There's no snark intended. Just concern for, I suspect, me and Aida alike.

Because she's right. I've ribbed all three of my mates mercilessly for dropping like flies this past year. It's been ridiculous, frankly, how fast and hard they've fallen. Even if our little Alchemy family has only got better for having Belle and Maddy and, I suppose, even Anton, as part of it. Even if I've never seen my friends happier.

So I've carried the flag for this glorious club and the particular delights it offers. Beautiful strangers and a wonderful buffet of varied, kinky, endless sex. I've partied and gorged and dreamt up events intended to thrill. To arouse. And I've been the life and soul of every party we've thrown. I'm that guy.

I was that guy.

And I can see why my apparent one-eighty might give Gen whiplash. It shouldn't—but I can see why it would.

'Yeah,' I tell her now. 'A massive change.'

'I just wanted to check in with you,' she whispers, 'to make sure you've really thought it through. I know it's none of my business, but I feel responsible for Aida. I couldn't bear it if she'd come here looking to gain confidence and she got her heart broken in the process.'

The mere thought of that happening is enough to make me feel sick to my stomach.

'No.' I shake my head forcefully. 'No one's getting their heart broken. Definitely not Aida, anyway. Maybe me. Who knows? And look. I haven't necessarily thought it through in the way you mean. I haven't sat there and obsessed about how different my life will look every single evening—and maybe I should, I dunno.

'It's way more instinctive than that, you know? I'm kind of being led by my feelings here. I'm not explaining it very well, but it's like I don't even have a choice.'

I pause. I get emotional even thinking about her, especially when I'm not with her. 'It's like this fucking massive tidal wave of, like, love and lust and adoration has just swept over me, and I'm being carried along, and I have no fucking clue where I'm going or which way is up, but I can tell you I am happy as Larry to go along for the ride.'

Gen's staring at me, her face soft and her eyes teary. She sniffs. 'Well, that's absolutely lovely.'

'So when you say *monogamy*, like it's some sort of intentional decision or even a commitment? It's honestly not. Like I said, I have no choice because I can't even conceive of another option. I don't want anyone else.'

I shudder, because the idea of being with any of the women at Alchemy now seriously gives me the heebie-jeebies. And if she'd wanted to use her time at the club to explore other options, I would have fucking died. Dead. No doubt about it.

Thank fuck I didn't emancipate her *that* much, eh?

'What I have with her is so…' I can't even find the way to

describe it. 'It means so much. It's a totally different experience from fucking random women. Why would I want to go near anyone else when I can be with *her*, you know?'

Her. It's a tiny word, but when I use it to refer to Aida, it feels like it should come with a capital H. Like she's God, or something.

Because she is fucking everything. *Everything.*

Gen's still staring, but she collects herself and puts her mug on the counter before closing the gap between us and wrapping her arms tightly around my neck. I reciprocate gladly.

You wouldn't think Gen's a great hugger, because she can come off as a bit of an ice queen if you don't know her. But she really is. First of all, her tits are amazing and cushiony, which always helps. She smells incredible, and she only gives hugs when she really wants to, like right now. She's squeezing me so tight.

'Yeah,' she whispers into my ear, 'the boy's got it bad. That's definitely love.' She sniffs again. 'God, she's a lucky girl. And our little Cal's all grown up.'

'Fuck off,' I say lightheartedly, and she hugs me harder.

'I'm so happy for you both.' She releases me and kind of squishes my face with a little slap at the end. 'Don't fuck it up.'

'I won't.' I have no intention of ever, ever messing this up. 'Now, I have to go take my girl for a very public lunch.'

73

AIDA

"The great end of life is not knowledge but action."
—Milton, *Paradise Lost*

A few well-timed calls from Mara to some of the classier society photographers pay dividends. Cal and I are photographed strolling along leafy Westbourne Grove together, his arm clamped firmly around my shoulder. As we stroll and chat, he keeps leaning over to pepper my temple and jaw and cheek with kisses so sweet I know they have nothing to do with the cameras.

Let me rephrase, because my boyfriend is an attention whore and I know he's in performance mode. They aren't *just* for the cameras.

I don't mind that we're being watched, though, because the sheer relief of being out and about with Cal is immense. Being able to go where I please with him is as important as it is delicious. I've endured the dark side of celebrity this year, but before John caused headlines, I could pretty much do as I please. I wasn't of any more interest than the dozens of glossy, vaguely familiar people who frequent this neighbourhood.

Our relationship couldn't have gotten off to a less traditional start, so it's crucial for me that we get *some* traditional parts, like strolling around, and window shopping, and just being—in a way that doesn't necessarily involve nudity or masks or bondage, that is.

We sit down for an alfresco sidewalk lunch at one of the area's chic eateries. It's pretty cold, but we're wrapped up in heavy coats, and the restaurant has outdoor heaters.

'I want to buy you something here,' Cal tells me, booping me on my nose.

'Let me guess. Underwear?' I ask.

'Not necessarily. Just something pretty.'

I smile at him, hoping my face reflects the warm, gooey feeling inside of me. 'You can always buy me something pretty. And maybe after, we can walk down Portobello and buy you a new gimp mask from the market?'

He lets out a hearty chuckle, and I love it. 'Aren't they more about antique spoons and Harry Styles posters?'

'You never know. You might get lucky.'

We're awaiting our coffees when two young women who can't be older than eighteen approach us. They're both fair-haired, very pretty, and carrying handbags no eighteen-year-old should be able to afford—if indeed they're even that old. It's so hard to tell these days.

I don't love being approached in public, but it would be churlish of me to begrudge it when this little stunt is an exercise in courting publicity.

'Hi,' one of them says while her friend giggles nervously. They're both looking back and forward between the two of us.

'Hey there,' I say warmly.

'Um, are you Callum?' she says, and I press my lips together to hide my amused smile.

Cal flashes them a grin that should come with its own hazard sign. 'I certainly am. How are you doing?'

'Oh my God.' They dissolve into a fit of giggles. 'That's so cool. Um, we follow you on Instagram. And TikTok. We can't wait for the show.'

I flinch inwardly, because these girls are absolutely not my target market, and the idea that they and their friends will tune into my very personal and age-specific journey is seriously horrifying. It rams home just how very public my story will be.

Maybe I should have fucked someone who'd be far less appealing to every age group out there.

Cal, on the other hand, appears not to be horrified at all. 'Ahh, that's so sweet of you,' he says. 'Thank you, honestly.'

'Do you think we could get a selfie?' the other one asks. 'If it's not too much trouble?'

'Of course,' he says, pushing back his chair and getting to his feet. 'With both of us?'

Their faces fall at the mere thought of me photobombing their selfie. 'Just with you, if that's okay?' the first one says.

'How about I take it?' I say briskly, to prevent embarrassment all around. They drape themselves over my boyfriend, who looks far too pleased with himself.

I hand the first girl back her phone when I'm done.

'Thank you so much,' she says. 'So are you guys, like, together?'

I glance at Cal.

'We're together,' he says with a firm nod of confirmation as he sits back down. 'Aida's my girlfriend.'

'Oh,' they chorus, looking totally crestfallen. 'Well, thank you and good luck with it,' one says feebly as they edge away backwards.

When I look over at him, he's grinning to himself.

'Just say it,' I say.

'I'm more famous than you.'

'You're such an asshole. And you're not. *They're not my demographic.*'

'You tell yourself that. And I have more Instagram followers than you do now.'

'That's because I don't take my shirt off constantly on social media.'

'Maybe you should. You've got great tits.'

'I'll take that under consideration, thank you. Anyway, I have more LinkedIn followers than you. I have, like, a hundred thousand.'

He attempts a straight face. 'I mean, that's seriously impressive.' He nods earnestly. 'LinkedIn. Wow. Yeah, you should be so proud of what you've achieved.'

I unfold my napkin and slap his arm with it. 'Fuck you.'

'Yes, please.'

'Ugh.' I throw back my head and look heavenward. 'I've created a total monster.'

IF LUNCH with Cal is a lesson in humility (for me only), then picking the boys up from their extortionate, elitist, overly British prep school is one big fabulous Fuck You moment.

I've had looks and comments all week at drop-off and pickup. The comments have tended towards back handed compliments and passive aggressive observations, heavy on the *you're so brave* and *presumably the BBC isn't thrilled about it* and *gosh, a sex club, really?* They've inevitably included commentary on Cal, too:

A younger man!

Doesn't the age gap bother you?

Just don't let him get under your skin, darling.

And, my personal favourite: *Is he taking on other 'clients'?* Like he's some kind of gigolo for hire.

I get that none of the above looks too devastating on paper, but when it's accompanied by wide eyes and raised eyebrows (where Botox allows) and bitchy, affected tittering, I can tell you, it starts to jar. It's all par for the course, but that doesn't make it enjoyable.

I've taken it in stride, and I've chosen to tell myself that my fellow moms' reactions are less the polite moral outrage they pretend to be and more what I've christened Lucky Bitch Syndrome.

I suspect the green-eyed monster has come out to play. There are plenty of divorced parents at this school, and even more attractive women married to very successful guys whose looks may not be their most appealing attribute, if you get what I'm saying. I wouldn't dream of telling anyone else how to live their life, but I do know this.

When you stick your head above the parapet, people are going to treat you as fair game.

And they're going to damn well take aim while they have that clear of a shot.

I guess, in the world of private school moms with too much time on their hands, partnering with a sex club and hooking up with a young, hot guy and *filming* part of that process is the gossip equivalent of climbing up on that parapet with a fucking bullseye on your forehead.

Back to the Fuck You moment.

Cal and I saunter hand in hand through Notting Hill to

the square where the school is. We're five minutes early, but there's already a line of parents and nannies running down the sidewalk. One of the dads, Evan, who runs a large institutional investment firm, raises his eyes from his phone long enough to nod smilingly at me before his gaze shifts to Cal. He jolts. The guy looks like he's seen a ghost. Cal throws a quick *hiya, mate* his way before Evan glues his eyes right back to his phone.

After we've walked a safe distance past him, I murmur, 'Do I want to know how you know him?'

'Probably not,' he says, squeezing my hand, 'but I bet you can guess.'

'Wow. I can, but I never would have.' Evan's divorced, so how he plays in his spare time is no one's business but his. Still, I'm glad I didn't run into him half naked at the Masked Ball, that's for sure.

Ew.

'I bet you know a lot of people's secrets,' I muse.

'You know it, baby. Including yours.'

'Nice.'

I bump my shoulder playfully against his and he halts, tugging on my hand so he can plant a kiss on my lips. It's light and chaste and school gates-friendly, but that sense of how natural it feels hits me hard.

This isn't some dark club.

I'm about to pick up my kids.

With my dreamy, sweet *boyfriend*.

'Why, Aida. Hi there.'

The fawning voice of Lucinda, one of the more self-righteous moms, and the expectant tone of her greeting have me turning away from the kiss. She's with a gaggle of her friends-slash-minions towards the back of the line, and they're all staring at Cal like he's a snow leopard I've stolen from the zoo and am parading around Pembridge Square on a leash.

'Hi there,' I say.

We all stand awkwardly.

'So you're hanging out with your... co-star,' she says. 'That's nice.'

'Um—' I begin, having no earthly clue what else to say.

'Co-star?' Cal says, a broad grin on his face. He lets go of my hand and throws his arm around my shoulder in what feels like a deeply possessive gesture. 'Aww, that's sweet. Are you familiar with the show?'

He just broke School Gates Rule number one.

Never call anyone's bluff.

If I didn't already love him, I would now.

'I—' Lucinda is a goldfish whose water supply is dwindling fast. 'Well, actually...'

'I mean, obviously there's not much to see yet,' he says, winking at Celeste, another mom who's staring at him like she's on a juice cleanse and he's a big fat spaghetti carbonara. 'But you need to tune in when it airs.' His gaze drops to her left hand, which is rammed full of diamond eternity rings. 'It's *very* educational. It might be something to watch with your husband. Or with the girls, if you feel more comfortable. Ladies' Night? You know what I'm saying? You're all exactly the kind of women Aida and her team are targeting with this. Right, baby?'

For once in my largely articulate life, I cannot actually form a sentence.

Lucinda rallies admirably quickly. 'We really don't watch much TV at home. There's far too much to do.'

'Tell me about it,' Cal says. 'Aida and I are usually getting stuck in at my club when we're not with the boys. Aren't we, sweetheart? But we'll also be running a huge social media campaign around the documentary to educate more women on how to take ownership of their sex lives, whether they're single or married. You might be able to fit in the odd "tidbit" between commitments.'

He draws out the word *tidbit*, making it sound downright creepy, and it's funny as fuck. Lucinda stares at him in horror. I think he's broken her brain with his verbal diarrhoea, and I feel a vague sympathy for her. But he's reeling Celeste in faster than you can say *balaclava.*

'So, have you two been filming today, then?' she asks, waggling her finger coyly between us.

'We've pretty much wrapped,' I tell her.

'No, just hanging out,' Cal says. 'Getting to know each other, you know? Sometimes it's healthy to take it out of the bedroom for short periods. Anyway, great to meet you all. Thanks for the support. Hope the programme gives you some inspiration!'

74

CAL

When I turn up at Aida's house to collect her for Rafe's engagement party, it's with an overnight bag and two VR headsets. It's less meanness that's stopped me from leaving the gaming stuff here before for the boys to enjoy than a solid appreciation for how much leverage they represent.

Aida's all dressed up, looking ravishing in a slinky red dress that matches her lips. I kiss her gently to avoid ruining them and follow her into the kitchen, where Kit and Pip are eating their supper.

'Hi,' Pip says, but Kit blurts out, 'Did you bring the Quests?'

'That's very rude,' Aida scolds. 'Greet our guest properly, please.'

He sighs. 'Hi, Cal.' There's a brief pause during which I'm pretty sure he's mentally counting, and then he repeats in a rush, 'Did you bring the Quests?'

'Hiya, guys,' I say. 'Good to see you. Yeah, I did. They're in the hallway.'

'Awesome,' Kit hisses with a glance in that direction, like he might bolt if he thinks he can get away with it.

I pull out a chair and sit down as Aida pours me a glass of wine. 'And you can play with them tonight when we're out, okay? Who's looking after you?'

'Ella,' Pip and Aida say together.

'She's a sweet local girl who's doing her A Levels,' Aida clarifies.

'Excellent. Well make sure you share with Ella if she wants a go, okay?'

They agree reluctantly.

I take a sip of my perfectly chilled crisp white and set it down. 'You know,' I say thoughtfully, 'there's only one problem. I'll have to come back here later and grab them, because I like playing with them on a Saturday morning.'

Kit groans out loud. Pip screws his face up. Aida stares into her wineglass, because she knows what's coming.

'Unless...' I say, looking around the table. 'Nah. Forget it.'

'You could leave one and take one home?' Kit says hopefully.

'I could.' I pretend to think. 'I had an even better idea, but don't worry about it.'

'What?' Pip asks. His forkful of meatballs and pasta hangs suspended in midair.

'Well,' I say slowly. 'I could come back here for a sleepover, and then we could all play with them in the morning while your mum has a lie-in.'

'Wow,' Aida says. 'I have to say, that sounds amazing. Pipster, that pasta's gonna fall, honey.'

I wink at her. I've got this. 'I just don't know where I'd sleep, though,' I say, pretending to grimace.

'You could sleep in my room,' Kit says. 'I've got a sofa bed.' He shovels a huge forkful of meatballs into his mouth.

'I'm way too big for that sofa,' I tell him.

'But we've got a spare room!' Pip shouts. 'You could stay there!'

'I could.' I frown thoughtfully. 'There's only one problem.'

They're hanging on my every word. Jesus, I'm good at this.

'What?' Kit says, mouth hanging open. It's full of masticated meatballs. Grim.

'Don't speak with your mouth full,' Aida says with the weariness of someone who's fought this battle a thousand times.

'It's a bit embarrassing,' I say.

'That's okay,' Pip says kindly. 'This is a judgement-free house, right, Mum?'

Fuck, he's cute. I glance at Aida, who's pressing her lips together.

'Right, honey,' she says.

'That's very kind,' I say. I feel a bit bad now about stringing them along.

'Do you wet the bed?' Kit asks, cocking his head to one side.

No, I do not wet the fucking bed. I shoot him a look of horror. In my peripheral vision, Aida is trying her hardest not to laugh.

'Absolutely not, mate. I'm in full control of my bladder, thank you.' I blow out a breath. 'Okay. Here goes. When I'm not in my own bed, sometimes I have nightmares and cry out for my mummy.'

I let that land. Kit and Pip both look openly torn between amusement and sympathy. Aida gives up the fight and buries her head in her hands. Her shoulders are shaking.

Time to close. 'So... it's best if I don't sleep on my own. I was thinking I could sleep in your mum's bed with her, because she's kind of old like a mummy, and she can cuddle me if I get upset in the night.'

Aida lifts her face and gives me her best *you're never getting laid again* glare. The boys' eyes are round as saucers, and I have the feeling a small part of them suspects they're being played. I maintain my expression of vulnerable sincerity with difficulty.

'But only daddies sleep in bed with mummies,' Pip points out.

I am so incredibly proud of myself in this moment for withstanding the solid gold temptation to make a Daddy joke. Happily, Aida saves me.

'We've talked about this, right?' she asks them. 'You know that adults can share beds with other people, not just their husbands or wives? It's okay for them to share beds with friends as long as everyone feels comfortable and respects each other. *And I know Cal respects me fully.*'

The last sentence is said through gritted teeth.

'It's just for a night,' I say easily. 'We'll be home late, we'll fall asleep, your mummy will cuddle me if I have a bad dream, and then tomorrow morning I'll slay you little chimps at Gorilla Tag, and you can show me which of your breakfast cereals is the most sugary.'

I sit back with a self-satisfied grin and pick up my wine.

And *that*, people, is how it's done.

75

CAL

Because my ugly mate is marrying a seriously elegant woman, it's no surprise to me that Belle has found a characteristically elegant solution to preempt any potential conflict between the Catholic extremists and the sex maniacs at their engagement party.

The wedding will be a whole other story.

Belle's very old, very frail grandma will be in attendance, and it's been agreed that she will turn up for the first hour or two, before Belle's parents whisk her and other family members off for a fancy dinner at some stuffy restaurant on Jermyn Street. This leaves the more debauched invitees to arrive fashionably late with little to no overlap.

Genius.

Aida and I do it the other way around, with a sushi supper first. By the time we rock up at the Mandarin Oriental for the party, the oldies and the more God-fearing of the invitees have moved on and Belle and Rafe's friends are pouring in.

A glance around tells me there's a good mix of City types and Alchemy members and friends of ours from uni, as well as glamorous twenty-somethings who are undoubtedly here for the bride-to-be.

A few weeks ago, I'd have been in my fucking element. Now, I give them the most cursory once-over before turning my attention back to my ravishing date.

We find the happy couple chatting with Zach and Maddy and some other dark-haired guy I can't place. It makes sense that they would have turned up early—Maddy and Belle have been friends for donkey's years, and Zach is, unlike me, socially acceptable enough to manage any social situation with aplomb.

'Well, don't you look gorgeous?' I drawl, taking Belle in. She's radiant in a long, floaty dress of palest pink that's tasteful and elegant while also showing off her slender figure. I kiss her on both cheeks. 'Congratulations, darling. He's a lucky man.'

She shoots me a wide, genuine smile. She's so sweet. 'Thanks for coming. And I'm so happy he brought you! You were so amazing on *Gordon Kay!*' The last part she aims at Aida and accompanies it with a little squeak of excitement.

I think I was pretty amazing on *Gordon Kay* too, given how many times the camera panned to me in the audience, but I'm not even bothered, because my girl has earned the spotlight far more fully than I have. I can tell I've been dismissed. I side-step so Belle and Maddy can swoop in and commandeer Aida's attention and presumably gush over what each other is wearing.

'Meet Belle's brother, Dex,' Rafe says, gesturing to the other guy. 'Dex, Cal is one of my oldest friends from school, and he runs Alchemy with me and Zach.'

Of course. I see it now. His hair colour is a lot darker than Belle's, but they share the same golden skin tone and striking eyes—green-gold, for want of a better description.

I hold out my hand. 'Good to meet you, mate.'

We shake.

'Good to meet you, too,' he says, grinning. I may be straight, but I have the unfortunate tendency to size up everyone I meet as a potential Alchemy member, and, on looks alone, this guy would be a shoe-in. He's broad around the shoulders and lean everywhere else—an ex-rower, maybe? He's also wearing a very fucking nice suit.

'I hear you're thinking about moving back—is that right?' I ask him.

'I was just talking about that with these guys,' he says, gesturing to Rafe and Zach. 'Goldman has offered me a promotion, running the Cash business for Equities in London in about six months' time, when the current head retires.'

'Wow.' I hold up my flute and clink his, impressed. 'That's a big job.'

'Yeah.' He makes a self-deprecating moue with his mouth. 'It is, and honestly, there are too many people ahead of me in the queue in New York. My only chance of a big break is London. It's also the easiest way I have right now to get on track for Partner.'

I know enough from my time in banking that if an opportunity this sizeable comes up, you take it. Even if it means moving your family to the other side of the world at a moment's notice. And, as far as I know, this guy has neither a wife nor kids, which should make his decision even easier.

'Sounds like a no-brainer,' I remark.

His smile is rueful. 'I suppose so. It's probably time I come back and keep an eye on my little sister, too.'

He shoots Rafe a mock glare, and Zach and I laugh.

'Bit late for that, mate,' Zach observes. 'She's walked right into the lion's den.'

'Yeah.' He looks down at his drink. 'Hasn't she just? I have to say, I've stayed away this long to put some distance between me and my dad's utter fucking toxicity, but I did *not* see my sweet little baby sis joining a sex club and getting engaged to its owner while I was gone.'

We all look over at Belle, who's in an excited huddle with Maddy and Aida. I'm sure when Gen shows up she'll get stuck in, too. My sister Annabel is only twenty months younger than me, but I can imagine my horror if a guy like Rafe had turned up, popped her cherry and swept her off her feet.

A guy like how Rafe *used to be*, I should say, because there's no doubt in my mind he'll make the best husband ever.

'Yeah, I get that,' I say to Dex. 'But never have I seen a man more in love than this fucker here is with Belle. She's in good hands, seriously. I mean, he even went head to head with your dad for her.'

His face softens, he and Rafe exchanging a look that suggests they've discussed the issue of his father at length. 'I'm well aware, and I'm genuinely grateful she's got you in her corner, mate,' he tells Rafe. 'I know you'll make her very happy.'

'Not as happy as she'll make me,' Rafe says gruffly. A month ago, I would have ribbed him mercilessly for spouting sentimental shit like that.

Now, I get it.

'You know you're welcome to stop by the club one night, while you're in town,' Zach says. 'Even if you just make it as far as the bar. I promise you, it's a fun place to hang out.'

'The fact that Zach is saying that is nothing short of a miracle,' I tell Dex. 'This guy is a lot more traditional than me and Rafe.'

Dex lets out a pained laugh and rubs at his temple. 'A sex club. Hmm—not sure I've made my peace with it *quite* enough to actually go along. No offence.'

'None taken,' Rafe says. 'And I get it.'

'The offer's there if you want it,' I add. 'If you're back in London for more meetings before you make the jump, feel free to stop by. I assume you're up to your ears in women—or men—in Manhattan?'

His laugh is easier this time. 'Women, definitely. And let's say I don't get lonely. But it's mainly Bumble dates. The dating scene is pretty fast and furious over there.'

'High turnover?' I suggest.

'Something like that.'

He takes a circumspect sip of his champagne and I eye him up. Zach, Rafe and I went to St Ignatius of Loyola, one of the most hardcore Catholic boys' schools in the country, so we all understand the endless hangover of guilt and shame a Catholic education can bestow.

I know from Rafe that Dex went to Ampleforth, which is right up there with Loyola in hardline teachings. I also know he left town and crossed an ocean to get away from his dad's overbearing ways and religious conservatism.

So the fact that he's seemingly fucking his way around Manhattan is actually pretty reassuring.

'Let me guess,' I say. 'You're working crazy hours, and you can't be fucked to date endlessly and wonder if all those interminable dinners will actually result in you getting your end away, so you rely on Bumble hookups instead.'

He screws up his face. 'Basically, yes.'

'We're one and the same,' I say. 'I mean, we were. I sold credit derivatives for years, and that was my MO, too. It's one of the main reasons we founded Alchemy, actually. Convenient, low maintenance, high quality fucking. If you make the move over, we'll hook you up.'

'Jesus, mate, stop pimping him out,' Zach says, laughing. He turns to Dex. 'Now Cal's madly in love, he can't resist living vicariously. Just tell him to fuck off.'

'In love with Aida Russell herself, no less?' Dex asks in a low voice, his eyebrow arched in a way that tells me he's impressed.

'I'm as surprised as you are, mate,' I tell him. 'But yep. She's been filming a documentary about female sexuality as women grow older, and she collaborated with Alchemy to do it. I was her mentor.' I smirk at the amusement on Dex's face at that idea. 'But if someone as respectable as Aida has deigned to cross Alchemy's threshold, it might make you rethink?'

He laughs and shakes his head. 'Jesus, you're relentless. Look, I'll bear it in mind. But... it sounds like a lot. I'm a pretty straightforward guy when it comes to, you know. Sex.'

I frown. 'You had a textbook Catholic education at the hands of Benedictine monks. There's no way there isn't a little kink buried in there somewhere.'

76

AIDA

"The world was all before them...
and Providence their guide."
—Milton, *Paradise Lost*

In the end, it's not Cal's shirtless Instagrams, or the 'candid' shots of us Alchemy's been dropping on its social channels, or any of the paparazzi shots we orchestrated that win the public over.

It's some footage from inside the nightclub we all went to after Belle and Rafe's engagement party, and afterward, as we stood on the sidewalk waiting for a cab. The footage is grainy and crappy and obviously shot on some random person's iPhone.

But it doesn't matter.

They've captured us on the dance floor, slow dancing together in a way that's also really dirty (this is Cal we're talking about), and then outside, Cal's arms around my big, furry coat, holding me in a vice as he kisses me. And I get why the tabloids paid up for this content, because no matter how low quality it is, it does an amazing job of showing our chemistry.

We look smoking together. I can't deny it. We're sexy and hungry and adorable and besotted. *We fit.* I guess I have to be grateful to the unknown person who invaded our privacy and recorded us without our permission—or knowledge. Because you can't fake this kind of authenticity.

When I was on the *Gordon Kay Show*, Cal sat in the audience looking handsome and adoring, and the cameras panned to him frequently while Gordon was interviewing me. Mara's verdict was that we did good: that the public was starting to tentatively ship us.

The headlines around this footage tell me the goodwill towards us is building. A lot of them are plays on the name of my show. *AIDA FINDS PARADISE WITH SEX CLUB OWNER* or *LOOKS LIKE PARADISE.* It's all gold for the show's prospects.

But is it awful that my favourite headline is in the *Mirror* and is accompanied by a still of Cal's head buried in my neck on that Mayfair sidewalk? The headline is *JOHN WHO?*

It's spiteful and mean spirited and vindictive, and I'm definitely a horrible person. But when your year has been dominated by lurid headlines surrounding the antics of your cheating ex, that headline is like a shot of crack to your veins. I laughed so hard when I saw it. If it wasn't for the boys, I'd probably frame it and put it in the bathroom.

John who, indeed.

The man who's come over to Shepherds Bush to drag me out of my office at the Television Centre and take me to lunch at White City House is most definitely not my aristocratic ex-husband.

Nope. This man is young, and stunningly good-looking, and so obviously dripping with carnality it should be illegal. Mara may have joined us for a debrief given today's press buzz, but I only have eyes for Cal.

My club is a phone-free zone, and for that reason, it's usually celebrity-heavy. But Cal and I have gotten a few looks, and our photograph was in full view on the stack of papers in reception when we arrived.

I'm openly admiring my hot boyfriend in his snug black cashmere turtleneck and jeans when Mara looks up from her phone.

'Huh,' she says.

'What?' I ask without looking away from Cal, who's returning my ravenous stare with his best *do I have plans for you* smile.

'If you could stop eye-fucking each other for long enough, I'll tell you.'

I twist my mouth in amusement and tear my gaze away. 'Sorry. What is it?

She jerks her head toward Cal. 'Looks like I've got myself a new client. GQ wants to interview this one.'

'Angle?' I ask, right as he shakes his wrist out in that universal male signal of self-satisfaction.

'Fuck, yeah,' he hisses. That warrants an eye roll, so I treat him to one.

'Looks like "real men fall for strong, powerful women" kind of vibe,' she says.

Well, isn't that nice?

Huh.

I like that a lot.

Cal's grinning, too. 'Hell, yes they do.'

'This is good,' Mara muses aloud, still scrolling. 'I can work with this. It'll definitely help with the messaging. You know what Lizzy was saying the other week about contrasts? Like, the outcome of your on-screen journey, and the person you've become, needs to contrast as sharply as possible with the starting point.

'So, yeah, if the press is working this angle that you've upgraded to a totally different relationship dynamic where your partner is fully supportive of you and wants you to shine, I'd say that's very fucking helpful. And John Fuck Boy Russell can go fuck himself.'

I can't resist. 'John who?' I ask sweetly, and Mara cackles so loud that someone from the next table twists their body around to see what's going on.

'You're such a bitch.' She shoots me an evil grin. 'I knew I liked you.'

Cal takes my hand under the table and squeezes it. 'I'm your biggest cheerleader, baby. You know I am. You are fucking spectacular, and I'll shout that from the rooftops if they give me a mic.'

I lick my lips, and his gaze drops to my mouth. 'I know you are, sweetie,' I tell him.

'Mara,' he drawls, not taking his eyes off me, 'don't you have somewhere else to be right now?'

'No. Why?'

'Because I hear they have bedrooms in this place,' he says. His eyes are dark and hungry, and his tone is low and rough, and all of it makes me shiver in the best way. 'And I'm feeling the need to drag my girlfriend off to one of them.'

77

AIDA

The final interview plays over the bacchanalian footage of the Masked Ball and that *walk with Cal down the Alchemy corridor.*

SIMONE: When you look back at this journey, would you say you've done what you set out to do and actually found paradise?

ME: Definitely.

SIMONE: And what does that look like for you?

ME: I'd say it looks like choosing myself and what I actually want over what I think I should want. We complain that society has expectations of us and makes us a prisoner of those expectations, but, really, I feel like we make ourselves the prisoner—often without realising it.

As we record this, Cal and I are in a relationship. That absolutely wasn't my intention, and I'm conscious that it might be more impactful if I say I've signed up to Alchemy and I'm so liberated now that I'm with a different guy every night.

And that would absolutely have been my prerogative, and it might also have made for a far better headline, but the fact that I've chosen my own happiness over any responsibility I might feel to deliver a message feels pretty meta to me. Meta, and also really fascinating, when I think about it.

I dreamed up this show because I knew it would be an incredible personal journey for me, and I expected it to be transformative for how I move through life.

But I did *not* expect it to bring me a great, staggering love like the love I've found with Cal—I never, for one second, expected that.

So, to think I might have let myself miss out on that love because my being a mouthpiece for a generation of women was more important to me? That is actually insane.

Ladies, go find your paradise. It might be monogamy, or adventure, or so-called promiscuity, or a really good look at your own sexual wellbeing, or even being happy on your own—it doesn't matter.

The only thing that matters is that you look inside of yourself, and you don't let society tell you what you should want.

Ask yourself what you want, and then give yourself permission to go and fucking find it.

EPILOGUE - AIDA

Stamina has to be one of the most fantastic, and unexpected, perks of a younger boyfriend. I don't mean in bed—Cal's ability to go the distance between the sheets would surprise no one, especially given how freely he boasts about his refractory period.

No, it's his stamina out of bed that's a fucking delight. Particularly when it comes to my sons, and the endless time and energy Cal devotes to playing with them.

Case in point: right now.

I'm lying poolside at Anton Wolff's insane villa in the South of France. The mattress on my sun lounger is wonderfully soft. The rosé in my glass is ice cold. The early summer sun is shining down in the most benign way, like the Côte d'Azur is its favourite place on earth. And this entire scene would be peaceful beyond belief if it wasn't for Cal, who's playing water volleyball with my boys and Zach's girls.

Playing Happy Families doesn't get much better than this.

God bless Cal.

He's been doing this for over an hour, now, with indefatigable cheer. I'd go so far as to suggest that his rowdiness and high spirits aren't even put on—he seems happy as a pig in shit with the kids. Far happier than when I tried to persuade him to take a rest earlier. He squirmed on that sun lounger like an eight-year-old-boy until he got back in the water.

Whatever. He can knock himself out in there. I certainly won't complain as I lie here with my wine and the glossy fashion magazines I grabbed at the airport.

Even Zach has given up on the water volleyball and is lying next to Maddy on one of the huge day beds dotted around Anton's stunning pool. They're getting married at the end of the summer in Puglia, and Gen and Anton are tying the knot here in a few weeks. We had Belle and Rafe's beautiful wedding in the Cotswolds only last weekend, and they're still away on their honeymoon.

Those Alchemy guys sure are dropping like flies, I muse idly as I feast my gaze on my boyfriend. He's far more attention grabbing than British Vogue, with his wet upper body and glistening muscles on display. He's raked his soaking hair off his face, and he looks like he could be on the cover of *Men's Health* with that tan and those looks and that physique.

I've made peace with the fact that the media loves my boyfriend far more than they love me, these days. They were firmly behind us by the time *Searching for Paradise* aired in January, and Cal's fan base exploded when the world met him on screen.

I get it. What's not to love about this guy? Women and queer men, young and old, are equally into him. He's filthy and funny and sweet and unashamedly himself, and it fucking works.

It definitely works for me.

This weekend is ostensibly about celebrating Alchemy. Not only has the show drawn a crazy amount of interest in the club from prospective members, but a tonne of those applicants are—get this—*women over forty.* How freaking cool is that? Gen and I are ecstatic.

More pressingly, the Cannes pop up opens tonight for its second season—a whole month earlier than last year, to capitalise on its popularity—and the grownups will go enjoy the debauchery tonight while Anton's butler, Céd, and his sweet wife look after the kiddies here.

It should be a fantastic evening. A huge fireworks display is planned over the Bay of Cannes, and Gen's gorgeous younger sister, Darcy, who's recently moved home from Australia, is dancing on stage. I've heard her burlesque performances are incredible. Hypnotic.

That said, I suspect this kind of gathering would have had a totally different vibe if the founders had done this a couple years ago. I'm sure it would have been hedonistic and carnal. Instead, if you put aside our naughty plans for tonight and the even naughtier things my boyfriend does to me when we're alone in our beautiful room, it feels like a lovely family vacation.

Cal takes a break from bashing the ball across the net at Pip and Zach's daughter, Stella, and glances across at me just as I'm checking him out. I lick my lips, and he halts.

'Break time,' he calls. 'Go get an ice cream, guys—you've earned it. But before you do, go and stand next to Zach and make sure you drip all over him.'

'I heard that,' Zach growls from where he's lying face down next to Maddy, and the kids all giggle as they wade towards the shallow steps at one end.

'I want to drip on Mummy!' Kit calls gleefully.

'No chance,' Cal tells him. 'That's my job.'

He vaults out of the pool in an alpha male way that I'm a total slut for, and I let my jaw drop open as he makes his way towards me, water pouring off his beautiful body.

Dear God, this man was made by angels. His red swim shorts cling to him, and I take in the broad shoulders, and the narrow, tapered hips, and the serpent winding over his side. He raises both hands and rakes his hair back afresh, but he's ogling my body just as hard with those dark eyes as I'm ogling his.

He is so. Fucking. *Hot.*

And then he leans down, showering cool drips all over my heat-warmed skin, and I squeal. Somewhere behind me, Kit laughs in glee at the noise, but my focus is on Cal, who's bending right down so his mouth is against my ear and his breath is warm on my neck.

'Baby,' my gorgeous, sexy, dangerous man whispers so only I can hear, 'come to our fucking bedroom *right now* so I can tie you up and get you out of that bikini, and I promise you within thirty seconds I'll have you even more soaking than I am.'

THE END

Want more Cal & Aida? Get the bonus epilogue here - it contains stepfathering (not a word), spice, and all the feels!
https://BookHip.com/QRDLQVR

Are you ready for Dex, Max and Darcy's MMF? I am!
Preorder Unstitch here.
https://mybook.to/unstitch_alchemy

And come join my FB group for some post-mortem fun and games!

https://www.facebook.com/groups/3060624120889625

AFTERWORD

Well, wasn't this a joy to write?! No religious trauma, bereavement or anything else to plough through. Instead, Cal came effortlessly streaming onto the page, his humour and filth and charm (and vanity) crystal-clear in my head.

Bless him!

I suppose after three other books in the series, I was always going to have a decent grip on him, but I'll let you into a little secret. I was pretty nervous about writing him! Firstly because writing the intense, grumpy guy comes to me more easily than the golden retriever-type energy that Cal has, and secondly because I know how many of you love him.

I hope I've done him justice and that you're happy with his HEA. It would have been easy to do another age gap romance with some hot young twenty-something girl, but I wanted someone who'd flip his world upside down.

Someone he never, ever saw coming.

Writing celebrities is so much fun for me. A lot of my MCs in my Sara Madderson books are famous, but Anton was probably the highest profile MC I'd written in Alchemy. I love that Aida is a household name who's at the top of her game (sorry about the rhyme), and I love how much Cal is dazzled by her.

Most of all, I love how wonderfully good and healthy they both are for each other. They're so unlikely together, but I'm in love with their dynamic.

For me, Cal's journey was the opposite of Zach's. Whereas Zach needed to embrace Alchemy to embark on his next chapter, Cal needed to get away from Alchemy and rediscover the joys of the real world, all the way from sexy moments in bars to whispering *those* three little words to someone in the intimacy of their home.

Cal may be the character you all know and love, but this was Aida's story as much as his—even more, possibly. I'm a year younger than Aida as I write this, and many of my loyal readers are older than me.

I lost a huge chunk of 2023 to undiagnosed perimenopausal issues and BOY was it hell. I'm on hormones now, like Aida, and I'm in the process of finding myself again. But I do think women in their 40s, 50s and beyond are less visible than they should be, even if we have stunning role models like J Lo and Jennifer Aniston and Jennifer Connelly and so many more leading the charge.

I could write a lot about this, but let me just say this to all my peers: this younger guy fantasy on steroids is my gift to you. *Enjoy* every delicious morsel! My hormone doctor recently told me she wished she could prescribe reading smut to her female patients because it's the most powerful aphrodisiac she knows—more powerful than any sex hormones she can prescribe—so go forth and TAKE YOUR MEDICINE like good girls...

Thank you for reading
Sara / Elodie xxx

ACKNOWLEDGMENTS

I was musing earlier that my author career today is so different from what it was last year. I'm so much more entrenched in the community and it's made the past few months an absolute joy.

THANK YOU first of all to my readers. You buy and borrow and share and shout, and you've made my books take flight. Thank you for loving my characters as much as I do!

In particular, thank you to my FB reader group, my Nerds. You are my favourite place to visit every day. You've seen me through grief and hormonal shit-shows and milestones and I'm so, so grateful to have found you.

Thank you SO much to Jennifer Brooks Brown and Lyndsey Gallagher, my amazing beta readers, for egging me on and talking me off the ledge and telling me to make the occasional scene dirtier... (I'll always be grateful for that, Jennifer!).

It was also Jennifer who sent me *that* Enrique Iglesias song (which I'd never heard) and casually suggested Cal might like to dance to it, which prompted one of my absolute favourite scenes to write.

Thank you also to my ARC readers, who are so good at dropping everything and reading. I hope you love Cal! I love our smutty group chat!

A massive thank you to my author community, in particular Bobby Kim, whose group I discovered back in May 2023 (thank you, Maddie Wade!) and who has transformed my career through his incredible wisdom and generosity of advice and time.

Through Bobby's Facebook group I've also met wonderful authors who I chat to every day and who have my back. I love my Stabby Seven and my Famous Five (Luna, Rosa, Isa and Ryan).

Thank you to the amazingly talented Wander Aguilar for this gorgeous photo of Cal looking positively lickable.

Thank you to everyone in this community, whether on TikTok or Instagram or Facebook, for taking a chance on me and my stories.

Finally, huge thanks to my family, Chris, Paddy and Tilly, for sticking with me when I'm so deep in my writing that I forget what's for dinner (and sometimes their names. Update: I forgot to dial in to Paddy's virtual parents-teacher meetings this week). Special thanks to Paddy for providing expert input on all things VR-related, especially Gorilla Tag!

You guys are the best! X

Made in United States
North Haven, CT
09 April 2024

51014716R00252